Also by MARK HELPRIN

A Dove of the East and Other Stories

This is a Borzoi Book published in New York
by Alfred A. Knopf.

Refiner's Fire

REFINER'S FIRE

The Life and Adventures
of Marshall Pearl, a Foundling

by Mark Helprin

Alfred A. Knopf   New York   1977

THIS IS A BORZOI BOOK
PUBLISHED BY ALFRED A. KNOPF, INC.

The description of the SS action in the Ukraine
is drawn largely from, and includes some exact
lines of, the "Affidavit" of Hermann Graebe,
Nuremberg Tribunal, PS 2992.

Library of Congress Cataloging in Publication Data

Helprin, Mark.   Refiner's fire.

I. Title.
PZ4.H478RE3   [PS3558.E4775]   813'.5'4   77–2575
ISBN 0–394–41273–7

Manufactured in the United States of America

FIRST EDITION

Damn your eyes, you ignorant beebuckle. This is no play upon the stage, a circlet, a doublet to unfold. And I have not written it. It is a Romance —written by the ravishing pace of five thousand years.

—Translated quite freely from *The Bee and the Thimble*, by Lapin of Rotterdam

Contents

Transportation of the Wounded 3

    I   A Coast of Palms 9

   II   The Hudson 49

  III   Columbine 79

  IV   High View 95

   V   Yorkville 141

  VI   A Lake in August 155

 VII   A Memory of the Plains 179

VIII   The Sea and the Alps 239

  IX   Settlement of the Dove 263

   X   Refiner's Fire 285

Morning at Hospital 10 369

Refiner's Fire

Transportation of the Wounded

It was one of those perfectly blue, wild days in Haifa when winds from Central Asia and the eastern deserts come roaring into the city like a flight of old propeller planes. Blue-green pines in the Bahai Sanctuary bent in the tense air, and tourists trooped like pilgrims to the top of Carmel for views both miraculous and mild in a full flood of gentle northern light. Moved by an astonishing high view, the tourists forgot themselves and all the many things which had troubled them. North along the coast, a delicate string of breakers rolled slowly to shore, leaving wind lines on the sea. Far to the north were mountains of white ice, silent and heart-filling. And there was perfect quiet, until suddenly and explosively within the hotel grounds by the promenade, black musicians from America struck up their New Orleans band.

From Mt. Carmel one can see for a hundred miles. Out to sea were ships coming to port and departing, each with prosperous cargo, each like a piece on the board of a naval game. Their progress fit the slurred elisions of the brass, drums, and woodwinds from the gardens, and their wakes seemed to freeze on the surface. The black musicians thought about the view, and the city, and the young country knee-deep in war and grinding along like an awkward but marvelous engine of the past century. It reminded the older ones of New Orleans and Chicago; of the muddy brown barges and steamships up from Mexico; of Lake Michigan's blue, seen from a high building. It reminded them of the trolleys (although in Haifa there are no trolleys), and the old-fashioned graces they had known before America had put on its skin. Because of these affinities they liked the new country—and its people liked them.

A country in war is a country alive. It hurts all the time and is full of sorrow, but is as alive as the blaze of a fire, as energetic and restless as an animal in its pen—full of sex and desires of the heart. The undercurrents are so strong that even the tourists take refuge in a larger view. To the east was a valley of industrial plants and enameled green fields leading to Jordan:

feed factories, concrete mills where the stones of the mountains were crushed and beaten, refineries, fields of wheat, long sinuous roads, power cables vibrating like violin strings, and the well-ordered camps of an invincible army.

In the north they saw mountains, the savage peaks of Hermon, and a sky so blue that it seemed to burn their eyes. To the west was the sea, and in between were well-tended fields, wildflowers, and heather-covered dunes. On the promenade an American Jew whose life had been a series of killing confinements said to his wife, "You see, if you come to this country you must understand that here it is the nineteenth century. These people, our people, have been left there by a combination of events. They still have the strength for fighting and building. They have a passion to clarify and to create. They are willing to sacrifice. Here, we are in our fathers' time."

Everyone knew that there was fighting on the Syrian border. The war was several days old and Haifa was still but for an armored column miles long winding silently like a collection of toys far below on the Jaffa Road. The tourists expected that the Army would win immediately and without trouble; but there was something unnerving about the quiet in the north. They were fighting there, carrying guns which hung heavily from their shoulders. It was unexplained, uncontrolled, and a world apart. Those men who fought at the foot of icy mountains and in windy forests would have given their right arms for a chance to feast in the gardens of the hotel. And, abandoned to their own devices in war and sleeplessness, they thought incessantly about women. In such circumstances, one receives a sudden burst of heartfelt feeling. One longs for a home with a woman who will shelter and perceive. One longs for children, and is intent upon them and haunted by them, candles burning up.

As the musicians continued, playing as endurance summons—a thousand years in the railroads—they heard the helicopters coming in from the battle. At least a dozen flew gracefully in formation at several levels, an angel fleet from the mountains, flying a straight and urgent course. They appeared first as specks and then glinting and yawing, hovering in the air, bringing in the wounded, the completely destroyed, those who had died while airborne.

An apprentice butcher could have done better when drunk. They were slit open and burned. Their limbs were torn, disjointed, covered in brilliant red. The rotor blades' concussive bursts drowned their screaming. Some died in the air, others hoped not to die. They had come from armor-littered plains and disassembled fortifications which had not lasted; they were the victims of ill-laid plans and the pride of those who conceive.

The helicopters were thick-bodied and heavy, of the most advanced kind, with stretchers inside on which lay soldiers soundly intoxicated by the ragged choppings of the motors. In one of them was Marshall Pearl, an American, who in the mountains had become the result of an artillery shell which had hit right and blown him apart, leaving him in remnants in a helicopter, trying to grasp some chance magic to make things whole again. He was only half alive, and he was pitifully open to the air, as if for sounding, when he rode to the trim Haifa hospital called Rambam. He shuddered at the others' screaming, and envied them for their painful superficial wounds. It was terrible and frightening. And yet, contrary to sense, like lightning-kindled forests which burn in heavy rain, he thought it was, in its way, sort of funny. He saw it as if from outside, and, surrounded by his own quiet, he smiled.

People in all quarters of the city stared at the approaching aircraft—a military color outside; and inside, a confusion of tape, blood, darkness, and exhausted doctors dashing about in small spaces. From within, Marshall Pearl imagined that he was strapped to the feet of the machine as he had seen in his childhood, in pictures of the Korean War. He could hardly breathe because they had tied him up so tight, to prevent him from spilling out. He didn't like that. It was contrary to the strange sense of humor he had about being where he was, and it seemed to constrict his efforts not to die. Even as he fell off into comfortable blackness and found himself in a deluge of memories and passions, he tried to get a hold so that he could begin to fight back somehow and in some way. They dared not give him too much morphine, though they gave him plenty, and the pain knocked him out again and again. But he awoke again and again, amused and fighting—for, being an American of the fields and mountains, of the ardent unlimitlessness, he fought in times when he could not even imagine strength.

Departing from the locust fleet, his helicopter veered in its turn and sidled down to a concrete platform between the hospital and the sea. They took him off the rack and carried him out into the air. He could hear the sea breaking against the rocks; he could smell it and sense the moisture, and his eye caught some particles of white which had been thrown upward and which hung motionless for a moment, as he imagined a bullet would do if fired straight up.

He was pleased by the proximity of the sea because he hadn't seen it during many weeks in the thin air of mountains. He remembered how on leave he had gone to a deserted beach and propelled himself through the clear green water and top foam with tireless speed, slapping the waves and then off again in a bound as if he were a porpoise. He reached with his left hand to feel the muscles of his right arm but he could feel nothing. Just before landing they had given him a very strong shot. His arm was there but his hand had no feeling, and so in the brisk winds by the sea and in the sun, laid flat on the concrete with a dozen others suffering the same apparel of gauze and four-cornered bandages, he realized that he had been reduced to a thought. His body was no longer to concern him, although it was frightening to imagine the pain of which he had begun to receive powerful intimations.

The grave rush of a dozen doctors and nurses, apelike orderlies, and helicopter crewmen coalesced, and in one movement he and the others were carried in absurd procession off the pad while the helicopter lifted just as it had lightly touched down. As he was wheeled through endless deep corridors he was glad to see men and women in trim uniforms—the nurses plump and sad in their nurses' hats and thick shoes, working hard and fast.

Being then so truly passive, he nearly enjoyed it. Wrapped in white sheets like an albino cigar lying on the stretcher, he was hustled into aircraft-like turns and banks around corners, being finally maneuvered with famed precision right to his proper berth. Despite interweaving pain and numbness he delighted in the order, in the physical actions of people and machines, in the long looks of loving eyes judging and fleeting, in the ecstatic tiredness and burning of work. He had always been susceptible to the play of light and motion. He loved, for example, to watch trucks driving on the road; the wheels turned, the engine was hot, and there was movement through the air. He felt that even the light and motion of a truck blasting down the sea road were at every moment linked to an artful and all-powerful God.

He was in an operating room. A nurse touched him on the head and said something he didn't understand. They prepared, ripping and tearing his uniform, cutting the bandages, assembling instruments and sutures, shifting trays, checking dials—with the pleasing strength and rhythmic speed which had made the country and all the civilized and mechanical things he had seen in his life. They moved up the tanks and placed a mask over his face. "I may not wake up," he said in English, and a doctor answered in English, saying, "Don't worry. We are fighters too."

They took him by the sea road down the coast to Hospital 10. This was a small military clinic on the edge of the Mediterranean, used before the war for the rest and recovery of soldiers wounded in border actions, or for those who had developed serious diseases or had undergone complete emotional disintegration. When Marshall was wheeled in past strings of Japanese lanterns and rows of cheap aluminum furniture, he was unconscious. He had fallen into a post-operative coma, and in the pronouncements of several physicians he had been declared lost. His metal tags had been separated from him and no one knew who he was. They calculated that he would need a few weeks to die, in which time his family might be found.

Though old-fashioned, and dirtier than Rambam, Hospital 10 was a finer place. Built by the British generations before, it had that characteristic solidity, coolness, and shade marked by leafy patterns of louvers and jalousies. It was in a style once designated "one world tropical," but as a concession to the Mediterranean, the eastern great bay of which it overlooked, red tiles covered the roof, so that a visitor might have imagined that it was a British building with an Italian hat.

Palm trees and thorns surrounded it, and a thin strip of beach separated it from a lovely green sea. No one was swimming. The previous occupants of the place (and seemingly of another era) had been thrown out and sent to their homes or their units a week before—all except an Orthodox aircraft mechanic whose legs had been broken by a snapping cable. For days he sat on the porch and prayed as he watched the dozens brought in and the dozens taken out. Few recovered. Hospital 10 had become a death house, a terminal for the hopeless cases of Northern Command. Scores of men died there after their operations, for they had been pulled apart more than anyone could put together. The mechanic worked at prayer and the doctors smashed their fists against walls and tables. All the hard cases had emasculated their skill.

Marshall was placed in the southeastern corner of a high-ceilinged room on the first floor, one of twelve silent men lying still in two frightful rows. Had he been able to see, he would have seen through French doors sidelong to the sea. Had he been able to see, he would have seen creamwhite walls, wood louvers, slowly rotating fans, a great double door leading to the hall, a shining black floor, and in the middle of the room a small table with a green glass library lamp which glowed even in daylight. Under the lamp were paperwork and medical supplies, a telephone, a buzzer, and magazines. A nurse sat on a chair next to the table. Every few minutes she checked each patient, and when she was not going from bed to bed she sat on the white wooden chair turning her head like a clockwork beacon to watch her charges. She worked too hard and was too busy to open her magazines. She wore one sweater over another, a green army kind and her own black cardigan. She was alert, exhausted, and frightened. These men were dying, twelve at a time, and she was a pretty nurse, very young, and had never seen anything like it.

Two orderlies brought Marshall to his bed. As they were leaving, one stepped to a window and looked out at several other orderlies resting and talking in the garden below. He flung open the shutter, stepped to the windowsill, and jumped out, hurtling through the palms to the ground. Rolling and skidding, he landed badly but then righted himself. He picked up two stones and challenged another orderly who was almost his exact counterpart and who, to complete the symmetry, took two white rocks and held them menacingly in his fists. They circled like fighting cocks and then rushed together, beating with the stones. The nurse called a military policeman, who was an exact third except for his more colorful uniform, his gun, and his club. He tried to reason with them but they were so busy smashing one another with the stones that they didn't even know he was there. He swung his club and knocked one of them out. The other didn't stop, so the policeman swatted him too and both lay insensible and bloody, four white stones near their faces, their faces almost touching. Other orderlies, drawn from hiding places ingenious and obscure, carried them to an ambulance. An officer appeared and was briefed, in the way officers are always briefed, as if by men who are pulling their own teeth.

"Take the one who jumped out the window to Prison 4, and the other to Hospital 9."

The orderlies looked at the two but could see no difference between them. "We can't," they said. "We don't know which is which."

The officer noted that indeed they were congruent, and he said, "It doesn't matter. Just take one to prison and the other to the hospital. Since they're both the same, they won't complain."

The military policeman jumped in the ambulance, a bunch of forms in his hand. The officer said, "If one wakes up, put him to sleep again or it could be dangerous."

"What if the innocent one wakes up?" asked the policeman.

"As far as the law is concerned," replied the officer, "one is guilty and they're both the same. Therefore, both are guilty. It is like the tale of the cat and the dog. But never mind; hit him on the head."

"Yes, sir," said the policeman, and the ambulance tore away, its back doors swinging wildly. At her chair, the nurse wept softly because the war seemed to be everywhere, and all the wonderful things she had known were gone.

But Marshall was dreaming. In the quiet room with a distant rumbling of tanks and trucks on the sea highway and the insistent sound of waves, she could not have guessed that in the bed nearest the window an unconscious soldier had the world opening to him anew.

Bright sun shimmered on the sides of the helicopter. Two nurses stood near him, leaning against the stretcher as the machine swayed. Compared to the intense light outside it was cool and dark inside the cabin. One of the nurses had an expression of terror; her eyes were wide but she worked nevertheless. The other was determined—incipient tears above a hardened beautiful face. Clenching her teeth, she changed Marshall's bandages. She was dark, with shining eyes. Marshall saw her in a diamond crown of sparkling sun. The engines roared. A soldier in the back screamed. As if in chain reaction two others moaned, and Marshall smiled like a dying young animal, numb and bewildered at the frozen light and color in the cabin enclosed within a great vibration. The colors pleased him so much, as they always had, and when the beautiful nurse crossed a floor littered with helmets and bloody bandages she fought to stay upright while the helicopter tipped. She grasped a handle above her, tightening her muscles to stay balanced. From the darkness in which men and women struggled he saw through the door down to the sea, which glowed in rippling light. Waves of deep blue light came in the cabin and filled his eyes.

I
A Coast of Palms

1

Riding in a new 1938 Ford through the March countryside of North Carolina, Paul Levy was astonished by the tranquillity and depth of the blue above. Every tree and field was sheathed in gentle, clear, warm light. Smoke from clearing fires rose straight and slow, and the speed and air were perfect as the car wound through the back roads, sounding like a perpetual chain of little firecrackers. He was sixteen, the son of a Norfolk ship provisioner, and in love with the Navy and its ships. His father saw them as delivery points for canned tomatoes and brass polish, but his father's son was struck as if by lightning at the sight of one steaming up the roads, bent forward, pressing on—a squinting bridge, high black masts and angled guns, smoke, wake, urgency, and water pulsing off the bows. And when they turned, with claxons and bells, and the stern seeming to sweep like a skater over mottled ice, he saw in them the history for which his tranquil boyhood had been created. And in the North Carolina countryside, joyriding in his father's car solo for the first time, he could not help glancing through the windows at the sky and thinking of the sea.

By darkness when he returned to Norfolk he had decided to join the Navy, which, after a year or so of arguments and heated wanderings in and out of the dance places at Virginia Beach, he did. At first he went to sea as almost a child, and the little experience he had he used badly, awkwardly, making more mistakes than he could count. But at nineteen he was an ensign in the Battle of the Atlantic. He used to come home every few months or weeks, and each time he was more solid, stronger, wiser. Being on the sea was miserable, especially in winter, and it wore him down. But it developed into his calling and during the war he had been off Africa, Normandy, and Japan. Because he learned fast and loved the sea he became a lieutenant-commander by the end of 1946, taking a year's leave of absence to rest and prepare: he intended upon a career in the Navy, but did not want to be entirely brought up in it. He thought that a year of peace—maybe some farming, a trip across the country to San Francisco, a month at home—would do it. His father had become prosperous, especially since the fleet had not been decimated and would not be dismantled as had been the custom after other wars. They lived in a big house and it was planned that the younger sister and brother would go to college.

Paul, though, was lost to the Navy; he was an officer with Southern ways and a fighting man's demeanor. They were proud of him, but having left

early and against their wishes, he was not very much like them. He had forgotten his Jewishness, almost lost it in the rush and conviviality of war. No
one knew he was a Jew if they didn't know his name. Even when he said his
name, everyone did not immediately know his origins, since he pronounced
Levy like the tax, or the embankment which holds back a river. He was by
appearance and dialect a Virginia or North Carolina farmer—and this delighted him. He was free as his father had never been to blend into the country and be whatever he wished, except for his name and except for his regret,
as he saw his father growing older, that he as first son would do little in continuing what began to appear to him in the quiet spring days of his extended leave, riding again in the Carolinas, as a very important line of
passage, a crucial tradition.

It took him a day to go from the balm of the internal Carolina lakes
and bays to Washington Square. New York seemed to him like rows of gray
teeth and he could not understand how people chose to live inside files of
concrete boxes in a city which was really not a city but a machine. To him it
seemed about the same as building a great engine, a thousand times greater
than the Corliss Engine, and then living inside. London too had gray teeth,
but in circles and enflowered by trees and promenades. This city on the
Hudson was like a shark's jaw—monotonous serrations thick and hard.

He had intended to seek out Jews, for the ones in Norfolk were in his
eyes predictable and Virginianized. But to his great surprise, the Jews
in New York would have nothing whatsoever to do with him. First, his
approach was confused. He walked into restaurants and ordered familiar
dishes. In this way he ate much and discovered that one does not retrieve
receding history through gastronomy. He sat next to an old man and looked
into his face, about to ask a momentous Jewish question, when the man said,
"Go avay, cowboy." He explained that his name was Paul Levy, but when the
old man heard the way he spoke, he fled. Paul kept on trying.

He chose a synagogue and went to pray, but when he entered they looked
at him as if he were a raccoon or a possum who had wandered in from the
Louisiana Bayou. He went to see a rabbi, whose advice consisted of coldly
instructing him to purify his pots and pans by boiling water in them and
dropping in a hot brick. "A hot brick?" asked Paul in disbelief. "Let me get
this straight. You want me to boil water in my nonexistent pots and pans,
and then drop in a hot brick? A hot brick! Rabbi, one of us is nuts, and it's
not me."

After a week or more of seeking out Jews in New York he found himself
at the house of a Roman Catholic law professor, lying on the floor of the
library, which looked out on a cold Washington Square where snow was
falling for the last time that spring, and next to the sooty buildings it tele-
scoped itself into a salt-and-pepper image like the tweeds in the livingroom
downstairs at the party. But the snow was twisting in cold whirlwinds like the

warm viscous air above the fire. He was roundly, rotatingly drunk, davening in his drunkenness before the fire, and next to him was a Palestinian Jewess whom he had beguiled upstairs to kiss; but she wasn't drunk at all. She liked him though and had never heard a Jew who talked as he did. When he told her he was a Navy captain (he blushed at the lie) she leaned over on the Persian rug and kissed him on his mouth in such a wet sexual way and with such great affection that he said, "Would you believe that I'm really an admiral?"

"No, I don't believe you," she answered. "But I want you to tell me about that you are a captain."

And he did, starting with his revelation in Carolina about the Navy and the sea, his love for the sea, how in the war he had fought and endured, how his father had not known him but had seen instead a tough stranger who did pushups and could fight, and how for him being a Jew was impossible since he could not get either in or out and seemed to be hanging in between worlds which would not have him.

They stayed together for two weeks until she took him in a turtle-backed taxi to Idlewild and saw him off on his way to becoming a captain, as he had said he was. He felt that he did not know his own mind. He was apprehensive about not returning in time to resume his commission, apprehensive about leaving the silent city which he had come to like and respect, apprehensive about rising above shafts of sunlight and clouds on a straining airplane past the rows of gray buildings in new prosperity—a good quiet place for infants after the war—apprehensive of rising into an empyrean of blue, apprehensive of heading east, apprehensive of challenging the British cordon with an old coastal freighter, and apprehensive of the dreamlike frame of mind into which he had fallen. He hardly knew what had happened, but he felt as if he were certainly rising upward.

2

He was lanky and well over six feet tall, with short blond hair and the remnants of a suntan he had picked up on the Albemarle. He was dressed in khaki pants, a white shirt, and a brown aviator jacket which he slung over his shoulder. Though only twenty-six, he had spent all his adult life in war. Darkness, danger, and combat did not bother him. It was a hot day in Brindisi. Children with nearly shaved heads and black shorts settled on the sea walls like rows of vultures. Heat was rising from the beige-colored stones, and prostitutes strolling under the palms were eyed by midget Italian sailors of the Adriatic Squadron. In the harbor, garbage scows and miscellaneous unkempt craft scuttled back and forth between ships, halting now and then to nestle against a cruiser or a minesweeper, not quite in the manner of a calf leaning on its mother but rather like the flies which settled on carcasses in the horse butcheries. Motors hummed and a brass band from one of the ships was practicing far in the distance, modulated by the waves of heat.

Levy had arrived at a pier in the old port, and there he stood staring at the Motor Vessel *Lindos Transit*, an appalling piece of junk by any standard, more like a bombed-out house than a ship. But if it could float and go, it would do. Air upwelling about him, he was immobilized in wonder, and a group of people on the main deck returned his gaze. There was a woman who looked Bulgarian, perhaps a washerwoman, in a print dress. Above her head and a little to the right was a dark man in a felt hat, a Polish or Czech army officer. Next to him was another thick-armed giant of a woman, with gray streaks in her hair, a face of granite, and a little child near her. The child had a tiny Japanese-like face with eyes as round and small as ladybugs. In her hair was a bright white ribbon which shone against the darkness and was in the shape of a perching bird. Next to her was another stout woman, with a worried expression—and the face of an Italian condottiere in a High Renaissance painting. Above her, leaning forward to look at the American, was a thin and handsome man whose arms were very strong. Levy could see this because the man had grasped one of the many ill-placed rails and pipes which ran overhead, and was suspended like an acrobat. There was a girl of about twenty-five, a pretty girl with black curls which were blowing in the hot breeze. Above her, more like a monkey than an acrobat, was a boy in an almost Alpine jacket and a flat cap. He was scared and bewildered, as if he had just come from a pre-war French children's book. He was, of course, an orphan.

Then there was a man who could only have been a waiter in a fashionable Budapest cafe or, and this is said without levity, a professional movie usher in Strasbourg. In the background were other eyes and half-hidden faces, old suits and hats. Levy felt very little, if anything, for these people and noticed mainly that the girl played with the rail and was the only one who did not return his stare. They watched quietly from the dark shade, as he stood in bright sun.

Some men were offloading coils of rope, barrels of solvents, and hundreds of iron poles with auger ends. Levy took possession, ordering them to return the material to the ship. They looked up in disbelief and weariness, for they had been working all morning. Furthermore, they had been ordered around too much by Teutons and Anglo-Saxons, so they each spit on the ground and went back to their tasks. "Jesus," said Levy, and ran up into the ship, where a man stopped him and then recognized him.

"You must be Pool Levy. I am Avigdor Avigdor." From then on, Avigdor Avigdor became his right arm and he became Avigdor Avigdor's left arm. No one would move unless told to do so by Avigdor, who knew nothing about ships. Levy became used to issuing orders and hearing them echo in half a dozen languages.

"The first thing you must realize," said Levy to his assembled seconds in command, "is that on a ship like this we will need every kind of equipment, material, livestock, and provisioning that we can get aboard. Since our cargo is human and hence very light, we can carry anything we require (if we can get it) without reference to weight. I want you to find what you can—food, medical supplies, ropes, scrap metal, lumber, tools, welding apparatus, fire hoses, wicker furniture, dowels, cloth, wire, a record player, tires, anything."

"What is wicker furniture?" Levy explained. "I can understand," said Avigdor, his left fist clenched and his right hand open, "food, livestocks, ropes" (he looked quickly about the bridge and superstructure to indicate his ignorance of nautical affairs), "but what please may I ask are we to do with scrap metal, tires, and wicker furniture?"

"We're going to make sure that we get these people to where they're going."

"But how with metal and tires and furniture?"

"How indeed?" said Levy, retreating to his cabin and leaving them speechless on the bridge. Though they had learned to call him Paul instead of Pool they resented his command and suspected that he was touched. Whereas they had expected him to stay on the bridge and turn the wheel, he quickly got to know every inch of the ship and went around telling everyone what to do. Most irritating for the more than three hundred passengers was that he made them move from where they had settled so that he could draw squares and rectangles on the deck plates in bright red paint. No one, he said, was allowed to stay or even walk there.

He noticed that the people, whether Poles, Germans, Czechs, Russians, or whatever, had a very peculiar mannerism. When he spoke to them they more often than not kept their lower lips between their teeth. He went to his cabin and stared into a round mirror set into a fake ship's wheel. When he did what they did he resembled a chipmunk, or a hamster. Depending upon their facial structures they looked variously like chipmunks, hamsters, rabbits, raccoons, and even a bucktoothed puppy he had seen once in Tennessee when his father had taken him there to experience the place before Roosevelt covered it with water. They used this expression to show their bewilderment, anger, happiness, and hope—a long and difficult string of things which drove the lower lip into the path of the teeth.

The Germans had beaten them so badly because, at least in part, the Germans were so well organized. But the Germans had been beaten badly in their turn by the Americans, who were savage and rich. America was clean; everything worked; everyone was sensible and fair; they had in America methods of organization as incomprehensible to Europeans as alchemy or a dead oriental language. Therefore, when Paul Levy covered the decks in red geometry, they deferred, for evidently he had some sort of plan, and who would dare to contradict him? For several weeks trucks rolled up periodically, and at the end of May everything Paul had requested was stowed aboard the ship. This astonished him. Though he had asked mainly for junk, in Southern Italy even junk was then in short supply.

He had refused to tell his plan because of an elegant Italian in a white suit. Paul noticed that he came to sit every day near the foot of Virgil's Column. Although this aristocrat was more than a quarter of a mile from the ship, lost in a sea of masts, spars, clotheslines, pigeons, vendors, and pedestrians on the steps and in the little piazza, Paul picked him out immediately in scanning with the ship's telescope because it was easy to recognize the front page of the *Times* of London. He couldn't be sure that the man was not simply reading an English newspaper and had no concern for the *Lindos Transit*, until he got up a head of steam and, as many ships in the harbor often did, vented it in a white cloud and a whistle which echoed off walls, buildings, and hillsides covered with hot brush and stones. The gentleman of the *Times* sat bolt upright and threw his paper down. Paul had his left hand on the whistle chain and his right supporting one end of the telescope. Each time he pulled the chain the man sat more upright and appeared more expectant and tense. Paul held off until his quarry picked up the downed paper and resumed reading. He called Avigdor to the telescope. "You see the man reading the *Times* of London?"

"How do you know it is the London *Times*?"

"The type face."

"Oh, yes. I see."

"Pull the chain and watch him come to life." Avigdor pulled the chain, and later let everyone know that there was good reason to obey their strange captain.

3

On the second day of June the *Lindos Transit* was fully stocked with refugees, food, and a hold full of junk and tools. People had continued to straggle in until their number verged on the counterproductive. Anyway, the sound of the words "second day of June" sounded to Levy positive and energetic. He fired up his engines, called in the Italian pilot, cast off at the tide, and with a plume and a whistle he signaled the port that the *Lindos Transit* was about to sail. For the benefit of the gentleman in white he tapped out the Morse symbols for Palestine, since he had always believed that homage was due to British agents in hot places.

In bright afternoon the ship drew out of the harbor and into the Adriatic. The pilot descended, and Levy took his first real command. The wind was fabulously strong from the east, as it most often is in Brindisi port, and the waves came in hard against the bows. He passed the last salt-eroded fingers of white rock, and then they were in open sea, rolling and pitching, out of breath, suddenly so much smaller, suddenly so much colder.

He knew that everyone would be going below, and he had ordered coffee, chocolate, tea, and biscuits for them even though the extravagance was bound to hurt later and disrupt some of his careful projections. Two-page census forms in Russian, Yiddish, German, French, and English had been distributed among the passengers. Levy had said to Avigdor, "Put jokes on the form, any kind of jokes." In the holds and corridors people were eating and laughing.

When well out to sea, the ship found its stride. Avigdor came to the bridge. "Now," he said, "tell me what you plan to do with all this nonsense we have put."

"We're going to fight the British—not just resist, fight. In other words, if when we approach the cordon we are attacked by a British destroyer, we will sink it."

"Ha! With wicker furniture?"

"Shields, Avigdor, shields and breastworks. Here, steer one-twenty-six. Keep it steady. If it starts to seesaw then lock it and wait, and make the adjustment little by little." He gazed deep into the smooth globe of the compass. "It can be done, but to do it everyone will have to work day and night for three weeks. Can they?"

"I believe they can. I believe yes."

Even as a child Levy had been obsessed with achieving the impossible. In geography class, of which he was by all measures the shining star, he often lost his position in a "bee," or other such exercise, due to his dreaming. For example, he had wondered if it would be possible to eat Borneo. Could you even eat just one little village in Borneo? A half a village? A quarter? How about a house? The picture of his eighty-five-pound four-foot self gnawing at the beams of a Borneo house staggered him. Could he manage even to ingest his desk? He calculated that powdered and mixed with conventional food it would take six months. "What is the capital of North Dakota?" asked the teacher. Levy, as runt of the past, was open-mouthed. Sometimes smart children drift away, but they always come back. The teacher abandoned him to an apparent dunce's reverie. "April, what is the capital of North Dakota?"

"Sacramento!" blurted out the little girl, eager for points.

If François Villon could write on the scaffold a poem swift and sure enough to save him, could he not have eaten the platform itself? If Pizarro could subdue the vast Inca Empire with a handful of men far from home and only one casualty, then surely people had wrong ideas about the possible.

In the war, he had wanted to be a hero and was forever trying to find the proper position. At a Norfolk bar he talked for several hours with an air squad mechanic from a carrier, about which parts of an airplane engine, upon being struck by a bullet, would cause the whole to fail and the plane to crash into the sea. Paul Levy's intention had been to shoot down an enemy plane with small arms fire. Given opportunity he would have stood in the open as the planes swept by, eyeing their engines and firing with careful fury until either he or they were crushed. It never happened. He used to lie awake at night thinking about ways for one man to sink a warship. He speculated that his obsession with the impossible would some day bear fruit or kill him. He could not restrain himself from consideration of that which was feasible mainly in the magical world and, strangely enough, sometimes in this one.

He had chosen quite a task. A ship out of port is a difficult creature to sustain, much less to convert; especially if it is crowded with children, the old, the sick, the dejected, and the insane; especially if it is a quarter-century-old coal-fired coastal freighter destined to match up with a contemporary imperial warship. But a cat can outrace the best thoroughbred horse if only it can grasp the idea of racing.

It was Paul Levy's moment, to tell the old ship how to do the right and proper thing. He ignored the cries and plaints, the colors and the sea, the beautiful women who go for a captain like a sea bird for water, the captivating children, the smashing luminescence of the bow waves, the rapid winds and the sea lure, and stayed in his cabin to concentrate on the plan. His lantern swayed back and forth with the ship; its brass flashings caught his eye in a circular dance, but he tightened himself and worked. Over the sea, bright angelic winds prodded up whitecaps.

After a night and a day the infant scheme coalesced. He had laid it out while in port, but several problems had persisted, problems he knew would submit when he was again in his familiar element and could marshal the genius of the sea.

The windows of the wardroom were sparkling with spray. All the men there were in khaki as in the military, although they had forsaken its precise and terrible beauty to convey east the men, women, and children who were the sweepings of the great European war. They took for their Midway or Coral Sea a ship loaded with cynical innocents. Paul Levy spoke as waves of white rolled and battered the ship in a night hour in the Mediterranean. His plan was quite complicated and quite correct.

"First, I want the census to be analyzed. Separate the people into those who can effect the skills they claim, and those who cannot. Appoint one able man for each twenty-five who are incapacitated. He will be their captain, and he will drill them in lifeboat procedure, response to instructions in English, etc., etc.

"As for the rest, they are the heart of the matter. I want you to pay particular attention to athletes and strong workers. They will be put in the combat sections. Welders, mechanics, engineers, smiths, tinkers, will form a technical section. I want four translators who are proficient in our five main languages. Appoint five cooks. It would be best if they were professionals, but it doesn't really matter, since what we eat is important but how it tastes is not.

"At the proper moment, about three in five of the engineering force will transfer to combat. The rest will be damage controllers. I want a medical staff of at least five, and one man, preferably an entertainer, to play records and to talk over the public address system. Oh yes, if there are enough musicians and musical instruments aboard, I want a little orchestra. It will change everything, as you will see if it materializes. When combat isn't drilling it will labor for engineering. Anyone who is double or triple qualified will do double work. But there will be priorities. First is engineering and technical; second, combat. The rest, even.

"Before tomorrow, I want two things. First, five of you will circulate among all the people to wake them up and tell them that we are going to fight the British. Second, another five will do a competent analysis of the census in light of what I have just told you.

"Remember, when you awaken someone in the middle of the sea, you are awakening him from a state of special dreaming, and he can rise to anything. If you tell him that he is to fight the British you may renew the man who was beaten down. Go and do it. Tell them that we will force our way past the cordon. Tell them anything. Tell them that their mothers and fathers are poised in heaven waiting, that now is the time for the dream of the Jews. By the love of God this ship rides eastward on moon-driven waves and with escort of heaven. Tell them that. With all they've been through, they are due for some sweet language."

4

The census proved a valuable tool. Four hundred and twenty people were aboard. Of these, sixteen were musicians but only ten had instruments. A ten-man band was set up on the main hatch cover. Its composition was especially strange in view of the rousing marches and bandshell waltzes it played: it consisted of four violins, a bassoon, a guitar, a trumpet, a concertina, a snare drum, and a harp. At first there were six alternating conductors, but then from the bundles and scraped suitcases came another concertina, two harmonicas, and an ocarina. Although it was difficult at first to get any of the musicians to play the ocarina (they sneered at it as if it were a dead animal by the roadside), eventually a complex rotational system evolved in which everyone shared his instrument, and from this arose an extremely attractive little orchestra which played a sort of harp-and-bassoon-punctuated, violin-laden ragtime—further exoticized because one of the violinists was a Greek and could play only in Hellenic style. They set themselves up each morning and played until five, and they played a small concert of favorites before everyone went to sleep. Little children, including the tiny girl with perfectly proportioned Japanese-like features, ladybug eyes, and the white dove of ribbon, danced on a wide canvas-covered expanse behind the conductor. They behaved exactly like small children at a wedding. Sometimes even their elders did dances of delight as the strange ship steamed over the electric blue Mediterranean, stacks trailing a constant unraveling cloud of steam. The music was good for the workers, the children, the fighters, the crew, and, some said, even the chickens. Although they did not dance, they seemed to lay a great number of eggs, and as maritime chickens usually veer toward the unproductive, this was seen as a good omen—even by the rabbis, who would normally have cautioned against such divining. But the times were not normal.

There were about a hundred and twenty of the very old, the sick, and small children. The group captains zealously overdrilled their charges by herding them into the lifeboats and marching them from one area of the ship to another perhaps a dozen times a day. Levy closed his eyes to this, letting the frail be driven, until they dispatched from their number a delegation demanding more consideration. He cut the drills by half, but only because he was convinced that entering the lifeboats was by then instilled into their natures.

A hundred, mainly women and merchants, were neither fighters nor engineers. They tended the animals, inventoried and rationed provisions, cooked, mended, watched the children, kept things in supply, and, most importantly, were an extraordinarily adept cottage industrial force. For instance, the wicker furniture was torn apart and rewoven into shields. It took the housewives only three days to create one hundred light and sturdy shields of various sizes, fashioned with strips of rawhide and sisal rope. Similarly, they finished the same number of lethal fighting sticks, turned on an improvised lathe, in less than a week. They sewed canvas garrison belts into which weapons were to slip. In battle, they were to serve as powder monkeys and medical auxiliaries. These one hundred worked very hard and were to be seen in only apparent disorganization laboring at a score or more of tasks.

Two doctors and seven nurses established fore and aft sickbays and took care of the ailing. Except for a few, those who had not been well quickly regained their health. After the seasickness wore off it became obvious that fresh air, decent food, sun, activity, music, and the promise of a place to settle were good medicine for the heat-oppressed souls and their thick ledgers of real and imaginary complaints. The decay of Brindisi and its garbage-filled harbor, where it was not unusual to find the corpse of a dead horse lapping against a quay, was replaced by long glimpses of chalk-white islands floating in a summer sea. Sweet pines and lemon trees grew on quiet terraced slopes. Resources of summer began to act upon shattered lives. At night after work, as the sea rolled and winds swept by, they felt satisfaction and equanimity.

Of twenty crew members, including Levy and Avigdor, ten worked below on the engines. The combat section sent regular shifts to relieve the stokers and help with heavy work. Eight deck hands took care of the rest—more than enough, since no one was interested in long-term maintenance: the ship was to be rammed against a beach south of Haifa. The deck hands climbed up and down the masts, supervised drills, and did watches on the bridge. Levy spoke through several translators. The newsletters also were multilingual, and the entertainer wrote jokes for them, sweetening the directives at Levy's command. Before dinner this same entertainer read the news in Swedish and Italian, and played scratchy opera discs over the public address system. Items of news were broadcast between the scenes of the operas—Madame Butterfly seemed most upset at the building boom in California.

Among those not classified in any major categories were three brothers who had been circus acrobats, two professional cocoa-tasters, and half a dozen rabbis who made the ship quite holy even though in many cases they were dealing with hardened atheists. Several refused the census and did not come to the bridge when summoned. When finally brought to Levy, they looked like criminals. They were criminals. He said, "I'm going to put you in the combat division. Any objections?" They said nothing, but some had expressions which meant that they intended never in their lives to do any work.

"You know," said Levy, "I'm the captain, and I'm the law. If you don't work and do what I tell you, I'm going to throw you off the ship . . . when we're far from land." He opened his desk drawer and took out a revolver in a leather holster wound around by a cartridge belt. The thick magnum bullets were somewhat terrifying to see in their dull symmetrical brassiness. Levy withdrew the pistol, snapped out the barrel, and turned it so that the criminals could see brass inside blue chambers. "Got news for ya," he said, chewing his gum fast, as sheriffs had done in his youth when they had questioned him. "I'm from Texas. Know what that means?" They were fascinated. "It means if you don't work and you won't jump . . ." and here he hesitated for a long time even after the translators had caught up, "I'll put a bullet through your head." Then he winked, but stood up and strapped on the pistol, with no intention of taking it off.

Including seven officers, the combat battalion numbered sixty-three. When augmented from other sections it reached over a hundred. They were divided into ten platoons of ten, each with an officer in charge. Every day they drilled for hours in fighting with night sticks, fire hoses, chains, long pikes, and their fists. They exercised and practiced climbing the masts and cables, swinging from ropes, broad-jumping from hatch to hatch, and maneuvering in unison. The criminals were especially aggressive, and this stimulated the others.

With almost fifty engineers, technicians, and artisans, Levy worked on the war engines. There were to be three corkscrew-type augurs on both sides of the ship. As well as rotate, each had to be able to move back and forth, up and down, and in and out. From the limited materials available, design and manufacture of wheeled and geared augur carriages was a feat. So was the installation of variable-length, angled power trains to provide turn for the drills, three of which would be operating at once. The two cargo booms were modified to slide at the base and lock down. At their tips huge weights were placed in opposition to conical projections with barbed ends of solid steel. These looked mysterious and dangerous.

Turrets were built on the superstructures, and holes made in bulkheads and decks in order to run hose to the upper fortifications thus created. The deck winches which were to power the augurs were taken apart and over-hauled. To get metal for these projects, for the hinged barbwire fences which hung off the sides of the ship, and for the various camouflage structures created to mask most of this from view, parts of the vessel were cannibalized. The effect was one of great sloppiness and disorganization, especially since the windows had been blacked out with an orange antirust paint and the wash fluttered from lines on all decks. The *Lindos Transit* looked like a fruit wagon which had rolled down a steep hill and crashed into a laundry truck.

Hundreds of people crowded the decks, practicing club fighting, doing calisthenics, peeling potatoes, welding, painting, putting out imaginary fires, calling orders, playing violins and an ocarina, praying, dancing, running with messages, nursing children, pushing around supplies, sewing, polishing, bathing, climbing into the lifeboats, climbing the masts, running lines, arguing, jumping from hatch to hatch, drawing plans, singing, sawing, rolling bandages, tearing up wicker chairs, weaving shields, piling rocks and rubble, erecting barriers of wood, metal, and wire, cutting apart rubber tires, treating the sick, hiding, laughing, doing everything except standing like a zoo animal behind bars watching as the world passed by. They had no tolerance for reflection; any motion seemed sacred. Only Paul Levy was privileged to look from afar. They had taken to movement unlike anything he had ever seen, and he thought that should this venture of the Jews prove successful, the new state would be filled with dancers and musicians, but especially dancers, for dancing like nothing else says: *I am still alive.* And although that simple statement will appear vacuous to those for whom living has always been a right, for those who have been challenged on this score, it is the most beautiful and momentous thing to be said or heard in the world.

Paul Levy would sometimes stand on his sway bridge and look backward over the sea along the ship's white wake churning up green water in a continuous noise that sounded like krill or dolphins. He remembered when early in the Battle of the Atlantic he had gone to the bow of the destroyer to hide his face between the converging gray plates and be alone. He had been so exhausted, so frightened, so tired, so cold all the time, and he had always had the feeling that he was going to die. That was when he thought the song "Speed Bonny Boat Like a Bird on the Wind, 'Onward,' the Sailors Cry" meant that the sailors were aforeship crying as they left their homes and country. They were in the mid-Atlantic hunting U-boats and hoping for contact with a surface raider. They were going fast through waters in which there had been a storm and the clouds were trailing rapidly across the sky. As he bent forward to rest against the bow and give his sadness free rein, he realized that in the preceding days he had not been paying enough attention, that his watches and interrupted sleep had left him ignorant of the ship's course. They had penetrated the tropics—a warm wind circled about him and he undid his coat—for the sea was green and thick. As he looked into the bow waves he saw the faithful and miraculous shape of dolphins, speaking to one another in chirps and whistles. They had great strength and endurance, and yet they were beautiful and not hard. By observing this he settled a conflict within himself, determining to be as strong as was necessary and yet not to be hard. One of them veered outward and in so doing made it possible for his eye to catch Paul Levy's eye, and both seemed to smile without smiling. From that day forward he knew how to knit together strength and love.

Almost as if by magic he was afforded another eye in which to look and by which to receive a reflected message from the sea. There was a girl amidships, sewing belts. She was small and delicate, with strong and graceful limbs. Using shreds from the wicker and reed she had woven a straw hat and it framed her gold hair and blue eyes in a rough warm cream color. She was pregnant. Levy could not help staring, so great was her beauty, so different from the saddened beauty of the others. She returned his gaze. The beams between them were as steady as a compass needle. The ship swayed, a water dancer, and the waters fumed and glistened to left and right. There was heat and love in the gaze, an aura of gold as with the dolphins, an interference locking them together for a moment utterly out of their power. Paul Levy felt as if he would go to her, but he turned away. She undoubtedly had a husband, and he was captain of *all* the ship—a rigor unquestioned, to which he had to keep faith.

He did not know that she had lost her husband and believed that he was dead, and that despite the vibrant light surrounding her, the flash of her golden coloring, despite her beauty and despite the captain's skill, she was soon to die alone. Her name was Katrina Perlé.

5

Sometimes in the frozen dry winters which made the Russian foresters fear for their young trees, Katrina Perlé's father climbed the stairs to her room directly under the roof, and there, as the wind howled and his little girl lay curled up under a cloud of silk and down, he would tell her stories. In summer she wanted fairy stories and tales of magic in the forests, but when the snow mounted its lethal attack she wanted to hear about those who had been before and survived. Her father knew little about his family, which had come on horses and mules from somewhere in Central Asia, perhaps from as far as Sinkiang.

"Where did we come from?" she would ask.

"From the land of Israel," he might answer, "but that was a long, long time ago. More recently, we came on a trek from the land of the Golden Horde."

"What did we do there? Did we grow trees?"

"Certainly not. There are no trees in that place. I can't imagine what we did. We must have been nomads or farmers of a sort, or maybe merchants. I do not even know what my grandfather was like, though of course there is that story. By the way, would you like to hear it, the story of Grandfather Shmuel the first (and last) Jewish Grand Master of the Sabre in Russia?"

"Yes."

"I thought so." This was always a favorite. He had told it a score or more times. She loved it and, until much older, she believed it. A long shriek of wind, and then sparkling silence like a snowflake was his signal to begin.

"When Grandfather Shmuel was just a little boy, his father was walking through a field one winter day as the snow swept across it, and the thought occurred to him that though he was a Jew, the land and the seasons upon it did not recoil, and crops planted by him grew as well as any other crops, and at night he could see the clear sky above. This, the delightful prospect of a normal life, made him extremely happy. He would use the lesson of the land so that in some generations (he thought) his descendants could breathe easy. He grew so excited that he danced homeward across the fields: his wife thought he was crazy.

"Little Shmuel was playing by the fire when his father rushed in the door and grabbed the child, holding him high in the air. 'You!' he said, 'are going to boarding school! There, you will learn to speak Russian like a Russian, to ride like a Cossack, and to shoot like a red-robed Grenadier!'

"Shmuel did not know what to say. He was only eight, rather plump, and he didn't know very much because he had spent most of his life arranging tin soldiers on the warm slate hearth. The mother was about to intervene to save

her child from the high responsibilities of being the first Jew ever to attend boarding school, but she saw him cock his head, stare into space, and receive into his eyes the glint of gray light reaching off the steppes. The little fellow had believed what his father had told him and, since he had been a totally blank slate until that very moment, he was set completely upon this mission— a lucky accident, because the only boarding school that would take Shmuel was the dread and infamous Ikrtsk District Military Academy.

"As Shmuel was swallowed into the spike-encrusted gates of the academy, he looked back to see his parents, barred from entry, standing outside on the road. They seemed so lonely—his mother in her fur hat and black cloth coat, his father beside her. Then the gate slammed shut and he was in another world. Did you know, Katrina, that the Ikrtsk cadets did not wear shirts or shoes even in the coldest winters?"

"No," she said, so gently and sweetly that it awed her father.

"That they slept on bare planks, and worked fourteen hours a day?"

"No."

"That they never spoke but only shouted, that they were hard as steel, and that they took baths in ice water?"

"No."

"Well, they did, and for years Shmuel could not grow used to such a life.

"The primary subject at Ikrtsk was sabres, but Shmuel was not allowed even to touch one. Instead, his father bribed the teachers with oranges and apricots so that they would pass Shmuel through to his senior year. The headmaster knew, however, that he could not permit a Jew to graduate from Ikrtsk.

"The headmaster was puzzled. Shmuel had learned and survived all the tricks. Though puny, he was fast, and attempts to surprise him with sword and pistol always failed. Then the headmaster realized that he had only to arrange a sabre match between Shmuel and Lugo, the Captain of the Ikrtsk Cadets—a three-hundred-pound muscle, a stayback forty-five years of age who had never graduated because he could not learn to spell Novaya Zemlya."

Katrina was delighted: she could easily spell Novaya Zemlya; in fact, she could spell anything.

"This was truly clever. Why? you may ask. I'll tell you why. Because . . . the best prisons are those that prisoners make for themselves. When they tried (outside of the rules) to get Grandfather Shmuel, he knew just what to do. But when the danger fell within the expectations of his daily life, it was another story.

"Shmuel began to feel helpless even in the face of these bovine vermin who were so stupid that, for example, they went running after the moon when it appeared to settle behind a small hill, hoping to capture it and sell it to the Czar.

"The match was scheduled for early June, when in the Ikrtsk District the color-laden landscape was wavy with heat and the fields were covered with roses. In contradiction of nature, the swamps around the academy were warm and brown and dotted with orchids.

"Normally, the sabre fighters were allowed armor."

"What is armor?" asked Katrina.

"Armor is like the shell of a turtle, but people wear it. Do you understand?"

Katrina understood.

"However, Grandfather found himself in only his muslin shorts, with a heavy sabre in his hands. The headmaster said, 'And now the Jew Shmuel will fight our dear Lugo. But first, Shmuel will approach Lugo and bend on one knee to apologize for striking a Christian.'

"Lugo lay in all his armor, reclining upon the floor of the academy's great hall, into which the summer morning light came streaming. Grandfather approached and asked for forgiveness. It took a minute for this to penetrate the many bony layers of Lugo's bullet-shaped head, but when it finally got to wherever it was going, one of his eyes flared red and Grandfather could see a tiny circular flame, like a continuous breaker at the beach, winding around the eyeball. Finally, Lugo grunted assent. Grandfather had not learned the many hard lessons of those years for nothing, and although he could not extricate himself by an act of cleverness, he was still not ready to be consumed in such an unequal contest. After all, they had never before given him access to a sabre, and the one they had just presented to him did not even have a handguard.

"He began to feel great rage. He knew that if he did not do something soon, Lugo would cut him to pieces in the wink of an eye. He wanted to escape, but the ranks of cadets were tight around the rim of the hall. He had to upset their lines so that he could run through them. He began to scream and he lifted his sabre. With an echoing cry, he attacked Lugo, who had not had time either to get up or to put on his bullet-shaped helmet of Mongolian design. Grandfather growled like an animal and brought his sword down on the flat, banging Lugo's head like a great gong. The sword broke, the ranks of cadets broke, and although Lugo was dazed he began to get very angry. This was obvious, because his teeth were clenched so hard that they started to break apart and fall out of his mouth.

"Shmuel found his rage dissipating in the face of tremendous fear. Not only was he standing barefoot and half naked with a broken sabre in front of a hog-muscled giant, but the rest of the cadets wanted to kill him. He ran out the door, every single Ikrtsk cadet in pursuit. Everyone knew that an Ikrtsk cadet could chase down a rabbit and, without the use of his hands, behead it with his teeth. Shmuel managed to reach an impenetrable swamp which, even so, he penetrated. He headed for the thickest muddiest bog and burrowed down into it like an anteater. His tracks quickly melted in the mud and thousands of red orchids obliterated his scent. He stayed for many days, not daring to move. From time to time he would see a flame-eyed cadet crisscrossing the forest, sniffing like a hound, crashing through the brush in great bounding arcs. They even tried to burn down the forest, but a rain came. After a few days they gave up and Shmuel made his way home. He never graduated, but then again neither did anyone else.

"His father wept and asked forgiveness. 'What can I do, my son, to gain your blessing?'

"Shmuel thought for a while, remembering how helpless he had been standing there in his shorts. 'Send me,' he said, 'to the Royal Danish Sabre Academy in Copenhagen.' It was done.

"His father paid half his fortune for a very special curriculum. The instructors drove Shmuel day and night for five years. A team of physicians was in constant attendance supervising his exercise, making sure that he was brought to absolute limits but without damage to his system.

"From six in the morning until ten thirty he had sabre practice with three great masters. From ten thirty until twelve he practiced gymnastics and weightlifting. From twelve to six the various masters engaged him in duels without cease. As he had his dinner a librarian read him the latest sabre magazines. After dinner he did gymnastics and went swimming, and then he had intensive fighting practice against an ever-growing number of experts. At the end of five years he spent fourteen hours a day with the sabres, sometimes fighting a dozen great masters at once. At twenty-four years of age he fought twenty-four great masters for twenty-four hours. He had become the greatest sabre fighter in the world.

"His regimen had caused him to grow to almost seven feet in height. He had 325 pounds of solid, lithe muscle, five pounds of regular muscle, and seventy pounds of other things such as brain, organs, etc. He could jump three times his height, run faster than a horse, and see better than an eagle.

"One bright June day he stood at the edge of the orchid-filled swamp near the military academy. He wore the finest black Danish armor, and his sword had been a present from the king. Across his chest were shining gold medals and red ribbons. Rays of light seemed to emanate from his face and eyes. With easy steps he ran ten miles through the swamp intending to fight all five hundred cadets and take on Lugo unarmed. But when he came out at the clearing where once the academy had stood he found only burnt remains— charred wooden beams enwrapped in clinging vines, and waving grasses on the windy floor where once he had fought. Losing many of their number, the peasants had come by the tens of thousands and thrown themselves against the academy, finally destroying it and its students. Shmuel was left in his shining black armor. He had become a jewel in fighting, but he found himself standing in a gentle field, his enemies gone, and soft things about which he did not know beckoning from all around him."

6

That was what Katrina Perlé's father told her. Being a little girl in a little bed late at night she believed him, and it gave her great courage in imagination. She loved her father very much, and since he was absent among the trees most of the time, this was a precious link to him. "Daddy," she would say, "tell me about Grandfather Shmuel."

Even a great revolution did not obliterate the things in Russia which give exiles tremblings of the heart when they think back to a past over which the moon rode and into which violent winds poured with no check except the beleaguered sense of beauty that still lives on. Katrina's father had been a landowner and manager of forests. Declassed immediately, he spent several years reliving his youth as a logger among the ever-present trees. Then he quickly rose and was made a manager of forests once again—perhaps because he had always been indifferent to politics, and even the most rabidly political could see no threat in him. He was convinced that whatever happened he was destined for the same profession, having been placed in it by accident of birth, his own skill, and then a Party committee. Luck restored the line and brought it from an altered course to its original path. His was a family of the forests and farms, and ever would be.

It had seemed to him at first that he might die in the timberland, for he feared partisans and antipartisans, and there was great strain amounting to small wars within the group of those taken from other professions and put into this, one of the hardest. Besides, he was not young, and after so long an absence the work was almost too much. He even dared say: "In its infinite wisdom, the Party cannot see that a man who has not been cutting trees all his life can easily die if he is old and put into the wilderness, and that a forester will surely die if removed to a watch factory or an office full of shuffling loose leaves. The beams for the tables in the offices will be crooked and slow in coming, and watches worn by the new foresters will not keep proper time. God may have been unjust, but at least He was intelligent."

He spoke like this only to former priests and aristocrats, and with circumspection. Then as if by miracle came the minor restoration, and with the few amenities he could usurp he sacrificed a little sacrifice and began once again to enjoy his life on earth.

The daughter was born in a house with a slate roof, gables, and many chimneys. It went unpainted because of the paint shortage and was bare inside except for a few pieces of furniture. There had been more but the Perlés threw it out so as not to appear wealthy. Perlé may have been apolitical, but he was shrewd. The floors and walls were shining and spotless. They repaired every little crack and chip, and found their elegance in cleanliness, order, and rows and rows of small treelets which were always in residence waiting to emigrate out to fresh tracts of timberland. The treelets had small labels on them and were set in terra-cotta pots.

"We are desirous of increasing production, so we have utilized this excessive amount of living space as a greenhouse." As functionaries and inspectors tripped over the trees they thought, in their functional inspectorial ways, how inconvenient and how correct. Let the man continue; he is an eager soul and wants to work for the people. So the daughter was born in a tiny forest, and her baby's cries echoed over the little trees.

As total and terrible as times may have been for most, she was spared, as some are always spared, and in a remote district near the White Sea they lived subject to God and nature, unbending to revolution or any other creation of man—not because they were strong (for they were frail) but because they stood in the eye of the hurricane, correspondent with mildness and awe. Though they had been mainly sad and unsuccessful, not heroic in any way, not great lords or particularly wise, not so strong, not so beloved, from their obscurity they were moved by the beauty of the world, often touched and often electrified by natural storms and colors, and they formed in their way a silent aristocracy—neither empowered nor bold nor ever known. They were to be born and to die in a long unrecognized line only rarely favored by fortune. In this way they suffered and were not distinguished, but they had one special power. They understood the light.

Katrina grew. As a little girl she worried about strange things, about what would happen were the White Sea to splash into the Black, if there were clarinets in the very north of Norway, how it would strain the eyes to see everything at once. She imagined that in the summer the interior of Russia was gold and warm. Railroad tracks lashed down the earth, for in its great goldiness it might easily have floated up to heaven like a balloon. Time passed rapidly over a childhood she remembered to be as still and beautiful as an engraving. And, summer or winter, when the family walked in the town people stared at the father, the mother, and the daughter as small and beautiful as a perfect icon.

A great cathedral stood in the countryside a little to the west. It had been built a century before in exact imitation of Chartres, and would not last the war. During Katrina's youth it had been converted into a grain warehouse and was taken care of by one of her father's friends. They often went to visit; Katrina was allowed to play in the mountains of grain rising high from the vast floor. When she was older she often returned on her own, walking through fields and over hills to reach the enormous room where she sat alone in the deep colored rays from the windows. The different panels were like patchwork, or fields seen from the Alps. Standing on the grain, she thought how much better a knowledge had the builders of cathedrals than the builders of a state, that the idea of a state is like restraining wire which cuts into the living fullness of the world. Moving in that replica of Chartres, the purple and rose lights playing across her face and dress and hair, she thought that the world was more than the sum of its parts, but that if she knew those parts and loved strongly and well she would come to know the world. It was sensible and logical. Know the elements, order them with love, and thereby know the great matter of things. She was too young to know that adversity would seek her out, and that she would struggle and fight, either to win, to lose, or to pass on the endeavor to the receptive innocence and awesome strength of a new generation from her descended. Thoughts of struggle were far from her mind.

But without warning she found herself mesmerized by the deep lights, unable to move, rigid, locked into the tiny waves pulsing from the glass. Her eyes were pulled up almost to the roof of their jurisdiction, and she felt the muscles of her face follow in pleasant numbness. A bolt of white surged through her, snapping her upper body like a whip, throwing her down on the grain, where she writhed in silence and amazement in the darkened cathedral. There she lay in painful intercourse with the spectrum, awakening finally to know that her life was not her own. She had gripped fistfuls of grain, and she cast them away from her as if to fight, but she was so exhausted that there was no fight left, or so she thought.

7

One night when it was raining and she lay in her bed listening to water on the tin and slate, she imagined Leningrad and its summer sky of cool whitened blue like the surface of a temperate sea. A powerful wind forced spray through the windowframe, and she fell asleep with the same rolling, easy sensation to which one abandons oneself in the clear night swell. She dreamed, but not of the sea.

She walked in the marketplace of a large city, where it was very hot and where the buildings and sky were of a similar heavy gray. Her breath was a mist and her eyes clouded with the thickness of July in the commercial back-streets. Pigeons washed in pools of dirty rainwater. A beggar said, "Give a carter a penny for a sledge." Before her was a street of carts with things of all colors. A large van at the end of the street was unloading the carcasses of lambs, and they were piled high—pink like clay roof tiles after many years in the sun. A man emerged from near the lambs and immediately he and Katrina were in communication. They came together slowly and the din grew greater around them; the people shouted and merchants held their wares aloft; a group of men rolled barrels down the street; a man was feeding a fire; green Amazon parrots screamed from their perches. But they converged slowly, she like an angel gliding unseen through Jerusalem on a feast day. Her legs and arms were almost bare. She seemed to glide to him. They embraced and kissed in the shadow of the lambs, and her hat fell off her head and rolled away on the ground.

She believed strongly that all dreams are remembrances of circular time, windows into a future which has once passed. In this instance it may have been true, for when she finished secondary school she left for Leningrad to study at a conservatory there. And she did walk in the markets, where she met a university student with whom she fell in love almost as if it had been a repetition of the dream. His name was Lev: he was good-natured and naïve. She had hardly begun to know him, when he was taken for the Army. Imagining that she would never see him again, she took it in stride because she was young and paid little heed to changes. After all, she had been used to looking at the trees in moonlight, and when she came to the city the electric lights seemed harsh and unnatural. But then she learned that in electric light the trees cast beautiful shadows as they wave and sway, and that the light washes the green into a very strange, almost new color. In the conservatory garden the leaves were like newly split emerald. There, lessons in the softest summer music were often shattered by the railroad whistles of a new military branch line which went right through the gardens, making the old professors despair of war.

Graduating in the late spring of 1941, she was sent to Riga for service in teaching violin and theory in a new Jewish secondary school. She had been put in charge of a summer session, which she determined to finish despite the threat of invasion. The children seemed extraordinarily beautiful. Their smiles and motions were her own depth unveiled. She watched them, loved them, and stayed with them even though she knew that they were all going to die. She taught violin in the little school (which had its doors flung open and was surrounded by planters and pots of searing red geraniums) as if no one would ever do so again. The students were just as intense; it was as if everyone had gone constructively mad, and they worked until all hours of night.

8

They passed slowly through the hot parts of June when boats seem not to move on the water, when old men lean on their chairs, when black spots on the screens are flies too hot to move. Nothing stirred. Lovers sat silent and still with their eyes upon one another. On the first of July the Germans entered Riga.

For the Latvians it was liberation, and they were happy. But for the Jews it was no liberation. They waited, debating in the councils about which was the best course, knowing full well that if they turned left or right, went forward or backward, or did nothing, the results would be the same. This frustration, powerlessness, and anxiety prompted the Sonderkommando to spread rumors that the Jews would be relocated somewhere in the Ukraine. "Why the Ukraine?" some asked. "Riga is a beautiful city. Why can't we stay? At least," they said, "we will not be sent to prison in Germany."

Katrina began to go to synagogue. It was quite unfamiliar to her, the girl who had convulsed with the greatness of God in a Christian cathedral empty but for grain, who had been outstretched on the wheat, stiff and trembling, a total prisoner of the light. There was no practical reason suddenly to become religious. Indeed, some deliberately stayed away. But she and many others joined together at a little synagogue on the outskirts of the city.

It had a red roof, Latvian decorations, a lot of warm-colored woods, and a brass chandelier from Holland. A fine sky could be seen through the windows; clouds passed smoothly and quietly; every now and then the nicest, gentlest breeze would arise and swing the door on its hinges just a little bit, always taking care to move it back again. When the rabbi spoke and when the cantor sang, the magic of the language made her sleepy and comfortable like the summer outside, like the child she had been not so long before in the little pines fragrant around her room under the roof. The candles were burning bright. Some dripped wax onto the floor, and no one cared. Everyone was happy and content; much love was to be found there.

Suddenly a man arose and ran down the aisle. He whipped around and faced the people, and he began to speak tightly and quietly. His eyes were twitching. He could have been a madman. "Can't you see?" he finally shouted, "can't you see that the air . . . I can feel the air; the air is starting to burn. The air is burning, burning, burning black." He moaned with a painful and dreadfully familiar sound, a cry from a long, long history, and they joined him, lamenting in the disordered remnants of their contentment, moaning in a frightening way which froze the children in fear and which became for them an initiation into their religion as they had never dreamed it would be.

Clutching a wooden rail, the rabbi had tears in his eyes and could not speak. The women began to weep, but a young man jumped up and walked to the door, kicking it open with such force that it sounded like a gun. He was more angry than they were frightened, the type to draw fire. "Let us go home," he said strongly, "and eat our dinners." It became quiet, and they filed out. Katrina Perlé sat motionless and afraid. The door was still open and through it she could see an evening star, a planet really, shining silver in soft fading blue. She felt love rising within her, and she kissed her hands and grasped the dark wood as so many of her people had done so many times before.

9

She continued to hope that summer would return and that the sea would again be like glass, even in a cold fiery autumn, a time for starting school or work or love, a season she had treasured. One afternoon on a bright day when she wore a white dress and shirt which glowed in the sun, and she looked as beautiful as she had ever looked—sunburnt, golden, and silver—she came upon a sign posted on a building.

> To all Jews. In order to populate the sparsely settled regions of the Ukraine, all Jews living in Riga on streets where this notice appears, and those with no established residence must appear at the Riga main station on October 5, 1941, at five in the morning, Berlin time. Each Jew can bring baggage not to exceed forty pounds in weight, including food for two days. Food will be provided in stations en route by the German authorities.

It was hard to believe that it would take place the very next day. Everyone was to be assembled and ready at five, meaning that they had to pack that evening, go to sleep early, and arise at four. Hurrying through the streets, she saw the white signs posted everywhere, and when at last she reached the synagogue, it was full. To see so many people in one place might have been encouraging had even one of them known how to avoid the deportation. No one, however, could think of anything. Fearing a pogrom by the Latvian auxiliary police if the order were not followed, they decided to cooperate. A student in tennis shoes pointed out that from a military-strategic point of view it seemed logical for the Germans to populate areas over which they had made lightning gains, and that undoubtedly the Jews would be used to farm and to run factories which the Russians had been unable to torch.

When everyone had departed and the Torah had been moved to the rabbi's house in preparation for the journey, the rabbi came to the empty synagogue. It occurred to him how very very beautiful it was, how wonderful it had been, how many clear nights and days he had spent there. He loved that hall greatly. With a pounding heart, he put out the candles for the last time.

For a day and a half the train went southward as they had expected but at about noon it pulled into a long siding next to a half-built factory and some sheds. Everyone was ordered off. Near the building were three ditches, each about one hundred feet long and twelve feet deep. Under watch of the SS Teilkommando detachment, armed Ukrainian militiamen herded the Jews into groups. All in all, about 1,800 had been on the train. An SS soldier with a whip forced Katrina's group to undress, after which they were made to put their clothing in piles which had been started long before and which lay partly covered with canvas tarpaulins. The pile of shoes was like a little mountain and would have filled a railroad car. Without weeping or crying the Jews undressed and stood together in families embracing each other and saying goodbye while waiting for a sign from another SS soldier who stood at the edge of the ditch, like many of his fellows, with a whip. There was not a single complaint or plea for mercy. They had been removed into a dream and they were dazed. The unfamiliar, half-finished place was hardly real. Katrina watched a man and a woman of about fifty who were surrounded by their children—an infant, a boy and a girl of about ten, and two girls in their middle twenties. An old woman who was obviously the grandmother held the baby in her arms, rocking it, and singing it a song. The baby was crying aloud with delight. The father held the ten-year-old boy, stroking his head. The mother grasped the girl so tightly against her stomach that it must have caused the child pain. The father seemed to be explaining something to the boy when the SS man near the ditch signaled to his counterpart. He in turn apportioned out a number of people, including the family and Katrina, and made them move to another part of the field. Katrina kept saying her number, "Thirty-three."

They waited for several hours during which they numbly watched other groups being formed and then marched to the ditches. In these ditches tightly packed corpses were heaped so close together that only the heads showed. Most were wounded in the head and blood flowed over their shoulders. Some still moved, raising their eyes a little and turning their hands. The man who carried out the execution was seated, legs swinging, on an old weathered board which ran over the ditch. An automatic rifle rested on his knees and he was smoking a cigarette.

More people, completely naked, climbed down a few steps cut in the wall of the ditch, and stopped at the spot indicated by the SS men. Facing the dead and wounded, they spoke softly to them. Many said the *Sh'ma*— then the monotonous rapid cracks of the automatic weapon. The bodies contorted. Their heads, already inert, sank onto the corpses beneath. Blood flowed from the napes of their necks. And this went on and on.

Finally the ditches were full, and Katrina's group was still alive. They stared with motionless eyes at the sky and the sun, which was going down behind smoke. It was getting cold, and they had no clothes. Then the SS man came around to them and half of the group was ordered to lie on the ground. This included the father, the mother, the boy, the girl, and others. Katrina watched with the two young girls, one of whom was holding the infant, as the rifle cracked and those on the ground convulsed. Then the girls and Katrina were made to lie on top of the corpses. By this time it was almost dark and the rifleman had begun to spray the bodies without really seeing them. He fired. Katrina was wounded in the leg, but nowhere else. When all became quiet there was a pile of bodies, like firewood, and just a few were still moaning. Katrina was trapped by the weight of those above her and could not move her arms. She blacked out.

In the morning she awoke to find herself in the same position, covered with blood. Those still alive stared into space with a set look, seeming not to feel the coolness of the morning air. Three peasants passed by, assessing the dead. They came to Katrina and pulled her out. It took all three to do it. Others who could begged feebly for the same assistance. Katrina tried to thank them. But she did not have to. They had pulled her out to rape her. And that was just the beginning.

10

Whether or not by design, and it seemed certainly so, a cardinal policy in keeping together the British Empire was the disposition of two types of force. The garrison, or police station, or, as they said, Tegart Fortress, was one half of the equation. It was found from the Hindu Kush to British Columbia, serving as an England in a box—the thick walls, bars, and peepholes for guns not unlike those of castles embedded deep in the English countryside and in history too. From these strongpoints embarked patrols riding victorious each time they rode, whether on horse or in armored cars or in trucks, up and down the traveled roads, through the villages, and over the wilderness. They could always return to the solid buildings whence they had come. However, as mighty as they were these bases were mostly small, manned only by a few, and not always as alert as they were supposed to have been. In short, nearly any one of them could have been taken by a determined force gathered from the several localities they were assigned to subdue. But then the rebels, or the peasant militia, or whatever, would have had to deal with the mobile character of the British forces drawn from other small points until they reached an impressive number. Of course, if the native populations had organized by country instead of by region, they might have succeeded in beseiging each small unit and in preventing every one from either giving or receiving aid. But then they would have been confronted by forces from other colonies and from England itself. Fractious populations could not accomplish national rebellions, much less world revolution. Thus the Empire lived. In co-opting local notables, making British justice felt in the interest of Britain, keeping alert to challenges which were likely to spring up anywhere at any time, and faithfully quashing tiny uprisings with reserve forces drawn from surrounding areas, a very small number of good-humored men was able to control the world, in their rapid actions surrounding and suppressing both unrest and general cognizance of it. If anyone was aware of this, they were; that is why they were so keen to do their duty and so punctilious about it. And as the Empire declined and they were pressured from all sides they often rushed to their stations with the eagerness and lack of complacency which marks devotion to an almost extinguished dream.

One such officer, impressed deeply by the miraculous character of a small nation exploring, discovering, and colonizing what had been an unknown world; devoted to conceptions of quality, responsibility, and fairness; a man not unpleasant in his demeanor or in his speech; a good and often tender man, was Captain Keslake of the Royal Navy, of the British destroyer *Shackleton*, of the General Naval Headquarters in Palestine, of a small office in a huge fortress high on a hill in Haifa.

His windows overlooked the sea, which he was able to scan for many miles. Being on a promontory next to Stella Maris, he could see Syrian mountains, Jebel Druse, Jermak, and others, and the Lebanon to the north beyond a vast windy coast of rising dunes. To the south was a long white beach flanked by small mountains. The winds whistled around the radar and the wire. At night a huge light played over the sea to guide ships to the harbor. Servants brought him lemonade on a silver tray—the lemon juice, sugar, and iced water unmixed. He had a positive sense of well-being there, high up in the thin air, suspended in blue, clean strong sunlight like that of the mountains penetrating a light beige-colored room, and yet all within the precinct of the sea. If he listened hard he could hear the white waves below. His ship, manned and ready, rested in Haifa port.

When not aboard *Shackleton*, he chose to stay at a rest center for officers, a building south a little down the coast road. He was a good-natured man but he liked best of all to be alone. Mornings saw him on the porch having his breakfast early, looking out at the sea. He would often walk down the glassine sparkling beach, wandering in and out of the hills and dunes. Once, a Bedouin who had brought his flocks to lick salt asked Keslake the time. Keslake replied in Arabic, "Ten after eight," at which the Bedouin was completely confused. Reacting quickly, Keslake corrected his answer to "Eight and a *quarter*," which the old man understood. The low mountains were good for wandering. When occasionally he would meet an Arab or a Jew he did not act arrogantly, as he might have, but smiled and made a little bow, and there was some fellowship. He wandered in the cemeteries too, for many of his friends had fallen and even at home he had been drawn to tombs as small stories of lives, encompassments terribly inadequate and yet calling for homage, respect, and not a little thought.

In the Muslim cemetery across the road from the rest center he felt entwined by the tendrils of Arabic script. He read the inscriptions, but it was as if no one were buried underneath. It was the same in the Jewish cemetery—he could not even *read* Hebrew. All these people and their aspirations perplexed him, for he had been too shy to fall in love with one of their women and he had not had the time to become enveloped in their culture as he had felt enveloped by the mere script on the Arabic gravestones. He could only respect them, and no more.

But a quick leap across a young hedge into the Commonwealth War Cemetery transformed him. There, were his people, though they were not all English or even Australian or Canadian. Buried under the Union Jack in immaculate garden splendor, as opposed to the sensual free-flowing vines and aromatic flowers scattered loosely beyond the hedge, were English and Scots, Irish, Sudanese, Indians, Egyptians, Muslims, Jews, Poles, Greeks—all the Allies except the Americans, whose wealthy government had transported them elsewhere. These were his brothers, fighting on his side in the great wave of war, participants in fleets and armies and the global span of the English endeavor. There were inscriptions which moved him as he went from grave to grave: 8351 SOWAR RAFI MUHAMMED, 13TH DUKE OF CONNAUGHT'S OWN LANCERS, 24TH OCTOBER, 1943, AGE 22. H. BELLEHE, SERGEANT MAJOR, GREEK ARMY, 14TH SEPTEMBER, 1944 (a Jew, with a great Star of David under the Cross of the Greek Army). CAPTAIN M. C. KISSANE, THE ROYAL IRISH FUSILIERS, AIRBORNE, 29TH JUNE, 1946.

It was quiet in that cemetery. Once in a great while a truck went by on the sea road. A goat was tied up outside the hedge, his nibblings on the rich grass vaguely discernible. The sea shimmered beyond. Behind Keslake were rocky green hills, and palms where the water collected in basins and curvatures. At night he watched the sky from a wooden bench, standing guard over the fallen men, alone in the close-cropped darkness. They were young and would soon be forgotten. But under the night sky he knew that he would not forget, that he would be strong for them, that he would uphold that for which they died, that he would guide his ship through the waters traversing and cutting like a mighty hound. He would be ever faithful to the sea for them; he would be faithful to the quick flash of their wasted lives which he felt in the open air above them, and even though he stood in wide open night under a vast ocean sky, he felt suffocated.

The following day he was invited to ride with a convoy north into the interior. A young Irish major had asked if he did not want to see some of the country. "It's very beautiful up there," he said, "quite like you've never seen before. We have fruit growing all over the place, and at this time of year there's a freshwater pool fed by the underground rivers from the winter rains. The water falls from ledge to ledge until it ends in another pool twice as large. Would you like to take a swim and have some good Arab food?"

Keslake could not resist, and they left the next day in a small group of armored vehicles, trucks, and jeeps. He and the Major shared an open car and traveled the whole way without a word. Keslake was in a beginning-of-summer reverie, when so much satisfaction is to be had from nature's luxuriant outpourings that the human voice and human needs seem thin, remote, and inconsequential. On the road up they passed under countless tall trees shadowing them as they went. The sky was entirely clear, and in the hills near the fort the sun beat down on blue-green brush in which wild boars crashed and plumed birds hopped from branch to branch.

Upon his arrival, Keslake went up on the roof to an open sleeping porch where he was to stay, and the Irishman joined him, bringing two gins and tonic, which they drank with enormous relief. The Irishman tried to broach the subject of home but Keslake would not hear of it. "This is home," he said. "That's the penalty for being English, and I'm not sure that it's a penalty. I will never, never go back to Birmingham, never as long as I live. It would be a disgrace." Then there was silence and they fell asleep in their chairs, the hot sun being tempered perfectly by a steady cool breeze. Through half-closed eyes Keslake could see Haifa miles away rising from the bay like a city of white castles and golden domes, which it was. It reminded him of Istanbul, which he had seen as a boy when it was Constantinople. In a near dream the far-away white columns of Haifa became subject to a more youthful eye, wild and untutored as it had seen Constantinople from the sea; like a huge inverted roc's egg split and painted, Hagia Sofia had drowned in its own quiet and waited for the umpteenth sun.

That night there was a feast. Local Bedouins had been commissioned to cook lamb, rice, hommos, and other such things, which were then served on good British plate with napkins, flatware, and glasses. Everyone ate too much and drank too much. In a frenzy of eating, the Irish major said, "You see, we take off a lot this time of year. The springs only last about a week, oh, maybe ten days."

"How do you know," replied Keslake, wolfing down sizzling chunks of lamb between swallows of iced wine, "that it's not poisoned?" He spoke loudly above the din in the courtyard lined with rifles on ready racks. Indian Muslim sentries (who would not drink) paced the walls above. "It would be rather easy for the Arabs to do us all in with a side of lamb, wouldn't it?"

"Nonsense! They're our friends. They wouldn't do it. Besides, I'd hang every last one of them."

"But you'd be dead."

"Then it wouldn't matter a bit, would it?"

"I suppose not. But what if they attacked right now, when everybody's drunk and stuffed?"

"They wouldn't attack now!" said the Major. "They never attack when we're drunk! They never attack at all! And if they did the chaps from up the road would be here in no time. It's only ten miles. Don't worry. Eat your poisoned lamb."

Keslake was always at the ready, or at least he tried to be. When the next day he swam in the clear pools, hardly able to tell them from the clear

sky, his pistol lay on the bank, always within sight. If he turned he knew at
what angle and distance he would find it. Even so, he would have lost himself
in the thunderously cool cascades had not a Sikh summoned him from the
most memorable bright water of his life to tell him that he was wanted in
Haifa that evening, and a convoy was just leaving. The Sikh had been
guarding when the message came over the radio on his jeep. It had come
from the fort. They had heard by telephone from the Army Command in
Haifa. The Army Command had heard by telephone from the Naval Command, which had heard from Suez, which had heard from Crete that another
illegal immigrant ship was making its way to the Palestine coast, as straight
as an arrow. Turning his back on the blue and white water, Keslake quickly
dressed, holstered his pistol, and set out with dispatch for Haifa port.

11

One morning the passengers of the *Lindos Transit* awoke to find themselves
in a dreamlike new land. The sea was azure and alert as they had never seen
before, the winds warm and fresh. To the south were the mountains of Crete
in steadfast order, swept back into a line of peaks which billowed like cloud,
so white were they, a blinding white. Many of the passengers had seen the
Alps, the Urals, the Appenines, but never had they seen mountains rising
from the sea. Preparations had been completed: Levy's plan allowed several
days of rest before the landing. The musicians were silent. Gulls wheeled and
turned in smooth waves around the ship. The passengers were transfixed.
They felt it possible that the gray mists of their lives, their dark cold histories,
could be cured from them, lifted out of them by the sun. They looked at
themselves—sunburnt faces, golden and dark hair, eyes green, blue, gray,
brown, and black. Perhaps in such a place they could again make themselves
whole. They had nothing. They were no one. Their fathers, mothers, brothers,
sisters, lovers, sons, daughters, and friends had been slaughtered like animals,
their homes looted and burned. The things they had had on their bodies had
been taken, their hair cut, their health stolen. But suddenly this landscape
had arisen from the sea. Levy had deliberately turned his ship and taken it
close to Crete. His charges fell in love with the abstract air above the mountains. They were resolute. A curtain of strength fell around them. No warship
was going to take them to camps on Cyprus. They would die first—willingly.

But matching the artistry of their determination was that of the British.
From the depth of the encouraging mountains they peered at the *Lindos
Transit* through a telescope twenty feet long. The great elevation and clear
air enabled a strange little detachment of Welshmen to scan a hundred miles
of sea. Levy had held his vessel within a few miles of the coast. The Welsh-

men were able to see the ship's name, and the white banner with the blue Star of David flying briskly from the mainmast. All seemed normal. The passengers were still and passive as they always were. The ships were invariably in shambles, and so was the *Lindos Transit*. Panels were missing, pieces of metalwork hung over the sides, and the windows were a crazy orange. The sergeant in charge of the post casually reported to his headquarters that the ship was in poor condition, overloaded, making only about ten knots. There were, to the surprise of the observers, quite a few sheep on board, standing on deck crowded up near the forecastle. Paul Levy had intended to slaughter them, but a delegation from the passengers had insisted that they be left alive, even were it to mean less food. And so it was that these Italian sheep were destined for Palestine, and they passed the time dreaming of the olive groves and bare meadows where they had been born.

Katrina Perlé slept on a hatch cover, the one on which the band had played in the more carefree days farther from the point of contact with the English. It was not the most comfortable place to sleep: the vibrations of the engines worked their way up hard and steady, and very often when the wind curled or backed, the stack exhaust settled amidships. A suffocating oily smell and taste in the air, familiar to mariners, was unwelcome to the twenty or so sleepers and sprawlers on the hatch cover, for its unpleasantness and for its associations. When Katrina opened her eyes she was shocked to see bodies lying around her, and she would not sleep again until she had seen some movement confirming that they were living men and women, and that therefore she herself was alive. But the sun had been of great help, as had been the views and the air. She was always partial to light and its various manifestations, messages, and tricks, and she could not help but share in the general good will and optimism. Her pregnancy was just beginning its seventh month.

At first she had wished to do away with the child, but then, like the magnificent rarity of a warship backing up, she reversed herself entirely and saw it as a great gift, comforting, the beginning of something better. She did not care that despite her beauty, which increased every day in the sun and air so that her hair was the color of burnished gold and her face roseate and dark, no one wanted her. It seemed not to matter. Though she believed the child's father to be dead, she was not alone.

A full day passed, during most of which Avigdor was at the helm—a strange new passion for him, of great utility to Levy. That evening as the sea got a little rough and the clouds broke into driven archipelagos, Levy was making his final plan. They would harry the boilers all night and through the following day when they would some time hit the coast. He knew that the radars on Mt. Carmel and on the destroyers could track him at night, but that in darkness no action could be taken short of blasting them from the water—something which caused him to be sure that they entered territorial waters during daylight. Besides, a night landing would be difficult for his passengers, too many of whom were old and sick. Everyone knew his station and job. The weather was off just enough to set them properly on edge. Levy wore his pistol almost ceremoniously, for he could not imagine how it might help. As the clouds passed, they called to mind all the geography of the wide world as he had always known and loved it. That night the ship made fourteen knots—the swan song of the old boilers.

It was a difficult night. The cabins and hold were silent and dark, but many in them were awake listening to the waves and the engines. Those who slept on deck looked up past the cables and shrouds and watched the smoke trail to stern past an array of mountain-flower stars. It was moist and uncomfortable. Even those who knew each other well did not speak. They just looked at the sky, toward the dark crashing and hissing which was the sea, and at themselves—rolled up in as many blankets as they could get, cold, sunburnt, thin, strong, and uniformly young even though they were of many ages and the young themselves were not youthful. This was something entirely different.

They had their own warship and were determined to fight and die. Curiously, they were in no way frightened, and looked forward with great anticipation to the battle. The unlimited expanse of the sea, the air, the nights, the military order in which Levy worked them (sensible, precise, and rigorous), and the sun rising to illuminate those upward-reaching mountains in Crete, had enabled them to throw over for a time the camps, the wire, the railheads, the minor indignities, the boxcars, the death, and the darkness. They were alive on a ship in the sea and they would arise in strength as if from myth. Death was familiar; they had already crossed over those lines, something the young sailors who would oppose them could not even imagine. A ship of the living dead—breathing, animate, and warm—was going to be quite a surprise for those who were simply manipulators of steel, engineers and analysts who could not delight in dying.

12

Dawn broke swift and hot. They were twelve miles from the Palestine coast and in the distance the Carmel Range appeared, a thin purple line dark in shadow. The immigrants imagined with a sense of mystery how on that thin dark line Jews were arising to the normal tasks of farming, factory, and fight. They imagined the cows being milked, the chickens scattering like idiots in the face of golden feed, the soft earth beneath barn doors, the dawn shadows, and the cry of the birds. The distant strip had so much import that they stood on deck mute and still. What moved them was not so much the legend and that they were at last coming home, but rather a simple vision of the sun coming up there on the beginnings of another day's work, morning light coming through windows in a warm and beautiful land.

At first light, Levy saw two British destroyers heading for him in perfect symmetry. He calculated their distance and speed, went to the microphone, and called general quarters. From his flying bridge he saw that the response could not have been better. In the time it took him to take off his leather jacket, tuck his shirt into his pants, adjust his pistol belt and ammunition clips, and put his jacket on again, they were completely at the ready. But completely at the ready meant that lines of laundry suddenly were strung across the decks, babies began to receive very long and luxurious open-air baths, and everyone ate with great ceremony and deliberation. They waited as the two destroyers, then in bright sunlight, approached and veered out to the north and south so that they could execute wide turns and come about parallel to the *Lindos Transit* and its course.

This they did, looking fast and beautiful. Avigdor was at the helm; Levy studied his adversaries through the ship's glass. They were twin ships (always a pleasure) of the S-class. Despite their efficiency and impressiveness they were no mystery to him. He knew them well and had been aboard. Completed at the end of the war, they were modern and extravagantly equipped. They had six boilers which collectively could bring up 40,000 shaft-horsepower. This in turn could propel the ship at 30 knots or more. There were four 115 mm. guns and (more to the point) half a dozen 40 mm.'s and numerous mounted machine guns. These ships had a complement of 250 men, and Levy assumed that they were outfitted with ingenious boarding equipment. An appropriate scan revealed about a hundred marines on the decks of each ship; gangways; hoses; and nets ready to swing. The marines were fully regaled in tropical battledress. Pan helmets, pistols, rifles, submachine guns, clubs, shields, boarding pikes, and battering rams cluttered the decks. The soldiers were smoking, talking, drinking from white mugs. They were calm, and must have subdued some tough ships to get that way.

Levy was happy at the sight of two trim new British ships. He tried not to be, but instinctively he felt reassured. How often had American and British ships ridden the ocean together in preparation for a fight. For a second or two he thought of surrendering to the nearby English-speaking, young, war-bred officers like himself. But when he remembered why he was in the Mediterranean, and that he could easily die at the hands of the Royal Navy, its blue beauty disappeared from his eyes and he returned to the boat of Jews.

By the time *Shackleton* and *Stanford* closed, running about 200 feet off both sides of the *Lindos Transit*, the group was nine miles from the coast. Timing was most important. Levy was hoping that they would not attempt to board before the three-mile limit. This would prevent many casualties. But he had heard that the British began their actions on the high seas, according to the premise that illegal blockade runners were outside the law and deserved to be treated in like fashion. The British were lords of that part of the Mediterranean anyway and could do what they wished, and they had had some outstanding failures when, like gentlemen, they had waited for the three-mile limit. Suddenly the dilapidated immigration ships could seem like speedboats and the docile Jews like polecats.

At eight and a half miles, Levy could see *Shackleton*'s captain observing him through a mounted telescope. He smiled and gave a little salute. When the reconnaissance was complete, Keslake was the first to speak. His voice was powerfully amplified and it echoed off water and steel in a particularly cold-sounding series of blows: "This is Captain Keslake of H.M.S. *Shackleton*. State your nationality and destination." Silence followed as precious seconds went by. Keslake again clicked on his microphone. "I would appreciate your statement, and advise you to comply." Still they did not answer. Keslake glanced at the coast upon which the small group of ships was closing. "One final request from me," he said, "is all you will get. I ask you for the third and last time to state your nationality and destination."

Levy replied in a deliberately irritating backwoods drawl: "I'm from Virginia . . . I'm going over there . . . yonder." The marines laughed and waited for their captain's reply.

"Very well for you," said Keslake. "You are a Virginian ship heading yonder. It is illegal to go yonder. Stop your engines and stand by to receive a tow cable."

"First of all," answered Levy, changing his tone to one of challenging argumentation to gain time by forcing Keslake to a lengthy response, "I'm from Virginia, but the ship isn't. It is in fact of Italian registry, but it is foremost a Jewish ship. I would like to advise you, Captain, and your crew, that you are approaching Jewish territorial waters, and are subject to arrest at my discretion. Turn your ships around, and go back to Britain." Then Levy motioned for one of his sailors to run up a string of signal flags. They read: *annuit coeptis*.

Keslake smiled, trying to remember his Latin; he couldn't. All eyes were on the signal flags. Keslake turned to the junior officers on the bridge. "Does anyone remember his Latin?"

"Something about beginnings, sir," said a navigation officer.

"Well, damn them, it looks like we'll have to·go aboard. We haven't that much time to waste it on Latin mottoes. Where do they get these captains? Next thing you know, they'll be challenging us to duels and spelling bees. Prepare to board." The claxon sounded.

Immediately Levy commanded stations ready. Laundry and washtubs were tumbled overboard, babies withdrawn, and the barbwire barricades winched to their protective positions. By this time the coast was only seven miles distant: the Carmel Range rose alluringly. It was Levy's plan to put his defenses in view or in operation not simultaneously, but as they were needed. In that way the British would never know what was next and would be forced to consider their own dispositions and responses at each juncture, allowing the coast to draw ever closer.

The marine major ordered up the wire-cutters. By the time the cutters were distributed and *Shackleton* drew closer, with *Stanford* in reserve, they were six and one half miles from the coast. Levy ordered up his final burst of steam. The destroyers adjusted their speeds. More time was gained. When *Shackleton* was about fifty feet from the *Lindos Transit*, Levy sent his main battle force on deck.

One hundred and fifty men emerged from the gangways and assembled on deck in fifteen groups of ten, looking smarter in their organization than did the British, who were grouped into rough lines. The Jews carried wicker shields almost exactly like those of their opponents. They had web belts from which hung clubs and (to Levy's surprise) knives. They were for the most part broader and more muscular than the marines, but much shorter. They had no firearms. However, four groups comprising forty men were lined up behind what Keslake had thought to be some sort of improvised chairs, which were actually rubber slings. Behind each slinger was a small pile of stones and a powder monkey, who dropped a stone into a breechlike contraption from which it was shot. The fifth group climbed into the two crow's nests and into the breastworks of steel and sandbags on the superstructure. They manned two steam hoses (from the breastworks) and three stations for throwing Molotov cocktails. "Good God," said the British as the little army took position. Keslake was astonished, and his marines were nervous; suddenly it was no longer a picnic. *Shackleton* sailors manned machine guns, and *Stanford* trained her 115 mm.'s on the *Lindos Transit*. The coast was six miles away.

"Put down your weapons," said Keslake. "We have vastly superior force, and are going to board."

"Keslake . . ." said Levy, waiting for a long time before he finished, "I would like you to know that my name is Paul Levy. I am from Norfolk, Virginia. I spent most of my adult life fighting the Battle of the Atlantic so that convoys of our men and matériel could get to Britain. I saw a lot of my friends die, we picked up a lot of British sailors . . . and you are a first-class compassionless motherfucking son of a bitch."

This angered Keslake, but not his crew. They had not been insulted, only he. And yet, in a spirit of anger, he then ordered them to board. He realized as *Shackleton* thudded against the port side of the *Lindos Transit* and gangways were rolled over and tightened to bolt the ships together that his men were not throwing themselves across as he would have done, but were proceeding delicately. As the British sappers began to cut the wire the Jewish steam men sprayed the fences with live heat, driving the sappers back. It was so effective that a few minutes passed with no progress at all. The steam men were proud of their work and leaned over their metal barricades uncautiously. Levy saw it, and he also saw the machine gunners take aim. He did not know the nationality of the steam men. They probably spoke several different languages anyway, and there was hardly enough time. "Get back," he screamed over his microphone. But they did not understand. A *Shackleton* machine gunner fired and killed them. One of them fell backwards and landed on the deck, injuring a slinger.

The sappers dismantled the wire very quickly, and when the *Lindos Transit* was still five long miles from the Palestine coast, British marines began to board her. As they started coming down gangways and cargo nets the *Lindos Transit* veered to starboard and back again, halting them just long enough for the slingers to take aim and fire. The technique was extremely effective. The slingers had had a week of organized practice during which they fired at dummies hung from racks in the locations of possible boarding ramps and nets, and they had developed excellent aim. The first barrage was one of small pellets, perhaps ten or twenty from each sling. In half a minute more than a thousand coin-sized rocks rained down on the marines. Some were knocked unconscious and lay on the decks; some were driven back; some held; and some kept on coming. But as they were too few they were quickly subdued by the battle groups. The slingers kept on slinging, having switched from shot to rocks and rubble of considerable size. These did not hit very often but forced everyone on *Shackleton* to be extremely careful, a harassment which did not last, for the *Shackleton* gunners sprayed the decks in front of the catapults with heavy fire. As planned, Levy ordered them abandoned, and the operators rushed to the augurs and specially adapted cargo cranes. The plan was to have been the capture of the British ship by auguring into its portholes and runoff vents, dropping the cranes onto the decks like grappling hooks, and looping steel cables over its chocks and then winching them tight. Levy was to have announced to the British that if they did not retreat he would blow holes in his keel plates and scuttle the *Lindos Transit*, capsizing the British warship in the process. The *Lindos Transit* was in sufficiently critical disrepair to sink in about five minutes. In five minutes, not even the British could cut through the several grasping augurs, cables, and crane hooks, and no one could prevent the *Lindos Transit* from going under.

Keslake had not thought that he would still be fighting at only four miles from the coast. That gave him three miles, since at a mile his seventeen-foot draft would almost certainly ground him. At fourteen knots, he had about fifteen minutes to subdue the ship. He still thought he could win, but he had Haifa informed of the situation and he requested that troops be sent to the beach. Whether they would arrive on time and in sufficient number was none of his concern. Were they to be necessary it could only mean that he had failed. So he combined his anxiety and his astuteness, and quickly recognized some sort of threat in the strange machinery on the deck of his quarry. The microphone clicked its hollow echo. "If anyone touches those machines, he will be shot. Captain Levy, inform your men about this in their own language. *Shackleton* gunners, carry out this order in one minute's time."

Levy too had been calculating. He thought that in less than fifteen minutes he could make it just by resisting with his deck force and keeping the enemy out of the wheelhouse and the engine room. His men were so positioned and drilled. He heard the echo of his own speaking machine: "Captain Keslake, you will have your way. Congratulations on guessing my plan. But I need at least three minutes to inform my men in their several languages of this new order, since we had not thought to practice it in English."

"Two minutes," said Keslake, to which Levy replied, "Very well."

The interpreters spoke slowly to fill up the two minutes. They were only two and a half miles from the coast and could see the white beaches, and individual trees at the tops of ridges. Before the interpreters had calmly and elegantly elongated the new instructions, the marines were pouring onto the *Lindos Transit*. There was nothing to stop them except hand-to-hand fighting —no catapults, no steam, no threat of capsizing, no wire fences, and Levy did not use the Molotov cocktails for fear of a great slaughter.

The real battle had begun, with Keslake informing his marines that they had five minutes to win or their ship would run aground. They fought like madmen, but the Jews responded in kind. Many were badly injured and lay bleeding on the deck. Some were knocked over the side, after which *Stanford* lowered some boats. Using clubs and shields, fighting on the deck of a ship steaming over a blue sea toward an Asian coast, the men felt as if they were in another time. But then in fear of running aground or losing his prey, or both, Keslake told his marine major to use any force necessary to reach the bridge and stop the ship. A squadron of marines with submachine guns fired into the massed defenders to clear a corridor to the bridge ladder. The Jews fell, their glossy yellow wicker shields rolling away from them over the deck and into the sea. There were gasps and cries. Sweating under their pan helmets, the marines winced at what they had to do. The coast was a mile and a half away, the beaches empty and white.

13

The lower decks of the *Lindos Transit* were silent except for the confused speaking of the wounded and dying. On wooden tiers of plank bunks, the old men, women, and children could not see the blue sky or the beaches ahead. Instead, it was hot and close and lanterns swayed back and forth as if the ship were simply delivering freight to a tranquil island in the South Seas. They heard automatic weapons fire and the occasional exchanges over the loudspeakers. For them it was not an unusual position or occurrence—to be huddled in a dark low place while the world outside fought and built-up things were leveled.

Europe was in ruins; two thirds of the Jews had been slaughtered; the rest dispersed, broken, and separated. And yet the remaining Jews could play music, write words, build, make children. Their insides were destroyed, but messages came to them from all about. Clocks ticked, light rays were refracted, fires burned, the sea rose. Nature persisted like a metronome, saying, Keep on, keep on, keep on. And one by one, piece by piece, the strong ticking was joined by hearts revived, by instruments of warmth and creation. The silence vanished and natural laws which had withstood all assaults appeared once again as ultimate guides, as they had been in the beginning and will always be—lines along which shattering can make itself whole. As they watched the lantern in its pendulum motion, light emanating from it, they did not know that they were slowly being healed.

In the long and difficult night before the siege, perhaps because of the tension, or her diet, or God knows why, Katrina had begun to feel the first labor pains. What she did was not surprising, especially in view of her years in camps and in hiding. She sought the emptiest part of the ship, where the lower deck met the slant of the bow, and she crawled into a rope locker which smelled of pitch and pine. It was dark and hot, but comfortable on the canvas and hemp, and isolated. She was alone, as if she had her own room again. The water against the bow reminded her of Russia and the rain on the slate roof. The smell of pine was like her house, and the pitch like the railroad tracks and new ties which had held down golden hinterlands. She wanted to have the baby, to nurse it, to sleep, to be in peace. She was also somewhat ashamed. It was as if she wanted to be the first to see the child, to make certain that she could love it. At the peak of the siege her pains came thick and fast, and the child was born in darkness onto the heavy ropes and canvas. There was silence until she opened the locker door a crack and the cooler air made the baby cry. It was a raw unbelievable scream laden with emotion and energy, and it shocked her because it was so new and so powerful. Where did he find such strength? she asked herself, and then she wept.

Before the marines had arrived on the bridge and taken Levy prisoner, he had given two commands. The first was that the engine room was to be bolted shut from the inside and that the motor men were to keep up full speed until the ship ran aground, no matter what they heard from the bridge. The second was that the rudder cables be cut so that the ship could travel only in a straight line. An English lieutenant rushed to the engine room telegraph and signaled full stop. He then took the wheel, which was limp and turned too easily to have been connected to a ship's rudder. Levy had a wide grin. They were a mile or less from the beach, where Palmach trucks were waiting and the British Army was nowhere in sight. For fear of running aground, *Shackleton* had disengaged but was still alongside, hanging back a few hundred yards. Only fifteen marines remained on board, and would be overpowered by the Palmach. Levy glanced at the wheel turning free.

Two children who had been playing below decks oblivious to the terror above, reported to their mother that they had heard a baby crying. At first she refused their entreaties but then followed them to the rope locker. They hung on her skirts as she cautiously opened the door, fearing that a rat might spring out. There was Katrina, holding her child too tightly for its own good. The woman realized that to save the infant she had to get it immediately into the light and air, wash it, cover it, and bring it to a doctor. The baby was so tiny and so feeble that she feared for its life. But Katrina became hysterical and would not let go, so the woman slapped her hard across her face and pulled the baby away. Katrina sank back on the ropes. The light coming through the hatch was a blur of colors because of the water in her eyes. The woman rushed off with the baby, intending to return for Katrina. Katrina was silent, for she had not understood.

The Lieutenant used Levy's microphone and informed Keslake that the rudder cables had been severed and the engine room would not respond. They were three quarters of a mile from the coast and between shifting uncharted bars. Keslake picked up his binoculars and glanced at the beach. He could see the faces and caps of the Palmach, but not one British soldier. Risking a great deal, he ordered full speed ahead and took the helm himself. His officers were numb with their own beating hearts. Feeling the surge of speed he had summoned, Keslake eased his ship about and pointed his lancelike prow at the bows of the *Lindos Transit*. The Palmach was rowing out in surfboats and rafts. *Shackleton* hesitated as at the top of a wave, and Keslake rammed her fiercely against the port bow of the *Lindos Transit*, opening a huge gash and knocking the ship to the side. He then veered off and made for open water. He had done what he could in the face of stubborn opposition. His day was over.

The bow of the *Lindos Transit* began to go under, and by the time the ship was several hundred yards from shore it dug into the sand and stopped its momentum with a great release of steam. The Palmach came aboard and began the evacuation. They had to leave half a hundred behind because the British had been sighted driving at great speed down the sea road from Haifa. Those abandoned included the two doctors, the wounded, the newborn infant, and Levy. They were seized and put in detention.

The two vigilant children rode away with their mother on the back of a farm truck. They pulled at her and said, "What about the mommy on the ship? Where is she?" The mother hushed them.

That day Keslake lost his passion for the chase and for arms as well.

Twenty-six died. Many more were captured. Some fell into the sea and drowned. About 350 immigrants had at last escaped the acrid soil of Europe, and they rode shaken but singing in old trucks under the sweet trees and warm air of a place where there were farms and endless orange groves full of green, fragrant, waxy leaves. Paul Levy became a Jew. Katrina Perlé died alone. And her son, Marshall Pearl, was born.

II
The Hudson

1

Marshall was not yet two months old when he arrived in New York Harbor aboard a French ship, the *Égalité*. A visa and "passport" were attached to his basket crib. No one would make off with them, since the photographs were of a prune-faced infant. Also in the packet was a letter addressed to Marshall's future parents, whoever they would be. It was sealed with red wax upon which were stamped a three-cornered hat, a duck, a crucifix, and a ring of blurred Latin. Inside was Paul Levy's narrative of whatever he could gather about the child's background, with the injunction that Marshall be informed of it at an early age. It had been written in the garden of the Dominican Sisters of Marseilles. Levy had gotten Marshall to Toulon, and found that the French refused to part with him except through official channels. The sisters had agreed to send Marshall to America as soon as they could. They were somewhat taken with Levy, and he paid them. Marshall was shuttled onto a great liner with his basket crib and envelopes. What passed for his birth certificate was signed *Paul Levy, Lieutenant-Commander, U.S.N.*

The Mayor of Marseilles was a passenger on the *Égalité*, and so it was greeted by an armada of fire boats and police launches blowing their whistles. The New York Fire Department Negro Band rode along on top of a big fire boat. They played jazz, and the conductor was swinging his arms and pounding his feet, saying, "Okay, my man, c'mon, c'mon, get them feets movin'." The Mayor stood on a high deck surveying the city. Tall needle-pointed buildings minding the sky's business in gray and green solitude would have been impressive, but on this hot day in August with jazz music and a dozen white water plumes, even the Mayor caught his breath. What impressed him most was neither the jazz-echoing cliffs in Manhattan, nor the high-wire heavenly bridges, nor the ceremony, but the staggering amount of traffic in the harbor. Manhattan's everyday was like the greatest of armadas, the choicest dramas of history, a million intensities. Giant ferries methodically plowed their ways crossing paths in all directions. Coastal tankers, lines of barges, freighters, launches, skows, tugs, river boats, sailing craft, yachts, and naval vessels headed up and down the roadlike junctions of the rivers. Faces were intent in the morning sun. Battalions lined the foredecks of the Staten Island Ferry, waiting to stream forth upon the Battery. On the wharves, goods and trucks were weaving in and out of each other. He could see various sports being played in wire cages atop tall buildings, trees growing in parks. There had been a great pier fire the night before, and one whole shore in Weehawken was smouldering rubble, white steam, and mist rising still in the excited air. But to the Mayor's surprise, barges and crews were beginning to clear it away, something which in Europe might have taken several years. The band leader was dancing as his fire boat pounded along, and he was saying to the rhythm of the music, "C'mon, c'mon, get them feets movin', my man."

On a deck of wide windows Marshall and other babies rested in their baskets, Marshall having been named by an American naval officer who was that day to take up his post on a destroyer and head into the Atlantic off the Carolinas, his face struck by the August North American sea breeze which he loved to breathe coming off the coasts of his country. Marshall stretched himself in rubbery contortions, his little fingers spreading and slightly buckling. He breathed a deep breath and lay back as was his constant wont, fully in need of a protector, the seven pounds of his human life as fragile as a gossamer, being carted in various baskets around the world uncomplaining except that on the Atlantic he had been exposed to a breeze and, as would be the pattern in later years, he had come down with a difficult pneumonia. He had high fever half from disease and half as his only means of insistence that he be taken into a human family.

When the ship docked alongside a great dark shed with shafts of dusty light structuring its interior like the cross-angled girders on the bridges, the musicians were still playing. The Mayor of New York was trying to make a speech, but the music drowned him out. His deputy turned to the pier boss and said: "For chrissake, will you tell them niggers to stop playing." A few minutes later the pier boss returned to report that, as the deputy could hear, they had refused. "Refused! What are they crazy?" Not only had they refused but they played louder and faster. They were civil servants and they had rights. The pier boss thought they had gone mad, but they played and played and played. Finally, the fire boat moved out into the river and amidst fading strains of music the assembled crowd watched the band transported to serenade the remains of the fire in Weehawken. The deputy said: "Those bastards are mad, aren't they? Just mad. Who knows what they'll do next."

Marshall was taken to the Foundling Hospital, another place run by nuns, who, seeing the cross stamped in red wax, were curious and impressed. As Sister Bernadine, the head of the adoption selection section, surveyed the infant she thought how strange a name, how weak and feeble a child, was he sick, and what of the (here she misinterpreted) Papal Seal on his dossier? All these questions formed in her mind to tell her that she knew just the parents for him. Mr. Livingston was coming down from Eagle Bay in a few days. His name was Livingston, but he was a Jew married to a Catholic woman who could not have children.

Sister Bernadine wanted the adopted child to be Roman Catholic. Otherwise, she feared that Livingston, despite his changed name, would somehow coax it into Judaism. The only trouble was that most of the foundlings were of indeterminate religion. Sister Bernadine rejoiced, as the glorious

Papal Seal made it crystal clear in her mind that this child was sent by higher
powers to be the solution for the Livingston problem. Outside the wrought-
iron porch of the Foundling Hospital a horse attached to a milkwagon
whinnied in delight.

2

Livingston had decided that any child was acceptable, and to please his wife
he had agreed to go to the Foundling Hospital. There were so many orphans
and DP children that it was no problem to claim one. She refused, however,
to walk down a ward and pick out a baby as if it were a can of Brussels
sprouts, so she sent her husband to do it. He didn't mind things like that. In
fact, he minded very little and was of a strange, quiet disposition.

When their house had been burglarized while they were in Yellowstone
staying at one of those huge log-and-beam lodges, Mrs. Livingston had cried
and fallen to her knees. Mr. Livingston looked around at walls denuded of
Impressionist paintings and at a safe with its empty mouth hanging open,
and went immediately to the phonograph to play a jumpy record. Then he
danced around Mrs. Livingston, who was sobbing on her knees in the middle
of the floor where a thick and colorful Persian carpet had been, and sang a
song he made up as he slapped his hands together: "They didn't take the air,
they didn't take the trees. They took the honey, babe, but not the bees."

They began to drink champagne and dance around the empty room in
dances of the twenties, which were the dances they had danced at dances
when they were young. Once, Mrs. Livingston remembered that they had
just lost all their movable possessions, and a tear fell from her eye, descending
from ledge to ledge, from high angular cheek to delicate wrist before it
stained the dark oak darker. But then her husband held her face in his hands
and said: "Don't worry. It'll be fine. Nothing's lost. We're alive." She had
not been privileged, as had he, to have been in a war for many years and to
have seen men blown apart and ripped up by bullets. So he held her to him
and remembered those times only a few years gone, and then they danced
until the afternoon sun came 'round and struck the porch, and they lay on
the lawn in their traveling clothes, only to awaken into a cool pleasant evening. They cooked some steaks on an open fire, and the emptiness of the
house made them feel younger and wilder.

Livingston arrived at the hospital by taxi. It was very hot in the city,
and Park Avenue was like an Alabama meadow—sheep grazed on the mall as
a publicity stunt for a charity ball, but the effect was pastoral and hypnotic.
He bolted up the stairs and into Sister Bernadine's office, feeling rather un-
easy at the sight of the several dozen crucifixes which covered the walls with
sinuous tendons. After Sister Bernadine's saccharine greeting and Livingston's

tortured smile, they got down to business. A nun wheeled Marshall in on a room service cart. Since he was used to the finest hotels, Livingston felt his appetite stir, and then chastised himself. Sister Bernadine smiled, revealing a mouth as wide as the Holland Tunnel. Livingston eyed the baby sprawled on the service cart. It looked like a little white gorilla. He turned to Sister Bernadine. She again smiled enormously, exposing a row of teeth like a large horseshoe of uneven piano keys. Livingston was expressionless. Sister Bernadine *widened* her smile and said, "Isn't he beautiful?"

Livingston looked again at the baby, who, as if he could understand the proceedings, returned his stare with suspicion and hostility. "Beautiful?" He wanted to leave. "Yes, I guess it is beautiful. I guess we'll take it. It's healthy and all that, isn't it, certified, all right in the reflexes?"

"Oh yes," said Sister Bernadine, "he's very smart for his age. He has a touch of pneumonia and his spine is a little bent, but he'll be all right. You see, he must have been premature. He's so tiny."

"Where does he come from?"

"He's French (*Vive la France!* as they say), from Marseilles; we suspect from a very good family killed in the war. Tragedy."

"What's his name?" asked Livingston, beginning to like the little thing, which was clearly suffering and hot with fever.

"It doesn't really matter. You can adopt him and he'll take your name."

"I want him to have his own name. I think he'll want it that way. What is his name?"

"Pearl."

"Pearl?" said Livingston. "I thought it was a boy." He peered at Marshall. "It is a boy, by God, don't you know that, Sister Bernadine?"

Sister Bernadine blushed deeply. Her heart beat like a jackhammer. "It is a boy. Yes, it is a boy. A boy, a boy. His name is Marshall Pearl."

"What the hell kind of name is that for a French aristocrat? Anyway, it sounds Jewish to me."

"Oh no no no . . .!" said Sister Bernadine in peals of nervous laughter. Livingston watched the baby punching the air, and assented readily to the adoption.

3

Livingston took Marshall up the Hudson in a sleeping compartment on the Twentieth Century. He had relatives in the Grand Central stationmaster's office who had arranged this short passage, and for the train to make a special stop in the woods which led from the river to his house. He had called ahead so that Mrs. Livingston could improvise a nursery and the doctor would be there when they arrived. The train left at seven in the evening. Livingston spent his time gazing alternately at the child and at the landscape. They passed the Palisades, and in his mind he saw long red files of British troops climbing to make a surprise assault. They passed the Tappan Zee—wide like an ocean bay—and they passed Croton Bay, where, in a spirit of daring and wild enterprise, the Colonists had pushed rafts of explosives up to the wooden walls of British warships. Livingston always leaped back to the wars. When the baby cried, he quieted it by stroking its forehead with his finger. Marshall grabbed the finger with his little fist, and although he could hardly hold, it seemed to Livingston that this was somehow a valiant act.

When it was beginning to get dark the train entered a curve of the river where forests descended to the shore and thick oaken limbs hung out over the water, in which were great boulders. Later, Marshall would have a rope hanging from one of the limbs onto a rock island that became his own. It was the end of August; the weather was hot and steamy. When the train stopped and Livingston got off with Marshall, black porters leaned out the exits to scan the dark forest. The stop at nowhere reminded them of earlier days on the railroad. Steam came up from the tanks and gaskets. A sweating porter in a blue hat with silver badge asked, "You live here?"

Livingston nodded. "Up a ways on the path. You want to visit, you're welcome to." He looked at the sick infant in his arms. "I mean that."

The porter smiled and touched his nose, and then pulled a lever in the vestibule. Steam rose as the brakes released and the train began to move forward slowly. The porter kept his eye on Livingston and little Marshall as the train inched forward with increasing force and speed. The porter himself seemed to draw energy and power from the accustomed momentum, and when he spoke it was as if he were in a preacher's pulpit. Livingston did not doubt the moment. "Chicago . . ." said the porter. "Chicago and the plains. Some day that child ride on this train all the way to Chicago, an' I'll be his friend."

The train started down the straight silver-cindered tracks, ticking off the joints in the steel. Livingston was left in the forest with the sickly child in his arms, surrounded by cattails, enormous boulders, pines, oak, and beech. He set out on the darkening paths to the house. In the distance the Twentieth Century sounded its whistle as it rounded the Oscawana Bend.

4

Marshall had need of a protector, and Livingston was just the man. First, his name was not really Livingston, but Lischinsky. He had changed his name not because he was an opportunist, and certainly not because he was ashamed of it, since he was neither. Rather, he felt confident in his identity and strongly attached to his history, and it mattered little to him if his name were

Russian, Yiddish, German, or English. He rationalized, and perhaps correctly, that the original name of his family must have been some sort of right-to-left Semitic hieroglyph. He did have a Hebrew name given to him at birth, and to that he would hold at the price of his life. As for Lischinsky, he reasoned, the family name had been changed *to* it, so why not change *from* it? He asked his father, a farmer and storekeeper, and his father told him that as long as he remained a Jew he could do anything he wanted—grow a mustache, wear a hat, change his name, invest in porkbellies, speak with a Chinese accent, whatever. He had altered the name for one reason only.

When the family got back to Newark from ten years on a reservation of Spanish-speaking Apaches in Arizona, young Lischinsky was eighteen and wanted to go to Harvard. After all, T.R. had gone there. But there was a quota. He knew that if he took his exams and did even extremely well they might still weed him out because of his blood. So he went to a judge and changed Lischinsky to Livingston, intending to change it back some time, but the new name fit well and he kept it.

He visited a girl he had met in a beer garden in Coney Island. She was a nice girl, who had a splendid body because she belonged to an athletic society and was a championess with the Indian clubs. Either Swedish or German, she had definitely beautiful hair and eyes, and an awesome complexion. He might well have gone to see her anyway, but he was spurred on by her magnificent breasts and by her address, a round even number on Park Avenue. There, she was one of the indentured maids. He asked her to tell the postman that mail addressed to a Mr. Livingston would be received by her. Thus when he applied to Harvard he was not Lischinsky from a Jewish ghetto in Newark but, solely by manipulation of paper, Livingston from Park Avenue. He did so well on the test that he feared drawing attention to himself, and to the amazement of relatives and friends he was admitted. Through a combination of work started on the day he received the miraculous letter, loans, and his father's help, he experienced Harvard as a Livingston might, except that each Friday night he went to synagogue in a poor neighborhood near the South End, where he was able to remember who he was and from where he had come. One of the principles of his life, and of his father's life, and later of Marshall's, was that a man must be free to go wherever he wishes. No place was off limits, and fences, whether of wire or paper or the mind, were for milk cows and chickens.

When Livingston was a boy his family had moved from the country in New Jersey near the Pennsylvania line to Newark, where the father opened a dairy business which sold the products of all the Jewish dairy farms in the Bucks County–Princeton area; and there were many, including his own, which he consolidated with those of his brothers. But in Newark Mrs. Lischinsky contracted consumption. Chances were that she would die—a lot of people did. A man other than Lischinsky might have seen too many difficulties and been unable to move—his means of livelihood, his children, the fact that they had already come all the way from Russia. But Lischinsky loved his wife and would be damned before he would fail to try and save her. He went to Washington, where for several weeks he made such a nuisance of himself at the Department of the Interior that they gave him a concession to run a general store in one of the driest deserts in the Western Hemisphere. The Apaches got a good deal, for he was an ethical man forever concerned with his wife's fragile condition. His compassion and sensitivity caused him to deal fairly with them, so fairly in fact that after ten years he could not break even, except that his wife was strong and robust and red in the cheeks—and that he deemed a great great profit. There were other benefits as well. His son became fluent in Spanish (although in an obtuse Indian dialect) and learned to ride and shoot expertly, as if by second nature. Since there was little but desert, mountains, and sky, the son spent most of his time in reading (there were no farm chores). So he did not become a rich man, but he gained strong healthy children—beautiful dark-eyed mysterious girls and a son who had the stealth and skills of a young Apache, and who had read through several government libraries.

At Eagle Bay were two quarter horses and a pony, a rack of rifles and pistols, ropes, blankets, and a thousand acres of surrounding forest, although Livingston owned only several and the rest was either state land or undeveloped tracts, the property of churches, syndicates, or the railroad. He had always wanted his son to learn from him not only skills of the intellect, but of the land. As he walked with Marshall's basket, in which rested Marshall himself and the fancy envelopes, he imagined what was to come, and quickened the pace. He passed the stable and began to walk over the rolling lawn toward the house. Lamps burned gently within, and terraces and porches with awnings and vined runners had dark shadow patterns thrown about them. With many windows and cheerful lights, the house was set in the darkness and placidity of a deep green forest, where night birds were beginning to sing and fireflies flashed. Livingston ran across the grass onto the steps of the library terrace. Having heard the train, his wife was standing at the window and she looked at the baby with an inbreathing of love, forgetting her fear that it was not and could never be hers. Husband and wife smiled radiantly at one another through the dark glass, Marshall held safely between them.

5

Mrs. Livingston opened the door and let them in. The doctor had just arrived and was starting to come down the long hall which led to the library. When he had been greeted they all mounted the narrow staircase twisting this way and that past landings lined with books and little doors leading to a maze of attics and secret passages. Marshall was fast asleep when the party arrived in his room. It had several windows; some nearly touched the floor, and others nearly touched the ceiling. Before Livingston had converted it, the house had been a huge stable with many odd architectural features. It had about thirty rooms, many of which were tremendous and others of which were closet-sized, and only half of them were in use. Enormous beams braced with cast-iron crossed the top floor. The windows were arched and they swung inward. Those near the ceilings had to be opened with long hardwood staves brass-fitted at the top; their shades were controlled by lengthy cords strung on pulleys, like the rigging of a ship. There were three stories. At ground level, heat was provided from deep pits in which gas was burned, the flames quite terrifying to see through iron grilles flush with the floor. Dogs (three Labradors—Wendel, Douglas, and Leon) dared not approach the hissing chasms of hellfire, and bayed as if at the moon when the thermostats popped and signaled new conflagrations. On the upper stories were vertical registers set in the walls to heat two rooms at once. Except where sex or privacy had dictated several heaters and no view, it was possible to look through the gas-burning apparatus and the flames from one room to another. The house was of brick, with walls three feet thick and a slate roof. There were many fireplaces, enclosed terraces, porches, winding passages, a small motion-picture theater complete with soundproofed projection booth, a chicken coop above the garage, a large workshop and storage area, hay chutes, overhead winching systems, a grandiose formal diningroom, and little places where a child could hide and literally never be found.

Outside, a deep horse trough was fed by a spring; several other springs were the cause of lakes, falls, and streams filled with watercress. There were a stable, an enormous root cellar which led like a mine into the side of a hill (and had been part of the underground railway), many stone walls, lawns leading to dense brush, and a great number of enormous trees, some of which were several centuries old and over a hundred feet tall.

Marshall's nursery had the expected baby amenities—crib, scale, cabinets, etc.—and African animals had been painted on the extensive spaces of brick between the windows. There were a giraffe, a lion, a leopard, a heron, and a tree, which is not an animal but was needed to counterbalance the giraffe and provide a bed for the leopard. The giraffe leaned over backward straining his neck trying to get one of the red apples on branches he could not quite reach. If he had been real, his coloring of dappled maroon would have made him king of his kind. All the animals were allowed to keep their nobility in deep colors, but they were friendly, as if they were looking upon their children. On the table with pins and cotton swabs and things like that was a lamp with a little lamb leaning against a tree, which held the bulb. Marshall later remembered being aware of it for a long time before he knew what it was.

The doctor began to examine the baby, and Livingston went downstairs to eat. By the time he had finished his steak, endive salad, glass of wine, and piece of chocolate cake, Mrs. Livingston and the doctor were coming down the stairs. He went into the livingroom to hear the doctor's report.

Now, the doctor was a plain-speaking man who looked like a broom—his mustaches were waxed and straight, as was his crewcut. He said: "This child was born prematurely, perhaps as much as two months earlier than normal. I don't know what kind of postnatal care he was given but it is surprising that he survived. I assume that he was immediately placed in an incubator. Anyway, he is weak, and he has a rather serious case of pneumonia. I gave him some penicillin, and that should clear things up. Mrs. Livingston, you will do as instructed regarding his care.

"As for his general condition—well, don't expect a strong child or, later, an athlete. It is probable that he will be sickly for a long time. I think he will have trouble with his eyes and with his hearing. His spine is slightly bent, in what is called Spina Bifida (this we will keep an eye on), and his legs, poor creature, will be bowed into parentheses. If he grows to be five foot six, he will appear to be five foot three. I have given him certain immunizations, and will give him others when he is well enough to come to my office for Roentgen. He must be given vitamin supplements and be fed as if he were a new acquisition at a prestigious zoo."

"I beg your pardon," said Livingston.

"It was close for him. He has to be strengthened or he won't survive."

This was, to say the least, upsetting news. But Livingston never put as much faith in doctors as did doctors and their victims. He had seen medical men gravely pronounce impending death, and the subjects of the pronouncements had later lived to sail around the world or climb an unconquered mountain. He planned to tell his wife, after the doctor left, his rather extreme views on the subject, forgetting that he had done so many times before. However, the doctor would not leave. Not only had he not been paid, but he was curious about the envelope with the red religious seal. He said that if it contained information about the child's history he would do well to hear it. So Mrs. Livingston got the chocolate cake, made some iced tea, and they sat down in the big livingroom to hear her read the contents of the heavy brown envelope. The seal itself must have weighed a pound. When the paper was cut, Mrs. Livingston pulled out some yellow-ruled sheets on which was penned a masculine hand. She took a sip of tea, adjusted a lamp (leaving her audience in deep shadow), and with the tree frogs and night birds sounding like waves at the beach, and the moon rising, she began to read.

"20 July, 1947

"I am sitting in the garden of the Dominican Sisters of Marseilles. My name is Paul Levy, and I am a Lieutenant-Commander in the United States Navy, presently on leave of absence. On the twenty-eighth day of June, 1947, the child Marshall Pearl was born on my ship as it approached the coast of

Palestine. Nothing is known of his father. His mother was a Russian Jewess who, from the ill effects of war, died immediately after giving birth. My ship, the *Lindos Transit*, was wrecked by the Royal Navy after a hard and costly fight. Most of its passengers, Jews illegally entering Palestine, managed to do just that. However, about forty were captured, including the newborn baby. Luckily, two doctors and a midwife were among the detained, and on the way to Haifa and for a week or so afterwards in the internment camp, they managed to care for the child. Since I was a potential cause of embarrassment and an actual cause of irritation, I was released rather quickly. I managed to convince them to allow me to take Marshall back to the United States. We traveled on a hospital ship as far as Toulon. Here in Marseilles I am told that I cannot take him farther, but the Dominican Sisters have promised to arrange for him to be sent to New York where, as a result of the war, they are in communication with various adoption agencies.

"I am a military man, due for a good deal more of sea duty, and unmarried. My parents are too old, and my sisters and brothers too young, to make good parents themselves. So I must give him over. I can explain a few other things, and make a request of you, whoever you may be.

"I was told by one of the captives that the woman who died was named Pearl. That may or may not have been the father's name, but no matter, it is one of the few things this infant has in his possession, and I am of the opinion that it should stay with him. As for the name Marshall, I chose it because I have always liked it. A friend of mine, a good friend, named Marshall, was killed at the Coral Sea. I thought that perhaps in his honor this child who was born in battle, a rare thing, should take his name. Also, of course, the words are a pun on the little history he has.

"His mother was most beautiful. I noticed her from the beginning, but I did not speak with her because I was intensely busy preparing for our violent landfall.

"I ask only one thing. His mother was a Jew, and he is a Jew. Whether he is brought up that way, whether you who read this are Jews, is not important. But you must tell him of this. If you do not, you will betray his people, his mother, and him. It will be confusing if he is not told directly of the facts. For he is what he is, and though he may grow up completely at ease in his chanced locale he will always suffer the interference of his origins. This I know well from my own experience.

"I hope that you take good care of him, and love him, and that someday he will visit me in Norfolk. I hope he will be able to find me. One last thing. I could tell by looking just once into his mother's face that she was a woman who had much love in her. I am sorry that we did not speak. Perhaps if the circumstances had been slightly different she would have lived. But that is over, and only the child remains.

"Respectfully,
Paul Levy, Lieutenant-Commander, U.S.N."

In silence, Mrs. Livingston looked at her husband. She had always thought of him as somehow magical, tied to a scheme of things that she did not understand—as if she were married to a Gypsy. Only he could go to a Catholic foundling hospital and bring back a Jewish baby with credentials embossed in symbols of the high priesthood.

They saw the doctor to the door; he was amazed, because it seemed that no incubator had been used. This he did not fathom, and he went away talking to himself. Though it was calm and (after the lights of the doctor's car had vanished) dark, though it was night and the moon was high, the Livingstons were as excited as if it were a September day in Manhattan when work begins after vacation, and cool air floods in from the north, and women buy clothes in department stores. They went upstairs and looked at the baby, calmly sleeping in his crib unaware that he had touched down. His new parents lay awake listening to the forest flooded as it was with night sounds. Even when the moon disappeared beyond Haverstraw, they did not sleep.

6

One day in June when it was so hot in New York that Livingston could not work and swiveled about in his chair staring out the window, he decided to cut back a little. He had some appointments scheduled for that afternoon, but just thinking of the stoked-up little men so miraculously skilled at the dollar and so overheated in its pursuit made him tired. On the street below taxis were rushing in both directions. It was early enough in the morning for the sun to cast a shaft of gray and gold light from the east, the special light in New York which comes down between the high old stone buildings and through which dust rises and pigeons turn in complex flight. It is a tired light; even though it shines early in the morning, somehow it suggests afternoon. It is a light which illuminates the past, and Livingston was reminded of the twenties and the thirties, of the El, although he remembered these times as if they were in a sepia print and not in the orange and green sunset colors in which he had truly seen them. He began to think of when he was young in New York, and had been wild and stupid.

During Prohibition he had gone to a party and awakened two days later in a lifeboat on the Staten Island Ferry, with no knowledge of how he had gotten there and no desire to leave. The way things changed, the differences in shading, how all the new buildings had become old buildings, how men he had known had died, how the Flatiron was suddenly a relic, how the misery and vigor of his youth seemed pointless and unwise, and the fact that the records were all scratched up and would not play on the new machines made him restless and upset. He went to the window and leaned out. The sidewalks, diamond sparkling, were beginning to heat, and he could see an ice cream wagon down the street on the corner of Fifth Avenue.

His secretary had come in while he was leaning out the window and thrown a batch of telegrams on his desk. He turned around and looked at them, deciding to get down to business. He pulled his chair up to the desk, clearing his throat and girding himself for work. Should he take a short nap? A cool leather couch the color of ox blood beckoned. No, he had already taken a nap—to work.

He picked up the first dispatch and opened it. It was from London, and was marked *Urgent*. It read: REPEAT STOP CONFIRM OR DENY STOP TAX UNFAVORABLE STOP PARLIAMENT FICKLE STOP REPEAT STOP CONFIRM OR DENY STOP SIGNED EDWARD. Obviously this telegram was the last in a series which had been delayed and mixed, so he opened the next one, which read: WHY WILL YOU NOT CONFIRM OR DENY STOP DEAL FALLING THROUGH STOP WE ARE AMAZED STOP SIGNED EDWARD. The next few were from California, and one was from Rome. The very last was another London cable, reading: LAST CHANCE STOP SIGNED EDWARD.

Livingston screamed to his secretary, "Do we have any earlier cables this week from that son of a bitch in London?"

"We have many son of a bitches in London," replied the secretary.

"But Edward. I mean Edward." The secretary checked and replied in the negative.

Livingston swung around in time to see a blue balloon, which had likely been lost near the zoo, ride up into the shaft of light. Then, as he did often, he began to think about the West. He remembered a dark little boy without shoes, riding an Indian pony along a mesa and returning to his rough house in time to light candles. He remembered the Indian agents and the resourceful lawmen who would sometimes pass through. Once, a Texas Ranger had chased a man as far as the reservation back country, several states beyond his jurisdiction. He had a Colt .44 and an Enfield rifle. He bought provisions from Livingston's father, who wondered how he could operate so far from Texas. The Ranger smiled, white teeth showing brightly in a face as darkly tanned as an Indian's. He threw his arm back and cocked his head, indicating the mesa and beyond. "I come overland," he said, "from Texas. And when I git 'im, I'll bring 'im back, overland. Nobody'll know."

Time passed in front of Livingston's eyes. He was immobilized. Certainly he could do no work. He jumped up and closed his windows. It was, after all, Friday, when it was natural to take off early. He looked at his watch, which said 10:30. There was enough time to get back home and change before the sun started downward. He left his office for Grand Central and the train to Eagle Bay.

Thin and a few feet tall, with a nice little face and some missing teeth, Marshall sat with the other children in the first grade reading the story of the dog Tip. Each child had his turn to recite two sentences. Marshall could read as fast as an adult, so when his sentence rolled around as *Mary calls Tip to pet him and Bill looks on,* and then *Bill sees Tip's white coat,* Marshall read them so fast that it was almost as if he had said nothing. Conscious of the remaining empty space in time, he read: "No skool llib dna mih tep ot pit sllac Yram. Taoc etihw spit sees llib." He turned to the teacher and said: "Esaelp Ssim Yggep, tel em daer erom," and burst into giggles.

Miss Peggy knew he was fast, but dared not skip him. For although in first grade he tested in reading like a senior in high school, he had no concept whatsoever of arithmetic. If he solved an addition correctly it was a gift of chance. Numbers did not make sense to him. It was as if the part of his brain which handled them had defected to the reading lobes. If the head of the primary school sat him down to try and remedy his numeral ignorance, Marshall could not concentrate, and squirmed around looking for a book. When and if he got hold of one he could sit mesmerized for hours. In his first year of reading he went through novels, history, geography, travel, comic books, railroad schedules, the telephone book (the Eagle Bay directory listed only a few hundred four-digit numbers), and anything else in print, including *The New York Times,* which he read with unparalleled devotion—paying equal heed to the front page, stock quotations, classifieds, clothing ads, the always ungrammatical divorce notices ("My wife Velma, having left my bed and board, I will not be responsible for any debts from she."), and Shipping/ Mails. "What's new, Marshall?" Livingston would ask, to which Marshall would reply with gravity that it was 86 degrees in Belem, or that the *Prudential Catassa* was sailing to Buffalo from Pier 42. He understood little, but was rapidly making progress. He learned to read so fast that he never learned how to spell, and this, plus his difficulty with math and his completely illegible, retarded handwriting, served to keep him with his classmates. In their interminable idiotic meetings the school officials debated whether to skip him or leave him back. The tension neutralized and he was unaffected. But Miss Peggy never let him disrupt the class. She put him in the closet.

He ended up in this closet at least once a day, and was instructed to leave his coat and lunch-box there instead of in the bank of assigned cubbyholes. Through a small window much higher than he could reach, he looked to the sky in the manner of prisoners. He spent hours in acute embarrassment and shame (worse even than the terrible moment in which the other children had discovered that he was an orphan), but he learned to read every nuance of the sky and clouds.

This day in early June was most humiliating, since there was a party, during which Miss Peggy completely forgot about Marshall. Marshall was too proud to ask for his freedom, staying instead crouched on the closet floor, staring at the window. The other children laughed, fought, and sang. Marshall had his clouds and changing light.

Just as the little party was drawing to a close, Miss Peggy remembered Marshall and dashed to the closet, fearing and wishing that he had been smothered, which of course was impossible because the window was open. When she unlatched and swung open the door she saw him in the corner, with his brown oxfords, blue denims with turned-up cuffs, black-watch shirt, and sandy blond hair. He looked at her when she asked him to come out, and said nothing. It was clear that he preferred to stay in the closet. He was being neither sullen nor obstinate. He simply preferred to be there alone. She made him promise to come out for his lesson, and eventually he did.

In the middle of the lesson some of the children looked up in fear. A tall man had come to the door. He was sunburnt and rough-looking, with a mass of black hair and a black mustache. He was handsome, standing on the swaybacked threshold in his Abercrombie & Fitch tough-guy fishing outfit the color of good gunmetal. The sun struck his face, and although he smiled at the children he frightened them with his imposing presence. He had a violent, strange, gentle look, tiny windows of light perceptible in the eyes, a willing readiness evident. He walked over to the teacher and conferred with her. There were only a few more days of school; Marshall had learned what he had to learn in the first grade; and the river was cool and blue. Miss Peggy was amazed at how immediately and graciously she gave in, numbingly charmed by outrageous and unheard-of demands from this laborer who interrupted her class by standing in the doorway in boots and rolled-up sleeves. Livingston signaled Marshall with a movement of his eye, and Marshall, who had been poised holding his breath, jumped up and rushed to the closet to get his things as if he had just been freed of a thousand-year prison term. The two of them left the class like a farmer and his son going out early in the morning onto the plains.

They were riding in the old wooden station wagon with a hole in the passenger door where a horse had kicked it, going up and down the hills toward Eagle Bay. Marshall had his feet on the seat, and was sort of half-standing-leaning to see through the window the churches and stores in town and the fences and farms outside. "What'd you do today in school?" asked Livingston.

"I dunno."

"How's the arithmetic coming along?"

"Awright."

"How 'bout the reading?" said Livingston, remembering that Mrs. Livingston had found Magruder's *Geography of the Despotic Asian Principalities, Protectorates, Colonies, Trust Territories, Mandates, & Secessionist Splinter States* under Marshall's pillow.

"Awright," answered Marshall, playing with wood he had plucked from the damaged door.

They turned into Eagle Bay and started going down the road to the house, when suddenly Marshall doubled up in storms of sobbing, unable to catch his breath, shaking all over, getting hot and red. Livingston stopped the car, got out, and went around to the passenger side. He opened the door and lifted Marshall into his arms. Marshall continued to sob, and Livingston sat down on a stone wall, holding him up close, trying to look in his eyes, rocking him almost like a baby. When at last he did see into the eyes of the boy he held, they were a mystery to him. They said so much and seemed so sad. Marshall told him about what had happened, and along with his resolution to see to it, Livingston was convinced that the little child was moved by currents deeper than he had thought.

At the stable they saddled up a horse and Antonio the pony, and Mrs. Livingston came out to give them a cooler of cold drinks and sandwiches. In her presence Marshall's color returned and he was happy and cheerful. She shared some of his secrets, and she could make him forget anything which troubled him. They tied wire-cage crab traps onto the saddles, mounted, and rode off into the woods on their way to the Oscawana Bend, where, when the sun was strong and high, the crabs bit like crazy and you could stand on the deserted shore and watch the bass leaping like silver. The river was glassy and flat as Marshall rode with Livingston along its edge hoping a train would pass by and salute with its whistle.

One did. They heard it in the north about five minutes before it arrived. It was going forty miles an hour—six black engines and two hundred fifty cars. The lead engine's light was visible far up the track, at first a tiny diamond, then like a mirror reflecting the sun. At night these beams were blinding. When the engine cab passed by, Marshall held the reins in one hand and pulled an imaginary whistle-cord with the other. The engineer was a lean squinting man covered with oil. He surveyed the father on his brown quarter horse, the son on a reddish Shetland, and their crab traps lashed to the saddles. Then he blew his whistle several blasts. The horses sidled. Antonio put his two left hooves into the cool lapping water. A short time later the whistle blasts echoed off the cliffs south of Haverstraw, but could hardly be heard over the rumbling of the freight. Passing them were the dirty saffron-liver-colored cars of the Pacific Fruit Express; boxcars from a dozen railroads—Georgia Pacific, New York Central, Rock Island, B&O, New Haven & Hartford, Pennsylvania, Canadian Pacific, CNR, Union Pacific, Southern Pacific, Illinois Central, Santa Fe; the company cars—Swift, Hygrade, Armour, Morton, United States Steel, Flo-Sweet; coal cars; oil and chemical tankers; flat cars; and cars loaded with hogs and cows going to slaughter. Each had a distinctive color pattern, and some had notable smells. When the caboose passed, Livingston turned his hand in the air and pantomimed something rising from it like smoke. Then he dropped his reins and flashed both hands twice. A man at the rail of the caboose saluted in thanks—he had been informed of a smoking hot-box twenty cars up. After the train passed, the smells of pig stale, rotted fruit, and grain remained, but the north wind cleaned things out fast.

Marshall asked, "Daddy, where does it come from?"

Livingston answered, "It comes from all over the country, from all forty-eight states."

"Where?"

"You want me to name the states again, huh." Marshall waited for Livingston to begin. Soon he would be able to name the states as fast as Livingston, who started at Maine, went down the East Coast to Florida, across the Gulf to Alabama and Mississippi, up through the Middle South and West, the Northwest, the West, and the Southwest. Marshall was dazzled. He tried, but left out Arkansas, Idaho, Nevada, and Minnesota.

A mile before Oscawana they set out at a canter down a stretch of narrow beach. Bass were jumping, and muskrats ran off into the weeds. Marshall had been taken up on a horse the day the doctor said his illness had passed. As far back as he could remember he had been sitting on saddles. At six he was also a tolerably good shot with a boy's lever-action Winchester, but as yet Livingston had not let him shoot from the horse. With his legs bowing out the brass-buckled stirrups and the rifle cracking in militant repetition, Livingston could shoot accurately and fast from his galloping mount, swiveling from side to side to deal with imagined enemies while Marshall looked on and drank it in to the smallest spaces in his soul as if in rigorous preparation for unknown or generalized vengeance. Only six, Marshall dreamed on occasion of slaughtering his enemies, though he had none, and in his imagination he could be cruel even if he were mostly kind.

They arrived at the crabbing place on the tip of the Oscawana Bend, and took the saddles off the horses. Marshall led them out a little into the sandy flats where they drank from clear pools. Down at Eagle Bay it would have been impossible for the horses to drink from the river and not get sick. But Oscawana was not too brackish, primarily because the Croton River (which they had crossed sinking up to their knees) intervened and blocked the salty bay. It was just a bit salty at Oscawana; horses like that. For several years Livingston had intended not to let them drink from the Hudson, since it was supposed to have been getting dirty—but for the moment it seemed clean enough. By the time Marshall got back and tied up the horses Livingston had baited the traps with gristle and meat scraps. They climbed the rocks and went to a deep place where with all his strength Livingston threw the cages out into the water. They took the lines and wrapped them around a stump, after which they sat down in the sun and ate lunch. It was very hot and humid, with the wind coming off the river.

The opposite side was flat before it became mountainous. High trees silhouetted in shimmering green made it seem like Africa, and it was quiet except for the small curling waves and the sounds of white herons as they took off along the water, splashing and then climbing on an invisible thermal. As it began its descent the sun hit Livingston and Marshall in their eyes, making them squint into the distance and keep still in the placid heat. Now and then they would pull in the traps and put the crabs in a big bucket. But they mainly sat and watched the colors of the distance and the white birds soaring over the river.

When they were somewhat dazed from this, a mirage appeared on the surface of the river. A little town from west of the Hudson, a town un-recognizable to them, was suddenly standing in the ship channel. White herons and gulls circled through steeples intense and wavering in the mirage, and a car moved across the water. It was extraordinary, and it made Marshall rise in wonderment. Livingston too was frozen in its power. For a full half an hour they stared at it, watching movements inside, watching it shimmer and change position. It seemed real.

Livingston had last seen a mirage in North Africa during the war, when he was a major in Intelligence traveling from Algiers to Cairo by truck convoy. They were south of the German pocket, bumping along the dusty road in white heat. Intermittently a song came in on the Allied radio. It was a sharp jazz tune with lyrics which went something like: "If I had a zillion dollars, if I had me just a zillion; when I get frisky give me whisky, give me whisky and I'll die." The driver was beating time on the wheel as he went dangerously and joltingly fast. A great white terraced city appeared, resting above the horizon in a bed of blue like the deep blue off the mesas in Arizona—so deep that it damages the sense of uprightness and causes one to circle without restraining force. The driver kept driving to the fast song, but the hair stood up on his arms and neck and he said, "Jesus Christ, Lord Almighty, white terraces, what the hell is that?" although he knew quite well that it was a mirage. They drove transfixed as minutes passed during which the white city danced in the sky ahead of them.

That evening when the convoy pulled into a little encampment, a captain in command of the American detachment called Livingston to interrogate some German prisoners. They were in a barn which smelled of hay and animals and was lit by a kerosene lantern throwing a golden light over the sunburnt faces of the assembled soldiers. There were a dozen or so Germans. Livingston approached a repulsively overproud young officer. Livingston was a good deal rougher, older, more authoritative, and bigger than the thin Afrika Korps lieutenant, but he felt nevertheless at a disadvantage when confronted by the hopelessly and meticulously ingrained worldview of the young Nazi. He began to speak and question in a German tinged with Yiddish and Yiddish intonations. It took the young officer a while to fathom the meaning of the American's fluent outlandish speech, and in shock and disgust he interrupted his interrogator, saying "You are a Jew," to which Livingston nodded in the affirmative.

The German spit in his face. Livingston slammed his fist into the lieutenant's stomach, collapsing him in a heap. The younger man was rather fragile, but Livingston jumped him anyway and was ready to beat him when he snatched Livingston's pistol from its holster. The guards came alive. As one of them emptied a carbine into the German, the German completed his last intended act and shot himself in the head. Everyone drew back. It had been so sudden, and he lay in the middle of the earthen floor directly under the lantern, a mass of blood and torn tissue. The prisoners and their captors were speechless in the sharp night noise of the crickets, and the lantern swayed back and forth.

Marshall had never heard anything like this, and looked at Livingston as if he were the key to a great many mysteries of which Marshall had not even begun to know. As the sun was getting low and softer over the mountains, he put his head in his hands and closed his eyes. Marshall touched him, knowing that he could not comfort him, not in a million years. Livingston was crying, something Marshall had never seen him do and would not see again.

When it became cooler and everything was quiet and calm as if in preparation for darkness, they arose, pulled in the traps, saddled the horses, and got ready to leave. Marshall had been thinking of the poor cows and pigs he had seen going to slaughter. They had cried and he had heard them. But then it had been bright daylight with the sun shining on him and the wind striking his face, so he had not noticed. Later, when dusk caused sadness even among the landed birds, Marshall remembered the terrifying cries of the animals packed together in the railroad cars. He turned to Livingston and said, "Daddy, let's throw the crabs back," and they did.

7

Not surprisingly, Eagle Bay was a residence of eagles, who had been there before anyone could remember and chose the forest and reedy bays as refuge for their last great eastern congregation. A score or more of them rested in the tops of the highest trees, on cliffs overlooking the river, in the dead branches of giant oaks. Marshall had trouble distinguishing the younger ones from hawks, especially in flight, but the old eagles had white hoods and muscular bodies unlike those of their air-slim competitors. These were the biggest and the most like the eagle in pictures or on silver dollars. All of them (eagles, eaglets, hawks, hawklets) hunted in the forest and across the river, and could be seen returning from the west in paired flight, a young one following his instructor.

One day Marshall decided to climb a cliff which rose about 150 feet from the river shore. He had frequently reached the top by descending Brandreth Ridge, but never had he gone directly up its face of jutting granite and loose rocks with trees rooted only here and there. He took a double lasso wrapped around his body as in pictures of climbers in the Alps or the Himalayas. He knew very well that there was no way to use the rope and that it would probably be a nuisance, but it looked good. It was a sunny day with some light breezes, and the river was choppy.

At first it was easy. Grasping projecting rocks and roots he climbed fast until he was about 75 feet off the ground. He rested and looked down. The railroad tracks were as thin as fishing line, and he could not hear the sound of the little waves. He promptly froze to the face of the cliff, sorry that he had been stupid enough to get as far as 75 feet. Imagining his dead body on the tracks below, he decided to retreat, whereupon he learned a basic anatomical lesson, that human beings do not have eyes in their feet. In ten minutes of agonizing distress he descended only a few inches. He would hang on to handholds which he knew he could grip for only a few seconds, and feel around with his feet until he found a ledge, with no way to tell if it would hold. His rope was indeed useless. He thought of lowering himself, but there was nothing onto which he could tie. The lasso was leather and smelled like a horse. He threw it down, noting that it took uncomfortably long to reach the ground. It was clear that he had to go up.

Past the halfway mark the handholds and crevices seemed to get smaller and looser as he got higher, and by the time he reached 125 feet he was soaking wet and trembling with exhaustion. He dared not look back, but the noise of a train passing directly below seemed distant and muffled.

Fifteen feet from the top he came to an outcropping which projected a foot or two from the pitch. He had to reach backward, grab the top of the ledge, and hang until he summoned strength enough to pull himself over. As he made past the jutting rock, every muscle in his body shaking violently from the exertion, he found himself face to face with an eagle which sat on an enormous nest Marshall had never seen from the top of the cliff only a few feet away. Marshall threw himself against the grass and lichen on the little plateau, and lay there breathing desperately, strengthless. The eagle was so surprised that it remained still for a long time. Marshall saw directly into its eye, in which the river and the mountains on the opposite shore were reflected in black and silver.

Then the eagle enacted all its parts and muscles into a rising so strong, slow, and furious that it seemed to Marshall as if the earth were shaking. The eagle rose into the air and swayed out over empty space, reached an apogee, and then swayed back, talons extended. Marshall began to run up the steep incline, and when the eagle made its first pass it had to veer because a gnarled tree between the rocks shielded Marshall's way. Marshall kept on, while the eagle flew up into the air, as if it wanted to clear its mind with high altitude and mastery of flight. The second time it came in, air passing through its feathers and talons made a screaming noise.

Marshall was at the top, and he turned around just in time to get knocked over. He rolled in panic, the eagle trying to hook and bite him, its wings folding and slapping the ground or beating in the air to keep balance. They were entangled in one another, and then as fast as it had swooped it took to the air and flew in a descending line downwind to the south. Marshall was intact, eyes, throat, genitals, and extremities still there, but he was scratched all over and cut in a few places, and he could not see out of his left eye because blood from a cut just above it filled the almond cup and blinded. He limped through the woods shaken, bleeding, and stunned. From that encounter he carried a scar between his left eye and eyebrow. People sometimes asked where he had gotten it, and because they did not believe him he learned to say: "A kid hit me." He loved the eagle, fierce and hard as it was. He loved the way it had risen and flown away. He envied its command of the air, and every time he looked at a silver dollar he felt a strange sense of pride. Having wrestled an eagle, he remembered what few would ever know, and that was the sound of its heart beating and its breathing as it fought. It sounded like a woman in love.

8

For each thirty or forty miles of mainline track the New York Central railroad had some kind of security man. Since Eagle Bay was not far from Harmon Yard, a major installation where electric changed to diesel (or steam, as the case had been), the roadbed running through it was in the charge of a full-fledged bull, a senior detective who had cased the tracks from Chicago to Boston before landing promotion to an easy berth near New York just outside the city limits so that he would not be troubled by the nests of vandals bred south of Spuyten Duyvil.

His name was L. H. Triggers, and in his declining years his strength was more than matched by intelligence and skill. He was thoroughly adept at all the techniques: fingerprints, telephone tapping, stakeout, acid gravure, revelatory footbaths, microscopic alignment, stool pigeons, plaster of Paris, tying little strings all over the place, etc., etc. It is said that when on loan to a Southern railroad he solved a major theft case in Biloxi by taking a fingerprint off a bean. And like all good detectives he had that instinct—a direct wire to the Devil—which led him down the right paths until he got his man.

Marshall first encountered him in 1956, when Marshall was nine. The Livingstons were close to a family of Russian émigrés called Gurkapovitch. They used to travel in the Gurkapovitches' old open car up the river to

Garrison, where they spent afternoons eating and drinking at a Hungarian restaurant set between a pine wood through which rushed a fast cold stream and the New York Central tracks. The Gurkapovitches were old, given to long meals and talk of better days in different places—the kind of talk to which Marshall had dozed off half his nights. But the Gurkapovitches had two strange children born when Monsieur Gurkapovitch was past seventy: Semyon, Marshall's age, and a six-year-old named Lad, for they had wanted him to assimilate. Lad (or as his father pronounced it, Led), his brother, and Marshall could tolerate reminiscences of Petersburg and Budapest for only an hour or two, during which they stuffed themselves with pastries and (from nervousness more than anything else) drank the dregs of wine left on the table. Monsieur Gurkapovitch was a wine aficionado and always ordered three or four different vintages as well as champagne.

As their parents sat contentedly watching the stream, the children busied themselves with pouring and fiddling, moving in their chairs, playing with the table implements and matches, and draining half a dozen wine bottles. Soon the three boys arose from the table and staggered out of the restaurant into a dirt parking lot. Lad's eyes fixed upon the railroad gates, miraculous engines at the roadside.

Thirty-five feet long, the braced triangular gates were painted in black and white stripes and fitted with wire-caged red lights. Having misjudged the potential of a country lane, the railroad had put them there to protect voluminous traffic which had never arrived. Staring upward, the two Gurkapovitches and Marshall stood at the base of one of the monuments. At its tip was a red light like a melon-sized cherry. That, and the promise of a view beyond the pines into the rolling farmlands and the mountains, set off their deep-seated urge to climb. But the lead counterweight was so massive that in the upright position it prevented access. They had drunk too much and could not make a human pyramid, so they sat by the side of the road with shoots of grass in their mouths, when from the north they heard the faraway steam whistle of a freight. In due time the wheels and gears of the gate began to sound and it lowered itself with a flashing of lights and a crashing of bells.

Marshall and the older Gurkapovitch straddled the tips of both gates. The train rumbled through the junction, shaking the wooden frames on which the boys nervously perched. When the caboose cleared the crossing the wheels and gears began to sound again, but the gates refused to lift. Soon the engines and transmissions were straining so hard and making such a cacophony that Semyon despaired and jumped off. His gate arose so fast that it nearly snapped. Marshall's was still straining, and white smoke began to come from the electric motor. Not wanting to give up forever the possibility of gaining the summit, the elder Gurkapovitch grabbed his brother and hooked his lederhosen around the top light. Marshall dismounted, and the gate lifted smoothly to the perpendicular. Lad had become the conqueror, but it did little good, for his vocabulary and experience were not sufficient to describe the afforded view. He was, however, quite content to be so high, safely held by leather straps, his feet firmly planted on a crossbar.

After a few minutes, his brother called for him to descend. Lad wiggled about but was unable to disengage himself from the hook of the light. The harder he struggled the more he became fixed to the tip. He was only six, and would have begun to cry for fear of being held up there until the next freight, but the wine kept him silent and happy. The two older boys were puzzled. As they sat down in hope of arriving at a solution, an old Ford truck with the New York Central oval came chugging down the road. Marshall turned to Semyon. "Distract him," he said, after which they began to dance the Charleston.

When L. H. Triggers pulled up to the crossing he stopped his truck, according to the rules, and stared at the two frenzied dancers. It seemed as if they were drunk, and yet it was afternoon and they were children. He turned off the engine and got out to investigate. Marshall and Semyon kept on dancing until they got a full view of the detective. He was six feet four and weighed over two hundred and fifty pounds. He was dressed in a black three-piece suit with a black bow tie and an enormous black hat with a brim as wide as a buzz saw. On the vest was a badge of silver which shone so bright and big that it was blinding. Across his middle a gold chain, almost as if of office, proceeded from Spain to Hawaii, where a gold railroad watch was half visible setting into the black Pacific. He had a great leather belt filled with bullets. A large pistol hung from it professionally, the wooden grip oiled from many years of handling. He smelled of tobacco and he walked regally.

Marshall felt like a dance-hall drunk staring down the barrel of a gun. But L. H. Triggers was only curious, and asked, "What are you boys doin', dancin' by the side of the tracks?"

Marshall answered, "Oh, we're just happy, sir."

L. H. Triggers leaned against the crossing gate and patted it with his detective's hand, saying, "You boys wouldn't try to swing birch this gate, would you?"

"No sir."

"You better not. The gears are delicately aligned. Any weight knocks them off kilter. Why, in the winter with all that ice, we have mechanics out day and night. It costs the railroad about a hundred dollars each time a gate needs fixing." Looking satisfied, he paused and started to turn, when Lad suddenly hiccuped. L. H. Triggers looked up. "Do you know him?" he said to Marshall and his friend.

Semyon Gurkapovitch answered, "He's my brother and his name is Lad. We were walking by. He got caught. Then the gate lifted and he went with it."

L. H. Triggers looked at Lad, a mass of blond curls, and at Semyon, as dark as mahogany with perfectly straight black hair and almond eyes because he had been born while his parents were in Singapore. "You say he's your brother? That's funny. You look like a colored boy. He's not."

"I was born in Singapore," said Semyon. L. H. Triggers went over to a telephone box, unlocked it, and rang up Harmon asking them to lower the gate. They did, and Lad was lifted off. He was so little that he paid no attention to Triggers, and just staggered down the road to the restaurant.

That was the beginning. L. H. Triggers warned Marshall and Semyon never to be caught again on railroad property. Semyon went away to boarding school and was not seen by anyone ever again, but Marshall remained in Eagle Bay, where the railroad was his playground. Not only was he fond of climbing signal towers and riding crossing gates, but he got hold of a key to the telephones and used to talk to trackmen all around the country. "Patch me over to Utah," he would command, and it would be done. But it was only when he was older and started to hop freight trains that he ran into L. H. Triggers enough to hurt. Until then it sufficed Triggers to chase him through the woods, firing the wooden-handled pistol in the air. Marshall always escaped.

9

In the town of Eagle Bay every other grown man called himself by his former military rank; that is, everyone down through sergeant. One man was left from the Civil War. Too old to talk, he sat in a blanket-covered wheelchair at the Methodist home and watched over the river. On Memorial Days they put a Union cap on his head and wheeled him in the parade. The poor old man drooled and trembled, and Marshall was saddened to think of the meadows in his memory, to imagine his recollections of a hundred years of hot days and quiet snows in Eagle Bay and in Virginia, where he had fought —only to grow old in the snap of two fingers while the world passed by in mercantile frenzy, the Brooklyn Bridge was built, roads came through the Hudson Valley farmlands, and the ones he loved died and were buried in the ground.

Marshall's nearest neighbor was the Colonel. He raised trotters and was a dangerous old fool who owned an enormous printing combine. When he discovered that he had outranked Livingston he tried to order him around, and received in return not obedience, but a famous gesture of Italian origin. In an Eisenhower jacket bedecked with half a dozen store-bought medals, the Colonel rode several times daily in a sulky from his estate to the town and back, the way paved with music from a portable radio tied to the graceful chariotlike frame. The horse left an astounding trail of manure, and the old man spit and gasped for air. Witnessing this pageant from behind a bush,

Marshall once heard the Colonel bark like a dog and say: "Sit right here honey. Let me reach in your dress. Oh Jehoshaphat!" After that, Marshall tried to stay out of the Colonel's sight, but he was not always successful.

For example, one day Marshall was ambling down the road, lost in thought, trailing a stick in the dirt and singing, "Hi-Ho, Hi-Ho—Hi-Ho Hi-Ho Hi-Ho. Hi-Ho, Hi-Ho—Hi-Ho Hi-Ho Hi-Ho," when the Colonel swept from behind in his sulky and scooped Marshall up as if Marshall had been a mailbag waiting for the train's silver hook. The Colonel explained that it was time for Marshall to pull his weight and serve his country, time to become a man, time to learn courage and bravery. With a lump in his throat, Marshall was resigned to the fact of impressment in the Eagle Bay firefighters, where he was conscripted into the Twenty-second Regiment as a hose boy.

Eagle Bay was a strange town, and its inhabitants were obsessed with firefighting. A population of just over 6,000 sustained thirty fully comple- mented fire companies and ten ambulance corps. The dominant sound in Eagle Bay was sirens. Each company had an average of five or six engines and auxiliary vehicles. Each of these had a siren, and on top of company headquarters was always a bull moose blaster, underneath one of which was a little sign which read: FOR T.R., AFFECTIONATELY. If burning leaves were wet and gave off some white smoke, three or four pumpers and an ambulance would arrive within ninety seconds. A grass fire meant thirty or forty vehicles. A forest fire would summon more than a hundred.

However, a fire in the Eagle Bay School's first, second, and third grade annex was cause for an apoplectic ingathering of fire engines and other vehicles. There were 180 engines, pumpers, hook and ladders, and command cars, 30 ambulances, and more than a thousand automobiles with sirens and flashing lights. By the time the alarm was properly received nearly 2,000 sirens and moose horns were blasting. The 2,500 firefighters, medics, and police submerged their equipment in a sea of uniforms and rubber coats. Twenty times as many people rushed into the burning building as had rushed out. Then they too came out, carrying their injured, while flames burned 300 feet in the air and the building was wracked by gas explosions. But when the engines (co-ordinated masterfully by the commander-in-chief from a special loudspeaker van) finally directed their full capacity at the inferno, the flames were extinguished in about two minutes, the building was com- pletely washed away, and several unwitting dogs were drowned in the rushing river, which finally found the Hudson and made Eagle Bay itself the color of ashes for about a week.

Marshall had been impressed as a hose boy and boot cleaner. He quickly rose to hose inspector, and then hose cleaning chief of the Twenty-second Regiment, or Black Rock Hose. In high school he transferred to the Eighth Regiment, or River Street Hose, an outfit which specialized in fighting forest fires and had 200 Boy Auxiliaries who dressed for the woods in leather hunting boots, fatigue pants, and plaid shirts, and fought brush and forest fires with shovel, axe, brush hook, and galvanized pumper tanks strapped on their backs. Marshall was quite early put in charge of his own 1,000-acre sector, which had fires at least five times a year. Sparks from passing trains caught in the dry grasses, sometimes kindling hundreds of acres. By fourteen, he had become used to fighting fires for days at a time without relief. He used an axe with incredible skill and strength for a boy his age, and learned the strategy and tactics of containment, cutting momentum, breaking up main thrusts, encirclement, and just dogged holding of ground. For years, Marshall was unaware that other towns did not share Eagle Bay's spirited defense against flame, or its resemblance to Allied headquarters for the Normandy invasion.

In this garden of former officers and passionate firefighters one was outstanding in his quality and in his effect on Marshall and scores of other children. He was an old man who wore thick glasses and had almost olive-colored skin and a ring of white hair. To Marshall, he had always looked a little like a fish with powerful jaws, since his face was squared off from biting the bullet and the big lenses magnified his eyes. His name was Major Pike, and he was married to the fifth grade teacher in the Eagle Bay School, where he himself was in charge of shop and legend. A Marine major from Norfolk, he had served in the Spanish-American War, World War I, Nicaragua, and the Second World War. Unlike the Colonel, who had been in charge of the Army's toilet paper, Major Pike had attained his rank in a lifetime of battles. An enlightened official of the Eagle Bay School had provided him with a large building, a budget, and a steady stream of students starting with grade two and ending with the sophomores of the high school.

The Major had assembled a collection of tools, materials, and mementos, with the object of instructing Eagle Bay students in technology, history, crafts, mechanics, and geography. His instruction hall was 200 feet long, 100 feet wide, and 40 feet high. A random and partial listing of its contents follows (these things stood on the floor; hung from walls, beams, and ceilings; were displayed in cases, on shelves, and in cabinets; and were spread about on tables): lathes; jigsaws; bandsaws; drills; milling machines; welders; a forge; grinders; polishers; sanders; winches; derricks; cutters; torches; automotive, cartographic, woodworking, aeronautical, and gunsmithing tools; a laboratory for quantitative and qualitative analysis; an astronomical telescope; ship's instruments; a sword collection; a rifle and machine gun collection; ship and plane models; kayaks; a wooden igloo; a collection of Moro weapons; buffalo, moose, and elk heads; hundreds of patent models; a printing press; a 1910 Ford; kites; a steam engine; an aircraft engine from a tri-motor; wings and wind tunnel models; rockets; gas masks; bayonets; electrical models; photographs and paintings of subjects diverse and miraculous, ranging from full-color portraits of Jesus and Black Jack Pershing and Sitting Bull to ship paintings, a photograph of FDR, countless pictures of Marine units assembled in tropical places, a Japanese screen, Remington prints, a diagram of the *Titanic*, and a picture of an alligator; dozens of colorful flags; and a thousand other things such as stuffed birds, Confederate money, a Van de Graaff generator, Magdeburg Discs, an aquarium, prisms, skins, arrowheads, clocks, bells, etc., etc., etc., etc. The most notable object was a Wright Brothers flying machine which hung from the beams fully intact and maintained. Every May Day, to counteract Communism, the Major flew a hundred feet across the girls' athletic field, a fine tan-colored Cuban cigar in his mouth, and American flags flying from both the top wings.

He had the place fully systematized. It started with second-graders who learned to work with wood on banks of jigsaws and drills. The Major moved from student to student, watching all. Anyone who made what was called a "basic operational safety mistake" (or, as the Major would say to mortified little girls, "a BOSOM") was condemned to chew a coffee bean. These were kept in an open box with a picture of a coffin on the side. In the beginning of his career Marshall chewed many beans, but the number decreased each year until he found himself to be a competent mechanic. As they advanced, the students dissected machinery of increasing complexity, starting with telephones and simple electric motors, and ending up in the last year with complete dis-assembly and re-assembly of the 1910 Ford.

Classes were suspended before each holiday, and the Major would appear in his uniform to tell stories of tropical and European wars; of decades of civilian administration in tiny republics; of the building of the Panama Canal; of the defeat of Yellow Fever; of Dewey's flagship *Olympia* at Manila Bay, where the Major had seen Gridley commence fire. So expansive was the Major's life in these and other areas that he never told the same story twice, and Marshall was to remember every detail of every one. The Major brought in his cronies—nonagenarians, visual encyclopedists, links to the past, upholders of tradition, liars, fabricators, and spellbinders. One old Irishman had been a boy making hay in the field when, in the searing light of the afternoon, a man had come running to report breathlessly that Lincoln had been shot. A railroadman of over a hundred was trooped in to tell about his friendship with Walt Whitman. He carried a conductor's leather bag in which were autographed editions and letters from Whitman to him, and he quoted the scandalous poetry (no matter, he said, he too was a bohemian) to the assembled children, who were electrified and enwrapt in the giant hall of machinery.

One of the Major's guests had spent the winter at Valley Forge, and was sought after by Lincoln during the Civil War because of his friendship with George Washington. "I'm going to see Eisenhower tomorrow," he said. "All the Presidents always ask me what to do. And I tell 'em. I just am real happy that George Washington saw me one day at the well and cast a charm over me."

It did not sound that unreasonable. After all, Teddy Roosevelt had gone to school in Eagle Bay, FDR had lived not far away, Melville had grown up within a stone's throw, and Audubon had drawn many a bird on Brandreth Hill.

Livingston himself had worked for Franklin Roosevelt, and had met Churchill, Einstein, William Jennings Bryan, Calvin Coolidge, James Joyce, Gary Cooper, T. E. Lawrence, King Farouk, and the Pope. Marshall could hardly imagine what this could have been like, for when the Mayor of Eagle Bay came to speak at the school, he shook Marshall's hand and saw an awe-struck child almost bent in two with reverence and shock.

10

One could look across the lawns, fields, and orchards of Eagle Bay and choose whichever part of the previous hundred years one preferred. History was quite alive, and had not been harried and compacted by a present which ranged totalitarian, usurping complete recognition, seeking out illogical will-o'-the-wisps to stamp into revision and conformity. The ice house was still there. Though not used, it could have been revived. Unassassinated royal families and splendid inventions were allowed to live their last days gently. There was room and time and quiet. It seemed to Marshall that the old furniture in his house and the view across sunlit snowfields into a tranquil winter landscape of ivory would last for eternity.

Thus, he dreamed in wide dreams encompassing every place and time, as if his life were gray and uneventful. He dreamed with love and longing of the corn-yellow towns on the flatlands in the Midwest, their silence broken only by singing locusts; of ships and islands; of the Arctic and Pacific, where he traveled in his imagination the trusted protégé of Perry, Parry, Peary, and Cook. Partly due to the Major's influence he fell into the habit of designing ships, fortresses, outpost towns, self-sufficient ranches, undersea chambers, and various utopias replete with geared and electrical mechanisms which would have made the Major numb with pleasure. These he put not on paper but in his mind's eye, designing in meticulous detail all his projects before he slept, so that he was lulled to sleep by a parade of unfeasible engineering masterworks and the slow unraveling of expansive imagination. He was quite willing to be drawn away from Eagle Bay, and he watched those who left and listened to those who had left, with admiration, taking note of the means they had employed to travel.

One day he was atop the cliff where he had fought the eagle, which rested below undisturbed. Marshall's feet hung over the edge and he stared at the mountains to the north and the horizon to the west. Often he came to watch the river, on which moved barges and tankers, sailboats, and the gleaming white yachts of rich men and senators traveling up to Albany. There was a channel, but north of the Tappan Zee the river was a hazardous route for big ships, which pushed on anyway. Suddenly emerging from around a bend, an enormous warship came steaming down the river. He had never seen such a tall or sleek ship. The weapons were angled and high; water was lifted in a roll off the bows; the ship's numbers shone in white; masts and radars in sky-touching black sailed far above the river. It was trim, fast, intent, such an athlete of a ship, like a great champion passing through city streets influencing children with the grace of his gait, tearing young boys a little away from their peaceful fathers forever. It passed without acknowledgment, buckling history in its path, gliding away as fast as it had come, the quickest teacher, a siren missionary pulling after it the love and loyalty of a boy on a cliff over the Hudson at midcentury, a boy who in later winters would look with wary eyes at the Victory ships in their shrouds towed downriver in fog and ice, heading for Vietnam; these prosaic wheat carriers were drawn in the slipstream of the beautiful warship years before. When a champion passes through the town in all his power and earned dignity, the children change.

Perhaps because he was immobile, Marshall not only dreamed of distant places, but found that he was susceptible to haunting. Images and thoughts, music, pictures, would flash before him compounding their original power by repetition and resonance. One of these haunting images was that of the mirage, which danced in front of his eyes and made him catch his breath long after it had vanished from the shining river. That night at dinner Livingston had described it in detail to Mrs. Livingston. It had grain elevators, old black cars, and many farm trucks. They believed that they had seen a wide main street stretching into an infinity of flat yellow fields. That which struck Livingston the most was the appearance of a clearly discernible checkerboard feed sign. In discussion they had dared to conclude that this vision had been lifted whole from the Midwest; Livingston had seen a thousand towns like it and not one east of Indiana. By the rules of physics it seemed unlikely, but its origin must have been other than the fields and rolling hills on either side of the Hudson. No one dared to speak, though, about the old cars which moved inside the glowing picture, and the resemblance it held to a town of twenty or thirty years before. No one dared, but the idea hung over the table in a silence as momentous as the mirage itself.

Marshall had read: "The atmosphere is a prism which bends and refines the light of the sun." Surely this lens, although potent enough to remove entire sunlit towns and set them in the middle of distant rivers, could not alter the solid laws of time.

There was such a lens, in fact, imbedded in the mass of machinery that was the projector of the Victory Theater in Eagle Bay. The Victory was a vaudeville house with a peeling screen, but the manager loved bright lights and had installed a great arc, so that no one noticed this imperfection, and the people of Eagle Bay were periodically raked over in light and color. It was so bright that it was as if they were rocks in its stream. Even blockheaded hoodlums from other towns who came equipped with dozens of firecrackers forgot their arsenals and stared open-mouthed at the screen. For the citizens of Eagle Bay the Victory was sort of a closed religious ritual. They never spoke of it, but the white heat and flashes of color from the powerful arc were like a steam bath or a good workout. On exiting the theater one felt light and clean, clear-headed. Even the blockheads felt clear-headed. Men, women, and children were here cleansed and calmed.

Late one afternoon Marshall escaped a cold March rain by attending the Victory's 50¢ Saturday matinee, in which the subject was from the Arabian Nights, scenes of wonder and astonishment inside a jeweled cave at the earth's center. Marshall was sunk in a worn brown seat, grasping a bag of nuts, bolts, and latches he had picked up at the hardware store, when Sinbad whirled about in the cavern and the camera focused, as if from his eyes, on the multicolored walls glowing and flashing. The strong light shining in deep ultraviolet and purples, the glinting of the emerald, a green washing out of the eyes, took hold of Marshall in a way he had always felt to be at the brink of his life, but had never experienced. His chair seemed to be revolving. Although he was upside down, the screen still met his gaze in exactly the same place, as it too circled in space. His eyes were fixed, paralyzed, held open, and his body followed suit, becoming stiff, exerting unnatural strength to remain frozen to the point. He had no idea what force was holding him, why he was frozen, why his muscles were as hard as iron or wood, why he felt so much pain. But the swirling colors were coming steadily and truly, with a sadness and expanse so magnificent that he could not hold, and there was a great white flash, after which was peace.

When he awoke, the theater was nearly empty, with the last of the children going out into the rain, and the usher plodding slowly up the dirty carpet. Marshall's hands were bloody, for he had grasped the bag of hardware with extraordinary force. The muscles in his neck were stiff and his body was shaking as he got up, exhausted, to walk to the door. There he stood looking at a wet brick wall in an alley and vines laden with heavy drops. The usher walked up the line, shutting the doors. When he got to Marshall he said, "Go home now," and Marshall stepped into the rain with the door closing behind him. The cool rain did him some good, but he was perplexed and angry at whatever had reached out and held him so strongly. He walked over the aqueduct, over the hills, and finally through the woods to his home, where he slept that night as the rain smashed against the roof tiles. He realized that like the enormous pieces of ice which glided down the river, he too was carried on a current, which would lead him from the things he loved.

Taking the warship as a sign, he assumed that he would go out by sea, since the Hudson was one of its familiar roads. He slept, not knowing that he was instead soon to chase down the mirage and find in it that which was forever beautiful and good.

III
Columbine

1

The last place Marshall would ever have imagined himself was in a train at two o'clock in the morning clipping past monstrous steel and rubber mills in Gary, Indiana, but he was there and wide awake. Through the window he saw cataclysmic platforms decked in white jewels and smoke, and the whoop whistles of donkey engines could be heard even over the train. For Marshall, night had meant crickets and the moon, and he was truly stunned to realize that amidst the deep-throated blasts and choking sulfurous air men worked in bright light as if it were day, that amidst their engines and furnaces and towers spread across oily landscapes they were like the laborers below the earth in *The Time Machine*, ignorant of the light, devilish, obsessed. But it was great nonetheless, this brutal beating heart of a steel-limbed nation, so different from his quiet river-bay country.

It was so late at night that the children were almost dreaming. They pressed against the train windows, some of which were open and let in a hot damp wind that had passed through the skeletal towers and picked up sharp disgusting smells. Many of the children were away from home for the first time, as was Marshall, trying hard to be unafraid and to let strange things pass in front of a cold objective eye. But that was hardly the case, for most of them had not been to Chicago, and could not imagine their destination—a camp in the Rockies. Marshall had never been up so late, or surrounded by so many strangers and girls. He reacted by staring at the night scenery with forced determination. It was all hard and noisy, hot and rough, and yet overshadowing the shock and wonder was the best and most exciting feeling he had ever had, or so he thought.

Sitting opposite him was a little girl named Lydia. She had tressed auburn hair and green eyes, and she was from the South. When she had boarded a train full of strangers at Union Station in Washington, she had been touchingly awkward and shy. By pure coincidence, she took the seat across from Marshall. They were young enough for the fact of traveling to Chicago with one another at two in the morning to be in itself a great adventure. The train rushed over steel bridges and oily streams, past structures angular and fierce. Nothing was soft, nothing was slow there, but Marshall was swaying rather gently in his tiredness, content because this beautiful girl had flowers on her dress, and even though he was used to the real things of nature these representations sufficed and were in themselves as enticing or more so than if they had been real. The steel mills eventually passed by unnoticed.

They reached Chicago in the middle of the night and were taken to tiny rooms in the Y. In the morning they assembled for breakfast in the cafeteria, where for 15¢ they got eggs, sausages, and potatoes. That day they walked about the city—a collection of sandstone planes and flower beds which reminded them just a little of New York. But it was hotter, flatter, quieter, somehow jazzier. You could feel through the walls that in the offices they were dealing in eggs and wheat, sheafs and bales, barrels and butchered beef. It was as if silos and bins had gone wild and migrated to the lake shore from all over the Midwest, agglomerating into tall buildings and independent spires. Surrounded by wholesomeness and good stored grains, Marshall felt as if he were on a farm. Then they would pass a night-club blaring jazz music in the middle of the day, and even the music seemed as if it had been harvested from the hot fields.

At the science museum they saw chicks being hatched, and a man with a hearing aid and a bamboo cane screamed at them a quite hysterical and desperate explanation of why the earth goes around the sun. Though the boys stuck together climbing fences and jumping hedges, and the girls had their concerns, Marshall kept glancing at Lydia, who, to his surprise and delight, glanced back. In the afternoon they rested by the lake, and after dinner they left the singing flat city on another train, bound for Columbine, Colorado, near the Wyoming border. There, a children's camp awaited them where the Elk River ran at the foot of the Sierra Madre. The places had names like Sweetwater County, Wind River Range, Mill Run Ridge, North Platte Fork, Encampment, Boulder, Larimer County, Piermont, and Fort Collins. Somehow, even before they arrived, the children associated these places and the windswept mountains which they had never seen, with the teaching of love and honesty. Even at their age they knew that such things had to be learned, and were grateful for an academy in the high air. Anyway, Chicago was so hot that even children were glad to leave it. The train began its long climb.

After passing over astounding inland seas of grain and wildflowers, after winding around foothills and valleys, crossing rivers as clean and fresh as the day they were born, and rising to air so clear and light that it dizzied the already tired children, they detrained at White Horse Junction, Colorado, a railhead at 10,000 feet primarily for the mines. It was evening, and there was great confusion as a hundred children, their trunks and duffels, and their books and small bags, were transferred from the train to a fleet of farm trucks with high boarded sides. Men in denim and khaki, tanned as bronze as Roman coins, loaded their impressed pickups, lifting little girls bodily into the back of the trucks, giving the little boys a brace on the behind if they started to fall backward as they clambered over the tailgates. The engine breathed heavily after pulling its cars up the mountain. It was one of the last regular-service steam locomotives—fourteen feet high, weighing almost half a million pounds, fired by coal. Muscular stokers with bandannas around their heads observed the children. Darkness enveloped them as a mountain cast a cool shadow in the sunset; beyond, the peaks shone like burnished metals, and the few snow-covered heights were gold in sympathy. The stokers got to work, and after a complicated release of levers and turning of valves, the engine backed off down the track to a water tower, leaving the children in the center of a white steam cloud, like immigrants at Ellis Island in the fog. After a head count, the trucks moved off in a windy evening convoy traversing forest and mountain roads, rushing through the little town of Columbine like an armored column, taking a dirt road encased by cathedral walls of pine, crossing wood bridges at speed, racing to the outer meadows of the camp. Led by recidivists, they sang a song:

> Sail along, the open road
> Under skys, so clear
> Sail along, the open road
> To Columbine, each year.

Despite the juvenile lyrics and the roar of trucks and wind, it sounded very beautiful as the choir of young voices sang to dissuade fears and to celebrate arrival in the wilderness once again for the beginning of a mountain summer.

They came upon a grassy common surrounded by a half-circle of wooden buildings, each with a large porch on which was a line of rocking chairs. In the rest periods and times before meals the children rocked on the veranda, gazing at a view so wide, long, and magnificent that it was, as someone said, "a peacemaker." They could see across valleys and plains, and down a white-tipped range to an infinity of alpine meadows. A herd of sheep ten miles distant looked like a tiny white glove resting on a mountain-side; a town with radiating roads and track was a starfish stuck in the valley. Great white clouds erupting in blinding billows sailed the range as a matter of course, not above them, but out from the mountain and level with their vision. The sun was pure and gentle, the mountain colors calm. Time fell away.

In the confusion of debarking—from the trucks a score or more of bright beams crisscrossing the dark field, diesel and gasoline engines clicking and purring, shouts and laughter—Marshall stepped a few paces into a field of dry grasses to look at space and the stars, which ran in belts and lines across the suede sky as he had never seen; they began to take hold of him, but he turned away hard and walked back to the trucks grouped like a herd of bulls with shining headlamps.

Once inside a huge, varnished, beamed hall of yellow pine, they sat at tables for eight, under clear bulbs in conical tin shades. They sang a grace which did not rhyme and caused Marshall to cock his head and look quizzical—"God is great and God is good, and we thank Him for this food" —and then delegates from the tables brought back enormous platters of roast beef, mashed potatoes, and carrots, buckets of gravy, plates of hot biscuits, and a tray of little jars containing honey, jelly, and butter. Thin air, exercise, and the natural growth of the children necessitated such menus at every sitting, and the counselors claimed that they could see their charges getting taller by the hour. This was much discussed at the first meal, and excited Marshall, for even though he was lean and rugged, stronger than two boys his age and as agile as an ocelot, he was small and feared that he would grow up (or not grow up) to be a midget.

On the long journey from New York they had crossed the Mississippi, which seemed to Marshall like a national date line, and he had lost track of the days. It was therefore quite a shock when at dessert the lights dimmed, the hall of kindly strangers began to sing, a cake with ten bright candles was trooped out by cooks in puffy helmets, and Marshall was cheered as if he were a hero. Embarrassed and moved in a way which befitted his age, he realized that it was the twenty-eighth of June, his birthday. He was told to pick someone out of the crowd to help him extinguish the candles. In the warm light shining on a ring of faces one stood out, the face of a seductively beautiful girl who was already breathing hard because she knew that she was going to be chosen. Marshall said nothing, but he had not looked at anyone else. She walked to his side and looked in his eyes. There were giggles from the crowd and the counselors' deep voices said something they neither heard nor wanted to hear. The children said, "Hold hands, hold hands." They did; they blew out the candles; and the lights went on.

That night in his bunk Marshall felt as if all the mountains and the height of the sky were in him, as if the world were a place in which entire alpine regions conspired to make children happy. And that night in Colorado the moon came up so bright that even sheep and horses could not sleep, and stood in the fields staring upward as confused as the first astronomers.

2

The second triumph was better. At the stables, two dozen children his age were assembled on benches overlooking a riding ring. The instructress was an octogenarian named Madame Zaragoza, whose Austrian dialect was so heavy it was a wonder that the horses could carry it and her at the same time, though she was so frail that she had to grasp the wooden rails whenever the wind picked up. At eighty she cared little for appearances and her daily outfit consisted of high black boots, jodhpurs, a pink satin shirt embroidered with Spanish proverbs, a sport fisherman's vest in which rode a multiplicity of tonics and pills, a police whistle at the end of braided snakeskins, and an army hat pressed down on what seemed to be a clown's wig. She often forgot what she was doing and leaned against the backside of a horse, fixedly staring at the nearest peak, which was called Mt. Cube. Most of the children had never seen anyone so old. When she became suddenly still they assumed that she had died, and knots began to form in their throats until a brave one managed to chirp, "Madame Zaragoza . . . Madame Zaragoza!" and she came back to life to continue where she had left off. Once, she had come across the shoe prints of several horses, some going north and some south. Because they had obviously passed at different times, their tracks were overlaid. Madame Zaragoza, however, concluded that phantom horses capable of passing through one another were riding her range, and she made Marshall and a bunch of other unfortunates erase the evidence and pledge secrecy.

She was explaining the parts of the horse and its tack, things which were to Marshall second nature. And yet he was so nervous that he could hardly sit still. Lydia was with the girls, and he wanted badly to show her how well he could ride. Madame Zaragoza adjusted the stirrups to what Marshall could see was suitable for him, and then asked for a volunteer to take the horse around the ring. In one motion, Marshall raised his hand, stood up, said, "Me," and jumped from the rail onto the horse's back. At last he felt at home, and for a moment he forgot even Lydia, for the movement and grace of the horse became all-embracing. He felt again as if he were twirling in head-over-heels flight through starlit space. He set out at a canter, gliding around the ring like cavalry. Then he galloped, and while so doing jumped on and off the horse from side to side, springing up and over. He veered to the center, and in slow motion the horse stretched his muscles in a graceful arc toward the sun, and Lydia saw horse and rider frozen in the air above the barrier—having abandoned everything for the laws of flight. Madame Zaragoza was stunned. From that moment she let him do anything he wanted, and trusted him with tasks such as running to fetch trail goggles from her little cabin, in which Marshall saw to his amazement about four hundred empty gin bottles lined up on the beams and horizontal members, stacked in corners, under the bed, etc., etc.

He fell as fast as he had risen. On the first Sunday they dressed in white shorts and shirts. Counselors inspected their fingernails and ears. Then they got on the trucks and traveled with blinding speed to Columbine. Marshall asked where they were going and was told, "To a clambake." This made him happy, since lobster was his favorite food. They pulled up in a row at the church, a beautiful white Alpine building in the middle of a meadow which came right up to the town. When they started to file in, Marshall asked a counselor if the clambake were to be inside or out. "Where's the food?" he asked.

"Are you crazy?" replied the counselor. "There's no seafood up here. We're going to church." By the time Marshall knew what was happening he was inside the doors, and from the starkly Protestant and mountainly interior gleamed the rays of a silver cross. Marshall began to back up against the stream of incoming people.

"I can't be in here," he said. "This isn't the right place for me. I can't be in here. Let me out." The counselor told him to shut up and sit down. He did, but when the minister came in he tried to get up and go out. A strong pair of hands grappled with him and pushed him down by the shoulders. It hurt to be shoved into the hard wood. So despite the fact that the minister looked like Eisenhower (for whom Marshall had always felt very sorry) and despite the pleasant-looking ladies and the gentle old men, despite the choir which had started to sing, the sunlight which came through the stained glass windows, the position he occupied in the middle of the congregation, the libertarian behind him, and the enchanting beauty of it all, Marshall submerged into a sea of legs and shoes and got to the aisle, which he ran up faster than a burned jackrabbit. There was a great stir. Eisenhower was (as usual) puzzled, and the Hound of God made his way with great embarrassment through an entire packed row.

Outside, Marshall climbed into a truck and breathed in relief, thinking that he was safe. But then he heard footsteps and the Hound of God appeared at the back of the truck. He was enraged, and he screamed at Marshall, who, like a trapped raccoon, looked back with a gentle poker face. "Get out of that truck. Who the hell do you think you are?" Marshall was afraid to answer. He didn't know this man, and it was therefore especially terrifying. "You live in a world of people. Do you think you have the right to go in your garden and close the gate?"

"Yes," screamed Marshall. "Yes. Yes. Yes."

"You don't!"

"Who says I don't?"

"God says you don't."

"God can speak for himself," said Marshall, "and you can go to hell."

That was it. The counselor boiled over. Marshall scrambled to the top of the cab. It was a true emergency. Hound of God threw himself over the tailgate at a bound. By the time he was on the roof Marshall was running over the meadow in panic. Even more enraged, Hound of God took some strides and caught him, and then, holding Marshall's hands and arms behind his back in a grip so hard that it hurt him to do it, he hit Marshall again and again and again and again and again. The more he hit the harder and angrier his blows became. The ground got full of blood. Marshall dared not cry out, for he feared that then the people in church would know what was happening and it would be to his shame. He was battered and moaning. Hound of God said: "Get back in there." Expecting to be murdered, Marshall bared his teeth and spit blood as his answer. Hound of God clenched his fist, and then suddenly strode away toward the church.

It was a beautiful building in a beautiful place, and the music was magnificent as choir and congregation together sang the chorus: "Oh thou that tellest good tidings to Zion, get thee up into the high mountain," and the lyrics reverberated throughout the valley. Marshall looked at the birds in the eaves and thought how small they were, how they could easily die by buckshot, an eagle, or the snow. They seemed ever alert, and devoted to the baby birds in the nests. He made his way back to the truck and sat in the corner. During the rest of the service he composed himself and cleaned off the blood, which had come mainly from his nose and mouth. His lower lip was swollen and there was a bruise on his face. He took comfort from the birds, the clouds, the mountains. When the church bells were ringing and the children came out he knew from their searching glances that he had lost his premier position. He said nothing.

Lydia climbed on the girls' truck and sighted him over the boards. He would not look back, and her truck drove away in the dust. She felt as if she would never see him again, as if he had died in the war, and this made a vast difference to her. She too had been taken there by mistake, and was furious that they had not considered her wishes. Marshall pained to be with her, but his truck was slow in leaving and he sat in the sunlight under a cascade of bells and blue air. All he could think was how much he loved Lydia, and how much he loved the gentle animals—the sheep, the birds, the moaning cows and pigs who hurtled down the New York Central tracks to their slaughter.

3

Every evening after dinner there was singing in an enormous room with a wall of windows through which the singers could watch night come upon the range and the lights of distant towns switch on. An older camper named Gaylord played the piano—he was something of a hero—and during the first few weeks the lyrics were displayed on large sheets of paper which two volunteers turned like spitted roasts. In this way Marshall learned about fifty songs of the "Marching to Pretoria," "Road to Mandalay," "Keeper Did A-hunting Go," and "St. Louis Lantern Rag" genre. When it was finally dark they would walk in groups to their cabins on the hill. Though attendance was compulsory, one of the finest things in the world was to go up into the high meadow and watch the sunset and brightening stars while songs floated upward and the warm brass-colored light of the

lodge made it seem like the best and most marvelous of Swiss music b
glowing in miniature on the mountainside below. When they sang friv
lighthearted songs such as the "St. Louis Lantern Rag" or "Sixpence," i
stamped their feet on the wooden planks. From the meadow it seemed a
the glowing box might come apart and seed the valley with music.

It did not take long for Marshall and Lydia to go up there together.
the lodge people were singing. Marshall and Lydia were in the meadow i
balmy air clear to the highest stars. They had thought that when the
would at last be alone it would be weighty and somber, but it wasn't. They
were almost whimsical, giddy, relieved. Everything was soft. Everything was
flowing back and forth as if in a warm wave, the grasses, the trees of pine
and fir and mountain ash, winds traveling invisibly over the great dark spaces
which were the mountains. They were alone on the hillside with the earth
spread before them. Marshall had always wanted to see the Northern Lights,
and had mistakenly associated the Aurora Borealis with high altitudes
rather than latitudes. Straining to see them, he finally imagined a crown on
the horizon—fiery crystals undulating against the dark—but Lydia could see
nothing save white stars, and when she realized that he was going a little
away from her because he was drawn to the Northern Lights, she was
saddened.

But the night was too fine for that and she reached out with her arms
and her eyes, and brought him back to her by saying, "You *see* the colors
of my dress," a gingham dress it was with a delicate frilly collar, and even
in the dark he could see her face and that it was full of color, and in darkness
he saw the stars sparkling in her eyes. For the first time, he was pulled away
from light and solitude, by a soft and knowing smile and the proximity of the
girl, feeling the heat of her body over the air, smelling her sweet hair and
skin. They wanted to kiss, but were too shy. In her look and in her words,
"You *see* the colors of my dress" (daring and intelligent words for such a
young girl), they had awakened. She remembered Marshall running up the
aisle, how she had admired his strength, and how in staying she had been
confident of her own. It seemed that on the high meadow two types of
affirmation were perfectly matched. They stayed until the moon rose and its
blinding white light, moon-bright, caused them to laugh and walk down the
hill, knowing that they had loved.

4

The most sophisticated penetration of Columbine was the sunshine. The
town was surrounded by borders of dark green pine and valleys which
dropped to ice-cold streams. It was a decade after the Second World War
and the men of the town had nearly all been soldiers. Fishing was the great

preoccupation. Wooden station wagons and winch-laden surplus jeeps parked up and down the main street, and in the theater Martin and Lewis chattered like monkeys in a technicolor tattoo. Marshall went into town in a camp truck. He had blond hair and he wore his characteristic denims and a plaid shirt with holes in the elbows, which didn't matter because he rolled up the sleeves, and didn't matter anyway. He had to ration out 50¢. It could go for an ice cream soda and a silver lure, or two magazines, or two rubber-band airplanes. He chose the ice cream soda and the lure—one to be enjoyed cold, sweet, and immediate, the other to shiver at the end of his line in the dark lake.

Afterward, he sat by the truck in the parking lot, holding his face to the sun. Great dark clouds were visible down range. He knew when it would rain and how it would feel. He knew what the forests would smell like before the rain, how wild droplets would be propelled in vanguard winds and strike only several at a time, how the sun would clear it all up again. From beyond the town came the whine of a chain saw. Marshall's friends emerged from the drugstore with new baseball cards. He knew the complicated values for this currency and the subtleties of trades and flipping. It was satisfying. There were so many good things to feel and think about, and it was good to lean against the rough plank bumper and feel warm in the sun. In these mountains he could sit absolutely still, concentrating for many hours on the color of the sky. He loved the landscape and the country so deeply that even though he was only ten he thought to himself that it would not matter if he died at that moment, for he had seen so much that was beautiful.

Then he was swept up again in the society of his fellows, something which invariably he regretted. Pleasant sociability made time fly happily, but when it was over he felt that he had been cheated. It was the same in the games they played. At the end he looked back like a man who has been asleep, and it seemed that he had been carried unconscious in the group, that he had learned nothing, felt nothing. But he did acquire a certain daring and roughness, which he questioned. For it seemed to him that it was daring but not true courage, roughness but not true endurance. Often in groups he found himself taking the lead—doing awful things of which he was later ashamed.

They were surprised. Instead of going back to camp they were to climb a mountain. Unknown to them, packs and equipment had been placed in the cab of the pickup. Spirits soared, for there was nothing better than ascent to a place from which they could scan over the tops of mountains that customarily were the borders of their sight. So when the truck pulled away they were jumping up and down, singing, stamping their feet like soldiers who have just had a victory and are leaving the battlefield for home.

On their way they leaned out dangerously and when they passed someone they waved a newspaper and screamed, "War! War! War is declared!

World War Three!" They had always taken it for granted that when they reached the age of conscription, a major war would break out and they would fight it. Their grandfathers had done so. Their fathers had done so. They would do so.

In the bedstead-sized towns and little junctions, some smiled, some were indifferent, some scowled. But when the joke was almost finished and their throats hurt from shouting so that they wished they would arrive at the mountain or pass no one else, they rounded a bend near a beautiful rapids.

On the shoulder was a station wagon, elegantly polished and well looked after. An old man, one of those old men of the mountains, with light tortoise-shell glasses, a tall lean frame, and silver hair, was fly-casting into the stream. Even from the truck at speed Marshall could see the beauty of the hypnotic black water flowing and ebbing. Surrounded by fine equipment, obviously a lord of the mountains, one who was part of the country, one who had come through, the old man turned and looked straight into Marshall's eye with a sadness which could have been saying only that he had seen war himself and was puzzled and distraught at the vitality of the death-head, rising as it did in the vigorous cries of young children riding through his green summer country.

The momentary grief on the old man's face told Marshall not to lie, that lies were bad not in themselves, but in the awful contrast they made with the truth. Then they went up on a high peak, reaching it after many hours, and the whole world was stretched out before them. Because of the perspective and the difficult route by which they had come, they crouched down and stared over the distances in complete and utter silence.

5

After they had been on the meadow in moonlight, Marshall and Lydia felt comfortable about exploring different places together, though not about the unrealized prospect of sharing an embrace or a kiss. Too young to know the unsurpassed communication of intimate settling in one another's arms, they chased through the beautiful landscape, making it surrogate to their yearnings. Small lakes and outcroppings of dry rock over rapids, silent groves, and heraldic pine forests were the sword between them as they moved from place to place with the swiftness of animals in a soft unstressful mating season.

In doing so, they forged a commitment. As children ineloquent and unable to frame exactly the sharp edge of their thoughts, even they knew that casual and joyful meetings can cast out heavy anchors. And they were ready for this. They knew little about one another except what they had seen and felt on the borders of the wilderness which approached the camp. They

believed very hard in pure and beautiful things. For example, they were convinced that when they became older they would marry, that though
separated by years and time, they would be brought together by the power
they sensed in the woods and on the mountain pastures. It made no sense
according to the rationality they were growing into and were taught in
school, but it was infinitely sensible as they spied in their differently colored
eyes a determination and recognition untenable in all but the strikingly
vivid world everywhere around them.

One night they went out during the singing, exiting secretly by different
doors, meeting underneath the lodge as the other children stamped the
floorboards above them in the singing of "Sixpence." From there they
rushed across an open field to the beginning of a deep pine forest which
seemed to lead all the way west to the Pacific. They ran silently over the pine
needles, sometimes losing one another in the tangle of black columns, but
always uniting after a mazelike traverse in fumes of resin.

They thought they heard a nightingale, but were not sure. Through
the net of needles the sky was dark blue. Thunder could not have penetrated
that green canopy. The forest floor was as soft and clean as they could have
wished. They settled by a large and perfect pine. From beyond the rim of
the woods they heard the campers' songs—hundreds of innocent voices.

They faced a dilemma, but the solution was provided. The problem was
obvious—how to last through years of change intercepting love and loyalty,
how to conquer the lock of powerlessness put upon children, how to be
united in the imagined future with the same graces they had found in the
Rocky Mountain forests. Well they knew that other children were drawn
into the breathless maneuvering of first loves, that others there were committed and caring as if they had been three times their real age, but they
knew also that time and distance would break apart these lovely connections,
and they did not want that. How then to overcome that which made others
believe that children do not forever love? They would have had no idea, had
their backs not been resting against it.

The pine, a thick-trunked black column standing in a sheath of green,
would be their emblem, for it in itself was perfect and exemplary. In nature
study they had learned that it prevented erosion, manufactured oxygen, held
back avalanches, and made good black soil. It provided resin, rosin, and
turpentine. Its lumber was invaluable, one of the pillars of Western Civilization, and it did all sorts of odd miscellaneous things, from serving as the
essence of cough drops to providing an essential and savory ingredient in
Japanese cooking.

But mercantile uses were slight compared to the life of the pine. It was
ever so splendid. It grew tall and straight as a rule, courteously pruning its
lower branches to make a forest gallery as extensive and lighthearted as a
Roman bath. Its symmetrical branches were better than a ladder for climbing
to the very top, which though thin and supple was strong enough to hold

Marshall and Lydia neatly counterbalanced high above the valley. The trunk was smooth and black, as if an artist had perfected his painting. It created a carpet on the forest floor, soft, clean, and fragrant. It was fragrant in itself, perfuming the wilderness with resinous draughts and clean air. When the wind passed through it a sound was created which made strong competition for ocean breakers or the hypnotic rapids sound. Its needles were soft and the boughs made lovely beds. A crackling pine fire was one of the joys of the world. And then, most important, it was evergreen and did not lose life or flex, in even the coldest most desolate of winters. When the snow came, there it stood, an essay in constancy and power, green, alive, continuing, forever.

They hardly knew one another: they could not have. But they took the pine as their symbol, and it brought them together in the strong solid way to which children are not normally accustomed, but which to the pine is first nature.

6

On a clear day at the end of August autumn began like a storm. The shadows were almost cold: only fat children stayed in the lake more than an instant. They prepared for the descent to White Horse Junction, to Chicago, to Washington, where, they knew, it would be hotter for a long time, and where the edge of the season then in the Rockies would not appear until mid-October. By December, the camp would be covered with snow and not a soul would return until the next May, when the owners came up from Kansas. Marshall and Lydia had won their battle, and on Sundays they stayed alone at the camp, with Madame Zaragoza, and the cooks.

Lydia became more and more beautiful as the summer passed and she was darkened by the mountain sun, so that in contrast to her smooth skin, the green of her eyes and the whiteness of her teeth became more apparent. She and her family were going to France the next summer to visit her older brother, who lived in Paris. She would not return to the camp. Nor would Marshall, for he was to attend a naval school on the Maine coast, and had registered the previous year for its grueling and popular sailing and survival program.

Marshall and Lydia were on the dock by the fresh cold lake, and Lydia was reading to him from a book about France. They wore shorts and dark blue T-shirts, and sneakers without socks. France, she guessed, was the first test. "And Maine," he added. "Two different things."

"It might be ten years," she said, "or more."

"Yeah," said Marshall. "I don't care."

At the finish of the season, activities dissolved into anarchy. They had several painfully clear cool days; then they were on the train riding over the heat-soaked prairie.

The men and women of the land in between were tall and gaunt. They looked too quiet, as if they had been placed in the stations and on the roads directly from photographs of the Depression. It was because they were filled with the land. The land held them from all sides. It was a singing, locust place, a sea of which they farmed the waves, foils of gold and blue light, a constant horizon which brought them far from themselves and made them quiet and unartful. Time was still and far too fast. Every movement there had satisfaction or countersatisfaction. The sameness made them elegant observers. Anyone observing them observe was filled with envy. And to them it was nothing, like the way they moved and talked—slow and loose with inimitable dignity. Outside themselves they were not much. In themselves they were more than good: they were magnificent.

Marshall and Lydia rode in a flood of daytime across the plains to Chicago. Summer had ended. They went through the gin car of beetlelike old men in black suits, train-bound salesmen more constant than Faraday's Law and no less corrupt than Egyptian referees. Lydia was so beautiful and suntouched that the gin-car men saw her as if she were a woman, and they were ominously silent when she passed. Marshall was ready to fight, and would have thrown them out the window even though they were twice his size. She blushed and pushed through the air crowded with leers and what she didn't want. They reached the back of the train and stood at the folding gate.

Wheat. Gold oceans. It smelled red and rich, full of life. The track clatter knocked them together rhythmically. They had to hold on to stay up. The end of the train whipped back and forth with wonderful sinew, pushing them closer. And they held each other tighter and tighter, until they pressed hard from head to toe and could feel one another's bodies and an entire hot clean summer passing through in an echo. They began to tremble. It was as if they were mixing. Electricity lashed around them as bright and sharp as the fleeing silver lines. The train was propelled in a hoarse power glide across the percussive flatlands. They ran through stations and claxoned crossings in a wheel of speed, continuing forward. Their hands were entwined. He put his lips against her light auburn hair.

7

When they pulled into Union Station in Washington the children got off the train weary and dazed, staggering on sea legs, streaming through the gates to enormous rooms where many parents waited. Those continuing north or south engrouped at food stands and sat hooked up to orange sodas and ice cream floats, the straws sticking into them almost intravenously. In one corridor dusty with age Marshall saw to his amazement a tattered poster of Smokey the Bear, on which someone had written: *This bear is a communist.*

Marshall went to Lydia. She was with a group of girls on an enormous wooden bench. They dangled their legs and spoke in a variety of accents. The end of that season was a special marker in their lives, and they had no choice but to grow up steadily and seldom look back. "Looka here," said Katy Barnow, a very tiny girl who resembled a field mouse, "Marshall the horse rider. I know why *he's* here." By some unwritten code, he was not supposed to show interest in girls. When he appeared, they held up their end of the bargain by acting put upon or coy. All but Lydia, who felt her heart rise uncontrollably with his. They knew her train would leave in twenty minutes. As they walked to the fountain in front of the station they felt that curious inhibition which rises between men and women when there is real love.

In the plaza around the fountain planted thick and treacherous with pink and white roses (the marble itself a sparkling white and alabaster as blue water passed over it), a high afternoon sun lit the great transom and shone in their eyes as if from a polished silver shield, obscuring much of the inscription, and illuminating some. They pieced out alternately and aloud that which the light illumined and did not hide: *Fire. Greatest of discoveries, enabling man to live . . . and compel . . . Electricity, carrier of light and power, devourer of time and space . . . greatest servant of man, itself unknown. Thou hast put all things under his feet, . . . bringer of life out of naught. The farm. Best home of the family, main source of national wealth, foundation of civilized society, the natural providence.*

In the train shed the reticulated vault was covered with half a century of soot. Leafy black patterns were engraved on the grated glass. A long row of cast-iron gates divided the room. Marshall was to wait another hour after Lydia left for the South. The noise and steam were deafening and white. The heat poured from above. They could smell the iron above and see black columns disappearing down the platform in a row like telephone poles on the prairie . . . tremendous excitement. Her train pushed vapor from under its skirts. She did not want to go. Red caps and pigeons flashed in the periphery of their vision, lines of luminescent color. Steel rails and steel wheels squealed and the sound echoed by and by. She was already beyond the bars. He would wait until empowered and then seek her out. He loved the way she spoke, the way that she was not quite confident in herself, and yet was the very best. He would find her and then they would marry, or rather, resume the marriage which had begun in trains and pine forests and by a rattling iron gate.

He put his head through the bars, noting that they were wide enough to allow an embrace but nonetheless would block passage. They did embrace. He thought he saw in her face the moment for which he had been born. More whistles and vast exhalations echoed in the train shed. The scale and geometry were overwhelming, for not only had time stopped, but past and future were brought together, and in a great spherical infusion they faced one another falling deeper and deeper in love, uncontrollably, like travelers to the earth's center falling through layers and layers of inferno. Then she stepped back into a beam of hot white light alive with dust, and he saw no more. All was suddenly a roseate flash, a waterfall of light and black. When he could again see, she was gone, and he felt his fists clenched painfully around the hard iron which had held him up.

IV
High View

1

In the dead of winter (and in those days there were indeed winters) the entire Eagle Bay School set together in wondrous precision to present *Iolanthe*. If the French socialist La Fournier had ever had a point in favor of his judgment that society's more unpleasant tasks (such as cesspool cleaning, dishwashing, and ditch digging) could be joyfully completed by adolescents and enthusiastic children, it was here illustrated. To be close to the players, the younger students eagerly did all the dirty work, and thought it a privilege. They mixed paint for the flats as if they were concocting hydrogen bombs, they pushed brooms across the stage as if they had just returned triumphant from Gaul, and they took out the garbage with the gait and expression of silent movie heroes.

There were several older girls in the chorus for whom Marshall would gladly have thrown himself off the high grid. The elegance of their costumes under strong stage lights, and the music, dancing, and color intoxicated him. To be even momentarily accepted by them as a junior, an apprentice, was beyond ambition. When occasionally it occurred, he was elated for days. For instance, to be close enough to Suzanne to smell her makeup, look at her hair sweeping downward over her shoulders, and see in the intense lights an expanse of purple hose as she did turns to the music was better even than long life.

Young stagehands (officiously directed by older boys who were socially unacceptable and so turned to the ropes, lighting boards, fishy paint, and high ladders) scurried about making examples for one another of their prowess at skimming catwalks a hundred feet up, riding sandbags from one grid to another, and manipulating the rheostats of the lighting board like Atlantic submarine captains. They imagined that the girls in the chorus were watching. They were not, but rather were hoping that they themselves were being observed from beyond the footlights. And if they were aware at all of the little stagehands it was as midget footmen in a well-defined hierarchy, monkeys in gray and brown swinging above them as counter-weights to their own fantasies.

But the monkeys of the upper galleries, in love and outcast, watched these lovely young girls, mouths open and eyes gawking from between ropes and belaying pins, charged glances traveling instantaneously downward onto the tempestuous color-filled stage. The girls' hopes went outward to the darkened auditorium, and the music and heat sailed up into the gray winter air.

Marshall lay back against brick and iron on a platform seventy-five feet off the ground. He was alone there, resting unobserved, and he felt like a bird in a tree at a nighttime garden party. But unlike the bird, he was thinking about what had been said in a class just before he put on his work clothes and climbed into the ropes. As was often the case, the teacher had ridiculed someone for liking that which was in bad taste, common, cheap. Arguments against it were strong. It was a short, bad poem by someone who had probably died immediately after writing it. But Marshall found himself pulled toward it, in defense of the indefensible and harmless, a strange combination which could boil him like a pot of tea.

He watched as the teacher formed a collection of students welded together against what they had been told was contemptible. But what then of the Irish woman and her grandchild Marshall had seen on Dyckman Street in upper Manhattan. He had gone to buy a fencing foil in a sword store. It was Saturday in winter with the snow packed onto the streets and the jingle of chains from municipal vehicles, and gusts of cold and colder air coming from the parks, from around the corners, and from the wooded snow-covered Palisades. The woman was great and fat and must have weighed 300 pounds. Her coat fit her like a tarpaulin slung over a Volkswagen. She had gum shoes and striped socks, a kerchief was drawn over her head, and she wore alabaster-colored glasses with thick lenses. The material of her coat was so cheap that Marshall could see the cold traveling through it. And her grandson of three or four was bundled in thin single-stitched cloth; an earmuff hat which covered his little head had slipped back. Marshall passed them as they stood in front of a religious articles store, its window crammed with garish unholy implements. The grandmother held the child's hand and pointed to one of the plaster castings, saying: "Look. Isn't it beautiful? A beautiful statue. Beautiful."

What would his classmates and the teacher have said about that? By absolute standards it was indefensible, and yet even if the love which the woman had for the plaster statue were formulaic, automatic, and artificial, it was all she had, and because of that the indefensible gained a great power and came up behind arguments assembled against it. It was all she had and she approached it with dignity and love, and as the little boy's hand stroked the cold window, learning the lines of an object of beauty, Marshall felt a strong bond. Sitting on his high platform shielded by darkness and beams of bright lights, he thought that not everyone can be schooled rigorously in art, not everyone can be lean and aristocratic, not everyone can win. But *he* would. And if he failed, he expected to die rather than live an uncharmed life. No Dyckman Street for him, and no contempt for it either, if he could keep his distance.

He stood up and looked across a dark chasm separating him from another, larger platform. The distance was about four feet down and four feet laterally—not excessive for a jump except in view of the considerable drop. One of the dancers below was staring past the hot lights into the darkness, and thought that she had seen a form sailing above her in the black. She had, and Marshall stood on the larger platform, his heart beating ferociously.

Humiliated in the role of monkey, imagining heroic action on the stage below, determined to be efficient and brave among the cables and pulleys, and always aware of the snow falling outside covering the ground and the dark English trees, he was momentarily sustained by the clocklike mechanism of the play—its form and discipline being love in counterpoint. The production was out of phase, awkwardly directed, bursting with energy. In a theater flooded with white light and washed-out pastels, they were all entranced. It got dark early then, and yet they often stayed until midnight. They danced below. The snow danced past the darkened windows.

2

Marshall was extremely restless. He was, of course, still a virgin, and as such driven to unspeakable fits of temper and longing. Who but a young virgin boy would walk many miles through thick brush and untraveled woods (even in the middle of winter) with the hope of coming upon a nude and lascivious widow-instructoress? He could not learn Latin, because Virginia Boar, a red-haired beauty fond of clothing with a revealing cut, sat (and bended, and stretched, and turned) in front of him in each class. The Latin teacher was afraid for Marshall. She thought that he had heart disease, because he often broke into cold sweats, and hot sweats, during which his face would become purple or red and his eyes would float upward in their sockets as he seemed to lose consciousness. He tried not to look at Virginia, but got a crick in his neck. Then he brought a bag of herbs into class, thinking that if he smelled it he would defuse his lust. Every few minutes he would take deep draughts from his herb bag.

"What *is* that, Marshall?" asked the Latin teacher.

"It's an herb bag, Mrs. Vouvoulis," he answered, dreading what he knew must follow, because he never lied in important confrontations.

"What in heaven's name is it for?"

He hesitated, but there was no way out. "It defuses lust."

Virginia Boar gave a long wanton sigh, and Mrs. Vouvoulis made poor Dinario Maravedis, the son of the barber, stand in front of the class and recite the declension of *oppidum* at the top of his lungs.

As if anticipating great changes he tried in still feeble ways to precipitate their occurrence. His experience and reading suggested that disease and sickness were weighty and majestic phenomena which imparted great wisdom. He tried therefore to catch impressive diseases. Once, he took off his clothes and stood in the snow for half an hour. He went to the filthiest restaurants in search of typhoid and botulism. He rode the train to New York to nap in garbage cans. He went to Times Square in search of syphilis but could not find her. He volunteered for medical experiments at more than a few hospitals but was too young. No matter what he did, he remained uninfected.

He dreamed of a time when the confusion and fear of adolescence would vanish in deference to understanding, excitement, and the flow of events. He thought that it would be like a mist lifting to show a sparkling city, or green mountains where every leaf on every tree was visible. He turned from searching out disease to the railroad and the river, where he could be close to danger and, by surviving, experience the changes which he thought might help to give him an adult's power and compassion.

Running along the railroad tracks which separated Eagle Bay from the river was a swamp of reeds and cattails through which muskrats, snakes, and spiders ran and burrowed in loam and mud. To gain wisdom, Marshall crawled on his belly through this swamp for about a mile and a half. He went in a straight line, crashing within the reed banks, where he frequently surprised quiescent muskrats and sunning snakes. When he came upon dead insects he ate them. After several hours he emerged entirely covered with stinking mud, gashes, cuts, puncture wounds, stings, and slime. His left eye was swollen, and his muscles were sore. Mrs. Livingston repressed her horror and asked where he had been.

"Just hanging around the village," replied Marshall.

In winter he rode ice floes on the river, teaching himself gradually in the shallows their characteristics and capabilities. Eventually, he was able to hop from one to another, in blue water. His only tool in this was a long pole with a spike at the end, which he used to maneuver and to secure his stance and, when the water was shallow, to push himself back to the beach. Knowing the currents (after heart-pounding experimentation in which he was often convinced that he would be carried down the January river out to sea), he rode the ice sometimes a mile into the bay, but was always swept back to shore. The danger was that currents and winds would vary, and that his chunk of ice would break up beneath him. But he had a good feel for piloting and traveled many numbing miles on those white rafts, never even wetting his foot.

Sometimes the river froze all the way to the channel, where ice-breakers kept it open. Above windblown river ice covered with crescents of snow were clouds of rushing powder like the atmosphere of Venus, howling past the hard mirror below at the behest of Canadian winds which scourged the valley. Once he stood alone in the middle of the frozen plain and looked shoreward. It was not the same as being in a boat, for then he was constantly busy with shrouds and tiller, and here he simply stood, legs planted in the rushing polar vapor, looking at his home on the hill and the woods he knew so well. Downriver, a moving line of confetti appeared, winding along the bank. It was a long freight, at a distance like a dragon of Chinese New Year—scaled and colorful, jointed, and yet smoothly traveling. Entrapped in a frozen moment of white and ice he saw the train come between him and Eagle Bay. He heard the rumbling, and felt the ice quiver and snap in response, as if a high-tension cable had parted. The cars were brightly lit by the sun, which had come low down and unexpected through a bank of lateral gray clouds, robbing it of its silver. It was cold and thunderous. The ice quaked. He wanted, like most of those his age, to leave. To his shock and surprise, he *did*.

Livingston was a little mad, as restless himself as an adolescent, and quite rich. He hated winter, for when he had returned from Arizona he had fallen through the ice on a lake in a Newark park, and remained up to his neck in the freezing waters until a brave, bearded policeman had pulled him out. One day Livingston told Marshall that he would not be going to school for a while.

"For how long a while?" asked Marshall.

"For a year or two," said Livingston.

They closed up the house, lent out the horses and dogs, had a last dinner in the cold North (the dinner consisted of roast chicken, potatoes, watercress salad, champagne, and chocolate mousse), called up a few goodbyes, slept fitfully, and then one silent winter morning left for several years in the British West Indies.

3

The new British jet quickly rose to 40,000 feet. Livingston suggested that they anesthetize themselves over the Atlantic and then, when the magnesium-white plane reached the Caribbean, wake up with steaming pots of tea. An informal vote was taken from Marshall at the window to Mrs. Livingston on the aisle, and a steward brought a tray upon which were nine glasses of champagne—four for Livingston, three for Mrs. Livingston (who did not protest), and two for Marshall. These were regular-sized wine glasses, not the disc types, and before long Marshall was enjoying the monotony of the engine's roar, content to sit still for several hours as the plane traversed a gray Atlantic—threatening in winter even to those high above it. Comfortable and warm, Marshall remembered the other time he had partaken of the drink.

A year before in early summer Marshall had been stalking in the reeds near the New York Central tracks. It was hot and humid. He wore khaki shorts and shirt, and carried a .30–06 rifle, with which he had to be especially careful because of its range. Making his way eye level with the soft cattails, he froze. Like an animal, he could hold for a long time in absolute stillness if for any reason he sensed a threat. Most of the time the perception came unawares. Perhaps he had heard or smelled it, but he knew somehow that sharing with him the hot and cushiony swamp was another creature of large size. He waited, and then after a while he heard it creeping through the rushes.

It got closer and closer, moving slowly and cautiously. When Marshall could see only that it was chocolate-colored or black, with sections which glittered and sections which were white, it halted behind the beige reeds. It then appeared to roll itself up into a ball and, in this posture, it advanced slowly toward Marshall, who had leveled his gun thinking that perhaps he faced a giant muskrat. As it closed he saw that it was not a muskrat. It was clothed in brown gabardine. Coming toward him were a man's backside and two legs. Not able to grasp the meaning of such a monster, he informed it to halt or be shot, at which an upside-down, snow-white, gold-spectacled, toothless head appeared between the legs and said, "Don't shoot. I'm ninety-eight years old."

Marshall put down his rifle in embarrassment and the old man, who had been dragging a heavy burlap sack through the swamp, straightened up and threw it over his shoulder. Even though the sack seemed to weigh more than he did, he carried it quite easily. Sticking out his hand, and with a thin but lively smile, he announced himself: "Triggers is the name," he said.

They walked together from the swamp onto the tracks. The old man was the father of L. H. Triggers. It seemed strange to Marshall that the detective had a living father so thin and so unbelligerent. Triggers pranced on the steel rail, a remarkable feat of balance at the speed he traveled, while Marshall tried to keep up the dizzying pace on the ties. "I got to move along," said Triggers, "got to move my behind before the day is done. Every night I like to get home early to my new wife. I just got married fifteen years ago. But damn, I said, I'd rather be dead than not be able to satisfy a woman twenty years younger than me. Boy, do you know what it is to satisfy a seventy-eight-year-old woman? Damn near kill a man of my age, that is most men of my age," he winked, "except for me. I was in the Civil War. I was a drum."

The coot hardly noticed his burlap bag full of ceramic and glass insulators and steel spikes and plates from the railbed. In fact, he walked the narrow rail with such a springy step that it looked like a pigeon race, his head bobbing up and down and back and forth, a silver watchchain similar to his son's clinking gently in the heat and quiet. "Every night I sit in my garden, where I have over twenty-five thousand insulators and fifty thousand spikes, and I drink two ice-cold cans of beer. I go on my expedition six days a week. I carry home fifty pounds of spikes and insulators. I been doin' it for years. Then I walk in and grab my wife and," he clapped his hands together like a third-class Swiss acrobat, "*Salamango!*" He gave Marshall a wry look, an expression similar to that of the swan on a merry-go-round. "I guess you wouldn't know about that."

"I'm surprised that you do," said Marshall.

"Oh! Is that so? I'll tell you something, young whippet. I was doing salamango eighty years before you were born. I have had the privilege, to do the salamango with the wife of a king, underwater, and in a balloon. I have done the salamango in twenty-three states and four territories. I have done the salamango on hilltops, in trees, and at the base of dams. Throughout my life, I have enjoyed the reproductive process."

After quite a while racing down the Hudson tracks (Marshall trying unsuccessfully to find out how Triggers had been a drum in the Civil War), they came to the bend. "Now," said Triggers, "I have to go up that way. So I tell you what I'm gonna do. I'm gonna give you my card blanch as far as this stretch of track goes."

"It goes to Chicago," said Marshall.

"Don't be a wise guy," answered Triggers. "I'd say from Eagle Bay to Oscawana. As long as it don't hurt anyone, you can do anything you want, and I'll clear it with my boy. He respects his father. He's not like those Lutherans. Now if I die, you're still covered. Tonight after the salamango I'll add another clause to my will, in which I'll specify that you are invulnerable. I have one thousand four hundred and thirty-seven clauses already. The railroad is your oyster, kid. I'm the only man alive who can tell you that; 'cause I been on it since 1870. I can walk right into Pearlman's office and sit on his desk. I ride in his private car. I smoke his cigars. I'm the spirit of the railroad. It's mine. It's as if one day I ate it and it runs inside of me, and then it ate me. I can touch the third rail, lift a locomotive, juggle freight cars over my head. I feel the tracks spread through the country like I feel the veins in the back of my hand." He bent down and touched the steel rail with a grandfather's affection for a tender babe. Then he walked into the brush, singing "Alice Blue Gown."

Marshall soon took advantage of his new invulnerability. Throughout that June (a month which passed with delightful lethargy until his birthday on the twenty-eighth and then melted into unconscious summer) he climbed signal towers, made heavy use of the railroad telephone system, rode crossing gates, hopped freights, and did other things which a railroad bull was pledged to eradicate. Triggers, who usually lurked behind every bush, did not appear for more than a year. The visitation had been legitimate, and Marshall was pleased. It was something in itself just to stand by a train thundering past. But to hang upside down from a signal tower while the locomotive, whistles shrieking at the sight, passed only two or three feet below, was ecstasy. Once, the Twentieth Century had slowed to a crawl at Red Barn Bridge. Marshall had jumped on and ridden on the roof until the trestle at Sisters' Beach, where he caught the girders and pulled himself up. He frequently traveled to New York on freights, and would run up to Albany for lunch, sitting happily astride the horselike sides of a tank car. By the next Fourth of July he had completely forgotten Triggers.

In fact, on Independence Day, when the population of the Hudson Valley mysteriously disappeared, Marshall was exploring lines of railroad cars which had backed up on the tracks and were waiting for maintenance at Harmon Yard. He frequently did this, climbing on boxcars, wiggling down into refrigerator cars in search of fresh coconuts (which he never found), and walking through vintage passenger coaches about to be torn up or sent to a Central American republic. Marshall would use the bathrooms, sit on the conductors' special seats, drink the rusty water, crawl along the hat racks, and spin the wooden fans. But there was little else to do. Of course, he always hoped to come across a naked girl reclining on one of the worn cane seats, her arms open to him.

That Fourth of July, after drinking a lot of rusty water and crawling over yards and yards of hat racks, he hit the jackpot. It was the finest moment he ever had on the railroad, and could beat even the thrill of riding the roofs of a fast-moving thunderous freight on a clear blue day. At the end of a long line of musty coaches, Marshall opened a reluctant door and came upon, of all things, Pearlman's private car. Almost as good as a naked girl, it was sitting on the track completely unprotected and alone, a rich Byzantine city to be sacked.

He was slight enough to climb in through the bathroom window. He could not believe that the bathroom of a railroad car could be made of alabaster and gold, and, in a false analogy with pearl, he scratched the gold faucet with his teeth to see if it were real. It seemed genuine, although he did not know what would have happened had it been a fraud. There was even a sauna, which he thought was an empty closet. The medicine chest was filled with bottles on which were unfamiliar French and Scandinavian names. Towels as soft as velvet puffed from golden rings. Then he left the bathroom and went into the living room. The carpet appeared to him to be a Shabooz of the highest quality. A Renoir hung on a partition. Mahogany and fruitwood desks, furniture and paneling, brass fixtures as shiny as the day they had left the factory, and Chinese vases were spread throughout in lean opulence.

Marshall threw himself down on a velvet-covered divan and stretched.

But he could not rest. He saw a player piano in the corner. After a while he managed to turn it on, and wonderful, sad, palm waltzes came from it. The bedroom closet was stuffed with tailored clothing. He took out a three-piece white linen suit, and the most beautiful beaver hat he had ever seen, which didn't mean much because he had never seen a beaver hat. It was three feet across and its fur glistened like the river bay. Struggling into this costume (over his own clothes) he added a few diamond stickpins and some silver cufflinks. He was thin enough, small enough, and young enough, so that his face fit in the expanse of the rakish and beautiful hat as if he were a lamb some children had dressed in a baby bonnet.

He went to the kitchen and opened the ice box. Twenty bottles of Dom Perignon lay at attention. He took one out and read the label, pronouncing the G. "Dom Perig-non," he said, "a good year. It will do. Oh, I feel so *blasé*." Grabbing a glass and a package of English biscuits, he tripped over his pants through the main salon and walked out to the speaker's platform—an open porch at the rear vestibule. There, he popped the champagne and sat with his feet on the rail, drinking, surveying underneath the brim of the beaver several miles of tracks from which heat was rising in undulating waves. The cattails and oaks were green and young. A very slight breeze came off the river.

Deep into the champagne (for the first time in his life), he began to imagine that he was an American President early in the century, crossing the continent by whistle stops, running to preserve his presidency and the bold policies he had created and carried out. He rose, the bottle in his hand. Standing against the rail, with the palm waltzes in the background, he addressed a rally of reeds and ties.

"My fellow men," he screamed in a squeaky adolescent voice, "and my fellow women, naked women, or clothed, however you may be." He swayed back and forth, posturing, posing, thrusting out his hand. "I want to tell you of the power in this new land. We have white battle fleets, transcendental philosophers, deep silver mines, music halls, and millions of acres of waving winter wheat. Let us take these mechanical things, the reapers, gins, sling hygrometers, Gatling guns, and steam plows, and let us thrust them throughout the world as if the world were a naked woman! Thank you. Thank you. This is a great country. Let us ride it like a horse! Let us enjoy it. If I'm your President we will move so far forward, so fast, that we will be like oats shot from a gun!" And then he waved his hat to the cheering crowd and sank back on the wicker chair in complete satisfaction—just in time to feel two strong hands, like the steel-clad hands of a knight and as thick as boxing gloves, throttle him by the throat dangerously close to the diamond stickpin. It was L. H. Triggers. He nearly snapped Marshall's neck.

"This is Pearlman's private car!" he screamed in rage and desperation. "He *owns* the railroad."

Marshall looked at him and said, "My people . . .!"

Triggers was dumfounded. He had collared Marshall for the first time. Even though Triggers looked like he had pillows stuffing his middle, he could run like a gazelle, but he had never caught Marshall. Now that he had him, Marshall didn't care.

"Okay," he said, "I'm taking you in. Keep on wearing those clothes. Bring that bottle. Move." He made Marshall walk in front of him up the tracks toward Harmon Yard. Marshall staggered and tripped over the too-long pants, and the beaver hat obscured his vision. In the distance the palm waltzes continued because Triggers didn't know how to turn them off. Somewhat sobered by the march in July heat, Marshall addressed his captor.

"My good sir man," he said, chin falling to his chest. Then he looked up and continued. "This is all foolish. Don't you know that I am invulnerable? Don't you know that your own father, the old fellow, granted me invulnerability in his wind, in his will?"

"You're full of creasap," said Triggers. "No one ever read it. It was ten thousand pages long in beer handwriting. We had to burn it. Besides, how could he give you invulnerability?"

"His decades on the railroad. He was the spirit of the railroad. He . . ."

"He was the spirit of creasap," interrupted Triggers. "He spent his life running a hardware store in Amsterdam, New York."

"He did?"

"Yes, he did. All right, he denuded the railroad of insulators and spikes. How could I arrest him? He was my father. We had to keep a repair crew on this section day and night. We juggled the books."

Marshall turned around, tripped on his heels, fell flat on his back against the ties, and said, "You juggled the books."

"What's it your business?"

"Say it to me again."

"We juggled the books."

"Again."

"Okay, we juggled the books."

"You can't arrest *me*," said Marshall, still so drunk that he couldn't lie down straight.

Triggers slapped his pistol and said, "Damn." He made Marshall give him the clothes, and Marshall vanished onto the shallow tidal flats where the Croton River empties into the Hudson. He spent that afternoon running after herons and gulls, trying to kiss them. When finally the running made him sober, he swore never to touch alcohol again.

As they flew over the Bahamas the steward brought steaming tea in silver pots. Looking down, Marshall saw a green sea such as he had never seen in his life, filled with blue and white isle crescents shaped like a lash or the inward curve of an almond. The water looked warm and inviting. That green tropical color was a sign to him, and he left his old life behind.

4

At Kingston the air was humid and thick. High mountains enshrouded in mother-of-pearl clouds and rain flanked the rear of the city, throwing out their chests. It was hot, and most of the people were black. In a corner of the dazzling white field, military transport planes were disgorging British soldiers and their equipment. Half a dozen pipers played songs which gripped Marshall so strongly that his eyes filled and his muscles tightened. Never had he felt such rich full heat. Never had he seen such green mountains. The soldiers came to attention, their weapons laid out for inspection. They were young and they looked like Marshall, who wanted to be one of them. He was shaken by the sight of the mountains, the palms, the sand-colored airstrip, and soldiers stiff to the sound of pipes. This was a new world, and he wanted with all his heart never to be the same—and he would not ever be the same. One sight of Kingston against the blue-green, and the Imperial soldiers rigid and fair, had changed him forever in just the way Livingston had known. For the first time, his history began to gallop up close.

Livingston had purchased a small blue Anglia, into which they stuffed themselves and their baggage. They started the drive across the island to High View, their estate on the northern shore, a lord's demesne Livingston had usurped by measure of wartime friendship and some semilegal deal closing. To shut the door on his proposition and convince Livingston to buy, the friendly lord had invited him to reside on his Jamaican estate for as long as he wished, "to show the boy a bit of the world, and holiday in the tropics." Unknown to the lord, the deal was so far weighted in Livingston's favor that Livingston had made a concealed troutlike leap and closed mightily upon multiple advantages.

Livingston was a sharp dealer and a good navigator, helped by Marshall, who could read maps with celestial perfection. So keen was his sense of direction and so lucid his feeling for terrain that Marshall preferred maps to pornography. On the outskirts of Eagle Bay was a disused quarry into which the state dumped illegal Danish pornographic mailings and sun-bathing magazines. Marshall used to wait at the bottom as dump trucks chartered by sober courts discharged their lascivious cargoes. At an early age he received full exposure to colorful images of copulation on bright beaches rimming the upward coasts of Helsingör. He preferred maps.

Driving through a tropical jungle, Marshall was impressed by a land-scape unable to fight the overwhelming intensity of color. Despite the tropic heat and the promise of creeping and crawling beings thickening the spectral landscape, he felt within his element. And of all the colors striking him like blows, those he most remembered were the blues and reds of the police—dark black men in white pith helmets, with black pants striped red down the sides, and shirts pale blue like the sky. They stood near narrow bridges over rushing tropical rivers, directing alternating streams of traffic. First left, then right would pass over the cool torrents hurtling down the mountainsides. On the concrete bridges the sound of water was white and trembling.

After several hours they passed the highest ridge, the top spine of the island. They saw a vast northern plain spread before them in glowing green. Canefields stretched like a smoky whip. The rivers were as straight as molten metal rods. Cows stood in dumb profundity, fecund matches to listless grazing clouds rotund and cottony above. They paused at the top, feeling like lords to the power driving out laterally from their eyes. The cultivation was stunning and alingual. Its heat rose to heaven.

Then they raced down to the sea. Abandoning the discipline exercised normally in protection of his family, Livingston drove the junky little car like a Spitfire, roaring past stands of cane, palm, and pineapple. It had been many hours full of sweet scents and blurred images. Entranced behind the wheel, guiding them, responsible, Livingston was formulating upon his days in war. The step back in time had caused him to reflect upon his military service. He was not surprised, for even a touch of liquor or sleeplessness carried him immediately back to the war, and always would.

Integral to the scheme, he remembered fighting not only in North Africa, but also in Europe. In these recollections he posited a universal bleak and cold, a soul cold, of armies and winter, the automatic and trancelike state of a soldier caught up not just in a given army in a given time, but in a phenomenon which is to man as waves are to the sea, working through the tapestry in solid unbreakable threads. That was why, Livingston thought, he in his tank shell of steel, knights in armor, and modern soldiers in armored carriers and halftracks had the same neutral faces, and went on like animals in herds and mystical migrations, part of a great calculated web. And yet even in a species parody of wild beasts, with steel weapons and sanctity and illusion, there was a beauty, an affirmation. Livingston had believed strongly in the white halls and green hills of the Hudson—horses and music, and pinnacles overseeing great river beds. In the depth of his despair on a winter field in Germany when blood was all around him, he had believed. Driving through Jamaican highlands and canefields, he hoped with all his heart that Marshall too would turn out to be a stubborn, steadfast believer.

In the thick of his dreams as he drove up a mountain by the sea and finally reached a great house of mahogany and porches and a red tile roof, he turned with emotion to his adopted son, and found him asleep. That night they ate fish from the Caribbean, and sat on a terrace high above the sea, enmeshed in the rich hard delight of a million stars in black. For Livingston it was a return to the timeless frames of Arizona, North Africa, the sea. It made Marshall think of Columbine.

High View was a property of five hundred acres on the side of a mountain rising from the Caribbean. Opposite the small town of Oracabessa, limited in the east by the Oracabessa River, and in the west by a porous rock escarpment, it dissolved rearward in the rain forest and found its northern border in a strip of reef-protected beach a quarter mile long. Due to the riverine effluents, fish abounded in quantities sufficient to feed the village and some of the inland population. Every day and night the small bay was filled with nut-colored wooden boats, from which spearfishermen ranged in the light, and on which at night compressed gas lanterns glowed splendidly two to a boat to draw the fish netward. Marshall learned to spearfish, and was frequently dispatched in late afternoon to bring back several large groupers, bass, or bluefish for dinner.

Every week the banana boat came through the inlet, a Swedish or British freighter which brought sharks in its trail. The wharves exploded with movement. As in war, the roads were covered with open trucks, but rather unwarlike, they carried only bananas. Scandinavian sailors sometimes left their ship for a minor debauch in the town, though not often, since they were usually tired from sex and drinking in Kingston. When the banana boat was in, so were all the people from the interior; and the ceaseless labor, massive lighters gliding in quiet precision to nestle against the ship (sometimes crushing a man's foot or arm), contests of strength, spider bite emergencies, romances, dances, shootings, and time passing in light and glory made much work for the constable and his several relatively dullard assistants. Music accompanied the loading. The ship stood off the port as white as an iceberg or a Greek island city on layered cliffs. The deep throbbing of motorboats filled the hot nights like drums, involving even black waters and unseen fish in the omnipresent fertile industry.

Their shirts were of pastel colors, and bristol blue or indigo. They worked as if they were shoring up the earth, and when day came they had some pounds and shillings and deep bodily satisfaction. As the generator grew sleepy, the electric lights would sometimes pulse, but never die. The generator would revive and the workers, fallen silent to a man, would upon hearing its resumed vigor echoing down from the town give a shout in unison and then start to work as if the entire family of man had just been rescued from the gallows.

Halfway up the hill was the small cottage of the estate foreman or, as he was called, "the bouche." He was a little brown man with brown hair and brown eyes. He dressed only in brown cloth or suede, wore a brown hat, rode a brown horse with a brown saddle, carried a brown-handled pistol and a brown leather lariat. One was not surprised when he introduced himself by saying, "Hello, I'm Brown," which was his name—Ismail Brown, an Egyptian Copt who had been shuffled around the world and somehow placed in a little lantern-lit cottage on the side of a mountain in Jamaica. It suited him. He felt as if he were in the Sudan.

5

Always tired from a full day in the sea or on horseback, Marshall went to bed early and arose to watch the dawn. He customarily entered the half-dark kitchen and made his way barefooted among the scorpions, or "lanwinkies," as some Jamaicans called them. Watching to make sure that they did not graze over to his feet, he would take a large white bread, cut off the crusts, and, with much exertion, mold the innards into a ball. He sliced this in half, coated the halves with margarine, and stood for ten minutes shaking salt, pepper, and Tabasco onto the two hemispheres, which he rejoined and further compressed. If he felt mean, he would break off a few pieces and feed the scorpions, who then died. Most of the time, though, he took a big knife, cut each scorpion in half, and swept the pieces out the door. He called his breadball "the Jamaican sunrise," for after chopping up the scorpions he always took it with him to the terrace—a thousand feet above the sea, nearly at the mountain's very top—and ate it as he watched the sun burn over the eastern hills. He drank from the swimming pool. The water was chlorinated, but the Tabasco was strong. On exceptionally clear mornings he could see Cuba ninety miles to the north, a pale green line, the Sierra Maestra taking in the morning sun.

They kept a spotting scope on the terrace. With it they could see ships plying between Jamaica and Cuba, hundreds of small inter-island freight boats still under sail moving slowly and gracefully like an albatross on the wind, sliding across the compacted emerald between the islands. Halfway through his spherical breakfast, Marshall was watching the palms and banana trees beginning to stir in the dawn wind, when his eye was drawn to what looked like a tiger moving on a path across the valley. It moved intently. Even though he could not make out what it was, he could tell that it was hurrying. Still chewing, he went to the telescope and swung it around toward the tiger.

Everyone was sleeping. He swept down the opposite hill until the path fell into view. Then he calmly took his eye from the aperture and sighted the moving image. Returning to the telescope, he followed the path in the direction of his quarry and overshot it. It had been a blur in the circle of his lens. With the patience of a gunner, he waited, bringing the instrument to sharp focus on large leaves near the path. Five armed men flooded the circle. As he tracked them he felt his heart go wild. Their long hair was covered with red clay. They had rifles and submachine guns, trident spears, sacks over their shoulders, urgent expressions, strong steady gaits, and something which made Marshall drop what was left of his bread. The second in line was carrying a man's head, grasping it by the hair.

Marshall caught the wrought-iron terrace rail to steady himself. Mr. Brown had said that he carried a pistol in case a cow or a horse broke a leg. Suddenly Marshall knew better. And the shots they heard at night were not drunks firing into the air. Then he froze to the rail. The path on which the raiders traveled led down into the valley, across the river on a rope bridge, and up the mountain past High View, coming within a hundred feet of it. It was possible to veer off onto other routes, but the main line of travel to the interior was right there. Its wonderful roof and dark woods standing out on the bluff, High View was beautiful and conspicuous. Marshall immediately thought of the automobile and the swimming pool, and how their presence might lure the bandits in for dessert.

Everything came clear, and the choices stood before him like a pilot's head-up display. Livingston was still sleeping, as were the servants. He dared not waste time in warning them, since they tended not to heed him.

His fear translated to pure speed and strength, and he went to his room, put on shoes, and then ran incredibly fast toward Mr. Brown's house. He moved like an antelope, leaping on the downhill run high over logs and walls which crossed the familiar path, flying on the steeper parts so that he felt as if he would be taken far into the air, just touching the dark earth briefly to spring up and out and downward. When he got to Mr. Brown's he beat on the door, shocked that he seemed to have lost no breath on the flight from High View. Mr. Brown came out in a nightcap. Marshall's face was enough, but he said, "The Rastas. Coming on the path. Five, with guns. They're carrying a man's head. Hurry."

Mr. Brown said, "The horse, saddle the horse. I'm coming," and went inside to put on his boots and get guns. Marshall ran to the stable and saddled the horse. He did it so quickly that he had time to saddle a second, and lead them out. Brown jumped the steps. He was wearing his pistol and he had two rifles slung across his back. In his hands were another rifle and bandoliers of ammunition, which he gave to Marshall, who slung them and mounted. Slower in mounting, Brown ordered Marshall to wait. He did not want a divided front, least of all with a boy leading. The horses were spooked like warhorses, and when at last Brown was up, they burst out of the compound onto the road galloping and thundering their hooves. The force of their start pushed Marshall deep into his saddle.

Marshall admired Brown. He was a responsible man. He was riding up the mountain with his guns, perhaps to fight, perhaps to die, when he did not have to. He was, simply, brave. Marshall was surprised that this bravery elicited from him great affection, something he would not have expected. When nearly at the house, Brown signaled Marshall to slow. Then they dismounted and left the horses to graze, running over a field littered with rotting mangoes. The cocks were crowing. Marshall imagined the Rastas in the house, and evidently so did Brown, because they ran faster, and, with weapons unleashed, charged in from the front entrance. Sweating, looking like madmen or soldiers in the heat of battle, they ran onto the terrace. Brown grabbed the telescope (which belonged to him) and skillfully scanned the path. Almost as if pleased (but it was hard to tell) he said, "They're coming. Wake your daddy."

Marshall burst into the Livingstons' bedroom and shook Livingston, who was rather surprised to see a Mauser and a strap of shiny bullets in Marshall's hands. "What's the matter?" he asked, and Marshall composed his first precis.

Livingston got out of bed. Mildly puzzled, he walked to the terrace. Then he lay down with Marshall and Mr. Brown and took up a rifle, methodically stuffing the magazine with cartridges. He had always regarded Egyptians as unreliable and overemotional, and with a touch of contempt he said, "Mr. Brown, what is this all about?"

"That," said Mr. Brown, pointing to the five men not three hundred feet away, the head bobbing up and down, "is what it is all about, Mr. Livingston."

"My apologies," said Livingston, as the three of them took aim.

"Don't shoot them," said Brown, "unless they come to the house. If you kill some of them, they will come back and kill all of us, as sure as God wills."

The bandits paused and unslung their guns. They looked at the house, and began to argue. Had they deployed to raid High View, lowered their shoulders, held their guns in that telling way of raiders, moved off the path toward the house which they thought to be innocent and asleep, they would have been felled to the last man.

But they moved on. "Shall we kill them anyway, Mr. Brown?" asked Livingston. The head, and their unkempt appearance, had aroused in him a positive dislike.

"No sir. We'd best leave them alone. They will not likely return."

"As you say, Mr. Brown. You know the country." After a while they sat up against the rail, Livingston in blue pajamas, Marshall in khaki shorts, Brown in boots, pants, and a nightcap. It had really been quite tense. They were shaken. In an unprecedented request, Brown said, "Mr. Livingston, I know it is only dawn, but could you get me a Bloody Mary?"

6

The phone rang as Mr. Brown was drinking his Bloody Mary. The constable wanted him to take the High View truck and evacuate casualties from Jacks River. The Rastas had knocked out the bridge to Oracabessa, but a runner had crossed the river and brought news of two women and a man who were badly off. Marshall and Mr. Brown set out in the four-wheel-drive truck, going over rough paths and streams to get to Jacks River by the back roads. Brown knew the complicated traverses and secret ways, whereas the constable did not. Presumably the constable was preparing for the chase, although everyone was aware that he would arm his frightened deputies, walk a few miles into the jungle, and be unable to find a trace of the Rastas, who moved in back country with the stealth of moonlight.

Marshall and Mr. Brown had their weapons. Having done so well that morning already, Marshall stood in the back of the truck in a near Napoleonic pose, eyes sweeping the jungle for ambush. Of course the noise of the truck and the thick cover made him an easy target, but Brown thought he deserved a reward for his vigilance. Smiling from underneath his nightcap (which he forgot to take off that day) he let Marshall stay, since by that time the Rastas were probably ten miles in the bush, pistols in their waists, their gaits still ferocious because of the cocaine and because they had been up all night.

Though it was early, the sun was murderously hot. Birds the color of red velvet flew through the patterned forest in swooping curves. With not a cloud nearby, a white and silver sun beat down hard as the truck chugged through the brush. Marshall sweated and the water dripped off him. He heard birds and other animals screaming: their chatterings were deafeningly loud. With the rifle in his hands and salt stinging his eyes he understood for a moment why the Rastas did what they did, although he could not justify it. The heat and light, the rhythm of a struggling truck moving on a soft forest floor, his beating heart, made him want to die. He wanted to die. It seemed a perfect thing to do in that hot jungle. And because he wanted to die, he wanted to kill. He wished that they would meet the Rastas, that he would fight them and kill some before they killed him. He wished that his body would be maimed and thrown to the side of the path to be consumed by crows and jackals. But this was dispelled when they sped into a clearing on the outskirts of Jacks River and Brown said, "Maybe they give us a cold beer in Jacks River." Marshall was put off by the idea of anything as wild and dissolute as drinking beer in the morning, and told Brown just that.

At Jacks River—a settlement on the road, a few houses and a little store outside of which fly-covered lamb carcasses hung for days—one of the women had died. The man who was supposed to have been wounded ran off into the bush when he heard the truck, leading Brown to believe that he had been a former resident of Kingston Jail, who did not need the hospital. The other woman was really a schoolgirl, who had a serious stomach wound. She screamed and writhed, and then would become entirely quiet and look around with a quizzical expression, amazed that she was still alive, not knowing quite how to act when wounded. Then she would buckle up in agony and behave in just the requisite way. They put her on a cot in the back of the truck and sped east to the hospital. There had been much screaming and hysteria, but the strange presence of a white boy as armed escort quieted the girl and her family. They stared at Marshall, not knowing who he was or why he was there.

At the hospital they took the girl into an open operating room and operated. Everyone waited in the courtyard, where relatives of the patients were busy cooking breakfast over open fires. The patients themselves lined the porches of the tropical buildings, looking wretched and sad. Every single one had a white bandage somewhere on his body. In one of the wards a dogfight began, and the mangy dogs were chased out by a man who ran after them gracefully, swatting them with his crutch.

After several hours they wheeled the girl onto the porch. She was sleeping peacefully, and the doctor told her mother that she would soon recover. The mother wept in waves, and the doctor put one of his hands on her shoulder and shook her. He smiled. She became silent as he rattled three lead slugs in his hand. "You should not weep," he said. "She is a lucky girl. And a strong girl. She helped me find the bullets. A fine girl. You can't keep the young down. You will see. Tomorrow she will eat like five strong men. In a week she will be dancin' again." The mother, a handsome woman with a light blue kerchief over her hair, wept uncontrollably, and smiled.

Looking at her face, high cheeks, and sweet eyes, Marshall was ashamed for what he had thought on the way to Jacks River. Even at fifteen, having been up since dawn and run himself to exhaustion in a hot, different, black country, he suspected that men without women are subject to the peculiar madness he had felt that morning. Its pressure was as deafening as the overwhelming cries of the animals. Those on the truck hadn't stared at him because he was white. They knew white men, and frequently saw Lucius Pringle, or his brothers, before all the brothers were killed by the Rastas. But when they had seen Marshall, he had had a savage, hard look.

Anyway, that night they celebrated with a big meal, and a jump-up, in which everyone danced, happy to be alive, in a kind of New Orleans funeral for the ones killed at Jacks River. Rifles were stacked in the corner, and Mr. Brown wore his pistol in the house. As always, the stars were as white as rocket flares, and cool winds swayed the large trees, in which birds slept. At about midnight a ship appeared near the horizon, blazing bright. They watched in silence as it moved off the curve of the world, and then everyone went home. Marshall fell asleep laughing, with a tear in his eye. He remembered the blood on the schoolgirl's dark blue uniform, the rush through the trees up to the hospital, the heat, the way she looked sleeping in white sheets, and what the doctor had said in his lilting bittersweet Jamaican dialect—"In a week she will be dancin' again."

7

Marshall began to range into the interior. Though young, he had passed the point where Livingston was able simply to tell him what to do. From the day of the raid forward, if Livingston were to direct Marshall he had to do it by internal politics, propaganda, economic pressure, pleading, begging, anything but a command—against which Marshall rebelled dragging in tow a full catalogue of ramlike adolescent insanities, and his own rather eccentric attributes.

One day he had asked Livingston quite nicely if he might hike into the back country. Livingston said no. Marshall asked again. Livingston said no. Marshall asked again. Livingston said no. Marshall disappeared that night. With an old Enfield rifle, some pouches of ammunition, a small sack of food and supplies, and a tarpaulin under which he huddled when the warm morning downpour shot mistily through the high pattering leaves, he stayed away for three days. At first he was terrified, but quickly learned that there were more scorpions in the house than in the jungle, and that if he didn't sing, make fires, or thrash around, he was more or less undetectable. Like darkness, the dense vegetation was the safest place to be, even if it were full of Rastas. In fact, the only danger to Marshall came from within. Because he did not eat or sleep properly for three days, he spent part of the last in contorted agony on the forest floor. An observer would have doubted his own eyes.

At the foot of a tall tree where he had rested his rifle, Marshall writhed as if he were wrestling an invisible boa constrictor. His clothes were black from sweat, and his skin glistened. He knocked over the rifle and it lay beside him. An ammunition pouch had opened; silver-and-brass-colored bullets were littered over the soft floor. His eyes were numb and would not focus. Bolts of light shot in front of him as if a night battle raged, and these tracers enwrapped the clouds of color which had overcome him and fixed him down. When it was over he was dry, exhausted, and pleasantly sleepy. He had contempt for nothing in the world except this all-powerful disease, and enjoyed surviving the murderous attacks. What great relief to come out of them. He thought that most people were fools for their ingratitude. They wanted money, they wanted justice, they wanted recognition, they wanted so much that their days were obliterated. Marshall was grateful just to be alive.

It became usual for him to go for a day or two into the bush. There, he had his favorite places, one of which was an open knoll of volcanic rock. Sitting on its edge, Marshall could see the distant blue strip of the Caribbean ten miles or so beyond a mass of stratified green. Near rapids cold from the feed of high mountain streams, Marshall thought that he was alone. He was not.

While reading C. W. Ceram's *Gods, Graves and Scholars,* he reached out with his right hand to pick up his rifle. It seemed impossibly heavy. He couldn't even move it, and he turned his head enough to see a legged boot standing on the stock. Lucius Pringle stood over six foot six, was armed with a classy automatic, and he said in a deep voice heard clearly over the rushing river as it curled about below, "This is my land." Marshall made no response and tried to lift his rifle and stand up, but Lucius put his foot down harder on the butt and said again, with a kind of madness, "This is my land."

Marshall finally said, "Okay, it's your land," at which the giant stepped back.

"I'm Lucius Pringle. I think I know who you are."

"Is that right?" asked Marshall, who was not so sure that he liked Lucius.

"You're the Livingstons' son, from High View."

"Yes, I am," said Marshall, who introduced himself with his customary explanations about why his name was not Livingston. Lucius Pringle then spoke for an hour about his land, his right to it, and how his father and three brothers had died in keeping it. It covered an immense portion of the back country, and part of the seacoast.

"In times gone by," said Lucius, "my father could ride from Port Maria to Montego Bay and never leave his own property." Marshall quickly realized that Lucius's obsession with his right to the land was cause for his armament. He was set for war, and in comparison Marshall seemed like a casual country hunter. Lucius carried many clips of automatic rifle ammunition, hand grenades, a heavy killing type of pistol, and a bayonet.

Mr. Brown had once said that Lucius Pringle was mad and would be killed. "He is really lookin' for it, I tell you," he had clucked. "Someday he gonna get killed. And then his mother and the girl will go back to England and the Rastas will take the land. And then we'll have Rastas right over the hill runnin' aroun' and shootin' and killin' all night. And then I go back to Egypt, and High View will be full of Rastas. Lucius Pringle is like a dam in the river. Some day the dam break, and the river wash us away. Then I go back to Egypt. High View will get covered with weeds. But it is good that he is a strong man, although only one bullet and he's a dead man like the others."

"Why don't you 'come with,' to Rica Vista tea. If we walk fast we can arrive almost on time. I hope you haven't been listening to Brown. He was with my brother when my brother was killed, and now he's afraid of his own shoelaces," said Lucius.

"No he's not," said Marshall. "He's brave. The Rastas came and we were ready to meet them."

"Yes, but not to chase them," said Lucius, his own designs quite evident. "Brown has stopped chasing them. And so, I am afraid, have I. At least for the present. Come, let's go." Had Marshall known that tea at Rica Vista meant several score people he would not have accepted, because he was fearfully shy. But he had no way of knowing the enormity of Rica Vista tea, was always hungry for biscuits, and had not been far in the direction to which Lucius had pointed, so he accepted.

They coursed through the jungle like scattering monkeys. Loose-jointed, wet, and hard-breathing, they pounded the paths, crossed slow-veined cocoa-colored streams, ran like horses in open places, brushed past slicing ferns and leaves, went mad with vines, and in a green rapid hour traveled miles across the hills under a light living canopy of plants which, like lace, trammeled the laser lines of quick glowing birds. For different reasons nevertheless allied, both Marshall and Lucius were convinced that humankind was to be eschewed, that real satisfaction was to be had only in the pure natural physics demonstrable in overwhelming volume everywhere at all times. Marshall was lonely, overcome by heat and stars, and in perpetual brush warfare with Livingston. Lucius had seen too many of those he loved die, and at thirty he felt far older than his years.

They broke out onto a red clay road which was hot and straight and led up a high hill. At the top of the hill Marshall was made breathless by what he saw below, and by the beautiful tolling of a bell. Lucius said, "That bell means tea," but waited for a few proud moments as Marshall surveyed Rica Vista.

It leapt from the throat of fierce jungle in an equally fierce, upright dignity. It was in appearance the essence of Marshall's obsessions about achieving the impossible and defending the indefensible. For there in a wide valley deep in wild swirling green was a prospect of fields, tall trees, sheep grazing as if in heather (but shorn cool), stone walls, dams, weirs, and a village of stone and mahogany houses which, though tropical in architecture and oriented to the Trades, had about them as indisputable a British air as a sergeant major in the Coldstream Guards. A dozen jeeps, tractors, and trucks were symmetrically ordered in a car park. Raw materials were stacked about worksheds as if arranged by the same hand. Four watchtowers made a square around the ten acres of the main compound. It was like a garden, a military camp, an English village, a tropical plantation. And the order was not oppressive because it was so busy. Even from far away Marshall could see so much movement and activity that he assumed it to be a thriving estate. Trains of tractor-drawn wagons wound in and out overburdened with cane and copra; red trucks from the fruit company in Oracabessa loaded up with bananas and drove out on the dusty road. As Marshall got closer he could see scores of people on the long wide porch of the great house. Perhaps seventy or eighty were standing in small groups or sitting with teacups on their laps. As Marshall and Lucius passed the wire a man with a rifle nodded to them. On the lawn in front of the porch were three groups of rifles standing upright like racked lamb, with satchels of bullets hanging over the ground inside the circular constructions.

The first thing Marshall sensed was that they would not keep their land. Especially when they were gathered, theirs seemed to be a losing cause, even though they had apparently seen some victories. With only one man of the family left and the rest workers or hired administrators, mercenaries, mechanics, and farmers, there was little opportunity to cultivate political power. Lucius had to watch the land—which receded gradually in satisfaction of economy, security, justice, necessity, or whatever, but was surely falling away. The bandits made it impossible for Rica Vista to harvest its cocoa, since the cocoa trees were on thousands of acres of leased land in the jungle of the interior, and the small farmers whose intensive labor had brought in the crop had fled to Shantytown in Kingston rather than be harvested themselves by Rastas and Rudie Boys mad on drugs in an inaccessible camp so far inland that they had to plan their raids a week in advance. Without the cocoa, and without the traditional lands, Rica Vista (already pieced up and falling) was in danger. Somehow Marshall knew that they would not last, and because of that, everything he saw there, all their actions, impressed him, moved him. They seemed to be artful in everything they did. He felt as if he had happened on a surviving court, a grouping of the Enlightenment, the anachronistic grace of another time set to be crushed by rolling justice, self-assured executioner of the old and the indefensible. Marshall always believed that people who wanted justice had the souls of killers. Despite these reveries he was beguiled to drink much Shandy Gaff, a mixture of beer and ginger beer, and he happily met the eclectic garrison at Rica Vista.

According to the trend of dissolution Marshall felt in his life, he stayed there—for an evening, a week, a month, a year, and more. The Livingstons left High View, and Marshall moved to Rica Vista. Swept away by relentless pressing climate, he forgot the river bay country and it seemed as if he would be trapped forever in the slow amber of eventless days on the land and over the reefs. He stayed because he knew that Lucius would have to go after the Rastas, because he did not want to return to school in Eagle Bay, because he was not genuinely the Livingstons' son, and because he wanted to find that which he had lost.

And then, Lucius had a younger sister who was rather extraordinarily beautiful. In fact, she was excessively beautiful.

8

He learned of Africa from a white girl. She was older than Marshall, though young herself. She had graduated Oxford with a first in history. Brown-eyed, blond, strong, Dash Pringle loved the rivers and the Caribbean, and could with Marshall stay in the water from morning until night, lost in the time of the sea. Though she loved England, she was to Jamaica as a prelate is to his own cathedral. She was open and warm, and could make you feel at ease and happy. She moved like a dancer. When Marshall met her at tea he fell in love with her so hard that he almost choked.

One night in September there was a wedding. Lucius had two friends who had become almost like brothers—Peter and Stanhope. They were black Jamaicans who had attended Oxford with him, where the three had come together as Jamaicans—the key link being their sweet disabled speech. Peter and Stanhope helped Lucius run Rica Vista, and together owned forty percent of it. Peter was married one night to a girl from Jacks River, and after the wedding they went to a house there to dance.

Marshall was shy, so Dash took him and led him to the floor. Once in a while they glanced at Peter and his bride, but most of the night they danced to the enlivening red music, holding close together through Dash's light silk dress. Marshall was astonished by the fact of her magnificent body moving against his for several hours at a time. It left him in a devilish trance. They grew very thirsty and quenched their thirst with cola wine and Red Stripe. Soon they lost track of exactly where they were and became oblivious of the other couples enough to kiss a little. Then the kisses grew hotter, deeper, and longer, until sometimes five minutes would pass and they would wonder who exactly was who, and where, precisely, each one was.

They ate the wedding cake like bulldozers clearing soft earth. They ploughed through it and polished it off in a frenzy. They drank more cola wine and Red Stripe. They huddled in the corner and laughed over jokes and stories while surrounded by a collection of jostling brown boards and red tin, and tables of coconut and cake and wine, and a hot rain outside. They went to the covered porch, where down among the splatterings of a thick night shower he kissed her lips and her neck and her shoulders and her breasts through the hot silk dress and she took him and lay back. She grasped some wide leaves which came over the porch, and as Marshall went mad in rhythmic kissing she said, "Africa, Africa, Africa," in Jamaican speech almost a miracle from her English face. They both nonsensically tolled the words, "Africa, Africa, Africa," with the long Jamaican A, while outside the heavy green leaves bent in the storm. A continent rushed through their imaginations as Marshall kissed her again and again. Then Lucius staggered onto the porch. They looked with their drunken faces. He lifted one eyebrow impossibly high, and then staggered back in. "You're too young," said Dash.

"Is this a joke?" asked Marshall heatedly. "I am not too young. I was, way before you were born, as a little child, in the Hudson Valley, quite old."

"Indeed," said Dash.

"Indeed," answered Marshall.

Oddly enough, this night wildness presaged days of exquisite discipline in which Lucius taught Marshall physics and mathematics, Dash taught him history, Peter taught him biology and agronomy, and Stanhope tried to teach him German. He learned history with kisses. "I'm going to tell you about Oliver Cromwell," Dash said, "and the Puritans, and the English Revolution," and as if hypnotized they placed their lips together and tongued and sucked for an hour or more during which Cromwell jumped up and down in his pewter helmet. But overall (and goodness knows it was much) he managed to learn, reading two or more books a day. Mrs. Pringle taught him literature.

She had come half a century before as the speechless Sheffield bride of a Scotsman made good in the tropics. She had seen many lives pass, including those of her husband and sons, and she had emptied the libraries and then sent to England for books. The first words she said to Marshall were from the poem of his name, of which he had never heard: "Pearl, the precious prize of a king,/ In all the East none equalling." To Marshall, it was suspiciously ambiguous.

At Rica Vista the farmers planned, the workers worked, the mercenaries practiced war, Marshall learned, Mrs. Pringle read, Dash dreamed of England, Lucius broke at the bit. It was confusing and would have driven them mad throughout the months except for the perfect sleep they had as arc lights played restively along the wire and sentries took their turns. It was because they worked and tried to do their best against the odds and the terrible heat. They knew that they would be defeated, but they were brilliant in their defense. Marshall was taken up with this and dreamed a dream; that he might sleep not alone but by Dash, and love her completely, as she had not allowed him to do in those dark nights thick with crickets. The atmosphere isolated them from themselves, creating exemplary portraits, shocking them with the stroke of love and time.

Lucius had learned his disregard for the things of man not from having father and brothers shot down like birds, but from his mother. She was a fiercely strong woman, though equally compassionate, and she knew that the beams of hard judgments allowed the soft things of the heart to thrive. Her speech was hard. She wanted peace, and would fight for it. She nearly capsized Marshall when she turned to him and said: "I don't like people who make waves. My sympathy is for those who stand against waves, who refuse to be overcome, to whom troubles flock, and who are brave in resistance. But I detest those who would destroy. That is why I will not allow Lucius to raid the bandits. We will stand here and fight them."

She believed in other than the primacy of man, saying to Marshall in her library as the sun flooded through the louvers and, by its intensity and beating, ticked off time like an escapement, "Some people see only the roots of trees, the base." She coughed and momentarily shut her old eyes. "They are moles, and belong tunneling in the seething earth. Others see just the shafts and trunks. They are the practicals—good for sawing and cutting and working the design. Others see only a fine canopy of leaves. They are the effete, and drop down in hard or cold times to beg."

"What can be done?" asked Marshall. "The parts of the tree are all faulted. If you see it from afar it is balanced, but close in, if you become part of it, you—"

"Exactly! If you become part of it you become lost to it. Go to the mountains. Take the high view. Then you will have the power, in looking beyond yourself, your race, your kind, to see the bold arrangement in things." She pursed her lips and took a breath. "Marshall," she said, "when I am in church I do not look at peoples' feet, nor even at their faces, though they are beautiful. I look at the pure light which floods through the white dove and which makes those faces what they are." She could see in Marshall's eyes that he understood, and then she asked him an impossibly difficult question about what they were reading, to make him forget for the moment what she had said, and thus see to it that her hook was barbed.

Lucius was going crazy. He wanted to mount a raid and capture the leader of the bandit camp, a man wanted on many warrants for murder. If he could bring him out alive, so much the better. If not, he would kill him on the spot. He felt little sympathy for him, since (with one shot through the window) the man had murdered Lucius's father when Lucius was only Marshall's age. The brothers had risen to place, and both had been killed. But his mother made him swear against his planned and daring mobilization.

Nonetheless, he had assembled the forces. They were necessary to protect the compound, and had daily to escort workers in the fields. Lucius, Peter, and Stanhope had served in the British Army in the same company, attached to the Royal Marines. However, there were two professional soldiers at Rica Vista, and they were the sinew of the play. Nielson was a Swede of fifty, as fit as a boxer, painfully experienced for having fought voluntarily throughout the Second World War, and continually ever after all around the world as it dissolved and flared at itself like sunspots. He was used to being in the thick of it, and though it is difficult to describe a mercenary as gentle, he was quiet and of a serene nature. On the other hand, his partner, a Northern Irish Protestant called Farrell, was a self-proclaimed son of a bitch whose overwhelming compulsion was to get things done. Farrell shared Dash with Marshall, unequally as befitted their ages and experience. He was repelled by any talk of goodness and morality, the notion of which sent him into a rage. It was his belief that people did more or less what they had to do, and that as a soldier his job was to absorb the hatred and contempt of those for whom he did the dirty work which allowed them ofttimes to live. He cared little for his life, cared little for anything except pure action and daring in itself and of itself. He had never killed anyone who was defenseless, or harmed anyone not armed against him. That was his code. He hated the constraints of those who would ponder and judge. He had left Ireland at sixteen on a ship bound for Malaya and fought for his living in a vast number of places. At times he grew sentimental for Belfast, but had never returned. He was not interested in money, in politics, in protecting the weak (though that is what he often did, and even though he would not admit to it, had consistently refused to fight for "bastard cutthroats"), but only in his job—which he did elegantly well even though he was rather small. Lucius had planned that Farrell would be the first to penetrate the bandit camp, knowing that he would love to do it.

They had automatic weapons, a mortar, and two jeeps on which were mounted .30-caliber machine guns. The five of them practiced marksmanship, personal combat, and tactics. They exercised and stayed magnificently fit even in the heat, but were restrained by the will of a lady who weighed a good deal less than their mortar—which, when disassembled, they could carry with them at a run for miles. They were a brotherly army, but her light hand held them back as if they had been the sad and speedy performers of a flea circus. Farrell cursed her but dared not let the words escape in front of Lucius, so that he often sounded like pure turbulence, or the gargling of an idling outboard. One day, though, she changed her mind.

Marshall was sitting on the long narrow porch, resting from hard work in the fields, dazed with the sun, listening to doves and afternoon birds, wondering how as tired as he was he would find strength enough to move, wash, and go to his hot little room and study. A dove swooped through the dark enclosure to the rafters—where it rested, glowing. The world looked so fine and rich that Marshall was once again reminded of Mrs. Pringle's words about the pure light and people's faces, reminded that except for his *given* nature, man was no more wondrous than a hamster.

Awakening from the trance of the afternoon, he heard voices in the library. He had seen Lucius enter the house shortly before, a submachine gun thrown over his shoulder, dark patches of sweat on his blue workshirt. Lucius had cleaned his feet, wiped his brow, and gone in. He was speaking to his mother, or rather, she was speaking to him.

It had been a fine and peaceful life, and she had been as sharp as a hawk in its protection when her men were alive and sound. She dreamed of the time when their problems had been how best to farm the rich land, how to emerge from a wrong and illicit love affair, how to keep England in perspective and bar it from magically enlarging upon their imaginations until they were like disenfranchised Jews dreaming of Jerusalem, how best to satisfy their expansive energies, how to ward off complete surrender to the beneficent countryside. To her amazement, her daughter faced the same embarrassment of ebullient feelings, even in the worst of times, as if it were again the best of times. Mrs. Pringle knew that her own mother had seemed worn and tired during the Great War, when Mrs. Pringle herself, as a young girl, had been almost overburdened with energy, love, and delight.

So she changed her mind, thinking that Rica Vista existed in a thousand different ways, and that if by ruling with a tired hand she tired it, she would be doing a disservice. For it was as well a brighter, younger patch of lands than she knew she could see. She realized that the meaning of their lives was much the direction in which history had pointed them. It would be better for all of them to die than to have abandoned course, for their line was like an arrow pointed and the back of the arrow follows the front as if from love and loyalty, but most certainly it does.

Marshall could hear them and visualize the scene, though he stared upward at the glowing dove resting in splendor on the dark mahogany beams. In planes of silence transferred on heat, with the plants and sunshot colors outside saying her message, with the deep white sparkle of her eyes, from a life in a foil of islands and seas, as if a great judge had rendered a great decision, as if the frenzied opening of a race of the finest straining horses, as if her husband and sons were in her and traveled with all their strength into her frail limbs—she took Lucius by the hand. And as all time coursed from her to him and her life came about steady and good, eyes opened, shining, she said from deep in her chest in almost a low moan, beams of sun cast against the black, dust rising and swirling silver on the air, animals of the farm heavy and sad outside in their numbers, she said in a stroke to compass her life and his and that of a thousand generations: "Lucius! Go!" and Marshall stared upward, electrified.

The dove swooped down again and with beating wings flew toward the white clouds and the mountains. He had been tricked, but how delightfully. His resolve upon pure light had been suspended for a time, as if in a stage play with many twists and much backstepping. And then, unable to sort the full complexity of it, Marshall stared with great pleasure at the high mountains where he knew he would soon try his hand at war and other things beyond his control.

9

They prepared for war, and entirely forgot themselves. It became easy for even the most tangled of them to glance skyward or at the form of a moving object and feel it shaking through him. Genuinely coarse men can't do that. Even the gentle horses stamped like cavalry mounts and showed themselves in statuesque profile, as if gray war clouds made them remember their horse-fulness. Stanhope, who if unchecked was biased toward the rotund, quickly grew uninterested in food and became thin in consideration of the plan. Everyone feared, including Farrell, for the strategy they chose was exceedingly bold, as it had to be in view of their small number.

One day, before Marshall had been allowed to go with them, Lucius, Peter, Stanhope, Nielson, Farrell, and Marshall were gathered at sunset on a part of the lawn boxed in by thick hedges. They were all in white for vespers, during which Marshall had stood outside the copse and listened, but had remained apart. Then when the loud, clear bell had rung they moved to the boxwoods and sat on canvas chairs around a map table. Though it was light enough to make out the green of the lawn, a gas lantern burned in an endless sprint to light the intricacies of the map.

The problem was the inaccessibility of the Rasta camp. It was between two swift rivers, at the foot of the Blue Mountains. The closest road was twenty miles, and then spies en route would make surprise out of the question. Without using the roads, they would have to cross thirty-five miles of jungle overland. That way they might very well miss their target but (even more vexing) they would certainly alert the enemy of their approach, since for many miles around the camp the country people had been terrified into informing. The camp was unapproachable. Lucius had seen it from the air. It was surrounded by open space and barbwire. Lying in the fork of the Rio Nuevo and the White Water, it was backed by cliffs and a high mountain range. Farrell suggested a parachute drop.

"There aren't enough of us," snapped Nielson, remembering the British at Port Said. "If one is injured and another must support him, we lose forty percent of our force, and that is assuming that only one is injured. We must reach the objective in perfect order. Besides, the bush farmers would hear the plane. Planes don't fly over there much."

It seemed impossible, unless they were to take a month and move through the jungle with triple the stealth of the Rastas themselves, something which, after having exuberantly sung resounding hymns only half an hour before, they thought they could not do. They were sure that silence was unbecoming to them.

Then Marshall intervened. Placing his hands on the map with betraying affection for the form, he cut the knot. It was not such a profound solution, and would later seem rather obvious. In fact, he wondered why Nielson or Farrell had not seen it right away.

"As far as I can see," he said pompously, and yet suddenly in command, "it seems to offer us the opportunity of coming down from the mountains. They will not be expecting us from the rear, as the Romans did not expect Hannibal, and they will think that we cannot pass the impenetrable cliffs and brush on the windward side of the Blue Mountain Range, as the French did not think that the Germans could penetrate the Ardennes with a large army."

"How will we get to the mountains without traveling the roads, Master Pearl?" asked Farrell. "If we go by the Kingston side every damned Rasta in the world will see us."

"We will go by sea, in Stanhope's launch. Leaving at night, in two days we will make the extreme eastern part of the island. After we are dropped we will head for the ridge, here, and get to the top so that our westward march will be unhindered by thick vegetation. In a few days we will reach this point, at which we will descend to here, and then, to avoid becoming fouled in the impossible windward country, we will ride the White Water down to the camp.

"It can be done, with our equipment in rubber flotation bags, which will support us. At the Rasta camp we will arrive without warning, at our ease. If the rear is unprotected we're set. All we need do is mortar over a lot of smoke and some high explosive shells to draw their attention. Then Farrell and Nielson can enter the camp and grab what's his name."

"Big Tub," said Lucius.

"What makes you think you can tell us how to do this?" asked Farrell, his face all twisted and his eye cocked.

"Because I have," answered Marshall, striking a heroic pose. The five of them eyed him dumbfoundedly. Lucius started to laugh, enjoying himself tremendously. Then Stanhope began to laugh as well, and the rest followed until they were rolling on the grass in the stark shadows of the map light, until they hurt and tears came to their eyes.

In between bursts of hilarium, Farrell said, "Tomorrow I'll start to teach Marshall how to use the weapons."

Marshall replied, "Tomorrow, Farrell, I'll teach *you* how to use weapons." They thought that this was the funniest thing in the world, and they would have been hysterical all evening had not the dinner bell sounded and forced them to migrate toward the house like a bunch of drunken sailors. Dinner was especially enjoyable—lobsters from the coast—and everyone had giggling fits, even Dash and Mrs. Pringle, who had no idea why there was so much whimsy.

Later, in bed, Marshall looked at the stars through the wide-open window and thought of marksmanship. He practiced, sighting in the pins of light, and assured himself that on the morrow he would awaken in one of those steelcast moods in which he sometimes found himself, when he could have threaded a needle on the back of a galloping horse, so precise and ecstatic were his confidence and belief. When he looked at the stars he felt bodiless and as if his power extended in a sphere. That night he dreamed of bullseyes, one after another.

10

Farrell too had stayed up late, thinking of how to test Marshall. It vexed him. Everyone knew that the five had been practicing, and that, though he had arrived with a gun in his hand, Marshall hadn't fired a shot in months. So, at breakfast, they decided to go easy on him. But partly because Dash was there, and partly because he believed that challenges were best faced when amplified, he cut in and said, "Oh no. If I don't shoot best I don't even want to go on the raid. In fact, I'll go back to New York." Getting himself deeper and deeper until his heart pounded and his ears burned, he said, "You must remember, Lucius, Peter, Stanhope, Nielson, Farrell, Dash, and Mrs. Pringle, that I am an American." Farrell smirked, but Dash was amused. "Americans shoot straight." They started to laugh, but stopped when they realized that Marshall was serious. It was getting out of hand.

"Perhaps in Texas they shoot straight," said Mrs. Pringle, "but in New York, Marshall?"

"Mrs. Pringle, it's true that Texas is bigger than space. That I admit. But the great marksmen of the United States live in New York. New York is not just New York City. The countryside is seven hundred miles wide by one thousand miles long. There's plenty of room for shooting. I have a friend who can throw ten dimes in the air and shoot holes in every single one. Once, we were about a thousand feet from a traffic light. There was an ant on top of the traffic light. My friend said: 'You want me to shoot that ant?' And he did."

"Marshall," asked Dash, "if the ant had been wearing a hat, could your friend have shot off the hat?"

"Certainly."

"That I'd like to see," said Farrell, always inclined to take things quite literally.

"Here it is," said Marshall, holding up a tiny crumb he had picked from the table. "I brought it with me. This is the hat of the ant shot by my friend Dabaloin in Fish's Eddy, New York."

They went to the firing range, where there were five tests—rifle, pistol, submachine gun, grenade, and hand-to-hand fighting. Farrell handed Marshall a Mauser, explaining the criteria. At fifty yards, Marshall was to put three holes as close together as possible in the center of a small black frame on the target. He had three shots in which to test trajectory and bias. Everyone took his turn while Marshall waited. The concussions made their nerves raw. Farrell had assumed that the many shots would shake Marshall's hand, but Marshall was used to the pressure of a firing range, and knew how to go limp and let the shock travel through him and out again. Nielson made the best score with a total spread of sixteen centimeters.

Marshall slung his Mauser, stretching tight against the cream-colored leather. Adjusting elevation and guessing the windage, he took careful aim at the center of the box and hit exactly. Compensating according to memory of where he had first aimed, he followed with two shots which came close upon the first. "That's it," he said, "I don't need to practice." His spread was nine centimeters, nearly twice as good as Nielson's.

Farrell grit his teeth and proceeded to distribute a half dozen pistols. Thirty bottles were placed on a plank. Each man had five shots. Lucius hit three, Peter three, Stanhope two, Farrell four, and Nielson four as well. They knew that the pistol would be heavy in Marshall's hands. Fourteen bottles remained. Before Marshall fired, he loaded another pistol and placed it before him. Then with only one hand (the use of two hands cramped the felicitous lateral traverse) he raised his weapon, knocked off five bottles in a row, picked up the other pistol, and knocked off *six*, getting the last one by a lucky fragmentation of the one before it.

Farrell was speechless. With the submachine gun, Marshall placed twenty of twenty-five cartridges expended in a silhouette target, a fine score. Throwing the grenade was foolish pleasure.

In fact, everyone but Marshall was astounded, since only he knew that from a very early age he had been taught by Livingston to sight and shoot, and that he had a private range on which to practice. But he was puzzled at the thought of fighting Farrell, who outweighed him by about fifty pounds and was hard and tough. Farrell had a mustache. Marshall was no more capable of growing a mustache than of growing a tusk. Farrell's muscles buckled and popped. Marshall was a boy. He swallowed hard and advanced to the center of a dirt ring where they boxed and threw each other about in training. He faced Farrell and began to circle like a fighting cock. He grunted and groaned, and made faces.

This proved too much for Farrell, who left the ring in disgust. "I can't beat up a kid," he said. "I give up. The little bastard is mad, can shoot like fookin' Robin Hood, talks like an instructor at Sandhurst, and isn't afraid of the bloody divil. Let the little fooker be chief of staff for all I care."

They made him clean the guns. "Do a good job," said Nielson. "They must be in good condition." Nielson had seen more than all of them combined, and he was the most anxious. Having seen nothing whatsoever, Marshall had no fear. The noise from the guns had quieted them, and they moved about in the blooming sunlight as if it were night.

11

They left in moonlight on a Saturday night when there was a dance at the banana wharf and everyone was drunk or dancing and would not notice the graceful green-and-white launch as it made out of the channel to a smooth black sea undulating with the slow sway of deep swells. Marshall glanced at Stanhope's gentle eyes lit mildly by the low compass light and red gauges. Stanhope turned the brass wheel precisely and rhythmically as they navigated through the coral to the high sea, satisfying requirements of course and recognizing the influence of a slow electronic tune coming from the wharf.

It was another time, another country, inhabited by men as strong as horses, who worked hard and talked like rapids. Strikingly set into the night sky and stars, the sea, and the fragrant hills, was the wharf, crowded with the colors they loved—red, indigo, pink like orchids. A table was covered with bottles of Red Stripe. The girls were in home-sewn dresses and patent-leather shoes. Lights sparkled from houses on the hill. The wharf moved like a drum of confetti, shaking. It receded in the distance as the small boat full of armed men moved to the open sea and its silence, with only rays and sharks slim and silver below. The stars showered down to Cuba, and as they turned eastward, Lucius lighted a cigar and passed it around. Stanhope took a puff and said: "Thank you, brother Lucius, and good luck to us." Marshall fell asleep almost as contented and happy as he had ever been. To be armed and at sea was very fine. A warm breeze washed over them. The boat pushed along toward Rigel and Orion, under constellations exceedingly bright.

When Marshall awakened, the constable (who was to take back the boat) was at the helm, and the others were sprawled on the deck, lying on the equipment, with tarpaulins and jackets pulled over them to keep off the mist and spray. Marshall washed in the salt water, ate some biscuits, and brushed his teeth. Then he took the wheel for half an hour, steering straight and steady. As everyone began to get up, he went to the bow. There he straddled the tiny sprit and extended his legs outward so that with every pitch the soles of his feet slapped against the warm blue water. Dolphins formed an escorting vee. In their streamlined promenade they came so close that Marshall tried to touch them with his foot. They chattered with dolphin fluency and he answered back in imitation as they vaulted the waves.

By afternoon the sea was sparkling and rough. As they were checking their equipment a ship appeared on the horizon, making from the direction of Haiti. It drew upon them rapidly, a fast collection of gray rectangles and black struts. Its bridge protruded like a brow; a round circle of color against the superstructure was like a compassed Sienese banner; and the guns and flags identified it as American. "Must be out of Guantanamo," said Lucius. "Only an American or British ship would cross Jamaican waters as if it were home." Marshall watched as it sped away resolute and swift, not even glancing in their direction, though the radars circled and twirled and undoubtedly struck them hard and invisibly. It moved toward Grand Cayman, cool, gray, and touched with fire.

At night they had hot cocoa and roast beef sandwiches, and listened to waltzes on Radio Luxembourg. Lucius said that the idleness was good. In fact, they planned to rest in several of the stages, so that their assault would be an operation of peak form. They would suddenly burst in terror upon those who had been so habitually proud of terrorizing them. By the next morning they had rounded the east coast, and lay beyond the horizon waiting to go in when the full moon rose. Naturally it did, and they made for an isolated headland where they found a gleaming cove and disembarked on a shining beach, only to vanish into the dark as the constable raced for the open sea, glad that he would not be with them.

It took all night to get to the foot of the Blue Mountain Range. There they slept during the morning and set off upward in the full heat of afternoon. Not a single farmer farmed the steep slopes. They were alone, struggling under seventy-pound packs (fifty for Marshall) to get a purchase on the trackless hills. Every hour they stopped under shady trees to drink, and to eat jerked beef and fruit. The birds sang deafeningly as usual, and the raiders sweated incredibly, panting upward under their paralyzing loads.

The most unfortunate of them was Stanhope. The sea air had further sharpened the perpetual razor of his appetite, and he had gained a few pounds on the launch. But he kept his place in the six-man line as they slowly climbed a sharp slope, went over a ridge, and into a steeper valley yet. Marshall imagined that Dash was able to see him, that he was in her thoughts as much as she in his, that she would look out in back of the house and let her eyes follow the fields leading to the mountains, and know that Marshall was there doing something heroic. She had been betrayingly concerned when he had begun to fight Farrell. He thought that by fighting, by daring, he would draw her thoughts to him like a rolling ballad.

But instead, he found his own activity hollow, at least while they made the difficult ascent with all the heavy equipment, and he discovered that he was lost in dreams of the great house and Dash within. As he labored step by step he imagined her in the hidden valley at Rica Vista and he knew that she was undoubtedly dreaming of Britain in much the same unrequited fashion in which he dreamed of her. He was in the center of a dream, a romance, and by his imagination he dispersed its energies as those without the dream concentrated their random scarcities into a rich image. He thought that those in Britain, for which Dash was longing, were longing themselves for the tropics and high adventure in mountains and jungles. If only the credits could be paid and repaid. The world was like a great reflective system of desires, a crystal so faceted and diverse that if he fell back he would be saved from the mountainous height by webs of dream-carrying light. He looked ahead at Farrell—stocky, blond, neat as a pin—and he said, "Farrell, just tell me one thing. Tell me the geographical location of your thoughts, not what you're thinking, but where."

Farrell thought for a moment and answered in Irish accents as green and flexible as a plot of saplings, "And don't you think that I'm capable of abstract thoughts? As it happens, I was thinkin' about physics, atomic particles, and all that."

"The truth," said Marshall.

"You won't get that from him," shouted Nielson from a ledge where he had put down his pack.

"If you must know, it was Africa, black Africa."

"Right," said Marshall, imagining a beam of light stretching across the South Atlantic. They rested.

After some minutes, Farrell jumped up suddenly and bolted off into the brush, cocking his submachine gun as he went. The others scattered, until Farrell returned leading a tiny boy of about six. Clad in only a pair of ragged shorts, he himself was leading a chicken on a leash. They did not think it was very funny. The boy would tell his father, who might pass it up the line so that on arrival at the Rasta camp Lucius and his band would be gunned down. "What are we to do about this?" asked Farrell gravely. Marshall felt a terrible apprehension. He could think of no answer, and suspected that Farrell, or perhaps Nielson, would kill the child.

But, seeing that the little boy was terrified, Peter spoke up, saying, "Vaitenzi eine Minute. Ich habe der Solution. Everyvon sprechen Deutsch. Sprechen Deutsch vehemently." They began to scream German words.

"Deutsche Grammophon Gesellschaft!" Marshall roared into the jungle.

"Deutschland über Alles. Willkommen auf Deutschland. Eine Kleine Nachtmusik," screamed Lucius. Stanhope, who had read German at Oxford, recited perfectly and madly from Schiller. Nielson sang the Swedish national anthem, and Farrell blasted out Gaelic oaths.

The boy began to shake in pure terror. He was so frightened that he closed his eyes. Peter took the opportunity to cut a short staff from a thicket of bamboo, and drape flowers over his head and shoulders. The child opened his eyes and stood frozen in front of them, clutching his chicken. They continued their German, repeating it over and over. Peter came from behind the boy and jumped into view, showing his teeth, eyes wide, flowers shaking.

"*Fiwa and obaca, takeel and manaca,*" he chanted. Then he motioned the others to silence. "We are *obeah* men!" he said to the boy. "We go to see the *devil!*" The child was shaking back and forth, and a small stream began to roll down his leg. "If you tell anyone you see us," said Peter, "we come at night and . . . the *devil* come!" The little boy was perfectly still. He had been drained. "You understand, human boy?" He nodded his head. "Then run home, and tell no one, o human boy!" He was too frightened to run, so Peter turned him around and gave him a pat on his backside, and then he tore off into the bushes at the speed of light, grasping his rumpled chicken.

"I give you my guarantee," said Peter. "He will not tell even Saint Peter on Judgment Day." He threw the "snake stick" into the valley and brushed the flowers off his shoulders. They felt relieved, and knew that the next day they would reach a high peak and rest on the summit.

"The poor little fellow," said Lucius.

"What about the poor chicken?" asked Farrell, and they resumed their ascent. It was so hot that memories and images were driven and set into them as if they were held over a raw fire by a smith to be seared and gleamed. They grew intent upon their march—so much so that there were times of steady pacing in which they forgot even women and the world.

12

Farrell stood against the world, was bothered by nothing whatsoever, and maintained that he had long been living on borrowed time. He was maddeningly contrary and unfriendly, which, to his disgust, tended to bring him adherents.

Lucius had ordered the best tropical camouflage uniforms from London, but Farrell refused to wear them, preferring khaki or green work clothing. "I don't like these camouflage suits," he said. "They make you look like a tossed salad; and they always attract attention when you're in the open or standin' up. I never wore them in Africa, and I won't now. Besides, I don't like the cut." Lucius shipped the uniforms back to London.

When finally they were armed to the teeth, Farrell turned to Marshall and said, "Now that you're armed, you're your own worst enemy. Why? I'll tell you why. Power is like a lion. It won't sit like a cat in a boudoir. Although the weak don't know this, when you have power you have to protect yourself from it. You're a strange little beebuckle, Marshall. But you've got a lot of growing up to do."

"What's a beebuckle?"

"That's just what I mean. You don't know anything. You're ignorant. Everyone knows what a beebuckle is."

They neared the summit of the highest mountain; their green clothing bobbed against distant patches of melting snow; sparkling white vapor clouds cruised at their level obscuring for a time the valleys and plains, and the thin line of sea beyond. Farrell ranted as if they were part of a city crowded with men and man-made things, subject to twisted social codes in which virtue stood on its head and feet were in the air. "Them!" exclaimed Farrell, "those bloody sons of bitches, the holy-mouth moral bastards, the apostles of comfort and weakness, the city-bred righteous vermin. They never seen nothin' but each other's asses. I'd like to crush 'em in my hand like soda crackers.

"And furthermore, they don't know the value of surprise. I look at one and I can tell you what he thinks about this and that. I can see it in his clothes and his ornaments (the bastards wear jewelry, even the men). They only eat soft foods, and never anything spicy. They don't even fight back when you hit them. They live in things that look like filing cabinets. No wonder they're predictable. It doesn't have to be that way. For instance, look at me. I'm a Belfast Protestant, but I hate the damned English. They're pompous bastards, but dear Lord if only England had continued to rule the world.

"That's the quick turn I like; that's why they call a snare drum a snare drum—it surprises you and the balance is good when it comes in on a march and changes directions."

Marshall thought for a moment, straining under a load of guns, rations, shells, and other equipment. "Contrary to all I know and think, I feel that you are right, and I too love England." The realization of this shocked him, to know that in the American Rebellion he might have been a Tory, unless, as probably would have been the case, he had been seduced by the notion of an army of farmers and brigands. But in either camp he would have tried for excellence in fighting throughout the unexplored woods and lightly settled coastal plains and savannas. In a stupor of exhaustion (driving for the top, they had not rested) he reviewed his own code—to love at risk; to explore; to fight when necessary; to hold tight and hard to the greatness of the West, loyal like a monk in the Dark Ages; to be fair and good and compassionate and strong; and to lay these things out, great as they were, like minor vassals before the Divinity. He could hear the ice crystals in the clouds, and the wind as it whistled past the highest point on the mountain.

They rested on the summit. Over 360 degrees they saw nothing but sky and clouds stretching above land and sea. Peter, Stanhope, Lucius, Marshall, Nielson, and Farrell sat or kneeled on one knee, breathless at having come so high above things, breathless at what they saw. Lucius dropped his pack and took out his pipes. No one had imagined that he would bring them, but he knew their value. They were silent and still as he blew up the bag, getting red in the face—but it was cool up there, and icy, and green. He began to play "Amazing Grace," the sound of the pipes damped among the clouds, his eyes fixed straight over the horizon. Different as they were, they were all moved, and their expressions showed it. It was not that they had come up the mountain, although that in all its meanings was part of it, but rather that they felt the power of the pipes. They were the West, and they were fighting for the West. Though Peter and Stanhope were Africans and Marshall a Jew, they had suffered and their generations had suffered and died and worked for the West, and like Lucius, Nielson, and Farrell they were wedded to it inseparably. A long time ago the ideas had been obscured, but not the facts, and not the feeling. Diverse as they were in that small band, they were fiercely loyal—and when Lucius played his hymn alone in the air their hearts and minds flew with it. The power and long aching presence of their civilization came to them with the sudden concussion of a snare drum. On a Jamaican mountaintop its order and variations had forged them into a single will. It was the climb, the thin air, the difficulty, the chance of defeat, all the troubles of Rica Vista, and the things they loved. They were taut and trembling as the cold air settled upon them and the clouds swept by. They were frozen as if in a photograph. Listening to the pipes, they felt the wide limitless glory of the West.

13

For two days they remained in a cave 500 feet below the summit. At night it was warm and dry as their fire burned brightly, shielded by a tarpaulin covering the cave entrance. Their meals consisted of dehydrated beef which they cooked in snow water, dehydrated potatoes cooked in the beef water, dried fruit, biscuits, and chocolate. Marshall loved these meals more than any he had ever had. He said, "When we get back to Rica Vista I'm going to eat this way all the time; it's delicious."

"Don't make me puke," said Lucius, not realizing that Marshall thought that the absolute best way to eat was while running.

They assembled their equipment one evening, went over the plan, arose the next morning, and cut through impossibly thick brush for hours until they got to the first tributary of the White Water. Whereas moving through brambles and vines had yielded a mile an hour, they went three times as fast when walking in the ice-cold stream bed. Soon they came to a point where they were up to their thighs, and here they met the White Water itself. They were not anxious to test Marshall's theory, especially since the water was so cold, but they blew up the flotation bladders, lashed in their equipment, and set off on the little river in a group—knowing that they would soon separate, but pledging never to pass Lucius. That way, they could consolidate as fast as the current brought them together. At first it was slow going. They had to stand up every now and then to clear rocks and push themselves over gravel beds.

But soon they were floating, sliding, running, and crashing down the leaping river. It gradually became momentous and terrifying, but they were not terrified, since they took it in stride by stages, which is to say that they were hypnotized and entrapped by it, and completely oblivious of the danger. The White Water was full of black pools, high waterfalls, and rapids. It was frothing, clean-smelling, frigid, green, clear, blue, and it ran through deep gullies and glades of thick jungle rising from the banks. Orchids, vines, and trees hung above them. They choked on mouthfuls of fresh water, and laughed when they collided with one another, or, when caught behind a boulder or a fallen log, one of their number cursed exquisitely and flailed his arms like an infant trying to escape his buggy. All the while they were aware of the contrast between cold rapids and green jungle, and of the dancing mist which hung over the river and reflected the hot sun in prismatic bands as thick as the vines.

The water was thundering. It had started as an insignificant white sound and, in the few hours that they drifted, had become utterly ear-shattering. They could not shout above it. It was not just one sound, but thousands of combined single sounds which changed continually—some gaining, some losing intensity—the pitch and tone forever varying. When they reached the canyon fork, where they would land several miles in back of the encampment (downwind from the dogs), the cold water, rushing sounds, flying spray and foam, straining logs and limbs (they were brown and continually wet and they moved rhythmically as if animate), and raging streams overwhelmed them and almost prevented them from reaching a tenuous point on shore, where they clung together against the current, holding as best they could to crags in the rock wall they had to climb. The canyon was like a numbing crucible of molten ice. It held them breathless inside while they bent their heads to look at the cliff top.

"How can we get up that wall?" asked Stanhope, hardly heard above the roar. He was obviously beside himself even though he had lost five pounds in the freezing water on the way down. Farrell pulled out his bayonet and rammed it between two rocks. They fastened a line to it so that they could hold on and not be swept away. This enabled them to rest before the climb. It was only about forty feet, but they were exhausted and numb and it was almost vertical, with few handholds. Marshall felt obliged to volunteer, but remembered the cliff of eagles. Nielson, the oldest, and seemingly the worst candidate, said, "Someone has to go up before we freeze to death," and began to pull himself to the first handhold. He knew how to climb and was not afraid to do what he had to do for getting up, including a frightening traverse to an untested ledge. The higher he got the better he climbed, because he knew there was little choice, and because the sun warmed his hands and made him feel human again instead of reptilian. At the top he pulled himself over a toupee of soft grass, and rested in the hot sun, due to which he immediately began to steam. He threw down a fishing line and pulled up a climbing rope, so that everyone (including Stanhope) scaled the cliff in good order. They quickly disappeared into the brush, moving quietly with weapons ready.

Half a mile from the village they climbed into an enormous vine-crossed sea grape tree. Perhaps two dozen buildings the color of wet straw were visible in irregular lines, between which were corrals of cows, horses, and pigs. Because they were downwind they could smell the animals, but the animals couldn't smell them. White smoke came from several dinner fires. Beyond the village a completely green expanse rolled now and then to right or left with the curve of the river banks. It was strange to be so entirely inland, and not see or smell the sea, which, even at Rica Vista, had always made its presence felt. In a band of a hundred yards around the thatch huts were cultivated plots protected by wooden fences and barbwire. There seemed not to be many men inside the compound, but those who were visible were armed with rifles and automatic weapons. Lucius shook his head back and forth, amazed that this pitiful grouping had defied the law for so long. Two companies of marines airdropped or heliborne would have served to take them prisoner a long time before, if hands had not been tied (Lucius did not make the political decisions of the Commonwealth).

It was five o'clock, not too long before dark. They smelled roasting meat and plantain. Lucius felt as if his small force were part of his strong arm and fist. They stayed in the tree until an hour before nightfall. Then they attacked.

They had rehearsed it at Rica Vista on at least a dozen occasions. Each time, Marshall had assumed that he would have to overcome great fear in the real situation. But, to his surprise, he was not at all frightened. In fact, he had the same pulse and drive as in the many school soccer games he had played against superior force (mainly military schools full of the violent, rejected, and disturbed), when fear vanished at the instant of kickoff and primal forces directed even the soft, small, Eagle Bay boys in their faded striped shirts and maroon shorts.

They had expected that the leader would live in conspicuous fashion. In the first confusions, Farrell and Lucius were to have crawled up to his hut and taken him. But his house was indistinguishable. Then, in a charged moment, Lucius caught him in the glass circle of his telescope. He was sitting in a little booth in front of which was a table covered with beer bottles, cameras, pistols, and transistor radios. It was absurd, but he was playing with them as if he were a child with toys.

They decided to capture Big Tub in a somewhat different manner than they had planned. Lucius climbed a tree and, when everything was ready to go, shot Big Tub in the leg. Big Tub bounded forward, knocking over his table of treasures. With the first shot as a signal, Marshall began to drop shells into the mortar. Soon enormous explosions and clouds of phosphor smoke filled an area on the other side of the village. Those inside began to shoot wildly at the smoke and noise, as if an army were attacking from the north, whereas Marshall and the others were on high ground in the south, completely unobserved. The half a hundred defenders looked and fired northward to a man. Shrapnel from the mortar shells, clouds of smoke, and falling leaves and branches (cut mainly by the Rasta bullets) gave them many targets and they fired in panic, increasing their own confusion.

Marshall dropped mortar shells steadily, one every ten seconds by his watch, changing elevation and bearing occasionally. There were twenty-four shells—the main reason for agony on the mountain—and his barrage lasted exactly four minutes. After two of these minutes, Farrell and Peter (who had crept up to the perimeter) rushed into the camp toward Big Tub, who rolled in pain over his cameras and radios. Covered at close range by Stanhope and Nielson, they were armed only with pistols hanging on lanyards. They reached Big Tub, hit him over the head, picked him up, and carried him out. Lucius was in the tree, ready to shoot anyone happening upon the scene. But no one came, and they began their retreat, dragging the mortar and Big Tub to the cliff over the river.

By the time they reached the cliff they could hear dogs howling and scores of men rushing through the bushes. Everyone except Nielson and Farrell was in near-panic. Farrell picked up the mortar and swung it like a hammer, letting go. It sailed in a heavy curve into a deep pool, where it crashed inaudibly. They lowered Big Tub to the base of the cliff. He weighed at least 300 pounds. Farrell and Peter were amazed that they had carried him so lightly. Marshall descended, followed by Peter, Stanhope, and Lucius. Farrell and Nielson had started to return the fire which by then came heavily from the brush. They had plenty of ammunition and the noise from the cliff top was almost as loud as the river.

When the flotation gear was set and Big Tub lashed in, Nielson climbed down the rope. Farrell remained, shooting. They pushed off, expecting Farrell suddenly to rush down the rope, or even to jump into the pool. They waited nervously, aware that the current was carrying them away from the landing place. Farrell never appeared. Above the sound of the water Nielson said, "He told me to go to hell. I don't think we'll see him again." And they didn't.

14

They rode down the White Water. Because Marshall had been first on the rope he found himself in the same raft as Big Tub. With two of them, one extremely heavy, they sank low in the water and moved more slowly than the others, who quickly vanished downstream. Tub was still out when they passed the village. There, two riflemen waited on the cliff, but Marshall saw them from upriver. There was nothing he could do, and he watched as they sighted him in. He thought of going into the water, but was sure that the rapids would drown him. Besides, he did not want to lose his prisoner.

As he got closer and they began to fire, he took out his pistol, thinking that he could try at least to drive them to cover. Bullets slammed into the water. Then he felt a shock in his right leg. His calf had been split down its length and it shot blood into the river. He screamed a shrill scream like that of a small child and fell back against the raft, only to feel a bullet graze his head and the blood pour down. As if this were not enough, his companion began to stir.

Big Tub was so big that he could have crushed Marshall with his fist. Marshall felt as if he approached his end. Then he became clear-headed and resolute, and angry. He raised his pistol in two hands and, to counter the motion of the river, moved it as in trap shooting, and let off a shot which dropped one of his attackers. The other promptly disappeared. On another bluff some more men stood with rifles. As Marshall went by he placed three good shots in their vicinity, driving them back. They too fired, and missed.

With his prisoner awake, his blood pouring from him, and the raft careening without control, Marshall found himself looking into a fierce, experienced, angry face. The man adjusted himself on the raft and began to move toward Marshall, who raised his pistol and pointed it straight at him. He saw a hideous smile, indicating that he was not believed.

Marshall set his teeth and drew back the hammer on the pistol; the click was heard above the waters. For an hour and a half they went down the rapids and then drifted on the big river—sometimes turning slowly, sometimes being submerged under a wave, sometimes being tossed like a chip down a patterned flume. All the while, Marshall kept his finger on the trigger. His adversary did not move an inch.

In darkness they approached a landing where the others were waiting and a purring diesel truck was ready to go. Nielson swam out and pulled in the raft. He and Peter had been grazed in the ambush, but not as badly as Marshall, who could not let go of his pistol. Nielson squeezed the trigger, firing a shot in the air, and then pulled the gun from Marshall's hand. They sped away toward Rica Vista.

15

It seemed to Marshall as if he were in an Eakins painting of a nineteenth-century operating theater. The light was exquisitely beige. All around were the grave mustachioed faces of serious young gentlemen. The white-haired doctor was English. It was night, and a full moon, or nearly so, shone in the window from over the mountains. Dash and Mrs. Pringle were there. Lucius and

Stanhope held down Marshall's shoulders. Marshall remembered what had happened. He had been given chloroform, to which he had proved allergic, and he had then suffered convulsions and unconsciousness. When he awoke the doctor had said, "Why didn't you tell me?"

Marshall was rather weak and could only answer, "You didn't ask."

They brought a bottle of brandy which Lucius had stolen from BOAC, and they began to feed it to Marshall. It was painful to drink the stuff, and he threw up. "Drink it," said the doctor. "I haven't any local anesthetics, I'm going to have to go in almost to the bone, and it's good French brandy."

Marshall drank. After a little while, when he began to say half words about rowing on a hot painted river in the summer in Philadelphia—next to a coffer dam with water flowing over and through it like flax on a comb—the doctor made the first thrust with his long curved needle, coming down deep and hard into the muscle. Despite half a bottle of brandy and the company of Eakins, Marshall screamed and tensed explosively, locking up like iron. Then it was repeated over and over again. He was sweating so hard that he could not tell the difference between the sweat and the blood running down his face from the newly opened head wound, on which Mrs. Pringle held a thick red-soaked gauze pad.

Sixty stitches were placed one by one until the moon shone in the opposite window and the servants stopped their wailing outside because they had become hoarse, tired, and sleepy. Marshall lost his voice on stitch ten, and then could only gag and move in pain. He fainted every now and then, and revived. He began to think that he was Eakins, and then he thought that Eakins was cutting him open to get color with which to paint. In moments of relief he would catch Dash's eye and smile. He knew that if he lived (at every thrust the doctor said, "He'll live, he'll live") he would finally get to sleep with her.

Dash, the moon, Eakins, a hot river in Philadelphia, the sharp needles, the three-star peach brandy, the blood and sweat on his face, the servant girls in customary wailing, the crickets, the white-haired doctor, Rica Vista finally safe like a jewel in the night, the cold currents of the White Water, the room's beige lantern light, the dark colors swirling from a century back, the water flooding like flax through a comb—delighted him despite the pain. For despite the pain, or perhaps because of it, he felt the world coming fully thick and lovely fast.

16

How close it had been. With Big Tub in jail, the government would realize that the Rastas were not invulnerable. More important, the Rastas themselves would see it. Most important, the country people would be encouraged to go back to their lands. Lucius returned from Kingston with reports that the constabulary were considering an expedition against the newly leaderless Rastas in the White Water region.

On his last day at Rica Vista Marshall went with Dash to the reef. Because the reef was so different from the summit views he had seen, and because he had paid dearly for his elation about the West, he wondered if he had not in fact suffered illusions at high altitudes. Perhaps, he thought, his idea of the nineteenth century was far from the truth—a purified miniature. Perhaps the Empire was in its order only dull, in form conventional, in justice not blind. But to remember those days on the mountain, on the river, and at the encampment as anything but what they were would be to err oppositely. They *did* do a great thing, and there was a time when great things were better understood. Marshall remembered his origins, raising barriers against the love he had felt on the peak for the British and their Empire. Like the stitches which had been painlessly pulled, those illusions gave way to the kaleidoscopic color of the reef and the days and days of dolphinlike abandon that he had spent with Dash, who was all the more beautiful as a result of the victory. They lost themselves in swimming, and copulated with the ease of water creatures, not knowing how to feel apart from the waves and the driven coral.

In the evening there was to be a special dinner. Lamb was roasting in the ovens and people ran back and forth on the drive of cracked white shells, which made a noise that seemed to stay after they had left. The table was decked with bougainvillea and hibiscus; candles burned in tall pewter sticks. It was a dinner not only for Marshall's departure, but for his recovery, and for the victory. They had a wonderful time. Lucius made not a few stupid jokes about Marshall's desire to eat only dehydrated foods, and the table was cradled in ease and happiness. They spoke of the questions Marshall considered, and Mrs. Pringle corrected him when he assumed that, to have dominated the world, the English must have been extraordinarily intelligent and sharp.

"Oh no no no," said Mrs. Pringle. "The reason the British conquered the world was not (as many think) that they were clever, but rather because everyone else was clever and the British were the only simpletons. Into the midst of prolix orientalism came the British singing four-line ditties and arising to take cold baths. Being simpletons, they went where no one dared to go, and fought against madmen's odds. Few could resist their clean-facedness, and they moved through intricate layers of opposition like a lance through a honeycomb."

She might well have continued, except that a car pulled up outside—unusual for that hour, since no one but the constable traveled at night in their section and, to be truthful, even he was afraid. It *was* the constable, and he entered the dining room with pith helmet in hand. His blue shirt was so well pressed and so airy that he looked like a piece of Dutch sky. Mrs. Pringle invited him to have a seat and partake of dessert.

"No thank you, Mistress," he said, looking at the festive table. "I have to say something very bad. They took him to the Ewarton Jail. Tonight the jail burned down. They had to let the prisoners go. He ran off into the bush and no one can find him."

Dash began to cry silent tears. Lucius was immobile. Nielson smiled. Peter, Stanhope, Mrs. Pringle, and the constable were frozen, not knowing what to think, although Mrs. Pringle knew that her daughter was crying for Farrell. Marshall looked at them and at the beautiful room and its dark Jamaican woods, as if it were a dream. Someone in the kitchen turned on a radio, and music could be heard faintly over the occasional clatter of dishes. The dining room was silent and the constable remained standing. Feeling awkward, as if he had intruded upon a family in mourning, he fixed his gaze on the beautiful burning candles.

V
Yorkville

1

Even in May, the wind above the East River was cold and strong. Marshall and his friend Alexander had gone to the Brooklyn Bridge; over their own reddened hands resting like talons on the railing, they looked northward up the great river filled with traffic and refractive waves. The day was blue and busy; tangled in sunlight, snapping flags, and people bobbing up and down long avenues compressed to see; its prospect like the shining side of a cool porcelain vase rich with running colors. The city before him resembled his image of Canton—ships in the harbor and merchants unloading wares at the foot of green hills covered with terraces, gardens, and trees which bent like centenarians.

Upon his return from Jamaica the previous spring, Marshall had found himself in a much-changed Eagle Bay School. The once lighthearted and eccentric students had been transformed by a race for prestigious colleges; they vulgarized their studies by ceaseless competition and flattered the teachers excessively. Marshall refused to participate, and was quickly drawn into an altercation with a bash-faced young biology instructor who made the mistake of grabbing him by the shoulders and pushing him against a wall when Marshall had refused to call him sir. Marshall fought a lively fight, driving the teacher outdoors, across the parking lot, through the nerve garden (worms were bred there for experiments upon their plexii), and backward into the lily pond. After being expelled, Marshall was sent to a private school in Manhattan, where he began to study in earnest. He often took the train upriver to see the Livingstons, to ride through the woods on the black horse, to ski on his old wooden skis down the long windy hill in front of the house. But when he arrived at Eagle Bay he was usually dressed in a dark suit, as if he were much older. Residence in Yorkville changed him as much as had his stay at Rica Vista. He could not go backward, and did not try. Although he had been familiar with the city, and although Eagle Bay was less than 100 miles distant, Marshall felt as if he had in fact been sent to China.

He lived with the family Pascaleo, of which Alexander, his classmate, was the eldest son. Alexa—a radiant beauty—was Alexander's twin sister, and Paolo was the youngest, an eager gardener of seven, who farmed a small plot in the park and brought home vegetables which were stunted, malformed, and delicious. Signora Pascaleo worked as a loan officer in the foreign department of Semple, Peascod, & Bovina; and Signor Pascaleo (an urban historian, expert on Florence) had somehow gotten to be New York City Commissioner of Public Works. Shocked by the sudden appointment (it was in the time of the tall mad mayor), his own family had questioned his suitability to the task. "What do I care?" he had said, shrugging his shoulders. "A sewer is a sewer, a pipe is a pipe, a light is a light." They had an enormous apartment high above Park Avenue, well, a little off Park Avenue, in Yorkville. They spoke mostly in Italian, and they kept a milk-white goat called Boofin. His hooves and horns were black as jet, because Paolo buffed them with shoe polish until they shined. It was his main delight, and often Marshall came in the door to see the goat perched on a big leather chair, Paolo hard at work shining the hooves. They loved to hear Boofin prance across the hard floors. He sounded like a team of tap dancers. When he got excited and could not restrain himself, it was like hail on a tin roof. He was a frightened, gentle goat. Petrified of dogs, he would not leave the apartment, but spent days staring out the window, his forelegs on the sill.

Marshall and Al were going to Harvard in the fall, and Alexa was going to the University of Rome. Mainly to her chagrin, her father had persuaded her to attend the semiannual Gotham Ball that June at the Plaza. She was so beautiful—tall and blue-eyed with shining blond hair—that she mainly got her way, and she had resolved upon wearing a black velvet gown and bracelets and necklaces of white gold. Though everyone had been instructed to wear white, she would not. Marshall, Alexa, and Al didn't quite fit into that stuff (Marshall certainly didn't), and they never knew exactly what to do about all the social events to which they were invited because Signor Pascaleo was a commissioner.

While leaning over the rail, Marshall had been telling Al about Jamaica. In the middle of his narrative he looked north at familiar skies and, even though no clouds were visible, predicted a thunderstorm. Al did not believe him and made him go on. For an hour they stood on the bridge, Marshall gesticulating and hoarse from a tale in which Al did not place much trust. No one believed anything Marshall said about Jamaica, but Al wanted to know what had happened. At the end, when frightening sheets, chains, and bolts of white fire were striking tall buildings to the north and the purple mass of a great Hudson Valley thunderstorm was sweeping ominously southward, Marshall hurried to finish his story, and they sprinted to the Manhattan side, drumming the boards and dodging pear-sized raindrops. Al pondered the similarity between his family and the Pringles, though he did not think that the Pringles actually existed.

Wet and breathless in the sullied blue of Brooklyn Bridge station, Al leaned over Marshall and grabbed him by the throat. He was much bigger than Marshall (not difficult) and he throttled him. "If you ever sleep with my sister," he said, "I'll kill you." Until that moment, Marshall had never imagined that he and Alexa could be lovers. She was too fine, too tall, too beautiful, too crazy, and too unpredictable. He had always regarded her as a sister—living in the same house . . . and there were other girls . . . the hospitality of the family . . . honor . . . death. But she was alluring and, despite her rebellion and feigned boldness, she was shy and gentle. That, really, was why he had thought of her as so delicately removed. Marshall caught a glimpse of his own face in the mirror of a gum machine. Though red from the throttling, he had an open, whimsical look. A subway thundered in, dripping and sooty. They got on, and by the time the door closed a vision of Alexa in all her beauty floated before Marshall's eyes, and he couldn't wait for that night's reading of *The Divine Comedy*, for he knew that he would share her book.

2

Signor Pascaleo settled into a pose of religious infallibility. Facing him were his family and Marshall, teamed up in pairs at volumes of Sinclair's dual-language Dante. The Pascaleos had completed the cycle nine times since Alexander's birth, and that June they would finish the *Inferno*. They read only one canto a week, going over it several times, translating, and discussing. Signor Pascaleo was authority and guide, a digest of all important criticism and an important critic himself. The more he read, the more excited he got, so that often at the end of a canto he paced the room like a spotted beast, arms alternately clenched and flying, a stream of Italian rhetoric issuing from him at such great speed that even his wife could not understand. How difficult it was for Marshall to work his way through the dark and savage wood of those rapidly uttered words.

Signora Pascaleo, whose braided and piled hair made her look like an Austrian basket, sat with Paolo, who, a few months before, had just started to understand vaguely some of the readings, but who squirmed and more often than not fell asleep while leaning against his mother. Al sat alone or, sometimes, with the goat, who had to be held when Signor Pascaleo became excited. Marshall sat with Alexa. That evening he realized that his enjoyment of the *Commedia* had not been entirely pure. He was in love with Alexa, but from politeness and civility to his hosts, and from fear, he had hidden it even from himself.

She had magnificent hands. He watched them gracefully embracing the text. On her right wrist were two tortoise-shell bracelets, and she had several small rings of silver and gold. From the corner of his eye he could see that some of her hair, though tied back, fell in delicate wisps about her ears and neck. When she spoke, he felt the process of it throughout her body and his, so close was she. As time wore on he felt a reverberating heat between them, especially if she were to laugh. When in turning pages their hands touched it remained with him long afterward. She looked a little frail and thin, but the sight of her full, stretched jersey reminded him that she was not. Al had told him of how as a child she had been deathly afraid of everything, of how she (a short fat girl) had stood at the window only a few years before and eaten boxes of chocolates while she watched her girlfriends cavort with boys on the street far below. Then, in a year or two, she had changed. They hoped that she would make good on her splendid transition, and be neither timid nor brash, nor exploitive, nor preyed upon. At the University of Rome she would be very much on her own, a delightful, frightening prospect. She longed for a city of fountains and green grass in January. She wanted to walk like a contessa down the worn and civilized streets, to pass by with a straight stare and high thoughts. She had determined that this city was for her, and though she shuddered in imagining it, the thought of living there alone on one of its hills in temperate Roman colors was as satisfying as a long embrace.

Signor Pascaleo guided them throughout Canto XXVI, the Canto of Ulisse, reading without emotion until suddenly he rose in his chair and the net of his vessels was visible in his hands. Though the storm had passed and it was mild and dry outside in the dark, with the sound only of a few taxis, they felt again the excursive cracks of thunder and lightning which had rolled down from Eagle Bay.

"O frati," dissi, "che per cento milia
  perigli siete giunti all'occidente,
  a questa tanto picciola vigilia
de'nostri sensi ch'è del rimanente,
  non vogliate negar l'esperienza,
  di retro al sol, del mondo sanza gente."

Signor Pascaleo felt his youth and history, when he had climbed the mountains north of Salerno and seen it as perfect and as miniature as a town on a postage stamp. The family was riveted, Alexa slightly quivering, the sweep of her shoulders and neck like the flowing main cables of a suspension bridge—in that the curve was perfect and hypnotic. The goat, who had been as immobile as a white stone, pranced up and down sneezing from excitement and had to be held by Al, who calmed him, saying, "*Shh, shh, caprone, non c'è niente.*"

Noi ci allegrammo, e tosto tornò in pianto;
  chè della nova terra un turbo nacque, ·
  e percosse del legno il primo canto.
Tre volte il fè girar con tutte l'acque:
  alla quarta levar la poppa in suso
  e la prora ire in giú, com'altrui piacque,
infin chè'l mar fu sopra noi richiuso.

Then it was sad, for it was dark and quiet and the boat had gone under even after Ulysses's great speech urging his crew to try for new lands in the track of the sun, beyond the Pillars of Hercules. Signor Pascaleo turned on a light, and remained with his hand on the switch. Signora and Paolo disappeared toward Paolo's belated bath. Alexander said, "Let's get outa here and go to a noisy saloon." Alexa didn't want to go. "C'mon," said Al. "C'mon."

In a place on Second Avenue—Julia's Cockroach Bar—a piano, a lot of rude bullyboy jostling, and a pint or two of beer made them forget the enjoining paradox which, without plan, had come to light in the reading. Everyone in the bar looked at Alexa, while Marshall and Al discussed their plan to explore beneath the city. In Signor Pascaleo's office was a set of forty master keys allowing access to every sewer, subway, water, gas, or steam passageway in the city. They were going to borrow the keys and spend a night underground. At night the sewer current was gentle enough to allow passage through all but the swiftest straits—the Fifty-third Street Flume, the West End Avenue Delta, and the great falls under the New York Times (absolutely impassable after lunch). They planned to return the keys by morning. They had already purchased miner's lights, high boots, a good rope, and a crowbar.

Alexa thought the scheme moronic. "The sewers smell disgusting," she said to her brother. "You would want to walk around in the sewers for fun."

"The sewers smell better than you do," Al snapped back. "Did you ever not see a nude mule?"

"How much beer have you had?"

"Half a glass . . . see. Did you ever not see a nude mule?"

"Are you crazy?"

"No. Did you ever not see a nude mule?"

"No!"

"You mean you always see a nude mule? Ha!"

"No!"

"You mean yes."

"Oh, all right. Yes. I did."

"Did what."

"Did ever not see a nude mule."

"When?"

"Most of the time."

"You have then, I take it, seen a nude mule, on occasion?"

"I'm looking at one right now."

"Then, did you never not see a nude mule?"

"When?"

"Ever."

"Sometimes."

"Not now?"

"No."

"Why?"

"When?"

"Let me ask you this."

"Go right ahead."

"Okay. Who?"

"Marshall, of course, who else?"

"Is that so?" asked Al. Then for half an hour they sat without speaking, while in the rolling bittersweet music Marshall did not realize that in the shorthand of brothers and sisters, Alexa had said that she was in love with him.

The May night was clear and balmy; they walked along the river and watched lighted sparkling bridges, viaducts, elevated roadways, trestles, and barges, which lately had been washed by pure rain. Between the two boys was a glimmering girl, and the skyline was like a great forest of fireflies. As so often is the case, New York could easily have been an idealized picture of itself in a quiet, contemplative future.

Marshall wondered how such great power could be still and mild at times, and thoroughly abrasive and destructive at others. Cellular and divided, the city's rooms, lights, squares, and streets could in their complexity put to shame the heart of a great electronic machine, or the whirling mosaics of the most colorful mosque. All of it could never be seen, and therein lay its great promise—its swarming variations were as valuable as an ever-receding geographic horizon. Beneficent distance was within, hidden in the turmoil, as if a monster had swallowed nature.

"Let's drive," said Al. He loved to drive, and prided himself on his knowledge of the streets, expressways, shortcuts, and detours through lost unknown neighborhoods. At night they often rode around the city, exploring the empty roads.

"Where to?" asked Alexa, as they climbed into the Pascaleos' vintage Dunderburg.

"How about a bridge tour? I'll take you over the Verrazano, Brooklyn, Manhattan, Williamsburg, Fifty-ninth Street, Triboro, Henry Hudson, and George Washington in less than an hour."

They put the top down and glided smoothly in the pulsing arteries, achieving precise transitions from one highway to another, taking corners with just the right G, maintaining near constant speed. Marshall and Alexa leaned back and watched the city lights, which seemed clearer and gentler than in winter when they sparkled and cut like diamond grit. Now, there was a fresh wind, and young trees had a chance.

Marshall felt as if he could stay in New York forever. He imagined making his way up the echelons to find ease and power in a high place. He imagined living in a loft south of Houston Street, where artists were beginning to set up studios as they had done long before in Greenwich Village.

He imagined entering ward politics with no protection or perspective except what he would get from the heat of his own effort. In summer the streets boiled and the air burnt his eyes, but he could always look down long disappearing avenues to the small blue square of sky at the end waving upward in viscous snakes of air. And if Alexa would return from Rome, or not go at all . . .

But as they flew across the wide rivers and had laid before them great important views, Marshall felt the draw of other times and other places. His origins seemed as well to pull him from the fine scenes that he often saw, so that within his own life he frequently felt like an observer. However, Alexa was too intoxicating to ignore, and he soon fell back into the mill of his infatuation, eyeing her delightful profile as the three of them did the bridges. The ways to love, it seemed, were as tangled and marvelous as New York's great network of roads.

3

One evening while Signor Pascaleo paced back and forth like a *marron glacé* in a dressing gown, Marshall and Al were tramping through the vast system of tunnels under Manhattan. They had given up completely on maps, which were about 800 times more complex than subway charts, and had decided just to wander. They entered by the basement of the Yale Club (accessible via an unlocked door in the Hotel Roosevelt tunnel) and quickly found their way to an enormous main through which knee-deep water was rapidly rushing. The conduit was so high that they would not have reached its top even had they jumped. Al had been right—it didn't smell, except for a dank odor like that of a sweating rabbit. They had the distinct impression that the water was coming from some specific place and going to yet another place of particular importance. Underground water seems issued from momentous chambers and destined for hidden seas. Actually, or so it was believed, the current came from countless gutters, sluices, and drains, and no Valhalla was at either end. But the rushing suggested a purposefulness that water does not have. They walked in the big tunnel, pushing against the current, and they stopped to rest, peering northward into the darkness, from which emerged a cool wind. Straight down the tunnel was a tiny yellow light. It flickered, and it was moving. "Look," said Al, "that light is moving toward us."

"How could it be?" asked Marshall.

"I don't know. Turn off your lamp." They switched off their miner's lamps and hid in a recess near an exit ladder. The light *was* moving toward them.

Marshall broke the silence. "They don't have night patrols down here, do they?"

"Nope," said Al, his throat tightening. "My father says that, except for emergencies, no one is ever here at night—no one, for any reason whatsoever."

"Then what's that?"

"Maybe it's debris."

"Debris? With a light on it?"

"I don't know what the hell it is; don't ask me."

As it drew closer they could see that it was a torch of pitch, burning with black smoke. They heard muffled sounds, words, and wood against wood, and then they saw that the torch was on the prow of a boat, fixed on a metal tripod. The boat itself was long and thin, crudely built of overlapping planks. It had a small sail of coarse, striped wool, and it went faster even than the rapid current. As it swept past them, they were speechless. A dozen bearded men in rags and tattered homespun manned little stunted oars and a seemingly unnecessary rudder. They spoke in a strange guttural language, and they were arguing vehemently. As soon as they had passed, the boat picked up speed and the torch got smaller until it vanished from sight completely.

At first, Marshall and Al remained frozen in place, jaws hanging open. Then Al got angry (he always got angry at things that he could not explain), and he jumped back into the main, sloshing ahead. "Before you ask," he said angrily, "I don't know. So don't ask."

"It must be beatniks going to the Village," said Marshall, "or maybe farmers who came from upstate in the aqueduct tunnel."

Al turned in disgust. "Maybe," he said, "it's a bunch of stockbrokers who have found a new way to get to Wall Street."

"That's a good theory," said Marshall, laughing nervously. "Just keep on coming up with theories. It's the only way I know of dealing with something like this. Use the data that you have. For instance, they were arguing. We know, for example, that they couldn't have been arguing about which course to take. We know, for example, that—"

"Marshall, forget it. No one would ever believe us anyway."

They could not see the end of the tunnel—which was many miles long— and they turned into a sizable tributary, slashing an underground mist with the beams of their helmet lights. A little down the road they came to a large platform fifteen feet above them in a high recessed well. Shining their lamps on it, they saw a door with a gleaming lock. Al leaned against the wall, facing it, and Marshall climbed him until he stood on his shoulders, Marshall's hands also on the wall. Then Al took both of Marshall's feet in his hands and backed down until his arms were straight, after which he slowly walked against the wall until he was standing at his full height, arms straight. Marshall was standing on Al's palms, a platform at least seven feet above the ground. Marshall stretched as much as he could, but his fingers did not quite reach the ledge. "I can't reach the ledge," he said. "Can you stretch some more?"

"No," said Al in a gasp. "When I count three, I'm going to toss you into the air. Jump on three."

"Wait a minute," said Marshall.

"One."

"Wait just a minute," said Marshall.

"Two."

"Thanks," said Marshall.

"Three," and Al threw him as he himself jumped. Marshall's fingers caught the ledge so slightly that he hesitated in space and then began to fall back. In complete panic he somehow threw his right hand up and caught hold. After pulling himself up, the entire right side of his body and brain contorted in a deadly cramp.

"What are you doing up there?" called out Al from below, where the end of a convention or intermission at the theater had caused the current to swell and rise to his thighs. Marshall hardly had the breath to speak.

"My ribs are scratching my heart," he scrawled with his voice.

"Your what?"

"My ribs are scratching my heart."

"Put your hands above your head and crack your knuckles."

He did this and was able to breathe again, just in time to throw down the rope, for the water was coming close to the top of Al's boots.

The lock was of stainless steel. They tried several wrong keys, and then began to work systematically through the forty. At twenty-nine the door opened and they stepped through as carefully as turn-of-the-century burglars with sacks and raccoon masks. On the other side was a clean dry tunnel through which ran steam pipes and cables. Spread over the floor were many pieces of zwieback and an occasional baklava. "What are these for?" asked Marshall of Al, who had attended high-level discussions of the sewers.

"Those are here to trap Specials. They're highly poisonous."

"Specials?"

"Yeah. That's what they call a live rat. Rats reproduce when they're two months old, have about six or eight litters a year of ten to twenty babies a shot. If two of them started in perfect conditions and none of their offspring died of hunger or poison, in a year they could produce five million. My father says that there are at least two rats underground for every person in the city. That's at least sixteen million. If something happened down here and they all came out at the same time, let's say in front of Bloomingdale's, it would be hell on earth."

"How come we haven't seen any?" asked Marshall.

"Are you crazy?" asked Al, shining his light on two dozen little ones tucked into a hole in the wall. Marshall knew that they were vile, but somehow he sympathized with them. Everyone in the world tried to kill them, when they wanted only to survive. They carried disease, but not intentionally. All they did was eat garbage, and squeak. Then, one ran up and tried to bite his foot, and he kicked it into the air with hatred and disgust. "That was a Dewey," said Al, "a live one which attacks. A live one which runs is a knocker. Knocker or Dewey, they're all Specials."

"What's a dead rat called?"

"A Beebuckle."

"A Beebuckle!"

"Yup. I don't know the origin of the term."

"I suspect," said Marshall, "that it's Irish."

At the end of the passage was a wall-mounted iron ladder which led up into darkness. They climbed for about ten minutes, until they were so high that they did not hear a penny hit bottom. They thought that they were close to ground level, when suddenly they saw a light from above. Switching off their lamps, they climbed quietly to the grate through which the light was passing. They could not believe what they saw, and they froze to the ladder.

In an enormous room the size of Grand Central Station, hung with draperies and spotlights and potted palms suspended in the air, were hundreds of nude women. Some lay on divans and ate fruit, or read. Some did gymnastics. Some were engaged at archery, while others bathed, worked looms, dived into a great pool of blue water with geysers and fountains spraying about, or played the lute. Others worked at desks, typing and making phone calls, while still others sat in poker games, visors of green their only apparel, the tables surrounded in clouds of smoke. Midgets of all races and colors waited on these women. The midgets were men, dressed in pea-green Department of Sanitation uniforms. A lone black piano player, bathed in spotlights and smoke, played a hypnotizing rondo from high above, and through clouded windows sunlight seemed to be streaming, even though Marshall and Al knew that it was night. The women were mainly beautiful, though some were very ugly, and they seemed extremely busy. Marshall and Al remained there, stunned and panting, until a midget with a tray of time drinks walked toward them and slammed a door on the grate. They could hear crushed ice dropping into glasses, and then a few footsteps. They poked their fingers through the grate, but the door was solid steel. They banged on it. Nothing happened. After a while they descended silently and made their way through the tunnel, in which there were then hundreds and hundreds of Specials, including a Dewey or two which tried to bite their boots.

After climbing through a shiny green ceramic tube they found themselves in Union Square at dawn. Millions of pigeons were strutting about, washing or eating. Marshall and Al peeled off their boots and removed their helmets. "They say," said Al, "that sewer gas sometimes causes hallucinations."

"Who's they?" asked Marshall.

"I don't know," said Al, and they began to walk home.

That day they gave up on the sewers and resolved upon bridge climbing. Summer was coming. Alexa was readying for the Gotham Ball and then Rome, and the furiousness and anxiety of her preparations drew the entire family after her. Marshall and Al told of what they had seen. The only one who believed them was Paolo, who, for the first three weeks of June, begged to be taken into the sewer, and then was distracted by the beginning of another dinosaur fad. June was hot, and Marshall took Alexa up to Eagle Bay, where they rode and swam and looked for early raspberries and dived into the fresh rapids of the Croton River. There, overcome by mutual affection, they lay together in protracted kissing as thundering water made them lose track of time.

4

Alexa's escort arrived in patent-leather slippers—she had said that he was a fool. Marshall asked him how he could walk the streets of New York in a tuxedo and ballet shoes. "What happens if you get in a fight?" he added. "How will you protect Alexa? She has a lot of gold and might be a target for muggers. How much money are you carrying, and what's your intended route?"

"Are you a security consultant?"

"No," answered Marshall, "but you need one. You're a robbery about to happen."

"I think we'll be all right."

Marshall followed at a distance. He wished that they would be robbed so that he could save Alexa and be a hero, but they walked straight down Park Avenue and were very safe. It gave him great pleasure to see Alexa fend off the escort's arm on Sixty-fourth Street and again near the Pulitzer Fountain. Hundreds of finely dressed people were there, some having arrived in Rolls-Royces and some in horse-drawn carriages. Entranced, Marshall followed them in. With great protestation, he had refused Alexa's invitation, saying that such things were not for him, and that he would never go near a full-dress ball. She *had* to do it, for political reasons—all the commissioners' daughters were to be there, and how would it look without public utilities?

He got into the ballroom even though he wore sneakers, khaki pants, and a white shirt. Perhaps because of the spirited dancing and loud rock music, no one had noticed him. He knew that he couldn't last long, so he walked over to a servant with a platter of champagne glasses and said, "I'll take that." The servants wore black pants, and white shirts not unlike Marshall's. Young people his age took glasses from his tray without even noticing him, as if he were a vending machine or a walking table. A few gave him tender patronizing smiles, which he answered by screwing up his face into the ugliest grimace he could manage. He maneuvered toward Alexa, who, in black velvet and gold, was a dark star in the collusion of music and marble. He was close enough to hear a Greek-looking gentleman at her table deliver a lecture on oil tankers. "Forty oil tankers is better than twenty. But sixty is not better than forty. International tax structure, especially for the Liberian fleets, favors a centralization of tax advantages in a medium-sized company which can write off depreciation as a function of its total operating costs. It is really fascinating, really fascinating. I will now list for you the fifty standard amortization writeoffs common to Panamanian tax shelters. One . . ."

Alexa drummed her fingers on the rim of her plate. Marshall stood at the edge of the dance floor, looking at her. Suddenly she raised her head and caught his glance. She turned red and flushed as if it were more than it was, as if Marshall had come back from the dead, instead of showing up dressed as a waiter at the Gotham Ball.

Marshall was a spectacle in his khakis and sneakers. An old maître d' bustled up to him and said in deeply indignant lisps, "*Where* are your pants and shoes?" At first Marshall did not hear, so loud was the music and so gorgeous the expression on Alexa's face. "Where are your pants and shoes?" repeated the maître d', astounded.

"On my legs and feet, dummy," replied Marshall, who was then ushered out backward, still looking at Alexa. As he was hustled through the grand pillars he let his tray drop to the floor. Because he was light in coloring and mild in appearance, two waiters tried to beat him up. He made quick work of locking them into a golden sentry booth, through the open top of which he poured a tub of loose dirt. On his way out he grabbed a stuffed lobster from a serving cart, wheeled about, snatched a piece of chocolate cake, and nearly overturned a woman who was making a pompous entry on the Fifth Avenue side. Three doormen tried to capture him, but he sprinted easily up the parkside, with the lobster in his right hand like a baton. Halfway to Yorkville a mounted policeman galloped beside him and said, "What are you doing with that lobster?"

"Treasure hunt," said Marshall. "Methodist Charities treasure hunt."

"Good luck," said the horseman as he veered off.

Alexa returned very late, and he did not see her until the next evening, when, in preparation for dinner, she was sifting confectioner's sugar over apple pastries. She worked at a counter in the kitchen, and when Marshall came in the first thing she said was, "Who knows, maybe I should go to Radcliffe." Marshall thought as she operated the sifter.

"Maybe I should go to Rome," he said.

"Better if it were the former," said Alexa, turning toward him and putting down the sifter, "although Rome would be interesting for us, I think. But I don't know if I want to. I've been in this apartment all my life, and I'm afraid. Perhaps I should go alone, like Ulisse."

Always uncomfortable with such questions unless, like a half-wit, he answered them immediately, Marshall was interrupted by Signor Pascaleo, who came in the swinging door. "Ah, *torta di mele*," he said, wishing that he could have a piece. They spoke for a while about Signor Pascaleo's latest problem and triumph—he had appeared on television during the successful cloture of a burst watermain at Rockefeller Center—when they heard Paolo's voice moving toward them in breathless panic.

"*Papa! Venga, venga!*" he shouted. "*Boofin il capro!*"

All six of them rushed from various rooms to the study, where they saw only white curtains blowing inward in a gentle June evening's breeze. Paolo went to the window and leaned out dangerously. Signora whipped him back in. When they put their heads out they saw the goat, Arctic white and nearly aglow, poised on the thin ledge. His eyes were intently fixed on a roof terrace across the way, about fifteen feet out and ten feet down. Though some wrought-iron furniture and potted geraniums were dispersed on the tiles, the terrace was mainly open.

The goat had all his feet together on the ledge, and was arched like a lute. It was amazing that he stayed on. The distance that he intended to bridge looked far too wide. Furthermore, he had no practice in jumping and was proceeding solely from imagination and will. They were afraid to coax him back, for fear that he would panic and fall the sixteen stories into the courtyard below. And even though they talked to him, they knew that he really did not know English. He began to lick his lips and quiver. Paolo started to whimper. Signor Pascaleo said, "He's a goat, Paolo. He knows what he's doing."

As they were wondering if he could leap, and if he would live, he leaped outward in a powerful perfectly upright movement and sailed through the air with his four legs straight. He looked like Pegasus, like a cloud, like something which flew, and not at all like a house goat. He landed right in the middle of the terrace. His legs went every which way, he lifted himself up after hitting his chin on the tile, and he began to bleat. Then he stopped bleating and walked over to a geranium, to which he helped himself.

Alexa went to Rome. It seemed to Marshall that not seeing her would be the hardest thing in the world, but when she had to leave, she had to leave. He knew that months and years make little difference, because when finally all goes dark, everything has passed as quickly as sparks. The vision of Alexa remained with him.

VI
A Lake in August

1

The years which passed were terrible, Coalbrookdale at night, a sulfurous artificial fire of intellect red within a tight frame, directed energy, over-burdening allusion, heroic rebellion, and finally a hardening as if to steel or iron untempered. On the way to Cambridge one steaming September evening, Marshall's train passed factories full of white clouds and fire, orange to the eye, with dirty furnaces in huge rooms with vast open doors, rooms di-sheveled and eviscerated like slaughtered animals. There was the printer's frame into which letters and words were locked by steel, and the locked leaded glass rigid in the great windows of Memorial Hall lighting a planked floor with shots of spectra. Train wheels over rails for two hundred miles had been noisy like a harbor full of ships with tall masts. Harvard was deceptive, difficult, kaleidoscopic, ancient, hard, and alive.

Almost like a battle, it exacted its toll in numbing, humbling, and killing some, while leaving many far behind. There, Marshall learned what it meant to walk down the edge of a sword. The unutterable resources of bound volumes would have been crushing; the thousand-faced Union; a flood of colors in galleries and chapels; a breathless white moon in perspective from Observatory Hill; the leathern authority of contemplative deans; red-booked revolutionaries running like gazelles from dawn-lighted police; a rapids course of young women more exciting than the White Water; a hundred formed philosophies as attractive as the gentle gleam from the old brass instruments in Dunster library; and the spread of the city as it pulsed throughout four voluptuous seasons would undoubtedly have felled him in demonstration of the frame and his predetermined positions, had it not been for the muffling snow, an insanity on bridges and high buildings, and the first-day piper.

At the very beginning, Marshall crossed the Charles on a September morning so hot that the water seemed to boil beneath the bridge, and the slim rosewood shells, oars extended, were like cooking prawns with sweating riders. This was not a river which flowed to the sea, but rather a lake in August. He went behind the deserted stadium, a prairie of soccer fields bordered by pale and fragrant grasses awaiting the lop of winter. Though protected by steel spikes and chained iron gates, the stadium was easily entered with a little vaulting, squeezing, bending, and jumping. A sign in-formed interlopers that it was the first precast concrete buildings in the world. From its top, Marshall surveyed Harvard's ring of brick and Byzantine towers. The university seemed too massive for one alone, and he wondered if he could survive its temptations and buffetings without going public, en-grouping, running in the packs he knew would be forming and which he almost could feel beyond the rim of protective buildings as the decade itself braced for pressure. He wondered if his place within the scheme would grind him down to synchrony, suspecting that time passing might, in making him old, take from him the spark and catapult by which it was thrown. And as he was thinking this, a furious figure appeared at the other end of the semi-enclosed field. A mass of Black Watch with bare legs and kilt, sparkling buckles, and pipes dark as ebony, he stood rigid, blew up the bag, and began to play. So perfect was the stadium's geometry that the sound was like a massed tattoo, and the piper marched stiffly and with spirit up and down the lines. When he came close, Marshall could see that he was an old man with a wooden leg. After he turned around and marched back, Marshall descended to the lowest bank of seats. Returning, the piper did not see Marshall until he was within ten feet of him. With a single tone of the pipes—as when Lucius had been too moved to continue playing and had stared out over the clouds at a thin rim of sea—the piper looked up and said, "I thought I was alone."

"So did I," said Marshall.

"How do you do. I'm Berry."

"I'm Pearl."

"Same general shape, at least. Please excuse me." He clicked his heels with a hollow sound and turned down the field at a march.

There was nothing greater, thought Marshall, than men like this who had lasted, who were old, whose passions had been refined in fire and in ice and yet whose love was solid and gentle and true. He recrossed the river and vanished into a single turbulent frame of four years, expecting to find his way between the teeth of hardness and compassion, and to survive the blasts of light. Those years were a composite of deepening dreams.

2

Although Al was almost as strange as he was, Marshall had looked forward to rooming with him in a freshman dorm full of noise, conflict, water fights, and discussion. He hoped to make friends, to enter the mainstream, and (by ending his isolation) to have some years without a certain formless responsi-bility which he felt always weighing upon him. He would put up a Harvard flag in his room, join the canoe club, try to last through a dance, perhaps even buy a pewter mug with *Veritas* written on it. Marshall was happy that most of the freshmen on his floor had crewcuts like the brushes on waxing machines, and spoke with *a*'s so flat that they could slide them under the doors. He looked forward to constructive assimilation. However, though Al stayed in Weld Hall, Marshall ended up living alone in an organ loft.

After he had been at Harvard for two hours, his proctor sent him to a dean who sat behind a rosewood desk on an ancient oriental carpet of ruby red. The dean was Australian. He moved in slow motion as if he were thinking hard, and said to Marshall over the exquisite silence of the marbled room decorated with Sargents and battered Persian muskets inlaid with pearl, "There is a prince, you see, from a small country in the Himalayas. His father, the King, casts in the General Assembly of the United Nations a vote equal to that of the people of the United States, and he has sent the boy to us. We are glad to have him. He's smart, an Etonian. And (to be frank) chaps like this always donate a million-dollar chair for the study of some impossible little language. But he applied after the deadline, and we were crowded anyway. I'm afraid . . . that . . . we're going to have to give him your room."

Marshall was displaced. He felt as if he were on a pastel road of royal palms, as if the room were full of halvah, marzipan, and jujubes, as if he were a slave who worked a fan and cracked nuts. "Why my room?" he asked.

"The Prince speaks Italian and wants practice. Your friend Alexander Pascaleo is perfect for that."

"Where am I going to live? I thought you were all filled up."

"That's just it, Marshall, there is no place for you . . . except in the Phillips Brooks organ loft. It's not exactly a room, but you have our permission to fix it up any way you wish, and, should you so desire, you can remain there for four years."

"Tell me something, sir."

"Certainly."

"When did the Prince apply to Harvard?"

"Yesterday."

"Then why doesn't he stay in a hotel, or buy a house on Brattle Street?"

"He doesn't want to be alone."

"Oh."

It was reached by two flights of circular stairs around a pole. He had terrible trouble getting things up there and had to work for a week cleaning and restoring, during which time he fell behind in his reading by at least a thousand pages. It was worth it, just for the sloped ceiling, beamed and white, a dark wood floor, and an enormous circular window with a nice view. The room was about forty by fifteen and ten feet high at the peak of the roof. Opposite the window was an organ of light-colored wood. Marshall spotlighted it. He had an enormous butcher block desk and a straight Chiavari chair, beautiful lamps that he had shipped from Eagle Bay, and a used but still pretty Kazakh carpet. He had a brass bed, and after he had bought only a term's worth of books, they lined the wall like the start of a mosaic. On Sundays he had to let in the organist, a beautiful girl giant from Blessing, Texas, and he watched her from his desk as she played, her bracelets clicking against the old ivory keys and stops. The best thing, though, was the painting. A minister several stories below had felt sorry for Marshall, winding alone up the stairs after his morning lectures, and had lent him for as long as he wanted it an Eakins oil bequeathed a long time before to Harvard. It was entitled: *Prisoners at Bala Cynwyd Build a Bridge.* An early summer's day on a glass-faced river held a score of men bent in consideration and service of the beamed bridge they were building. Though guards with shotguns in arms stood like windmills on the banks, the men working were no more prisoners than the painter himself. They were ecstatic over their bridge; they did not even notice the water lilies and the thick green banks. Once, Marshall, and Wendy from Texas, watched the painting for an hour after she was finished with her music and shaking from the beauty of it, and the rain came down and pattered on the gray slate roof above them.

His isolation complete except for Al, and Wendy the organist, Marshall developed a taxing routine—two books a day, furiously worked papers, and lectures from (among others) Professor Berry of Oxford.

He was tall and handsome. He was so clean that dust flew to him as if it abhorred a vacuum, and it was rumored that he changed his shirt three times a day, shaved twice, and brushed his chalk-white teeth as the clock tolled each hour. When he entered a room the air began to glow and it smelled like an herb meadow or a pine forest. A shiny and bejeweled gold watch that was hypnosis itself dangled from a spangling chain. Because its face was so clean and clear, even from across the cavernous hall, nearsighted students could see time twirling on its chain.

Professor Berry taught exploration, but spent most of the time in digressions informally delivered in response to casual questions. Marshall awaited him in the midst of several hundred cynical students reading newspapers and eating anise cookies cut into the shape of trees. After he entered, he limped up to the pulpit and banged his leg against it for silence. He unfolded a small scrap of paper upon which were inscribed the notes for that year's lectures, and said, "Well!" as he slapped his hands together. He knew that his students—mainly athletes with cataracts of the intellect—made it impossible to proceed as planned, by deliberately asking tangential questions (they called his course "Boats" and they boasted of having "thrown the commodore off the track"), but he took up their challenge, since his lectures were about taking up challenges diverse and tremendous—none too small, none too large, as he might say.

He began that morning with great enthusiasm, hoping to teach them about Pizarro and the Incas. Chuck Wazeel, a shotputter, spoke. "Professah Berry?"

"Yes?"

"I don't mean to lack a propos, but yesterday you grated me into action with your mention of one Cosmas Indicopleustes. I harrowed the library, and of references to the aforementioned individual I found none. Were you in fact creating a Potemkin Village in your mention of this quaint individual, or has history obliviated each of his memorials? I would appreciate an answer to rectify the vistula in my yesterday's transcrible. And could you also tell us about rattlesnakes?"

"Well, Chuck," answered Berry very crisply, abandoning the podium to pace to and fro on stage, "I'm glad you asked that. I'm afraid, though, that I don't know anything about rattlesnakes." He spoke clearly, since most of his students had difficulty understanding British English. "Cosmas Indicopleustes, or the 'Indian Traveler,' was the author, in 550 A.D., of a geographical treatise entitled *Christian Topography*, which, according to Gibbon"—he looked skyward past the busts—"was 'to confute the impious heresy of those who maintain that the earth is a globe and not a flat oblong table.'" Wazeel laughed like a monster, for he had fathomed Gibbon's joke, even if he did think that Gibbon was a Civil War photographer.

"Although Cosmas had visited Abyssinia, Socotra, and the Persian Gulf (he never did reach India), he envisioned the universe as an arched rectangular box under a vault of crystal. On the floor rested Asia, Africa, and Europe, with Mount Ararat rising from Asia. Circling Ararat were the sun, moon, and stars—a sweet picture though not accurate. If only the world were such a simple glassed-over box. Cosmas rebelled against nonbiblical geographical hypotheses, saying: 'Of what use is this or that knowledge of this earth, if by it our Faith is not enhanced?'

"He was particularly adamant about the flat-earth theory. When a child, I had to memorize his works. About the roundness of the earth he said in derision: 'For if men, on opposite sides, placed the soles of their feet each against each, whether they chose to stand on earth or water, or air or any kind of body, how could both be found standing upright? The one would assuredly be found in the natural upright position and the other, contrary to nature, head downwards. Such notions are opposed to reason and alien to our nature and condition.'

"You see, Chuck, Cosmas was right. Newton was more than a thousand years in the future, the theory of gravitation and mass completely unknown. *Logically*, Cosmas was entirely correct. Rain does not fall upward. Nor do trees grow on the ceiling." He paused; the room was hushed. "That is why logic and science are not the final arbiters of *any* question. And that is why you must not bend like a flight of starlings when your leaders, antileaders, or abstainers call for you to do so. The self-righteous as often as not go the path of Cosmas Indicopleustes, encased in the suffocating box of logic, not knowing the airy wonder of future discovery."

Another athlete spoke up. "Uh, Professah Berry?"

"Yes, Fletcher."

"My remembrance of things past deposes the incunabula of a certain personage mentioned in the last lecture, a personage by the name of Atawalpa. After breathtaking scans of the library, I could not unveal mention of this personage. Could you be so kind as to further exchequer along the lines of his existitude?"

"I'm glad you asked that question, Fletcher," said Berry, and so it went until they all exited into chilled puddingesque streets of wet snow—visions of globes and maps, ships and apples, ancient geographers and sugar cookies dancing in their heads like basketballs.

Marshall returned to his loft and hung from a beam by a Whillans harness, slowly swaying back and forth. He imagined a school called "The Cosmas Indicopleustes School & Academy of Opposites" in which pupils were taught from babyhood that up was down, stop was go, red was blue, and so on. Though most would wilt from the agony of opposition and some would be struck down in simple accidents at traffic lights and stop signs, perhaps a few would survive, and throw some light onto modern conundrums descended from the flat-earth theory and other such things.

Wendy came up the rounding stairs, her hair shining, and Marshall reddened with floods of affection. He was not tall enough for Wendy, and he knew that she loved Al. If only he had been a foot higher, or she a foot lower. Hanging from the beam, red as a plum, he returned to dreams of geographers and blue seas on which to sail, although when her bracelets clicked, he felt hopelessly in love.

3

He rose one perfect day in May to run fifteen miles. In white shorts and shirt, his keys hidden under a painting of Teddy Roosevelt, he set out in the strong sun. After a little distance, he decided to get a drink of water in Memorial Hall. It was dark inside but for the sunlight through stained glass which struck wood walls and pale marble. By the time he was halfway across the darkness, alone on a day when not a soul wanted cathedrals or silent halls, he was taken by the light and he lost his balance, falling to one knee. He fell to the side, but put his hand out and pushed up. He thought that he had been a fool to walk amid those sparkling lights, and he was angry, as well as fearful that someone would discover him. At Harvard he had been all right. The dull boxy diet, compulsory exercise, and steady hard work had always kept him from falling. He reached out in emptiness to find balance; his face was bent in pain. It came upon him in waves, a massacre by the all-powerful panes. The blue of a woman's robe, and the red light in a crown, the white from an emperor's name, the gold edging of a cloak, and even the muted coat of a hart—cut him down as if there had been firing squads in the galleries. He felt himself hurtling through the ray-pierced black until he came down hard and unfeeling on smooth stone.

Then the characters and colors seemed to come alive, running and flowing throughout their lighted circles. The entrapped dead women, having held still for so long, began to move their limbs, and they smiled, and they rose and floated to the center of the room busying themselves naïvely in ancient movements and courtesies. There was no way to stand the light coursing through them in their glowing. It was so strong that they were silver at the edges. And then their movements took shape in the vastness of the hall. The decorative equations of suspended angels appeared above, magnetic and enveloping. Christianity, or its symbol (but it was one), swayed him to the West—a gleaming crown of white, crystals shining, a blinding aura and fast blue rivers, fire and ice and shocking energy. If by its art it were to appeal it would certainly enliven. It appeared to his left a round, white, silver, and blue halo suspended on a plane in space, circulating and flashing gently. He loved it longingly, as in a dream of opening waters and the freedom of the sea.

But then in a graceful movement both a smile and a sway, the suspended angels turned his eyes, and on his right the space was filled by a red and green attraction of soft colors like the view into an Easter egg. This was the Jewish East, a loyalty and love which had reached into him like a strong hand and pulled at his heart. It was the softness and memory of a windy palmed coast, the enveloping heat of history. The images—and he regretted that he had been schooled profoundly in images and light—glowed on either side to the obliteration of all other sight. He was rent by the power of their pulling, and afraid that the two would come together. The chiefest woman among them smiled a third time with charity, and the images did begin to move together. Marshall was shaking in terror, but she looked gently at him from above, and the lights met in front of her. When they did, their power was a great spark, a void of white, and every part and piece was saturated with rich red fire. He awakened into a quiet smooth-running world, exhausted but full of quivering energy as if he had just lasted a mortal combat, as if he had just been beaten, and just been born.

One of many miniature rotund Sicilians in blue work uniforms, employed by Harvard to sit on steps and smoke cheap cigars, or lean for hours against the handles of rakes, was opening the great door. Sunlight washed through the hall as if a dam had broken, and was met from the other end, where another maintenance man, rake in hand, opened the facing doors. They met in the middle and disappeared through some swinging panels which led to a staircase going down. Marshall heard one of them say: "Just anothah weahdo . . ."

Marshall stood and felt his balance as sure and strong as if he had had a gyroscope in him. He went to a high railing and mounted it. Standing on one foot, he exercised as if on a balance beam. Though he leaned out seemingly beyond grace, he remained true to center as if he were bolted on. He jumped down and began to walk through the hall, upright and steady.

There, were engraved the names of those Harvard men who had fallen in the Civil War. They were many, and the dates were overwhelmingly burdened with the feeling of seasons a hundred years past. The inscribed Mays and Julys were billowing with early summer and midsummer; the March was windy and full of crows; the January crystalline and numb. The names were so charged and breveted beyond simple designations for town or field that they seemed sunken into the marble-like eyes on an old, old man —Antietam, Manassas, Second Bull Run, Vicksburg, Cold Harbor, Wilderness, Malvern Hill, Chickamauga, Kelley's Ford, Spotsylvania, Brandy Station, Gaines's Mill, Port Royal, and a dozen others. Marshall had spent weeks in the endless stacks of Widener, lying on the floor, imprisoned by *Official Records of the War of Rebellion*, a hundred strong, aligned like troops, dusty and unused. But when he opened the covers the war came flooding out in startling prose. To his surprise, he read in those volumes as if he were reading his own past. This was surely a mystery, since he knew that he was the first of his line in America. It seemed unlikely that he was descended from a Civil War trooper who had somehow cast his seed back to the Old World. But as he read the dispatches he was certain that he had been there; he knew the names; at mention of some places he found himself shaking his head as if in knowing confirmation of a severe battle, or delightful recollection of a starry night, camping by a cedar fire. And once, in leafing through a book of photographs, he had come across a young Union cavalryman gaunt and thin from fighting and fatigue, in what was obviously early summer. The young man appeared to know that Marshall was looking at him. To Marshall's amazement, their faces were the same.

He feared the angels, and the soldiers of the past, for connections were too solid and fluent. There were too many memories where there should have been none, too many messages, a disturbing unreliability of time. He ran from it. Thinking to burn it all out, he ran for miles and miles, hot and deep-breathing, feeling clean and muscular. He ran along the river, vaulting bicycle racks and trash barrels, and he ran through parks and streets. After several hours he loped into the cemetery which overlooks the Mount Auburn bend in the Charles. There he passed the grave of Colonel Higginson, commander of the First South Carolina Volunteers (black troops fighting for the North), the grave of William Dean Howells, and the graves of Henry and William James. He came to rest in a yard for the Union dead and lay down in the shadow of crossed cannon, against the worn headstone of one Nims Burros, who had died in Virginia more than a hundred years before. The government markers were fading, but on Nims Burros's Marshall could make out: *Gone into the world of light.* After his seizures, Marshall always ached as if he had been on a succession of mounts for several days without rest. Exhausted from his running, he lay back in the strong sun and slept, only to dream.

The line of wagons groaning southward with Lee's wounded from Gettysburg had been seventeen miles long. On July second in that battle, the First Minnesota Volunteers lost eighty-two percent of their number after fifteen minutes of fighting; the fighting was as quick as a hardwood fire on a summer's day, the gunfire crackling faster than shingles being nailed down. At Gettysburg alone 51,000 were reported dead, wounded, or missing, and at a simple country church where the wounded lay, they drilled holes in the floor to drain the blood. Marshall recollected these facts in his dream as though his memory of them were real, as though they were true. Lee's lines had been so long stretching northward that Lincoln had said, "The animal must be very slim somewhere . . . break him," and they had.

Wars had been common. The Florida War, the Mexican War, and the wars with the Indians had made soldiers of many, so that "the animal" had hard experience upon which to develop. The Rebels in South Carolina took lead weights off fishing nets and melted them down for bullets, and a lot of Yankees rode out of New York and Washington wearing sheet-metal "invulnerable vests" soon discarded with a fatigued curse. Marshall saw streams of soldiers descending on the Potomac and Rappahannock from country farms in the Berkshires and from the Mohawk Valley, from the light-colored ash woods of Ohio, from Alabama, from West Texas, and from the Blue Ridge Mountains. One of them said, "The old blue Northern's gonna blow." Another said that when the war would end, "Silence and night will once more be united." And they had had something good about them, something young perhaps because they were mostly young, but even the older men and the generals were mysteriously benevolent. "You have to get it out in the open," one had said, "and then everyone gets calm and kind. Wars make for kindness, 'cept of course to the other side." And yet at Vicksburg during the siege there was a neutral place where relations and those who had been friends could meet and exchange news of family and home. Two young soldiers sat for several hours as if there had never been a war, as if that night there would not be the crack and mitre of star shells; when they left they were overcome by genuine affection and regard, and they surprised one another by saying simultaneously, "You take care of yourself now," only to vanish into woods with two fleeting armies bivouacked briefly among oceans of small lean trees. In his dream, Marshall was moved and could not find his place there, but only pieces, as if his sleeping eyes were the flue for buried spirits and they had been dreaming voluptuously of summer battles and the Union Navy off the Carolinas or on the western rivers. There was Jennie Wade, the only civilian to die at Gettysburg. A girl of twenty, she had been making bread in her kitchen when a bullet passed through two doors and felled her. Marshall saw the freshened white wood in the doors where the bullet had torn, and was uncontrollably sad for her, and yet he sensed redemption among the flat fields and lowly rising hillocks.

And then his own tinder began to catch, and his own memories began to come alight, allied to physical pain. First it was deft touching, an incomplete picture, a lighthouse on Chesapeake Bay, a white frame building on piles in the water, a boat full of young soldiers, theater in the capital, candles burning in tin shields, inflated acting, a winter when snow whistled through the cracks of a lean-to, night fires leading to spring, and June, when everything fell into place as clearly as a view from high mountains. He was in cavalry, a trooper, and his horse was named Secesh, a little brown Virginia with alert ears and love above all for fresh corn and cresting the top of a hill. He was there, happy to be with Secesh.

His family had lived next to John Worden, an officer in the Navy, and by means of Worden's influence he had become (strangely enough) a cavalryman. He sailed down to New York and took the train for Baltimore. They went into eastern Maryland and got horses, among them Secesh, and crossed the Chesapeake in a dozen boats. His had twenty men in it, and just for their pleasure they stopped at a lighthouse. An old man greeted them. Inside was a sullen young boy. They had lunch there. The floors were shining and spotless, the room breezy in the autumn, and the table held a steaming cauldron of crab soup. There were loaves of bread, and a cask of red wine in the corner. Throughout the lunch and the cold voyage afterward when the sun was low, he had thought of the horse and how much he loved it, especially since he had just left everyone and everything he had ever known and felt as empty, cold, and purposeless as a detached soldier in his first days of service. But the next morning he rode to Washington, and the warm brown shoulders of the horse were a comfort to him.

Cavalry was stationed throughout the Potomac to protect the capital and converging supply routes often disrupted by partisan raiders of the Confederacy. Led by Turner Ashby, Morgan, Mosby, and Forrest, they rode all night and day deep into the Union and struck like hunters. When intercepted by Union detachments they split up and scattered over the countryside, or sometimes stood their ground, making for the sad sight of dead horses, and the unbearable sight of dead men littered on the fields, toppling over stone walls, weapons discarded beside them, hats off, mouths open.

The Union cavalrymen were more restless than their horses, and they craved speed on the roads and the crack of bullets. In the beginning of June they prayed that Mosby would whip his forces north and wade into a supply train, tearing up the track bed and laying the steel on bonfires of ties, so that the rail would bend of its own weight over a sunlit, face-drying fire. They knew that if *they* were restless, Mosby would be thrashing. Their commander—a major who rode with them—was no fool, and moved them early to the south. When Mosby raided they would hear by telegraph and leap to cut him off. The Major was a Bostonian who sat insanely straight on his horse, studied maps and countryside all day, and said: "Mosby's gonna go in and eat 'til he's fat. And then when he's cruising south with women in his eyes we will ride him down from where he heads for shelter. The only way to stop a raider is to raid. The best way to counter his daring is to out-dare him. Who wants to come with me as I burst out of the woods on Mosby and his troop?" They cheered their acceptance.

In their redoubt dangerously close to Confederate lines May passed like a wave, peacefully, though they had sentries out all night and day and slept with their rifles by their sides. They camped around the Major's head-quarters in a church—a hundred horses and a hundred men clustered about, the church straight and boxlike, echoing inside, upper windows open, tall trees like white columns, pennants and guidon flags wounding the stillness of the ashen deep-set wood. Then on 5 June a man on a sleek distance mount galloped past the cooking fires. He hurried into the church. The Major came running out buckling on his pistol and sword, and he screamed: "Let's go!" The hair on the back of his neck was stiff and his eyes looked as if he had just had a vision. "Let's go!" he said, legs apart, standing firmly to keep himself up in his excitement. "Mount and ride after Mosby!" He was the first on his horse and sprinted back and forth through the trees to get them clear. It was midday, and birds swarmed high in the branches. Secesh was mounted, and when he and his rider moved off, galloping down the road and turning onto a meadow to cut across country, they felt the day and they smelled the last of the pines. His rifle banged on his shoulder. The dark wood, which had been stained by much handling and too much gun oil getting all over the place, was frightening and comforting at the same time. They rode eastward, since close in that direction Mosby was chasing a panicked supply train. Cavalry was coming from the north: Mosby probably assumed so and was prepared. But he undoubtedly thought the south tranquil.

Galloping on Secesh was easy, and it was easy for the horses to run. The rush of the troop, a hundred thundering in blue with weapons and flags, made them stretch and bound effortlessly. He expected to come up on a rise and look past fields revealing a long civil prospect to the sea, but instead they turned north and followed the railroad. They galloped for two hours, then walked quietly, and were fresh by the time they came to a knoll over the top of which smoke was rising. The Major spread them out and they proceeded up the hill. They crested it and looked down.

An overturned locomotive hissed a steady cloud of steam vapor. Scores of freight cars were smashed or burning. The Confederates were dismounted, all except for Mosby himself, who wore a wide plume in his hat. He was scanning up and down the tracks while his men gathered the best of the looted supplies—lobster salad, sardines, Rhenish wine, new repeaters, bolts of smooth blue cloth, jangling hardware. The Major said: "I want him to see me first." They drew their short sabres. A hundred silver unsheathings, a smooth ringing sound, turned Mosby's head like a bird's. They charged down the hill without a word, breathing hard, falling upon their capable enemy, who mounted dismayingly fast, but who were at a disadvantage. Thumping up and over the rails and ties, the attacking cavalry cut many of them down and chased others. The Confederates used their pistols, firing just as often at the horses, who toppled screaming and cracked their ribs on the rails. There was smoke all over from the burning cars. Two officers sat on skittering horses, banging their swords together with no effect. Then they smiled and disengaged. A young Rebel was deeply slashed in the neck and, the wound horrendously open, he staggered toward the wood, certain that he would die.

Secesh was felled and he stumbled into the cinders, rolling over his rider. Everyone went past them. Each step forward was taken with difficulty, as if the fighters stood against breakers or an undertow. They could be heard stepping hard for position. Secesh made no sound. When the rest of the troop lit out after the remnants of Mosby's band and Mosby himself, Secesh lay still on his rider, whose lungs held a bullet.

Breathing was nearly impossible. They took him by train all the way to Armory Square Hospital in Washington. Days later in a trance of white wood and beams in a sunny air-filled room, they told him that the Major had died, that Mosby had gotten away unscathed, that his horse, left for dead, had been discovered grazing quietly by the tracks, and had been taken to a cavalry depot to recover. "Give him fresh corn," he said. A hemp carpet ran through the wide room, which was as clean and well-proportioned as the lighthouse on the Chesapeake. But the lung wound only got worse.

At night they boiled water in a copper cauldron, and there were gas lamps to light the room. They kept him clean, read to him, and gave him opium, but then he died as thousands and scores of thousands had died, wishing only for someone with imagination to contemplate his grave and feel the heat and light he had felt in his fine time, destined to pass too quickly. A photographer came to photograph the ward. In the morning light of early summer, his exposure was very rapid. A man wheeled himself away in a cane wheelchair because (with his leg gone) he did not want to be photographed. But then a nurse persuaded him back and they all stared into the camera, hopeful and delicate as patients will be. And outside, the bees were humming and the soft summer ground waiting. Time had raged about him. He had moved through it coolly, and often with love. He died well, and was remembered, even if only for a time—for rememberers are not immune.

4

A year later Marshall returned to the cemetery to see how the notches in stone which said *Nims Burros* had weathered, and he looked at a tall oak, imagining himself straddling its branches beautifully balanced, leaning into the long telescopic sight of an octagonal-barreled Sharps rifle. There had been thousands of Union and Confederate sharpshooters in spring, summer, and autumn, balanced that way, a rake to their limbs, in fragrant pine branches or in oak. Their balance played and replayed—the delight of getting a good perch hidden in aromatic green, up above the clouds of gnats. They were there, and they were there again, and he remembered so well, or the memory was given to him so well, or so well had he dreamed, that (he concluded) time took its place among the many contravenable forces. Like gravity, inertia, and momentum, time worked its ways and could also be manipulated. Well.

The Prince was named Nataraj Patna, but soon came to be called Nat. In sophomore year he moved to a great Brattle Street mansion surrounded by formal gardens. Nat had a Rolls-Royce in which he explored the country-side, a leather-bound specimen book lying on the seat beside him. He was not one for expensive restaurants and clothings, but he was filthy rich, and would often allow himself rare and unusual things.

Marshall and Al often attended Nat's poker games, in which literally hundreds of thousands of dollars were won and lost of an evening between lethargic and corrupt sheiks, sons of dictators, and the pale hamlike children of the American super rich. Because Al had been Nat's roommate, and because Marshall had been pushed out of the room, Nat allowed them to play poker at the rate of a dollar per thousand. Even so, Marshall and Al had had some tense throat-buckling moments when they had bet far beyond what they could afford, although Nat would have bailed them out, for he was ingrained thoroughly with the habits and mannerisms of a munificent despot, and did not like to see strife or embarrassment. It was hard, though, for Marshall and Al to get along with incognito princes and the confused progeny of billionaires. Nat took to having them over in the afternoon, quite informally.

It was raining tremendous drenching thick wet drops. Al and Marshall splashed through lakes and puddles on Brattle Street. Everything was green and soaked and water began to accumulate in silvery sheets upon which could be seen reflections of trees and bushes. Sometimes the landscape smelled like a wet dog, and sometimes like a sweet garden. Professors sped along on bicycles, their briefcases propped on the handlebars, the rubber wheels splashing through water so soft that it seemed lubricated. At Nat's house, the butler brought them hot towels and slippers so that the highly waxed floors and the intricately worked carpets would not suffer from their dripping. Standing at the fire, Nat looked quite sad.

"Hello Nat. What's the matter?" said Al.

"I don't like the rain. It's dangerous."

"It's not dangerous," said Marshall. "And besides, it cleans everything. It keeps people out of the streets. You can see the architecture."

"Have you ever ridden a horse?" asked Nat.

"All the time," said Al, who had never even touched a horse.

"And you, Marshall?"

"Yes, of course."

"Would the two of you like to come to Beverly for a round of Bushkazi, Chabtal style?"

"What is Bushkazi?"

"A game with horses. It is the ancestor of polo. In the Chabtal style there are three players to a side. Three fellows are up at Beverly already, despairing because no one in the West is or ever will be interested in playing or watching Bushkazi."

"Oh, I don't know," said Al. "Look how fast bowling caught on in the fifties."

"Yes, but there isn't a single floating Bushkazi game in this country other than my own. Ravi Garhwal flew in from Washington just to play today. I couldn't find enough men to make a contest. Would you . . .?"

"Sure," they said. "What can we lose?"

The ride to Beverly was beautiful even in the downpour. Wonderful trees hundreds of feet tall posted and skeined wufts of turbulent fog. Horses danced in the privacy of the rain. The light green and the soaked forsaken browns vanished in supine Icelandic mist. All the way to the Bushkazi, Nat played taped ragas and was lost in a dreamlike state, into which Marshall and Al quickly followed, rolling their eyes distractedly in complete oneness and harmony with the Rolls-Royce.

The hunt club was almost deserted, and Marshall and Al were the only Westerners. The rest were Gurkhas, Persians, Afghanis, and Sikhs. They wore turbans and tunics, and their mustaches were turned as neatly as the curl of a sea nautilus. A vast yellow-and-white striped tent had been set up next to a field of new grass. Inside, on camp chairs, were several older men— mainly Gurkhas and Sherpas. Their eyes glowed. "Thank the Highest One!" they said. "We will have our Bushkazi today, and it will be as if these clouds have plummeted down from the mother of all mountains to spray the land in cold and green."

"We've never played before." Marshall felt quite young.

"And I haven't ridden in a while," Al added.

"That is all right," answered Garhwal. "Bushkazi teaches itself and

takes its players with it. You will move like lightning. In two minutes you
will be as fierce as lifelong players."

"Fierce?"

"Bushkazi," said Garhwal, a man of middle age with a graying mustache
and an enormous frame, "is a savage game. In Chabtal style, very often,
several are injured. In Chabtal style, we use not whips, but staves."

"What do you mean, not whips but staves?"

"In Chabtal," answered a tremendous Gurkha, moving his hand to
indicate great distance, "the inflated skin of a goat is placed in the middle
of a playing field, and the six players rush to it. A goal is scored when a
player tosses the goatskin into the ring on his end of the field. The staves
are weapons with which to knock and smash one's rivals."

"You must be joking."

"No!" replied Garhwal. "It is holy."

"You could die that way. Look at these things. They're thick and
heavy, and long."

"Many die at Bushkazi."

"I'm not playing with staves. No. It may be holy to you, but not to me.
Whips are one thing, but staves can kill."

"You would not be afraid to play with whips, then?" asked Nat.

"No, not with whips."

"Splendid! Mount!"

Before Al and Marshall knew what was happening, they had sheepskin
jackets, leather boots, and stubby whips. The horses were so tall that they had
to be mounted from stepstands, so strong that their muscles felt like steel
cables. The field was covered by an inch of water. Nat led them. His teeth
clenched and his eyes wide, he raced for the goatskin. At the instant he
seized it, Garhwal's whip fell across his back and tumbled him out of the
saddle into the water. Marshall and Al felt their blood boil. They cinched
their legs about the horses' hard girths and galloped toward Garhwal.
Marshall slashed with his whip, panting and spitting, his teeth bared and
the muscles around his eyes making a tight ring. Garhwal threw the goatskin
to the tremendous Gurkha, but Marshall whipped it down in midair.
Almost before it struck the ground Nat galloped up and snatched it. Garhwal
wheeled around and threw himself at Nat, beating with his whip. The combat lasted until Nat threw the goatskin to Al, who had been trying as best he
could to control his horse as the animal turned in circles and dipped its
neck. Al screamed, "Jesus!" and kicked the horse. The horse sensed that he
did not know how to ride, and ran off the field into the meadows.

"Cheating! Cheating!" yelled the other team. They were very angry, but
did not move until Garhwal spurred his horse, saying, "My honor!" and
burst out in the direction Al had taken.

The five of them gave chase. These men (but for Marshall) were tall and of royal stature, their horses were enormous and classically beautiful, and the trappings, bridles, saddles, and costumes were splendid to see on one alone, much less on all at once as they galloped in a thunder after Al, who rode ahead jostling on his crazed horse. He held the goatskin as if it would save him. Marshall watched breathlessly as Al's horse took a high fence. He was sure that everything would stop there. But Al stayed on, and did not lose the goatskin. They could hear his screams, which had changed from those of fear and terror to those of complete physical ecstasy and excitement. They took the fence several at a time, tons of horses and men sailing over a light wood frame, a wave of brown and a chorus of backs bent in fleecy pelts. Al looked back. He had learned by trauma how to ride, and something in him had snapped. (Marshall knew exactly what it was. *He* had had the same madness after the Rastas had come to High View.) Al clutched the goatskin and bent over to lessen the pressure of the wind, urging his horse on to escape his pursuers. They saw him whipping desperately. His mouth was curved in a snurl. He had become a Himalayan bandit.

In his madness, Al directed the horse to the highway. He raced along the shoulder, passing slow-moving cars. The five came after. They were by this time heated and enraged, and had decided to chase him down and kill him. It was neither dark nor light when Al broke through a hedge onto the lawn of a large brightly lit house. Half a dozen men and women were sitting on a porch overlooking the enclosed copse into which Al had burst and around which he raced trying to find an exit. They had been drinking. The men were wearing plaid pants, pink shirts, and canary-yellow jackets: it could easily have been a reunion of the St. Paul's Class of '37. The house guests and their hosts sank numbly into their chairs as Al and the other riders pounded across the slippery lawn and made circles around lawn furniture and bushes. On several occasions, Garhwal and the Gurkha jumped their giant mounts over a garden tractor. Finally they caught up with Al right in front of the porch. The audience gazed in wonderment as Garhwal, the Gurkha, and their teammate—a huge dark Sherpa—exchanged fierce whip blows with Al, and Nat nearly broke his lungs pleading with them in his own language to stop. Marshall made circles about them and, when Al began to draw blood and it flew, spattering the people on the porch, he charged the knot of horses and men. Then Nat charged, and it was a battle royal. Sweat and blood mixed indistinguishably. The horses gasped and tore at one another, their horsey teeth protruding like old surgeon's tools of whalebone. The animals screamed and the men cursed hoarsely in several guttural languages.

The agony and greatness of this was brought up sharp by a sudden blast. The master of the house had taken out his shotgun, and, while loading, had fired prematurely and blown a hole through the roof of the porch. He trembled, unable to comprehend the presence of Sherpas and Gurkhas in skins, the whips, the bloody mounts, the goatskin, the large elegant mustaches, the flashing eyes. Battle over, Al still clutched the goatskin. Nat addressed the man with the shotgun. "Excuse us," he said. "We apologize for the disturbance, but we have hurt no one. My father, His Most Illustrious Majesty Sawatni Patna, is fond of saying, 'Everything that rises must converge.' We are sorry to have converged on your private grounds, but perhaps you should strengthen your hedge, and besides, we have diplomatic immunity."

Al threw the goatskin onto the porch, and the band of fierce horsemen turned about and raced for the darkness and rain as if they were heading for a camp on the wet silver slopes of the Hindu Kush. They thundered back across the fields, faces red, wounds stinging, the wind whistling through jackets and saddlery.

5

Object lessons abounded in Cambridge, though they were mainly examples of what not to be. There was, for instance, the bread. On the bakery shelf of Sweet Tobin's emporium was a sign which said: BAKED FRESH DAILY, THESE LOAVES CONTAIN ONLY FLOUR, WATER, SALT, AND YEAST. NO TWO ARE THE SAME. Marshall could see that they were clearly irregular: they were not the same, and yet he could not tell one from another. So with the many people who pridefully cultivated their differences without being different at all—people who wore bells and shaved their heads, who dyed their eyebrows pink and filed their teeth into circlets and moons, who dressed in skins, wore powdered wigs, went nude, tied logs to their backs, crawled on all fours, wrapped themselves in black satin, carried monkeys, walked ocelots, and put bones in their noses (and there really were people like this in Cambridge, so many, in fact, that it challenged the sanity of many students—and won). These people changed their identities with fashion, and the fashion at the time was to be revolutionary. Marshall was not that.

He was not against change if it were to perfect rather than replace. One might argue that, had the inventors of engines merely continued the development of steam power, there would be no internal combustion, rocketry, etc., etc. "Imagine though," Professor Berry had said on one of his diversions, "a steam engine of the year Two Thousand, having been perfected for more than two centuries with utilization of new metals, materials, and the recent discoveries of pure science. It would be like a shining jewel, as efficient as the geometry of a crystal, something so pleasant to behold and operate that it could in itself be an entertainment, sparkling and miniature, silent and clean, and such an old friend. ☉

"What I am talking about," he had continued, the shafts of dusty light a vital invasion of the wood-dark room, "is the difference between serenity and noise, between deep colors and none at all. If the English had settled in the Arctic for the sake of 'forward movement,' or to satisfy a conceptual model, they certainly would have been mad. Common sense made them reject this prospect. They took the good fertile lands. This is the difference between exploration and revolution, and I would have you keep it in mind. Exploration rejects in a process as homely as a living man that which is lacking in graces and which is unconnected to the scarlet thread of history. Revolution lies amid the cold rocks and cuts the thread. Exploration proceeds along lines of beauty. Revolution is a knife which severs them. And besides, most revolutionaries from good universities become effete, epicene, whining, hermaphroditic muffins, fit only to write for the *New York Review of Books.*"

Witness to countless riots and demonstrations, aware that in political organizations machinelike psychopaths emerged as leaders, Marshall became (among other things) an anti-revolutionary. He saw that power casts a sterile seed. He took as models men like Professor Berry and Ariosto Ben Haifa, his professor of Jewish history—dragonate and of genius, and often quite nasty, as geniuses and dragons tend to be. Jean Jacques Lumineuse, his tutor in English, was a better example than any of the vaunted revolutionaries—despite the wonder that he had written a 600-page Ph.D. thesis entitled "Landscaped Walks and Cracked Shell Drives in Seventeenth Century Rhapsodic Epitaphs," and was at work on his first major tome, "Milton's Depiction of Insects." Then there was Boccaccio Bancamuli, with whom Marshall studied Dante for three solid years—a man who had in one fat gesticulating finger more skill and knowledge than Marx, Lenin, and Rosa Luxemburg combined. Even Bancamuli's nervous assistant, Fango Della Mente, was a tower of virtue, though he did little but long for his fiancée entrapped forever in a minute Sicilian hill town called Centro Biftecca. The list was long, the backbone of Harvard, men who had risen not by politics or conspiracy but by their unadorned brilliance.

Marshall's years at Harvard were not weighted unfairly to action. He often lost himself in the perfect mechanizations of old art and new science reaching out with fingers and hand to feel what the ancient heart had known long before. This convergence was satisfying—to see science flesh unknowing the path of literature as sure and steady proofs rolled in, to see in the infinite lens of a university of minds a deeply moving orchestration of history and its meaning, and the revival in imagination and toil of times almost forgotten—not to accomplish an end, but to keep free a path for grace. All things tied into one flow, as the Florentine had known—the insistent forward metronome, the light tan coat of a hart in miniature or in glowing glass, the reverberating infinite spectra of Whistler oils within the

Union chamber, the heart-snapping ruby lasers pulsing at near full purity, wooden oars rhythmic in the river bay, the wavelike motion of a girl upon her bicycle, the symmetry of the Common and its long lines of trees in ballet, the thunder of trains across bridges across planes of hard white ice across cold black water, or a leaf sadly uncoloring as autumn passed. The images flooded and burst upon Marshall and he saw that they were set within a matrix perfect and unfailingly vigorous. To see each day a hundred thousand views as bright and touching as fine painting and not be blinded or collapsed took much stamina. Art and intellect were the construction upon which the weight was held, though its strength came not from classrooms, concert halls, or the many great libraries, but from physical courage, and imagination of physical courage. Under attack, neglected, placed aside as if it were not a virtue but a vice, it was a balance for the unceasing flood of images.

These taxed him physically. He exercised and learned to accept pain and seizures so that he could continue reception. Like all good things, they came hard, and often seemed overwhelming. Then, his eyes would flash in remembrance of sharp struggles, hunting, combat, and that which had driven men outward beyond their last breaths, beyond their little strengths, chasing upward fueled by spirit. That was one lesson, there were a thousand others, and most drew some blood in one way or another.

Marshall reached the fall of his senior year not realizing that he would leave before he had planned, that in the spring he would not be dressed in a blazer and white pants, squash racquet in hand, thinking about his thesis and graduate schools. Instead, by March he would each day stand knee-deep in a pit of blood, a weapon in his hand, his breath condensing in the cold air of a place full of deathly screams.

6

Autumn lasted only a week. It was summer until the twenty-second of October and winter by the twenty-ninth. Marshall remembered a class in between. As was his custom, he sat near the door—last in, first out. He spent the entire hour looking at a gold doorknob in which the cream-colored floorboards stretched in wondrous perspective to the same vanishing point as a green blackboard (the latter being one of the major paradoxes of education). The lecturer was very tall, and looked even taller in the golden convex mirror—he was easy to track as he bobbed up and down in the white fluorescent light. Outside, summer was dead and fall was dying, autumn—with its leaden light and clean air, its shades and cool afternoons, no insects buzzing, the dead grasses as crisp as cereal. The professor in the doorknob was an historian of diplomacy, the pride of a famous family, Dudley Waldwin

Buce III. In his office he kept long fire matches, one of which a visiting student was obliged to strike and hold level while completing his requests or (in the case of radicals) demands before his fingers were burned. Marshall did the obvious—coated *his* fingers with liquefied asbestos—and spoke at leisure.

Then it was winter. Suddenly it had become white, muffled, frozen. People went from street to street on packed ice and snow. Plow trucks jingled their chains and dark fell early. It was so cold and still that he sometimes expected to see horse-drawn sleds racing down Mt. Auburn Street, and a profusion of many-colored scarves and caps made the whole town resemble the bottom of a Christmas tree. But inside the gymnasium the pool sparkled like a lagoon in the Marianas. It was in a several-hundred-foot blue hall, high enough to keep echoes, banked with spectators' galleries under arched windows. Marshall swam a mile each day. Young men and women in the lightest tank suits churned the water into rapids. They did laps, spun from the high board, flew on the trampoline, worked exercise machines in the mezzanine. There was so much activity that it looked like an ant farm. Divers in silver bathing suits seized Marshall's eye as they whirled into light stars over the water. They revolved like hovering discs and they went off the board one after another as if they were orbiting planets. Under the tutelage of a diving coach with a crimson hat and a whistle, they had become disembodied spirits.

Marshall and Al spent most of their spare time poring through travel books, airline calendars, and atlases. They yearned for the Pacific, for New Zealand, China, Japan, even California. Though it lay 3,000 miles across a whitened winter continent, they thought they could make it, and sometimes found themselves walking west over the frozen river.

They faced a particularly bad exam in January. Their Arabic professor, a chocolate-colored Egyptian who could not say *j*'s (for example, he said "virgin" instead of "version": "Do you know that virgin?"), had gotten overstimulated and required them to memorize a fifty-page economic speech by Habib Bourguiba. They spent days and weeks clucking to one another in Arabic. At dinner they rattled off an hour or two of the text and stayed up far into the night driving it into their heads. They hadn't time for other work. They had become obsessed, neglecting to shave, shower, or sleep. Then one midnight in January, it left them. They had worked up to page forty-five, but found that they could not recall even one word. They couldn't remember how to say basic Arabic sentences such as, "The President of the United Arab Republic studied the matter," and they realized that their other courses had been sadly neglected. They felt pilloried, exhausted, and relieved. "We blew our fuses," said Al, glassy-eyed. He was very tired, tired enough to look like Van Gogh's painting of boots.

"There's only one thing left," said Marshall. "Australia."

"No turning back."

They dressed in good mountain climbing boots, heavy twill pants, and down-filled canvas parkas. They loaded light rucksacks with jerked beef, chocolate, and dried fruits. They took essential documents, fifty dollars apiece, a compass, lethal knives, and paradise cookies (the kind with a chocolate bar on top). In a blizzard at one o'clock in the morning, they walked to the freight yards.

A train came trundling along, shaking the ground. They ran and caught hold of a ladder. Once on top, they lay flat across the roof for fear of being killed by unseen bridges and signal structures. Snow flew into their faces and the acceleration of the hundred-car freight meant that there was indeed no turning back. The train was moving fast enough to convince them that it was not headed for a local siding. They began to freeze, and risked a blow from an unseen bridge to walk the catwalks in the blinding snow and try and find an unlocked hatch. Twenty cars and twenty jumps later they found one and let themselves down. The car was only half loaded, and though cold it sheltered them from the wind. Striking a match, they made out the nature of the cargo—chess sets from Luxembourg destined for Los Angeles. In the darkness they felt afraid, but could only wait for light and the new landscape they would see upon emerging from the hatch.

They sensed from the roar that they were going much faster than they had ever gone on a freight. They could hear alleged thousands of kings, queens, bishops, knights, rooks, and pawns vibrating against their boards, as if they too were shivering. As they passed through the Berkshires and New York it must have been near zero. They exercised to keep warm, and consumed a portion of their supplies. Dawn struck and lit the car faintly gray. They climbed to the hatch and stuck their heads into the bitter cold. As far as they could see were snow-covered fields and rolling hills. Not a farmhouse or a fence intruded. On both sides of the train, fields stretched white like an enameled clasp, the horizon of blank cloud like mountains of snow. The only black was a thin trail of diesel smoke from the engine. Apart from that, the air was fresh, and smelled a little like apples. For the first time that year they looked at the landscape just as it was, empty of human works except for their train, quiet and cold, fleeceless and melancholy, but giving of strength. To see it open in front of them as they crossed it, to see the banded light changing in the distance as clouds swept by in high winds, to feel the untouched air as if on a winter sea, gave satisfaction and enjoyment higher than a world of degrees.

Then they descended, broke into a carton, and played chess until, in half delirium, they imagined that they were the pieces. The train kept its speed; the fields were endless, and Marshall and Al were so cold that for two days they thought they would freeze to death. They were going too fast to jump off, and they imagined Charybdian monsters in the engine and caboose. Several nights out, having exhausted all rations, they lay miserable and groaning on the boxes, bunched up in fetal positions, looking like two kidney beans or a pair of boxing gloves. Marshall remembered one summer in Eagle Bay, when he went into the hills and found a lake surrounded by willows. There, he lay in the hot August sun imagining light wood boats sweeping past. The sun was surely marvelous, moving inside itself like a harpsichord or a heart, and he had slept cradled in its heat.

Shivering and numb, he was grateful for the shattering cold. For it was part of the same wave in time by which he had come once, and would come again, to a lake in August.

VII
A Memory
of the Plains

1

By the fifth day they did not even know their own names. Just able to reach the hatch, they looked past the rails to an open sea of snow. These were the plains over which Marshall had ridden with Lydia from the Rockies to Chicago, through an endless wealth of wheat which shone at them fierce and dazzling. The train had rocked back and forth sharply from day to night. As much as he had fallen in love with her, sunburnt and green-eyed, he and she had also fallen in love with the land. He remembered what he had seen through the window glass a little dark and thunder-colored. Combines spun wheels and paddles in a steady swaying dance. The sun was high and they looked to infinity. They felt as if they could reach out and touch the states, as if Kentucky and the Dakotas were forever, and as if they had been once before and would again be alive, passing through limitless rich cycles. Marshall remembered that summer as quieter than a night without wind or crickets, a time that he knew to be hot and slow. Even failure and death appeared beautiful in the end—so intense and quick-focused was his vision of their form. He was someone's son, and she was someone's daughter. They felt small and inconsequential, but the outside had rolled into them.

Though they had parted as children and twelve years had passed, he shuddered in memory of her. He loved her achingly even in the midst of his ability and independence, and he felt passion for just the thought of Union Station and its vaulted ceilings where birds swooped in the light.

"You know," said Al in a daze of hunger and cold, "when you see this, you realize that despite all the crap that goes on in the cities, despite all the words and accusations, the country has balance and momentum. The whole thing is symmetrical and beautiful; it works. The cities are like bulbs on a Christmas tree. They may burn, swell, and shatter, but the green stays green. Look at it," he said, eyes fixed on the horizon, not unmoved by the motion of the train. "Look at it. It's alive."

"Do you think this train will go all the way to Los Angeles without stopping?" asked Marshall.

"I don't know. I can't see how it could go three thousand miles without changing engines or refueling."

"We must be west of the Mississippi. That's fifteen hundred miles and we haven't stopped yet."

"Maybe we were asleep."

"Excellent," said Marshall.

"We can't be sure. Do you think we should risk arrest, and get up to the engine?"

"What engine. I want the caboose. It has the stoves, blankets, and stew . . . I'll spend a year in jail for that."

"You may have to."

"Look, the snow is at least three feet deep, and it's just flat prairie here. We could jump when we see a town."

"When did you see a town?"

"There has to be a town."

"There has to be a town. Show me a town."

"There," said Marshall, pointing across the snow to a collection of upright rectangles from which came plumes of smoke and steam.

The train was going just as fast as ever when they took their haversacks and climbed outside, where the wind threatened to turn them to ice. In descending the side ladders they found that the steel was painful to touch with ungloved hands. They leaned out two or three feet above the ground, scared to jump. Al said, "Okay, this is like jumping out of a parachute," and flung himself into the air, backward. When he hit, he made a cascade of rising snow like the rooster tail of a speedboat. Then Marshall used the same technique. When he landed, he bounced and came up with a mouthful of white powder; icy crystals covered him.

Al had some blood on his lip. Otherwise, he and Marshall were intact. The train passed, and from the caboose came the scents of a hickory fire, beef stew, sweet carrots, and roast potatoes. They turned toward the town and began to make tracks in the thigh-deep snow. There was no wind. Clear sky, high sun, and their movement made them hot for the first time in days. "I'm hot, I'm hot," said Al. "I love it. Let's get to that town and eat." They walked steadily for hours.

On the outskirts of town they came to a little diner and went in. A lineman, two police officers, and a small businessman who walked on blocks were bent over the counter eating tomato soup and individually wrapped saltines. They turned to look at Al and Marshall. The police glanced at one another and went back to their soup, their brains and hearing ready to spring them into action should the strangers break a window, smash a plate, or talk dirty. The waitress said, "Whatayou-boy-swana-eat?"

Al answered, "I'll start off with a bowl of Hearty Beef Soup. Then I'll have the Icy Cold Atlantic Shrimp Cocktail, and the Thick and Juicy New York Cut Gourmet Steer Beef, with Crispy French Fries and Garden Fresh Salad. With a side order of half a dozen fried eggs easy over, a loaf of toast, grits, and a pot of tea. I'll have three beers, a sardine sandwich, four slices of Rich Fudge Cake, a piece of Homemade Apple Pie, and Hot Chocolate with Luxury Marshmallow." The waitress wrote and calculated.

"That'll be sixteen dollars and eighty-five cents with tax," she said, "and you can pay me now." Marshall finished studying the slate.

"I'll have the same," he said. As she began to cook, one of the police hopped off his stool, adjusted his holster, and walked over.

"You boys sure are hungry, aren't ya?"

"You said it," answered Al.

"It makes me suspicious," said the policeman. "It's irregular like. It suggests."

"It suggests what?"

"That's what I mean."

"What?"

"Talkin' back."

The other policeman came over. It took half an hour of detailed explanation of who they were and where they were going and where they had been and why, to prevent their arrest. At the end, when their mouths were dry and the food was in front of them, the second policeman said, "Just passin' through?"

"That's right," said Al, "on our way west to join the Marines, just like we told you."

"Come here to work?"

"No, we're on our way to California to join the Marines."

"You wanna work, or what?"

"Don't think so," said Al. "We're on our way to California, to join the Marines."

"Come here to work?"

"Nope. We have this idea, see. We want to go to California. When we get there, we want to join the military and fight for our country."

The other policeman spoke up. "Tell me somethin'," he said. "You boys come here to work?"

"Yeah," said Al. "We don't want to go to California. California stinks. The Marines stink. We wanna work."

"You want work, huh?"

"Sure. We want to work our guts out."

"After you eat, we'll take you over to the factory. You'll have to work with niggers, but they won't mind." They laughed as only sheriffs can, and sat down to watch the eating. An hour later, they led Marshall and Al to the back of their patrol car and drove them off toward the enormous complex of buildings that Marshall and Al had seen from the train—tall towers, many-storied quadrangles, grain elevators, tanks, silos, domes, rail sidings, a hundred miscellaneous sheds. As they made for the factory, Al said to the second officer, who had been belching as they sped through the quiescent snowbound town, "I don't like to defame the animal kingdom, but you remind me of a tapir."

"What's a tapir?" asked the second officer.

"That's an animal which can't defecate unless it's standing knee-deep in water. No water, it explodes."

"Where'd them tapirs live?"

"Mainly in Africa."

"Africa!" said the officer. "You callin' me a nigger?"

Al leaned back in the seat and let some time pass before saying, precisely and contentedly, "That's about it."

The officer tried to turn in his seat to strike, but his meal had been too rich. "Damn it, Otto," he said, "stop this car so I can beat his brains out."

As the car was slowing, Marshall spoke up. "Hold it," he said. "Wait a minute. My friend gets a little crazy after he eats too much. He didn't mean it, really. I apologize on his behalf. Please don't do anything."

"I want *him* to apologize," said the fat policeman, pointing to the road ahead because he couldn't bend his arm in Al's direction.

"No," said Al.

"Stop the car, Otto!" screamed the policeman, thrashing.

"Hold it," said Marshall again. "He's crazy, insane. You can see that. I'll take care of him. If you beat him it'll give him fits, and then he might kill himself. Just don't pay any attention to him."

All was quiet and the police were satisfied when Marshall broke the silence. "You know what?" he asked the second officer.

"What?"

"You're a jerk." By that time they had arrived. The second officer jacked himself out of the car. He ripped open the rear door and pulled Marshall from the back.

"You bastard. I was doin' you a favor and you called me a nigger and a jerk." He held Marshall in the air and banged him against the roof of the car. Just then, a call came over the radio.

"Breaker-One-Seven, Breaker-One-Seven. This is KN 8897 Control to Unit Eight. Give me integrity Unit Eight."

"Cut that out, Aldine," said Otto. "You know damn well there's only two radios in this town, and we talkin' in 'em."

"Unit Eight, proceed to section A-2 on a 10–90."

"10–90. That's rape!"

"Negative, Unit Eight. 10–90 means when a washer in the laundrymat is overflowin'."

"I thought that was 10–80."

"10–80 is if a rabbi comes to town."

"We'll get right down to the laundrymat. KN 8897, Otto clear."

"10–4, Unit Eight. KN 8897 Control clear."

2

They walked into a small brick building and found to their amazement that they had entered a great hall. Al stepped outside to survey dimensions. It was little more than a shed. But inside it was no less than an echoing cathedral, empty and dark except for a fire at the other end, burning bright with a heavy metallic flame. They walked over a smooth stone floor, their footsteps resounding in the unseen heights, until they approached the fireplace and a dozen men grouped around it. Some sat on rockers, some on barrels and boxes. All wore bloodstained white overalls. All were old. All were black. They stared at Marshall and Al as if they had been expected.

"Where's Monroe?" asked one.

"He's in the fire," came the reply. "You want me to get him?"

"No, no, I'll get him." He stood up and walked to the fire, shielding his eyes. "Hey Monroe," he yelled into the flames. "Monroe!" Al looked at Marshall, and then they both rolled their eyes. "Monroe, c'mon outa there. We got two new boys."

A man of at least a hundred years stepped from the fire. Partially blinded by the light, Marshall and Al did not see that he had come from a passage in the flue. "It's warm back there," he said, surveying the newcomers. "I go there 'cause I'm so old I can never keep warm in the winter. Now what do you want, if it's not work?" He spoke with gentleness and benevolence, and they felt at ease.

"We do want work."

"There's plenty of work here. Do you know what we do?" They shook their heads no. "We kill animals. It's a bad job, a bad thing. But someone's got to do it. So we do it. We need help 'cause there's lotsa animals around here—cows, pigs, sheeps—millions. You could help us for a time. Then you'll go, but that's all right," he said, smiling. "It's all right with us."

"What are the wages?" asked Al, leaden and serious.

"When you leave, we give you seven hundred and fifty dollars. When you're here you don't have to worry about what to eat or where to sleep. You can go into town sometimes and go to the bar and see the whores. That's paid up. When you leave, you'll have seven hundred and fifty dollars in your pocket."

"How long do we have to stay?"

"You stay for a time, just a time. You won't know how long, no one does, but everyone who leaves thinks the money was good. I promise that."

"When can we leave?"

"You leave at the end."

"When's the end?"

"Whenever you want."

"Sounds like a good deal to me," said Al. "What if you get someone who leaves after a day?"

"Don't got days here."

"How do you mean?"

"Well," said Monroe, shrugging his shoulders, "when you start to work, you can't feel time. But don't worry, we won't take anything much from you."

They accepted, and were led into a room of clean white work clothes. They put on overalls, hats, knee-high rubber boots, and gloves. They were given blue and gray sweatshirts with hoods, and told that sometimes it got very cold. Then they were led outside, where it had gotten dark and they could see blinding stars in clear frozen air, and they could hear the black ether rushing above them between the stars and earth. At times, Marshall thought that he could see it waving like a black scarf, agitating above them. The cold pushed them down as they padded in their rubber boots over the snow past many buildings. At one of the buildings, certainly the largest, they paused before entering. Monroe said, "What you see, you never have seen. When it's over, it's best to forget. While it happens, make yourselves as dead as the winter sky. Never think of the ones you love, not here. When you leave you'll see how good it is to work a day. But now, don't think of children, or womens, your fathers, your mothers, or anyone. Move without thought. Survive."

An eternity after they had started, Al turned to Marshall and said, "Are we in Denver? Is it winter? Is it night? Has time passed? Has it been a million years?" Then he wiped his sweaty blood-soaked brow, and grasped a wood grappling pole. He and Marshall pulled until they thought they would die, eviscerating a steer, with snaps and crushings like a bulldozer moving through brush, as the innards were severed from the carcass. The animal's head lay on its shoulder, bobbing in death with wide-open eyes as the two of them pulled the carcass apart. Its stomachs, intestines, kidneys, bile, bladder, heart, and blood forever spewed from it. When the cows were led inside from the cold winter where they had languished in darkness, they mooed in delight. Then they were penned, a man with a heavy hammer walked up to them, bent his frame, showed his teeth, and struck with all his might. They lurched backward before the blow, pulling in their forelegs with bent joints, banging the iron walls. Then they fell forward with an exhalation and sigh, folding their legs, turning their heads strangely upward. A chain was attached to them, and they were dragged, sometimes with their lives flickering, and an eye open despite a crushed skull and spilling brains, to Marshall's and Al's pit.

Because Al was tall, he cut open the belly as Marshall turned a blood-covered winch. Then they pulled it apart, shoveling flesh and fluids down a sucking chute. They heard from Monroe that pigs were sawed in half while still alive, and they did not know about the sheep. They themselves moved dreamlike, not eating, not sleeping. And time passed as if they had been riding drunk on a cross-country train bombarded by the sight of a hundred thousand houses and enough corrugation and ditches to choke the world. They never caught their breaths. It stayed night and absolutely cold. A great furnace provided heat. It was behind them and it sounded like a water-fall of oranges. They saw it each time they turned, or reflected and glowing in the orbs of the cows' eyes—fire by night to fight the freezing, blasting in tongues to drown the nonlingual animal moans.

Every cut and pull drove them down and yet strengthened them. They thought of how in the East their rich clean friends had spoken pridefully of necessities, of how it was merely sentimental to care about animals, of how man was pre-eminent and all that mattered. If they could only stand here knee-deep in warm blood, thought Marshall, and pull out the occasional fetal calf hardly dead itself; if they could only hear the cries, and see the expressions, then they would say how wrong they were. Sentiment implied weakness. Marshall grit his teeth, bloodstained, as the blood splashed his eyes, and felt the great power in his arms and chest as he worked the winch and cut. Let them be hauled in here and winched up, he thought, if they think this particular compassion sentimental, the bastards.

They wound in and out of moods as if they were running a river with bends. Al said, "You work all your life playing by the rules, honest and fair, trying to be good and to achieve excellence. Then a law is made and the whole damn thing turns upside down and you have to turn around and start upward again, from the bottom."

"It strengthens you," said Marshall, straining.

"Or kills you."

"No. *Strengthens* you. I'm not going down on that, never. The bastards can swivel the glass a hundred times and I'll start up again, by my rules, for what I love." He was hoarse. "*Nothing* is going to keep me down, *nothing.*" He pulled at an enormous spilling carcass, tears in his eyes, sweat coursing down his temples, an expression of horror, fighting, and live battle on his face. "Not until I'm still in the grave, not until there isn't a breath left, not until I'm dark dock dead—*damn.*"

It is hard to imagine how thin they became, how gaunt, and how ridiculous. They could never understand why night continued on, why the stars and furnace were unceasing and unbending. Nor could they always fathom Monroe, or heed his advice. Sometimes they did think of the ones they loved. And then it was a blazing pain, as if the cows they butchered were themselves. Al almost quivered at the thought of Wendy, sweet and tall, far away in another world. The ride west over the same land that he and Lydia had used to forge themselves together had caused in Marshall a sudden and almost frightening upwelling of her image. He was shaken and surprised, and he dreamed of her, frustrated and angry that he had never seen her as an adult. When they thought of those they loved, it almost killed them, and they entered a band of numbness, doing their work with only the hope that they would survive.

"If I could pick up my father and hold him in the air, and pinch Alexa until she attacked, I'd be so happy," said Al. "This is a mean trick in time."

Marshall could only agree. Lydia was too distant for anything other than deep memory. But in the cries of the cows, in blasts of fire, in the thundering doors which rolled open to reveal a winking black sky, in defiance and tension, in blood and reduction, in lack of time, in Monroe's slow gentle talk, in the brightly colored flags Marshall sometimes imagined that he saw, and angels descending to comfort the cows, in the inescapable flatness of plains and sky through which time skipped and pivoted without control, skidding across the countryside, in the elements of the place, and in his exposed memory and heart as if he too had been torn and opened to the air in the high, giddy, beam-filled shed—he found that he loved Lydia (even if he could only imagine what she had become), that he was directed to her, and that his resolution in the station would be the backbone of his life, as steady and sure as a steel rail. America was spread about, round like a compass rose, and though it was winter, spring was somewhere. In his anonymity among the steaming carcasses Marshall thought that spring would come to shatter the prison. Monroe had said in his slow speech, "Never talk down the power of gentle things. They come from underneath and open up the earth, like shoots and flowers."

3

After what seemed like several lifetimes, Monroe came and called them to the furnace, where he stood next to the open door. "It's half over," he said, "and now you can go outside and walk on the snow. The top is frozen and will hold you."

"But why?" they asked.

"Simple," he answered. "Your time here is half over, and you have something to show for it. It's like a clock. They turned the furnaces outward so the air above the ice won't be cold. Don't stay long, but climb the little hill and look to see spring. This is the night it makes itself known in the mountains. I think you should see."

They started to put on their sweatshirts, but he stopped them, saying, "Look. Look at the furnaces." He took them to the door, from which they saw an orange glow over the factory grounds. Manifolds had been directed to the outside, and currents of warm air flew about the courtyards. They found it delightful as they walked slowly in the dark toward a small hill. Looking back, they saw the factory, which stretched for miles. They had not imagined its great size. Hundreds, perhaps thousands of chimneys steadily gave off smoke. At their bases were licking rondels of beating flame. The line of these lights stretched to picket half the horizon. Black and silver towers were just visible against the sky because they blocked out stars. It remained busy; the fires burned with a pounding noise.

Having turned from the factory, they continued to the hill and arrived at its top. A flat plain fled for hundreds of miles, interrupted only by the factory. As if they had been in the center of a round card, they saw around them a perfect circle. Along the entire perimeter were low mountains, jagged and full of visible angles, like the mountains of Mars. Across their peaks, in a full circle, rose-colored fire was strung in lines of spark. It appeared as if the world's rim had caught in warm flame. Garlands of it made the mountains glow.

The turbulent breezes which crossed and folded above seemed also to be mild, despite the clarity of the air. Had they closed their eyes, they could easily have imagined palms. They had never realized that spring announced itself by running rings of lapping fire. It was half over, and they slid down the hill and began their walk to the factory.

They expected to resume the slaughter. But Monroe came to them and said, "Tonight they stopped it. You can wash in the baths, and go see the whores. Are you tired? You see, I told you. Some times, they go to the whores two times, or three times, or none at all. You can go once." He smiled, and padded away. Then he turned, saying, "C'mon, I'll take you to the baths."

They came to a little wooden door at the end of a walk which wound between the giant buildings. Monroe opened it. It seemed as if no one had been there in a long time, though it smelled quite fresh. He groped around looking for the lights. They thought that they were at a workmen's bathhouse, with gritty floors, missing shower heads, and forty-five seconds of almost hot water. "Here it is," he said, flicking a switch.

A hundred and fifty heavy floodlights positioned around a vast ceiling of Finnish arches and cedar beams projected thick penetrating rays throughout the baths. A central rectangular pool of bright blue water took up most of the room. Monroe said that it was 200 feet long and 100 feet wide, and that at one end it was seventy feet deep. Around its edges were smaller pools—a thrashing whitewater mechanico, a little blue ice cube over which vapors condensed, a mineral hot spring, warm and shallow rivers interconnecting the static bodies to feed and refresh. At one end of the main sea stood a permanent scaffolding of heavy aromatic beams, on which were staggered diving platforms ranging to seventy-five feet, chutes leading into the water, tilted trampolines, ropes and trapezes on which to swing out and let go, and a wire on which one could glide by hand trolley high above the pool, choosing when to drop. Waterfalls and fountains poured into the main and small rafts had drifted to its edges. Gymnast's rings and a high bar were suspended over the far end.

Monroe went to a great armoire to fetch a load of supplies, which he set down before him. "This one's for you," he said, "and this for you," handing them green velvet towels, soft, new, and blanket-sized. Then he handed each of them a piece of soap as big as a melon.

"What's that?" asked Marshall. Monroe squinted at him, as if Marshall were crazy or from another civilization.

"That's soap. Ain't you ever seen soap?" Marshall looked at the turkey-sized mass in his arms, which weighed at least fifty pounds, and said nothing. "What influences you?" asked Monroe of a sudden. It surprised them.

"What influences us?" echoed Al.

"Yeah, what influences you? Don't bother to answer, 'cause I already know. Now you can stay here for a time, and then you can go to the bus, and the bus will take you to town."

"How long can we stay?" asked Marshall. "This place looks better than whores to me."

"You can stay for a time. You come again before you get paid, to wash up. So only stay for a time. You have to be clean for the whores. Disease. Use the soap to wash. I'll be back in some time." He left, carefully closing the door behind him.

First they had endless showers, wrestling with the soap. Then when they were clean they put on bathing suits that Monroe had left for them, and began to work on the amusements. What a delight it was to sail through the air and crash into the clean water, to climb the beams, to fly on the trapeze and then release, traveling like a dolphin into a broken front of white wave. Finally they were so tired that they fell asleep on rafts, only to be awakened by Monroe, who stood at the side of the pool and tapped a gourd. They dressed in black pants and white shirts which were baggy and did not fit, so that they looked like Russians. They were apprehensive, for they had never been with whores and did not want to be; but it had been an eternity without women, so they went to a little bus full of other workers in ill-fitting clothes, and sped to town. Behind them the factory was lit like a crown of flames.

The bus let them off in front of a bar. Inside was an enormous purple room, in the center of which hung an electric sign which read: ST. LOUIS. Music and light were so profuse, and the atmosphere so wild and deep with sex that Marshall had the overwhelming feeling of being on a rock in the midst of fast-running, breaking, thunderous rapids; with trees being felled and cliffs collapsing; houses, cars, and logs sweeping by; and the observers stolid in the middle. Light smoke coursed through the room, rising in eddies like mist from the rushing river.

It was filled with whores of sex, who sat blinking in satin draped over their revealed bodies. A thousand-lensed sphere turned above, tapping out interruptive rays. The color violet and the flashing lights began to defeat Marshall's will. He hoped that any convulsion or battering would come later, upstairs, or wherever they would take him. He was ripe for the taking. In a minute he was glossy and gone.

Sensing deep ecstatic breathing, a purple sister glided across the darkness smooth and iridescent as a shark. She sat down at their table and stared at Marshall's eyes. Al was negotiating a treaty with a long-legged black beauty. The woman of flashing lights stared Marshall into liquefaction. She seemed just loose and lithe enough, and her face was lit with the intelligence of sex. He could not see if she were in any way beautiful, because he was too moved by her other elements. Normally, he linked love with love. But lost in the revolving ultraviolet of that bat cave, he said what the hell, and when she took her breasts in her hands, stretched her neck upward, closed her eyes, drew in a breath, and said, "I want to be sucked," there was simply nothing to do but stagger after her to the far end of the room, where they mounted a circular staircase to the second story. A small chamber had a floor of glass bricks through which purple light from the room downstairs came darkly and thick. She unhooked and dropped all her shiny satin in a moment and lay on the bed, moving. "The ocean is coming up here," she said, pointing to the end of the bed. Marshall had always loved the ocean.

4

On the way back to the factory, heaters puffing over limp, exhausted men heading once more into endless night and work, Marshall had a luminous memory and, like an old man, was overcome with affection and love for a moment in his past. Remembering it, he understood that nothing vanishes, that between the mirrors of heart and mind is a meditation long standing, infinite, and full, that Jamaica still lay hot and lush, as green as a bird of green feathers, slow-moving like Jamaican speech. He had it precisely, a locking incision. Dash's kiss tasted like apricots. Even Farrell's death and the arrival of the constable had not altered the bloom of his rosy trust. From High View he could see that ships were shearing across a blur as green water hissed through the reefs.

When they arrived, the other workers left for their stations, but Al and Marshall were told to go inside and see Monroe. They expected the worst, for it was said that after the first visit to the whores, a new man was sent to the killing chamber, there to bludgeon the steers. Inside the cathedral room they approached the old men, one of whom said, "I suppose you came to see Monroe."

"That's what we were told to do," said Marshall.

"Okay, I'll get him." He hopped up and walked to the fire. "He's in the fire again. Monroe! Monroe! Come outa there!" Monroe appeared.

"Oh," he said, "it's you. You been gone for some time."

"That's right," answered Al. "We've been gone for some time. Monroe, some times it's irritating to listen to you, since you have no idea of time."

"Do *you* have an idea of time?" questioned Monroe.

"More or less."

"Then how long you been gone?"

"About ten or twelve hours," answered Al.

"Ten or twelve hours!" Marshall said in astonishment. "It was no more than forty-five minutes."

"I haven't seen you boys for some time," said Monroe. "That's all I can say." He looked around, and then said, almost under his breath, "You boys interested in a short card game?"

"Short!" said Al. "You see!"

"What you mean?" asked Monroe, genuinely puzzled, taking a stubby deck of cards out of his overalls. "We plays with short cards." He held one up. "You can get a credit of two hundred and fifty dollars on your pay for the card game. You want to play?" The old men were poised on the edges of their boxes and rockers.

"Why not?"

"Yahoo!" they screamed, moving like greased lightning to set up a table, lower a gambling lamp, and put a big mesh grill on the fire. "That's for shrimps and bacon," one said. "When we play cards, we grill up shrimps and bacon, and drink beer."

"Suits me," said Marshall, for he loved shrimp cooked on an open fire. "Got any soy sauce?"

"Any *what* sauce?" asked Monroe.

"Soy sauce."

"What's that?"

"It's a sauce they have in Japan."

"Is this Japan?" queried Monroe.

"No."

"Then we ain't got no soy sauce."

Quickly is not an adequate word for how fast they lost their $250, and they didn't get one bit of shrimp or bacon, or one sip of beer. In what seemed like the most superbly co-ordinated collaboration in the history of mankind, the old men conspired to distract, cajole, and waylay them, depriving them of food and money. Just as Al or Marshall would reach for a sizzling lean shrimp, a man would pick it off the plate, and another would say, "Call!" They carried this off with unimaginable skill until Marshall and Al were completely skinned. Despite the smell of broiling seafood, neither Marshall nor Al was hungry. "Now you only got five hundred dollars in your paycheck," said Monroe, "but that's all right, because spring will come, and you won't need too much money."

He looked at Marshall and said, "I said you'd ride to the plains, and you did. And I'll tell you that by the time you get to the mountains, you won't need money at all. And then you'll go away, but in some time, you could be back." He laughed. "What's that stuff? Joy sauce?"

"Soy sauce."

"Like I said, this ain't Japan." He disappeared into the fire, and they walked through the darkness to get back to work pulling apart the sad-looking bodies of slaughtered cows.

5

Al schemed to resist the timelessness. He offered a nearby worker his pay for a watch. "What do you want me to watch?" asked the man. They decided to observe the course of the moon, but there was no moon. They counted cows and, after some time, compared figures. Al said they had processed three, and Marshall said a hundred and twenty. So they gave up.

They were working hard when they heard a singing noise in the distance, like the vibration of high-tension wires. It got louder and louder. They dropped their knives and rakes, and rushed to the door.

The sun was coming up fast and big, as if it were in a telephoto lens. They could hear musical tones and reedlike vibrations. In a vale of gold, it mounted steadily to a natural position high in the sky, where it seemed not to move but rather to beat and pulse. Steam covered the landscape as the snow melted and the fields became spring green. They could smell cows in the holding pens, see white clapboard houses in town, hear distant freights. The sun was warm, and the steam from straw-colored ground was good to feel. In the west, a range of mountains appeared as a light purple haze on the horizon. The plains flowed in all directions like a windy gulf.

Waving his arms, Monroe trotted down the path. "C'mon with me," he said. "C'mon. Spring came. It's time. Gotta wash up, wash up." They ran after him to the baths. The door was open and a ticket-taker stood in front. "Okay for these two," said Monroe, and they went inside. It was packed with screaming children, adolescents, women, workers, and even old people crammed into the mineral baths. Sunlight streamed through fifty-foot windows, and puddles from the children's splashing covered the floor. They received watermelon-sized soaps and green towels, and soon after they had washed, shaved, and immersed themselves with the octogenarians in the hot brine pools and fresh-water rinsos, they went outside into an emerald of a prairie day. Flowers had arisen on the fields. The climate was perfect. Their clothing had been cleaned, and Monroe gave them each fifty brand new ten-dollar bills. "You feel healthy, don't you?" he asked. "The mountains there are west, as any fool can see." He made them kiss him goodbye, and then went about his business. Al had decided to head south. He wanted to see the Andes, but Marshall was to continue west. They agreed to meet on top of the Eiffel Tower at noon on July 4, 2000. Then they shook hands and parted.

Marshall walked silently through the courtyard of the slaughterhouse, past brick walls and smoking chimneys, past dozens of men in gray and blue hoods and bloodstained clothing, men who did not see him while they worked amid the carcasses and trucks and black smoke rising upward in a coil of bitterness. He walked as if in a military review, or graduation from a European war academy. But no one looked as he made his way past the brick and the wood, on which shone a golden sunlight as if from underneath a ceiling of storm clouds. He had lasted the slaughter intact, he was as solid or more so than he had been, and he hoped to leave it forever, graduating from that school with a full beating heart, heading west on a day into which a piercing ray had penetrated decisively. Monroe had said that spring would come—it had.

6

His warm parka was neatly rolled and lashed to the strap of his rucksack. They had not only cleaned and pressed his clothes, but repaired and waxed his mountain boots. He traveled across a flat, endless prairie, an ideal picture of a man walking. Healthy, somehow well-fed, clean, strong, and happy to have lasted his slaughtering task, he walked with buoyant step toward the mountains. He knew that eventually he would come across railroad tracks, and there he could jump a freight. Meanwhile, in the sunshine, he thought about Monroe and Professor Berry.

They had curious similarities. One snowy day in Cambridge, Marshall had been winding from room to room in Kirkland library and had come across Professor Berry alone in a firelit study. The strange thing was that Professor Berry had been standing practically right in the flames. He quickly hopped out, and made some excuses about having lost his watch in the fire.

And once, a hairy ruffian had invaded Professor Berry's famous lecture on Magellan, and shouted him down. This ideologue had beaten professors, stood nude in the Yard, and shouted obscenities at children. In these activities he received thorough support from many not on the scene. But he did not dare touch Professor Berry, whose health, strength, and willingness to fight deterred him like a battalion of Gurkhas. Professor Berry looked at him with compassion, understanding, hate, and disgust. After uttering some nonsense about colonialism and imperialism, he turned to Professor Berry and said, "Like, look at you. Like, you're looking at me like I was like an animal."

"Like you are an animal," replied the good, one-legged professor with such severity that the room vibrated. "And you will like remove yourself from my class or I will like murder you and tear you into like small indivisible pieces uglier than your original self." The ruffian didn't budge. Professor Berry was suddenly galvanized; his face beat with red and purple blood; and he charged with unstoppable ferocity, his wooden leg thundering against the floorboards. The ruffian ran out the door. Professor Berry remounted the podium, straightened himself, and resumed his lecture despite the wild heart-pounding applause of his students, who loved their professor for his courage in the face of the wave.

Then Marshall recalled what Monroe had said. He had been standing amidst the screaming half-slaughtered calves: "I been in every state in the Union, on the railroad. That was before I retired, some time ago. First, I worked in the dining cars, when I was young. In those times, rich men rode in cars bigger than houses. You wouldn't know about that. And we used to serve them all kinds of fancy dishes—Forfit of Cheese Mongolian, Paté of Turk, Larchmont Birch Beer, roasted Plant Pappy, Honeymoon Bungalow Cake, and Log of Chocolate Byzantine. But we never did what was dishonorable. We never bent our necks, no sir, and we always bucked trends. I say, fuck 'em. It throws you down and knocks you out, but when you get up again you feel twice as strong. I know. I did it. I do it. I been from Alaska to Alabama. I seen babies born. I seen bullets stop dead in the air. You always got to fight trends. You get alone, but it strengthens the heart." He thought for a while, knitting his brows. "Britain stood alone. Lord, there is a texture in life, and a reward."

Marshall caught sight of a magnificent, earth-shaking, three-hundred-car freight shuddering across the sunlit plains. He began to run, pounding over the flat ground. It was a joy to run, and, like a horse in effortless gallop, he came even with the train. He took hold and sailed onto it. Once on top, he sat on a catwalk and looked at the rolling grasslands and distant mountains. The landscape was nearly maritime in its expanse—like a Homer painting. He bent his head and lifted his eyes to the slit of the horizon, making a clean thought of the colors. They were so strong that he could almost lean against them as the train started up the western grade to the mountains.

Proceeding to vast areas of thinner air, he found them quite different from the Hudson. At Eagle Bay Marshall often looked through his white-framed windows into a green and humid landscape suggestive of a badly managed terrarium. The trees were wet and entangled, with corky bark and a sense of lizards. The fields were rich and loamy. But in the cool mountain range the trees were mainly evergreen, their disciplined quills as neat as a good hardware store; the dry pine scent inseparable from the wind whistling through their needles. There were some poplars and some ash, their leaves rippling the light like sun-covered water or bronzed sequins. He could tell that the water was fresh, just by looking at it. He was excited to be approaching once again alpine country in which bear, elk, and mountain goats bolted across unknown pastures close to the stars. The train went around bends, through the trees, over bridges of match-stick steel—vertical nets of metal contoured against red ravines with streams of white foam leaping down the crease.

Rather than cross the Continental Divide, Marshall left the freight on the eastern side at about 10,000 feet. He headed southwest along a great valley between mountains on which snow rested in patches near the summits. The land was so perfect that he made no mistakes. A bias right or left brought him either way to deserted meadows surrounded by blue spruce. On one of these meadows he discovered a small herd of mountain goats, or perhaps they were bighorn sheep. Who could tell? With the excitement which always comes upon seeing a wild animal in nature, he walked to them in slow, measured step, as if by negotiation he could approach and finally take them in his arms. He wanted to pick up a little one which had snow-white wool, ribboning curls, a palpitating heart, and an astonished, abandoned look. He would sit in the meadow and rock it until it slept, while its mother and father surveyed the distance.

At first, they froze. Only their great brown eyes moved. But when he was about 200 feet away they rose; the rams and the ewes, and then the lambs. As he was quietly tacking toward them, they suddenly started in combustive motion and (strung in a line like a rosary) vaulted and jumped into the forest, smashing down brush like a panicked infantry company, heading to some deeper meadow known to them for its safety. He loved their alert faces bent in arches and cheeked over like chestnuts, with sole-purpose eyes and razorlike gazes.

He spent that night in a meadow, curled up in his down parka. As it darkened he had nothing to do but lie back and watch massy white fonts of cloud illuminated and outwardly tumbling as they sailed by. The strange thing about the mountains was that hunger, thirst, cold, and other deprivations meant little. As long as they were not extreme, they served to sharpen the view. Marshall's supplies ran out two days off the train, and yet he walked rapidly and well. He subsisted on cold water, berries, and his southward momentum on the ridges. Dark as a brown penny, he grew nearly as thin, and began to remind himself of the way he once had been in the Rockies, in a world he perceived as a paradise saturated with adversaries.

7

Marshall came upon a saddle between ridges, in which he found a small, perfect cabin, a corral, a meadow where two horses were grazing, a shed, and a stream channeled into a trough and out again past a waterwheel in a little generator house. The place was so neat that it might have been Switzerland—cords of clean split pine lay stacked in rows; the horses' hay was like combed hair; a small kitchen garden was tilled in straight tracks, immaculately weeded, and organized with the touch of science. Birds were singing; the sky was clear; and it was ten o'clock in the morning.

He could see no movement. He came out of the woods, walked past the horses (causing them to neigh and skitter), and went to the water trough, waiting for someone to appear on the porch. He was sure that by venturing into the open he had telegraphed peaceable intentions. A tin ladle hung from the side of the trough. He picked it up and dipped into the fast water. As he bent his head to drink, a rifle shot rang out from the house. The bullet passed so close that he felt the turbulence of the air. But, to reaffirm his peacefulness, he did not budge, and only turned his head a bit and smiled tentatively. Another bullet whined past; the crack of the shot reverberated against the trees. Still, Marshall did not move.

A tall black-haired woman kicked open the screen door (she had been firing from a crack near the window) and stepped onto the porch. As the door opened, Marshall saw and smelled a pine fire. The woman was holding a lever-action rifle, which she kept leveled at Marshall. A pistol hung from her belt. She wore a white blouse with ruffles at the collar, and her teeth were as white as the New Mexico moon.

"Take off your damned wig, Felipe," she commanded.

"This is my own hair," answered Marshall. "I'm not Felipe, either."

"Well you don't look like Felipe. Where is he? Who's with you?"

"No one's with me. I don't know Felipe. I'm alone, no weapons." He raised his arms and turned around and back. "See."

"Where are the provisions?"

"Provisions? I don't know. I wish I did."

"Aren't you one of the delivery boys?"

Marshall looked about at the uncompromising wilderness. For days he had seen neither a road nor a human habitation—not even a cable, a distant structure, or a fence. They were high in dreamlike mountains, and she was talking about delivery boys. Perhaps she was mad.

"Look," he said, "I'm not a delivery boy. I don't even know exactly where I am. I mean you no harm, and, if you'd like, I'll just keep going, if you'll point to a place where there's food." She softened, and leaned the rifle against a post. As Marshall breathed easy, she drew her pistol. She did not direct it at him, but held it pointing to the ground, her finger on the trigger.

"There are these delivery boys," she said breathlessly, "these crazy craphead delivery boys that bring supplies up here every two weeks. The university has it contracted with a general store in Santa Fe. They cheat like hell. I get all the old vegetables and dented cans; and they come in the day, in the night, anytime they want; and they try to rape me. I shot *two* of them," she said, holding out two fingers, "but they keep on coming back. They like to get shot. The last time, they were drunk as dogs and they returned my fire. It was a gunfight. I was afraid for the horses. The delivery boys loved it." Marshall's mouth hung slightly open. "The dirty bastards open my mail. That's a federal offense! But they don't read it, because they can't read. They think that if a letter comes for me from, let's say, Berkeley, it'll have dirty pictures in it. They must imagine that the people there walk around naked. Actually, they do." Marshall loved her breathless energetic speech. He wanted to tell her that he understood why the delivery boys were willing to die for the chance of touching her, but decided that she might overreact. "What university contracts for your provisions?"

"This is Pinnacle Mountain Biological Station," she said, "of the University of Chicago. There's no sign because no one ever comes here. I'm the director, secretary, chief scientist, and support cadre. Who are you?"

"I'm Marshall Pearl, no titles. Except, perhaps, ex-student of Harvard College—didn't graduate."

"*We* know," she said, like a six-year-old. "I'll bet you're just another goddamned delivery boy. I'll bet I'm going to get raped."

"No."

"What's the name of the big library there?"

"Widener."

"Who was Rimbaud?"

"Rimbaud?"

"That's right, Rimbaud. Everyone I ever met from Harvard brings up Rimbaud, Gascoigne, and Goncharov within a minute and a half." Marshall gave brief histories, and she approved.

"All right," he said, "who was Cosmas Indicopleustes?" Her face went blank. They sensed an engaging tension, a playfulness irreverent and private, which had sprung up between them already. For the next hour they discussed Cosmas Indicopleustes and other things, and at the end they were sitting on the porch, leaning against two posts, facing one another, at ease. Her name was Nancy May Baker. She said that she was from Kentucky, and this seemed to be confirmed in her speech and stride. She offered to feed him, so he followed her into the cabin.

It was a single large and airy room with six or seven crossbeams from which all kinds of equipment were suspended; its floor was of shiny pine. Along two walls were shelves of reference works in the sciences, and probably every book ever written about eagles. In half a dozen languages and all colors and sizes, they filled one entire wall. The other wall held the more general books and about 250 looseleaf binders. These contained observation records. On a long heavy table a few feet out from the book walls were an IBM typewriter, a fluorescent lamp, office supplies, dictionaries, a slide projector, and bird magazines. Telescopes, tripods, 1,000-mm. lenses, cameras, folding blinds, and mountain climbing and camping gear hung from the rafters. In a corner stood several large jars of formaldehyde with unrecognizable shapes within. Against the back wall were an iron stove in which burned the last of the breakfast fire, supply cabinets, a counter, a sink, and a small refrigerator. Underneath a large window which gave out on distant ranges and a narrow valley disappearing into sidestepping infinity, was Nancy's bed. At its foot was a camper's trunk and on a table beside it were books, a lamp, and a radio. "Only country music," she said, "but it suits me fine up here. When someone dies they play Beethoven, and then I realize what I'm missing." The bed and the dining table were covered with blue-and-white checked linens. On the walls were portraits of aged scientists, extraordinary telephotographs of eagles, and a picture of Nancy when she was a small girl, a ribbon on the top of her head, her chin resting on folded hands. "That's me when I was five."

Facing the bed was a rifle and pistol rack with a shelf along which were stacked boxes of ammunition. "I took all the cameras and optical stuff and hung them from the rafters," she said. "They used to hang on the wall, but those nuts line up four and five abreast and run against the door to try and break it down. The first time, I was at the table eating, looking at the wall, thinking about *Buteo buteo* (that's a hawk), when all the equipment suddenly jumped into the center of the room. I thought it was an earthquake, but then I heard drunken laughter. The moon was up, so I grabbed my pistol and ran outside. That's when I got one of them, in the leg."

"When was the other time?"

"The other time," she gasped. "The other time I woke up and they were standing by my bed, with idiotic smiles. Felipe had his pants off. They grabbed my arms and held me down while the animal climbed on the bed and began to grope around. I laughed and said, 'Don't you fellas want me to put on my tikla?' 'What's a tikla?' they asked. 'I'll show you.' So I got up, went to the rifle rack, took out the pistol, and sprayed them with bullets. They left hurriedly, but I got Felipe in the chest."

"How long do you stay here?"

"From the end of April to the first of November, at least during this year. That's six months."

"And no one else is ever here?"

"Oh yes," she said "Denis drives out from Chicago every month or so and stays for a few days."

"Denis?"

"Denis Frog, the head of the department. He's English, and next year he'll be eighty-five, a little too old to make it up the mountain. Last time, he climbed so slowly that he had to spend four nights on the trail. But he rests and takes notes in the process."

"Forgive me," said Marshall, "but what month is this?"

"This is July. How come?"

He slapped his head and began to count on his fingers. "January, February, March, April, May, June, July," he reeled. "I was in that place for seven months. It seemed like a few days, a long, long night. Seven months." He told her about the factory, and between that and her stories of her solitary life up there, they talked until they looked out the big window and saw the stars. Marshall was very dizzy. She said that she would make him a special dinner. They had steaks, corn and radishes from the garden, and blueberry pie for dessert, for the mountains were covered with early blueberries. At the end of dinner Marshall ran to the edge of the woods and was sick. Deathly sorry, he washed his face and brushed his teeth in the numbing waters of the sluice, and, feeling better, looked up to see Nancy Baker bent over him. "I'm sorry," he said.

"That's all right," she answered. "It's hard to eat after four days without food. That's all right."

In the noise of the sluice they walked back to the cabin over a slope of pine needles. She looked about, checking the horses and the black perimeter. "Everything's okay," she said. "You can rest tomorrow. Maybe you'll read a little about eagles. We can talk. I've been thinking about some things and I want to tell someone. Then the next day or maybe the day after that, we'll hike up to the observation chimney and stay for a while. Up there you can get the most beautiful classical station. I'm glad you came."

That night he slept on the porch. He was already bedded down and nearly asleep when the lights went off in the operations section of the cabin. She had been typing the last of the previous observation reports. He watched as she walked to her bed. The little lamp went on, casting a warm light. He could just see her against the white and beige of dried grasses she had arranged above her bed, and against the black sky through her window. She took off her blouse by lifting it over her head in a quick motion, and put on a cotton nightgown almost as quickly. She had a beautiful body, and she was as brown as the brown penny of which Marshall had been thinking several days before when he had looked at his reflection in a still pool. She was so beautiful that he wanted to hold her, without moving, throughout the night. She was slim, graceful, a dancer. Then he was amazed, because she fell to her knees and leaned against the bed to pray. And she prayed for a long time.

He could see only the sweep of her black hair against her long smooth neck and the pale blue gown. When she finished, she rose, she turned out the light, and he saw stars burning through the cool swirling glass of the cabin windows. "If you come in here," she said, "I'll have to shoot you." He smiled.

8

The next morning he awoke to the sound of splashing. It came from within the cabin, where Nancy May Baker was bent over a large tin basin, washing her hair. For this operation she was clothed in a slip which had once been rose-colored and had become nearly white, and she had the pistol on the table beside her. As she leaned forward a chain swung out from inside the silk and a locket dangled over the water. Vaguely embarrassed, she looked up at Marshall and said, "Hi, I'm washing my hair."

"I see."

"I lather it up and stuff in here and then I dump the dirty water in the latrine. But I rinse in the pool."

"The pool?"

"Didn't you see?" She pointed to the woods. "There's a natural pool up there, so cold that if you stay in for more than a few minutes you'll faint. It's painful to put your head under. Luckily, Felipe and his friends don't know about it, so I can swim anytime I want, without a bathing suit." She hesitated. "But now I guess I'll have to wear one."

They went before breakfast. The water was as clear as the mountain sunlight, and in the glade the temperature was perfect. Where the sun did not strike there were dark brown and black shadows, in which the air was cool and dense. The pool was within a rock kettle about fifty feet across. "Its twenty-five feet deep," said Nancy, as they stared at a few alabaster-colored trout hovering in slow eddies. "You can see right to the bottom." She brought him to a high ledge overlooking the water, which was still except where it came in over a fall. "Just jump in."

Together they jumped. When he hit the water Marshall thought that his nervous system would freeze and shatter. They gasped and shrieked in their rush for the bank. Even as the water was falling from them in glinting pearls, Marshall looked at her. Her arms were long and brown, her expression sweet—he leaned over and kissed her lips. She kissed hard, and then withdrew quickly. "Too soon," she said. "Jump in again." He did, watching the empty sky as he was suspended in flight before a dashing penetration of the icy pool. Fish shot to and fro in brown spangles. When he was more used to the cold, he dived under and tried to catch them. Their sides were flecked with trout colors and caramel. He said, "Trout," underwater, and glasslike bubbles passed to the surface. He stretched a numb hand in their direction, as if they would volunteer to be clutched, and deep in the cold water he had a perfect picture of them in an iron frying pan with butter and the mushrooms that Nancy could safely gather because, she had said, she was a scientist.

When again they climbed out onto the rocks they felt completely fit, like just-matured raptors trembling in air for their own perceived delight. They understood the perfect bodies sketched by Leonardo, and the interface of aerodynamic force and a lean muscled wing. Their eyes and faces were clean and ready enough to sense pulses in the sunbeams striking them. Almost as if by numbers and seconds the light was divided into beats striking off time, and Nancy knew by intuition (admittedly skew to the laws of science) that the biological clocks about which everyone spoke were calibrated by light, even if invisibly. She sensed the exact division of the sunlight louder than their heartbeats as they watched it divide and diffuse on the tan rocks and in the water. It hung in the air in its split state, like mist from a fall. And then it reverberated warm and cloudy, but with an edge so fine that the veins of the stream glittered with sharpness and definition. They stared at the views across the cliffs.

"I remember," she said, "an August day in Illinois. It was flat and hot. Henry and I were in a car, and had pulled into a gas station by an access ramp. A high concrete wall had been built at an angle from the ramp, for no reason that I could see except perhaps to shut out the cicadas and the cornfields which flanked the road. A man began to clean our windshield. 'I'm giving your car some treatment,' he said, 'treatment.' It was murderously hot, and a train was roaring past, and other cars were lined up. He opened the hood and began to work on the engine. I looked at him. He was absorbed in the running of it, and when he put his thick oil-stained hands inside he lost hesitancy, as if he were cleaning a fish and did not fear the entrails. The engine moved silver; it made sounds like popping corks, and the clickings seemed to spread over the prairie. I thought that the engine's sounds would eventually be snared in some high oak on a riverbank. Henry wanted to speed onto the turnpike and head west. But I was fully satisfied watching the man with his hands thrust into the silver and black engine. It was alive, hot, in time, moving, and I felt as if the world were a circle around us. I felt the heat rising from the coarse concrete. I smelled the fields. It was as if I had tacked down everything I knew and it lay sturdily battened in the full blast of a light storm."

She herself lay back in the sun, blinking. "And then we left the station, and for hours and hours and hours that engine carried us at speed through a tube in the prairie, falling toward a horizon of running colors. I saw dozens of raptors on the wing to left and to right, wheeling in permanent axes they had just taken up. It seemed to interconnect—the stroke and clattering recession of the engine rods, the axis of an eagle's flight, the path of a dim disappearing road saturated by August heat and moving like the patterning of a piano. And then I looked at Henry's teeth, and at his eyes fixed on the road. Physical laws were so apparent and omnipresent that I wondered of what we were made, and if our dissolution would really bring darkness, and it seemed to me that it would not, no more than the fall of water and its infinite dazzling changes the stream. I realized then that raptors are not independent fliers, but that in their aerial turning and their wide flight, they are merely indicators of lines which have always been. It drove me to a shaking conclusion. I tremble at the thought. It filled me, and I was amazed."

"And that's why you pray."

She quickly looked at him, and held her gaze. "That's why I pray."

9

"It takes six or seven hours to get up to the observation chimney," she said. "When fully loaded, even in this near-zero humidity, you're going to sweat like an Alabama hog. The more we carry, the longer we stay; the longer we stay, the more work; the more work, the better for continuity and integrity."

"Scientific integrity?"

"Scientific integrity," she echoed.

He did not believe her warning until he saw her loading his pack. She put in food, cameras, lenses, and five bottles of wine, explaining that they could not use lights at night because they would be in the center of a valley of eagles, and that after dark the only entertainments were music, astronomy, and drink. "I usually tie myself down and stare at the Milky Way. My pack weighs ninety pounds. Unfortunately, yours weighs a hundred and fifty."

"How far do we have to go?" he asked, terrified.

"It's not how far; it's how high. We're at eight thousand feet, and we're going to eleven thousand feet. We have to go three thousand feet straight up, eventually, which for you will be the same as taking a hundred and fifty pounds on your back up a sixty-story skyscraper five times. You'll lose twenty pounds, and we'll have to sleep for a day."

"What about water?"

"Luckily, we have a cistern up there which collects rainwater, so there's always enough if one is careful not to waste it."

They set off at a stumble, but once they took the path upward, gravity steadied them. It was extremely difficult. The straps of the packs dug into their shoulders. After ten minutes they were sweating, and they walked for many hours. As the air thinned and they fell into a stupor of exhaustion, the world, too, thinned and sounds were hardly heard, as if a spell had been thrown across the pines. They saw dust particles, bees, things hovering in air.

They were wet; they sweated; they breathed hard for hours. "The chains and chain ladders jingle against the rock," she said, "and the rock is brown and terra-cotta as far as the eye can see. It's worth it."

Halfway through the afternoon they rested by a stream, where the air was screamingly thin, a high frequency for breathing. "This is the last stream," she said. They drank. The water was nearly iced it was so mechanically cold. Muscles aching, they lay back on a terrace of pine needles to listen to the trees hissing in a steady western wind.

In late afternoon they came to a curving flint ridge about five miles long. At its end were high rock chimneys toward which they traveled walking on a path near the edge, looking down a thousand-foot cliff and then much farther into a valley which seemed to run toward the rest of the continent. Though the day was clear, the horizon was blurred. Had it not been for the imperfections of air and the human eye, they would have been able to see for many hundreds of miles. A queer spectrum began below the cliff with yellow sands dotted by brush—a tan haze with strata of orange was the undulating floor of desert, and in the distance bands of blue and purple gave way to blue and green and blue once again which finally cleared to the sky above them. Birds other than eagles swooped and darted above and beyond the cliff face, singing strangely and beautifully. They could not see one sign of man. The enormity of view, the complete absence of any challenge to natural order, the effulgence of horizon colors, and the strange sweet sounds gave to Nancy May Baker and Marshall a sense of being on another planet or in times prehistorical. They could just make out the curve of the earth. When they looked up from their flinty plain of brown rocks they felt as if they were looking outward. The planetary sense derived from this made them feel (in contradictory fashion) that they were on a small moon or asteroid.

They leaned their packs against the wall of the highest rock chimney and attached them to a nylon rope which hung down several hundred feet from a gantry at the top. Then they took a circular path winding dangerously along the outside to a plateau halfway up. On several occasions they had to press against the wall, so thin was the path and so formidable the drop. A chain ladder led to another plateau forty feet farther up. After a terrifying walk along a ledge, gripping a companion cable, they came to the last chain ladder—190 feet to the top. "This is very difficult," said Nancy, "and you must observe several rules. First, never look down. As you can see, halfway up the rock pushes out. If you look down at that point, you won't profit. Second, before and after the bulge, rest for a count of a hundred, putting your arms through the rungs and flexing your hands. Third, remember that Denis used to climb this when he was seventy-five."

They felt like flies. Rounding the bulge, they hung outward over a drop of more than 2,000 feet. Marshall was almost faint, but Nancy's pace was exemplary. Because she too was breathing hard, he knew that for her it was an act of courage. At the top, they lay panting until they recovered. "Who put these ladders on?" asked Marshall.

"Two Swiss rock climbers made the ascent, tossed down ropes, and pulled up enough to make a crane. Then they hoisted up a team of iron-workers, and more materials, including an engine. They rigged scaffoldings, and drove the best steel alloy five feet into the rock for anchor pins. A geologist laid out the pattern. It's not humid up here, so nothing rusts deeper than a protective coat on the outside. Every few years a metallurgist and an engineer come from Chicago to inspect. The ladder is rated to hold ten thousand pounds and Denis says it can take five times that."

"Is it true that Denis climbed this, at seventy-five?"

"Yes. He says he comes from a long line of tree Frogs. He's so sweet. Every girl in the department is in love with him. If only he were forty-eight instead of eighty-four."

"How many girls are there in the department?"

"Three graduate students. Me, Bonnie (who's married), and Angela, who looks like a manta ray. Her body is shaped like a hammock. She's in the Philippines, studying *Thorax thorax*."

They used a winch to hoist up the knapsacks and the bottom of the ladder (which hung free). Alone in an impenetrable fortress in empty terri-tory, they mounted fifteen iron steps to the upper deck from which the world appeared before them in Himalayan style. This place was nearly perfect, because it was both exciting and completely safe. A waist-high fence and lightning rods had been installed, and these made the upper deck look like the flying bridge of a warship. "In lightning storms you go into the utility room on the second level."

At the second level were a higher fence, some optical mounts, the cistern (full of cool water), a heavy wood picnic table, and a canvas sunshield pro-jecting outward like an awning. All around, rings were attached to the rock. "Because of the wind," she said. She drew a brass key from her pocket and opened an iron door which led inward to the utility room, hewn into the rock underneath the top deck. They took out canvas chairs, kitchen equip-ment, telescopes, the radio, large mats on which to lie, safety harnesses, cameras, and a pelorus. All of these were clipped to the rings or mounted on provided supports.

"You can't work or sleep in there," she said about the one room they had, "because somehow, even when the wind is high, it's just a pocket of dead air. When it gets really rough though, I have to write my notes at that table." After filling the stove, arranging the supplies, opening the log, and loading the cameras, they took out and grilled their only two steaks. The sun was beginning to set.

When they had had their meal they looked from under the canopy to a world where eagles returned to cliffside aeries in graceful lines of flight, the sun diminished in a perfect sphere beyond the curve of the horizon, the stars appeared at first mildly and then blindingly bright, and violet bands stretched from heaven to the face of a darkened peaceful earth—a planet of cool high desert and ruffling insistent winds. After they cleaned up, brushed their teeth, and splashed cool water over themselves, they went to the top deck, clipped on their safety harnesses, and reclined on the mats. The view was so black and bright that it was as if they were traveling in space. Gravityless, they looked outward, and they slept entwined in one another. Marshall awakened deep in the night. He saw the stars from 40 degrees below the platform to the top of the sky for a full 360 degrees around, as if he were lying on a pedestal thrust into space. The wind was mild. Nancy May Baker looked quite wonderful when asleep. He listened to her breathing—an even, steady, and miraculous sound.

10

"There were thirty thousand of them not long ago, and now there are fewer than ten thousand. Two thirds of *Aquila chrysaëtos canadensis* have been shot from planes or the ground, poisoned with insecticides, and who knows what else." They had awakened with the sun, and they sat clasping their knees as they watched some eagles hunting in the dawn. "I think that wholesale extermination has had a profound and subtle effect on the remaining population. Certainly, from their point of view, they have inherited an empty though beautiful world, and if they could think the way we do, they might be confused by the riches in game afforded them after so sad a decline."

"But they don't think the way we do. They just hunt and travel from one day and one season to another and another."

"No, they don't think, but I feel that the vast silence influences them. I believe their movements have changed, their expressions, just the way they are—subtly of course and most likely unbeknownst to them—and if we could enter the world of eagles, we might not know the heart of even one. Anyway, that's not scientific. Later, we'll get so scientific that it will hurt."

That afternoon, a storm arose. They noticed that the horizon had grown plum dark, and was bristling with miles-long lightning bolts. The storm approached rapidly, tumbling and turning like stirred wool, gray and white in the folds, purple and black deep down, a crest of white at its round and alpine top. They saw sharp flashes, listened to their hearts strike a number of beats, and then heard the rolling thunder as it swept across the desert and echoed in the canyons.

A mounted horde, the massed clouds charged over miles of desert.

Lightning was everywhere bright and thick, and at times the sky looked like a zebra. As they stowed away the last of their equipment, a minor bolt struck one of the lightning rods, and the thundercrack made every part of their bodies tremble. Great drops of rain flew past in steadily thickening sheets. Purifying lightning and thunder attacked so viciously that in their room hewn of rock they felt as if they were in a barrel going over a falls. They sat quietly on canvas chairs, a light like silver illuminating their mountain-dark faces. Water dashed off the second terrace into the air.

Their primary tool in observing *Aquila* was the 12,000-mm. lens/ telescope with SLS (by which it was possible to see in starlight, although they knew that eagles spend the night at home). More than forty feet long, the lens moved easily on a titanium-magnesium mount. Two could look through it simultaneously. Nancy controlled the camera, photographing intermittently in her dictation of notes and observations. Marshall frequently checked through his eyepiece to coordinate his understanding of her narration.

The power of the lens was astounding. On a cliff five miles distant perched an aerie of *canadensis* in which yearlings were about to fly. Marshall could easily make out the pineal structure of their feathers, and the individual fibers of lint clinging to their snowy chests. One night, he and Nancy climbed up to the observation level and swung the lens in the direction of Albuquerque. They didn't see anything, but a few degrees' turn and Santa Fe was theirs for the taking. They could read signs and movie marquees, and (with the SLS) they could watch people in the streets and in their houses. The images were mere shadows, but by skilled deduction they saw lives playing out—fights in bars, night workers scrubbing walls, police sleeping in their cruisers, children reading under the blankets with flashlights and animal crackers, and a uniformed brass band playing in an adobe kiosk. A green streetcar passed in the background. By turning on the SLS Marshall could see that inside were many women in long frothy skirts, that their hair was done up, and that they smiled. The interior of the streetcar was dark, paneled with fine cream-colored wood. The women looked at the brass band and seemed very pleased, and the green trolley disappeared into the darkness.

They wore out their eyes following eagles ringed with the azure world. *Aquila chrysaëtos canadensis*—holarctic and monogamous, a lifespan of fifty years, its feathers and beak of finer and smoother flow than the once molten gold of the Abbot Suger's golden porphyry jar. As the eagles soared above and below, Nancy gave a random dissertation.

"I find it difficult to speak about this," she said. "It's the one thing in the world I know something about, and so much gets in the way. But as the eagles move I'll tell you about them." And then she proceeded, interrupted by her notations in the Ornithology Department's shared codes and jargon.

"Three quarters of the time they do nothing. They need rest for the kind of life they live, and are not of the working class. So they sit on their perches and contemplate the horizon, like philosopher kings. They spend a lot of time food-getting and, related to that, in soaring and acrobatics—the connection being obvious yet difficult to describe fully. We do not know how closely hunting and soaring are dovetailed (perhaps the wrong word), nor do we fathom the subtleties of the crossover. They are relatively asocial, an ephemeral presence over the landscape. Because of this, they do not suffer destructive sweeping epidemics, and their populations are fairly stable over extended periods. They have several nests, sometimes more than a dozen, and go from one to another according to their pleasure, prey availability, weather, and changes in territoriality. Often they'll green the nests, so that when we band the birds we work in a bed of fresh pine branches. Their vision is the keenest of all creatures', with visual acuity perhaps eight times that of man. Rochon-Duvigneaud reports a million cones per square millimeter of eye in *Buteo buteo*. Eagles can spot their prey (never very large) at two miles. I've seen that, and I hope to show it to you. Now look up there, you see, you see that speck? He's probably close to fourteen thousand feet. They fly so beautifully that it can take your breath away. He might be food-getting, migrating, playing, giving a territorial display. Whatever it is, it's gorgeous.

"The complexity of fixed-wing flight (and there are volumes of equations which hardly begin to explain the forces engaged) pales before the infinitely variable contortions of wings, adjustments in emarginated and primary elasticated feathers, the spreading tails, legs, beaks, muscular tension and trunk attitude, feet, and talons. *Aquila* has been clocked in stoops of two hundred seventy-five miles per hour, and an eagle can brake smoothly and suddenly just before it hits the ground.

"The daily food intake of *canadensis* is about seven percent of its body weight, far more efficient than dogs, but less so than lions, which average two point five percent. The lions' social organization allows them this. The eagle, though, is fairly efficient for a loner. You know, they arrive at the sound of gunfire, having learned to associate it with flushed prey. But not up here. They're too wild. I can fire away for an hour and the darlings don't blink. On the edges of the Asian deserts, in places like Kirghiz and Samarkand, some people depend on *Aquila* for their livelihood. The eagles are sent after foxes and wolves, for the pelts. In medieval times, only a king was allowed to hunt with an eagle. They are the perfect hunter, and they have little trouble in dashing in to grip an unwitting bird or mammal, piercing to the heart. What Whitman—"

"You mean *Walt* Whitman."

"I mean, what Walt Whitman called 'the dalliance of eagles' is really a sexual display in which the male and female tumble through the sky after the female has turned on her back and presented her talons to the male.

Sometimes, though rarely, this is combat. In 1948, a pair of golden eagles were found in Scotland, quite dead, locked in one another's talons."

An eagle flew by at their level and dropped a stick, which fell through the air until he dived after it and caught it soundly. Nancy was delighted, and quickly began to snap photographs. "This is just what I want," she said as the eagle repeated the trick again and again until finally he was lost in the distance. Her face was pressed against the telescope. Marshall was entranced by her smooth dark skin and the convex form of a blue eye as it peered into the black tube.

"Sometimes they'll swoop down on some poor bird and frighten it to death, just out of habit, or in practice, or in play—we don't know. Sometimes they kill and don't eat. You see, the need to kill is intensified in certain stages of the breeding cycle. Males, the provisioners, develop the habit of killing far more than they themselves need, for the nest-bound females and young. I'm sure there's a link with play. I shouldn't put it that way. Perhaps there is a link. I'm observing young males who haven't yet been required to provide for families, to see if they indulge in such highly aggressive diversions. As you can imagine, this question has many complex implications. My greatest fear is that if I can fashion a decent dissertation on the subject, some idiotic behaviorist will use it to arrive at a tart psychological explanation which other behaviorists will claim mirrors the soul of man. They are fools, you know, behaviorists. They don't understand—not at all—religion, nature, art, or birds. As far as I'm concerned, they're as convincing and attractive as bats."

"Yes," said Marshall, "muffins of the lowest caliber."

"Indeed, and I fear even more that a sociologist will get ahold of it. Then my ideas will cretinize in the news magazines. I'd have to go to some place where they don't have *Time* or *Newsweek*."

"Doesn't exist," said Marshall.

In the days they watched eagles glide, and at night they lay facing a raft of stars. Sometimes they turned on the SLS for the silent band concert. The green streetcar always rolled up in the darkness and the women looked happily at the concert. But as Marshall and Nancy became better observers, they realized that the expressions of those women were very sad as well, as if they were longing for the unyielding past. One night, they had been observing life in Santa Fe, when the streetcar came around the bend and did not stop. The women inside were tearful. Nancy began to cry, and Marshall held her, his shoulders spotted with hot tears. He didn't know exactly what was happening, but she said, "I have a confession to make. I'm not from Kentucky. We didn't have a ranch or a breeding farm. I never rode horses until I came to Pinnacle, and then Denis had to teach me." She looked sad and burdened, as if she had done him a great disservice in creating the myth of a Kentucky girlhood.

"We grew up in Chicago, near the elevated line. It was a Polish neighborhood. I even know some Polish. Daddy worked at Swift. The most I remember about nature is looking at the orange sky beyond green trestles. I thought that it was a fire from a purer place. I thought that if I could fly, I could get there. That's how I came to love birds. In summer, we used to sit outside the door, in the heat, and watch the streetcars go by. They were green, just like the one in Santa Fe. Is it wrong to cry when I think of how little I knew, how much I loved, how much simple things meant? I remember that little girl, in clothes that were always too heavy and never fit. I was so hopeful. I didn't really know who I was or where I was. And yet, those times seem to be the center of the world, the root of everything. Am I wrong? Am I wrong to love the little girl that I see in a sweet, tortuous, slow-moving vision of the past," she got her breath, "in Chicago, in the summer, far away from eagles or anything like them? We were very poor. Am I wrong?"

"No," said Marshall. "No. You're not wrong at all, not at all." He held her so tightly that she had trouble breathing, but she loved it, and pulled him to her even harder. The little girl who was, who would never be again, came in front of their eyes. And there they were, way on top of a high rock chimney, breathing heavily because a vision of Chicago had leaped out of time and taken hold of their hearts as suddenly as if an eagle had fallen from above and gripped them in its talons.

11

In the last nights they waited for the wave of Chicago to come rumbling in as if a commuter train with tracks on air left the city each day and raced across the plains to Nancy Baker, whose eyes clouded as she was subsumed in a mist of the past. Sometimes it was pleasant. Once, they found themselves on a wood porch overlooking a hot street. It was so quiet that they heard the faucets in a neighbor's house, and the grinding of streetcar wheels many blocks away. A potted palm sat in the corner, its fronds pressed up against white rails. Where was that palm? And where was the heat, and the glances? Where had they gone? It was painful to discover that she would not see these things again, more painful when she saw them in their true colors billowing out of the air, and still more painful when somehow other people's memories and sadnesses were spliced in. Why did these things return so surely and strongly?

Marshall said that it was because the stars were so bright. "You see, we're lying here and all time is passing through us, echoes of light from the past and the future as well. The whole thing," he said, moving his hand to indicate the sky, "is a vast complex of webs and lances. The lances are like needles, and they thread the past after them. Wherever you are, you are completely hemmed in with events that have happened and events that will happen. It's like being submerged in water. You can't see it, but you're pressured from all sides. Air, too, is like that—you feel it only if there is a breeze. We are trapped in this molten crystal, and sometimes the surge of waves allows us to sense a chain of events. Sometimes, you can even lean into it and not fall. It is communicated and revealed by light. You need not see it, but you have to be in it. I'll prove it. If you want the waves of Chicago to cease their pounding, come sit in the storage room and we can discuss practical matters divorced from memories. And you'll see that, away from the light, the past recedes."

In the rock chamber they felt as if they had gone behind a waterfall after passing right through it. Nancy threw her hair back and stared into the darkness, knowing that a cascade of light and time beat against the rock as busily as a heavy rain. It came from all angles and struck rhythmically, arhythmically, with surprise, insistence, and humor. They could have been in a cave of Spain, in cool white rock, while all around the lightshower chattered like clucking animals, castanets, plucked strings. In quiet places where the stars shone or the sea rose, the lightshower was always strong. She looked at the black wall, where a line of booted cavalry in white galloped over a ragged hillside while, beyond, a plain covered with red flowers appeared telescopic and grainy. The cavalry rushed along in searing colors. "I thought we were to speak of practical matters," she said, as dust flew from behind the horses and sabres and metal equipment danced about and jangled.

"Just a second," Marshall replied. "It will undoubtedly fade. Must have been drawn in after us. They're Mexican, late nineteenth century, wouldn't you say?" She strained after the fading image.

"It's hard to tell, but they are South American. They have those flattish hats, and they're dark in color." When the image left, they discovered that they were exhausted. They went to the top level and threw themselves down on the mats. Their supplies had run out two days before, and they had been working on spirit, devotion, and lust. But they dared not descend the great ladder in too much of a trance, and had decided to leave the next morning. Marshall was pulled east, though he could not explain the attraction, for Nancy May Baker was certainly enough to keep him at Pinnacle forever. Within him was a pressing desire to confront his past, the way Nancy May Baker had begun to do. The period of observation was over.

It was not easy to leave, but certain images arose to claim fealty, images mysterious and powerful, which he knew that he could no longer ignore. And one only moved to the West, and could not grow up there, whereas the East was real. The East was substantial, the West only a dream.

But then there was Nancy—dark, quiet (though often quite voluble), and so beautiful in and out of her sex that she entranced. Her interest in the objective world brightened her beyond belief. She and her kind, scientists who followed a pure cord of sense, were destined to discover new dimensions, an order apart from and superior to the decadent mechanistic notions of the avant-garde. It would be, perhaps, a new faith, an iridescence in the bell of the universe. In pursuit of the absolute, in attention to things such as the flight of eagles, and in travel of great distances, new laws would become manifest. Legions of scientists worked throughout the world in enviable integrity and wholeness, charting the processes by which, someday, earth and its sucking gravity, a constraint (and balance) for the mind as well, would be escaped.

In her study of raptors and eagles she had soared beyond fashion and trend to learn the inbent lessons of a million years within the cabinet of perfect nature. Others who had seen the strange and penetrating lights had left record in music and painting. It had been their way and the only means. And then the wave of exploration had transferred to the back of the mundane, and, by pure logic (they thought), astrophysicists broke upon the time sphere of musicians. It was a strange alliance—sunburnt young men and women in Africa and elsewhere giddy in the noonday heat, their seniors in laboratories of the West, and all the minors doing their part so that by the small steps of technological advance, a pure science was directed on its way as straight as a lance. Nancy did not know her role, but Marshall realized that were he to travel with her he would feel the enviable momentum of a priesthood in ascendancy.

She was not only lovely, but tall, and the direction of her life was very important, touching as it did upon the outermost reach. The day that he left they hiked ten miles to a rail line and waited by the tracks for several hours, talking nervously. A freight rounded the bend; she stepped back because of the noise and vibration; Marshall started to run, and then jumped on. Nancy May Baker and the ethereal world of the Far West, traced above by warlike eagles, receded in the distance as he was carried to the solidity of the East.

12

He rolled south into dotted desert flashing with the larcenous grins of gila monsters. The track bed was nearly gone, necessitating a pace slow enough to permit hopping on and off for exercise and pleasure. Instead of panning to the east at the base of New Mexico, the train halted on a siding at a deserted crossing point near the border. In the bright light of a silver midnight, a triple-edged party of U.S. Border Patrol, Mexican Federals, and railroad bulls began to work down the long line of dusty cars, opening every door. At first, Marshall didn't know what to do. He had no desire to travel into Mexico, and yet, to set off in the desert without water was not attractive either. Finally, he decided to go with the train, and he hid in the brush until they passed.

The diesel started up in oily sparking convulsions, and Marshall headed into the Mexican desert in the deep of night. He could not believe that it was so brown and never-ending. For days the empty train beat south with hardly a stop. He ran out of food early on and there was no water anyway. Soon he was sallow and starved, with the complexion and demeanor of a hermit. The endless flats were most discouraging until, finally, he saw a palm. It looked as if it were dead from arthritis, but it was a palm. Then a few more appeared, and eventually he saw stagnant rivers and ragged fields bordered by uneven rows of banana trees. Marshall left the train for a minute to steal bananas, but the trees were stripped. Leaning out of the boxcar, he checked ahead for farmhouses. If one appeared in the distance, he jumped off the train and raced past the locomotive and its Mexican engineers (who seemed not to notice or care), until he came to the farmyard. With only two or three minutes to spare, he shot out the few words of Spanish he knew, trying to communicate his urgent need for food. "*Frijoles! Tacos! Enchilada! Tortilla!*" he screamed loudly, as if he were introducing himself to someone who could not hear. Faced with a breathless American waving his arms up and down, reciting a list of foods, and pointing to a handful of U.S. money, the farmer's wife and her sweet smooth-faced nut-brown children were thrown into panic. The white-suited peon began his dash from nearby fields to confront the intruder, and only once out of a dozen times were food ready, the train slow enough, the peasants sharp enough, and a container present, so that Marshall got a substantial meal. He ate it with his fingers while his legs dangled over the dust and the steel wheels.

Mountains framed the far distance with cool icy crests like a bird's crowning plumage. The food was hot and it burned his mouth. He was full of grease and had not washed or brushed his teeth for days. He had no idea of where he was going; he realized that he had forfeited his degree and that all his friends were just then entering medical or law schools; he did not particularly like the way he smelled; and just a few hours after the chili and hot peppers, he began to feel his stomach catch fire. It was so hot even in September that sawdust in the boxcar began to smolder. He lay on the hard vibrating floor in great physical pain, staring at the mountains.

He did not speak Spanish. He thought that he might come to a violent end or, what is worse, end up in a Mexican prison. But despite his seemingly horrendous position he was ecstatically happy and even whimsical. With nothing left and all opportunities missed, he was standing on pure nerves, and he felt lean, strong, and alive. He liked the rough growth of beard, which was quite different from times when he had simply forgotten to shave. He liked the dirt on his face and hands, his dusty gnarled boots, and the expression he imagined that he had—as open and clear as the mountain plateaus to the southwest, as if whatever he was had begun to come out after years of submersion in a life of supplements, adjuncts, opportunities, and provisions.

He discovered that his arms were badly cut from charging through ranks of thorns and cactus in his sprints to beat the train each time he saw a farmhouse, but it was all right. The train slid eastward into a hot grainy landscape and at night he sweated and could not sleep, but it was all right. He held up his cut and infected arm and swept it across the brightness of the Milky Way, moving his fingers in a wave. He could feel the muscles in his fingers, his arm, and his side, and he moved his hand back and forth over the stars as if to music. It was not the first time that he had been electrified by a soundless shower of stars, infinitely distant and untouched. It was not the first time that love had arisen from nowhere and given him strength, sustenance, and peace. He was hungry but not hungry, hurt but untouched, tired but full of paced movement. There was a sweet smell of cane and mangoes, just as in Jamaica. Looking up at the stars from that southern track he remembered courage on the White Water, and all was clear. He was carried over rivers and through many miles of greenery toward Vera Cruz and the Gulf. Although he thought that he was low and tangling in his raw wits, it was just a practice run, and he had survived rather easily. After all, in Mexico, or anywhere else, the stars were always high and the heavens an inviolable, unconquerable blue.

13

Wandering half-dead among the river-colored mud walls of Vera Cruz, Marshall wanted only to sleep on a bed of clean sheets. He found a hotel for a dollar a day, and checked in. He was given a steel locker for his bag, and led to a small room with French doors which opened on the plaza. It wasn't a bad room, but there were eight beds in it jammed up one against the other. Marshall climbed over soldiers and whores to the center cot, where he pushed a bunch of rifles, whisky bottles, and pornography to the edge and lay down.

He slept for twenty hours, his face resting on the barrel of a Belgian automatic rifle with an atrocious French accent. When he awoke it was dark, his jaws were sore, and a new and different set of soldiers had come in. Marshall left to wander through the decay and the wharves, where he found a shrimp boat headed for New Orleans. Despite rumors that the captain was notoriously storm-prone, Marshall paid him $100 for passage.

Then he wandered back to the plaza and sat in a straw chair, drinking Japanese beer and listening to the marimbas and electric gourds. In a place like Vera Cruz, people always seem to be living their very last day. This was especially true concerning the prostitutes. As if they were suffering from advanced beriberi or kwashiorkor, they appeared obviously starved of love. It could be easily seen in their eyes. Even the hardest among them felt the tick of every second like a dull pain—deficiency of love, inner leprosy, a profession only for those with organs of porcelain, and the rest beware.

He stayed in the plaza until dawn. Even near the wharf, the sea was blue, green, white, and loaded with glossy swells. Marshall went to his berth on the *Louisa,* and when he awoke they were in the center of the Gulf, with a burning sun, no birds, and whitecaps as crisp and foamy as sugar. They plowed across midsized swells, and gathered for a meal.

Although 110 feet long and properly provided with bowel-like chugging and tugging machinery—winches, pinchers, grinders, obloons, balugas, concors, and glackpoven—their African Cape shrimp sloop was toylike in its roll and appearance. The shrouds were as tight as harp strings and the gleaming machinery was coated with special dirtless oil. Mounted amidships near the machines were recreation slats for gazing at the moon. A sailor put his head and neck in a slat and, as the ship rolled and pitched, his eyes danced like bouncing balls to follow the bright undulations of the moon, thus providing recreation. The crew was composed of Jamaicans, Mexicans, and Americans. Of course, the Jamaicans had familiar Jamaican-style names—Ambrose, Dexter, Wilson, Birdie, Evans, Harlan, and Sterling. The Mexican names were too long to remember (and thus the Mexican crew was numbered from one to ten), and those of the Louisianans, if not as engaging as those of their island neighbors, were at least somewhat striking—Toughmello, Pinckney, Starbuck, Crispin, Belchasseur, Close, and Duckworth. They paired up in strange conflagrations—Close and Crispin, Belchasseur and Pinckney, Starbuck and Duckworth.

They were heading straight for New Orleans at full speed to disgorge a frozen cargo of Giant Gulf Shrimp. The holds were as icy as Greenland, and the sailors went about with rubber boots and shovels, adjusting the shrimp. So it was a leisurely voyage except for some routine shrimp shifting and machine cleaning. Everyone was happy, and when they gathered for Sunday dinner abaft they looked delightedly at a blue sea as smooth as oil and as rolling as West Texas grasslands. A steel barrel cut in half from top to bottom and laid sideways on metal legs held a bed of white coals. The cook was grilling shrimp as thick as a boxer's fist. Occasionally, he threw quartered Mexican lemons on the grid to sizzle with the shrimp and scallions. They had water biscuits, beer, and Vera Cruz mangoes, and they sat in a ring around the fire and took what they wanted. Marshall asked if there were any soy sauce. "Any what?" asked the cook.

"Forget it," answered Marshall.

The captain, whose name was Grafton Burnwhite, questioned Marshall

carefully, thinking that he had taken on either a fugitive or a drug addict. Upon discovering that Marshall was sound, upright, and innocent, he wanted to aid him.

"How much money ya got, Mowshil?"

"About three hundred and fifty dollars, Captain."

"That cain't last lawng."

"I know."

"Wha done yew wake whin ya git ta Niew Orlien?"

"Ah thowt Ah would," replied Marshall, swayed by the rolling speech.

"Wha done yew becalm a god?"

"A god?"

"Shuwa. Ah know the chief god a the Nut Shoal frayt yawd. Whin we reach pote, Ah'll give'm a cawl."

"What does it pay?"

"Pays good, but you wake awl nat on a trayin. Yew eva wake awl nat on a trayin?"

"Yup, but not for pay."

"Nut Shoals is the biggest yawd in Morka, an ma fren is the chief god."

"Oh."

"Now yew wrat doun his naminadress: Meesic Simmons, Chief God, Nut Shoals. Tell him that Grayafton Boyinwhat sintya."

"What kind of name is Meesic?"

"Ah thank it's a bee name."

"Oh."

After a few days of skidding down friendly swells, they passed over the continental shelf. Production and drilling platforms covered the sea like dragons astride dragons. Monstrously orange, they spat smoke and vast skeins of conical flame, red and blond in daylight, burnished gold at night. Weaving amid the fiery towers, the crew of the *Louisa* watched flamelights reflected on their faces. The sea was thick with these steel cliffs and the rumbling and rhythmic booming of their massive flywheels and pumps.

"When I came to America for the first time," said one of the Jamaicans, "I could not help but shake. I was thinkin', what kind of country this, that even a hundred miles in the sea before it there are factories and steel towers ablazin' high an' mighty."

14

They wondered why the sea was urgently green. Water and waves came directly from the north in parallel lines as straight as polarizing glass, as if they were traveling an infinite warp of loom cloth. The wind grew steadily

stronger and smelled like almonds and uprooted cane. Grafton Burnwhite
went to the radio and tried to raise the Texas coast but could garner only a
white falls of static. The barometer was palsied, and by the time Burnwhite
had gone over his charts and weather maps, and finally stood at the door of
the pilot house, he was faced by most of the crew. They knew his reputation
for running into storms, and they looked at him accusingly. "Theyas gonna
be a mahty big one," he said sheepishly, and put them to work under Starbuck and Belchasseur.

All the machines were covered with flexible pastaglese which locked
tight to the deck, assuring waterproofness and buoyancy. The flat rattling
hatches were fastened with turnbuckle catches, and the half barrel full of
coals was tossed into the sea, where it went down with a dying hiss.

After an hour they faced a great emerald storm wall, a frozen wall of
green cloud, in appearance as solid as a rock cliff. Driving toward them in
horseshoe shape, it was miles high, disciplined not to exceed the front of its
power, marching steadily, preceded by winds which sung in the stays and
made open lines into the terror harps once thought by oarsmen under decks
to be sirens. "We goin' backwahds," said Burnwhite, even though it seemed
as if they were racing forward. "It's just the wind and wowta. We makin'
boat tracks a fifteen knots on the suface, but the suface is movin' south
'bout tweny!" The horseshoe closed, and they found themselves in the center
of a ring on a tranquil sea. They began to move north, charging the wall.

Others cowered sternward and amidships, but Marshall decided to stick
on the prow. He chained himself to the bow cleats, thinking to find protection in the natural strength of a sharp arch. Though it would be the scene of
exploding white water, and though it would travel the greatest distance to
complete pitches and turns, it might be the best place, he thought, because
its knifelike shape would cut the blows and pass them out to the flanks. It
had the smallest area to be pounded, and he could get good holds on the
narrow bulkheads, cleats, and chocks.

He passed several lengths of chain through a foul-weather harness, and
secured himself to the deck. The emerald wall approached. Grafton Burnwhite was determined and rigid of face. Sailors lay about the decks with
stares upturned at the roll of fleece about to break upon them. The wall was
threaded with veins of lightning like a tangled wood. The swells were five,
ten, twenty times the height of the boat. When they entered, those astern
could see the prow disappear as if the boat were being fed into a grinder or
passing through a dark curtain. It had been broad daylight, but Marshall
could no longer see. Every few seconds, a flash of lightning revealed the deck
full of terrified men, and Grafton Burnwhite, locked in the pilot house,
steering by compass.

The prow was lifted with the force of rocketry. They hesitated at the
summit, and heard the disheartening slench of water falling away from the

hull. They flew, propellers spinning free, and then crashed onto the sea with splintering shock. Marshall was battered about and thrown like dough onto the hard deck. He ached, and could not get hold or stand stable. The bow dipped into the waves, and, for a minute or more, the ship became a submarine. Just as Marshall brayed out the last of his air and was about to take in a column of water, they shot upward in a concussion of foam, white sides, bubbling breakers, and cries from those who had been able to hold their breath.

Marshall's eyes stung, his throat was raw, and his belly was swollen from the pressurized inrush of brine. He had welts on his waist and on his forearms where he held the spreading chains; and he was stunned in the bones from all the smashing. Not a single sparkle remained on the surface. Instead, it was gray and green, tangled like wet wool on a dark night. For six hours they were tossed and beaten, the losers in a brawl with the sea.

Finally the boat went completely mad. It could no longer keep rudder and keel plowing through the ridges and it was turned and thrown in movements like those of a bucking horse. A yellow sheet of lightning revealed the shattered glass of the pilot house and a freely spinning wheel. Grafton Burnwhite was not to be seen. The strain vibrated the timbers like a live wire, and ripped out stays and fittings. After the *Louisa* had been revolving on the cap of a giant whiplike wave, it was thrust deep into the water and turned upside down. It was quiet under water. Marshall thought to free himself in case the boat did not turn upright again, but couldn't escape the harness. His fingers were too cold and numb to work the bronze buckle. When they had gone down he hadn't been able to draw much breath. In want of relief he had already expelled the air remaining in his lungs, and seen air bubbles like wiggling mercury glide upward past his face. Then the *Louisa* turned upright with a thud, and he breathed. "It *is* the hurricane season," he said to the storm. "I hadn't thought of that."

Though he saw that no one was left on the deck, he assumed that he could ride out the rest of it, for the bow was indeed the best place. Perhaps it had been a day, or two, or three—there had been a lot of darkness and he could not judge the time. Then he heard a familiar sound. In a salty delirium, he thought that he stood amid fragrant pines in a dry meadow, where he had just watched Livingston fell a tall fir, from which they would make timbers for a new south gate. The air was dry and gold; autumn; a good fire in the kitchen; waving evergreens; dry grasses. When the fir went down its sound was splintered into a thousand breaks, like a roaring fire. That was the sound.

But it was really the boat breaking apart. It tore into itself, disintegrating into light-colored soft-looking shreds. The deck machinery amidships sank into the hold. A wave jumped in after it, and the boat got heavier and lower in the water. Caught in the trap of two contradictory rollers, the bow parted from the stern. Marshall threw himself clear, hoping not to be smashed

against the timbers, and the two halves went down like plumb bobs. He was
swimming on the sea, but not alone. Hundreds of thousands of shrimp had
been liberated from the freezers, and slowly thawed uncurling on the surface,
floating amid chunks of hissing dry ice, the vapors, and great masses of sliding
foam. The shrimp stretched and flexed, and then began to swim about,
crackling in communication. It seemed to Marshall that they were laughing,
and that the way in which they circulated and grouped could only have been
joyous reunions.

After the hurricane scattered everything, Marshall was alone in a world
of green. The rain and lightning ceased. Great winds propelled him through
valleys and down smooth oily slopes. He came to like it. After a while the
swells cleaned up, clearing of foam, and the clouds lifted to form an angry
ceiling. He was content to swim along until exhaustion would put him to
sleep and he would go down and under. But, to his astonishment, he saw
beyond the breakneck ridges a sandy coast of dunes. A half hour passed, and
he was spat upon the hard sand as if the sea had tired of entertaining him.

15

At Nut Shoals freight yards in New Orleans, Meesic Simmons had an office
high in a tower. At the end of switchback iron stairs, Marshall walked in on
a little man with an upturned nose and blond hair in a waxed crewcut. He
had blue eyes, and was wearing a yellow-and-black striped polo shirt.

"What can I do for you?" asked Meesic.

"Grafton Burnwhite sent me. He thought you might have a job."

"Grafton Burnwhite. Did you know him when you were a little boy?"

"No. I just met him. He's dead now, unless someone fished him out of
the Gulf."

"You talkin' about Grafton Burnwhite, master of the *Louisa?*"

"That's right."

"Grafton Burnwhite went down with the *Louisa* in 1958. Everybody
knows it. It's in the public record. I have jobs, but not for liars."

"A piece of information for you, Meesic Simmons," said Marshall, leaning forward over Meesic's desk, teeth clenched. "I'm no liar. I just came from
Vera Cruz on the *Louisa*. We broke up in a bad storm. Everyone died but
me."

"That what they teach you up in Yankee land? How to lie and get angry
at the same time?"

Marshall pulled little Meesic from his swivel chair and hauled him over
the desk. "I don't want your stupid job, you dumb little bee. Take your job
and shove it. But I was on the *Louisa*, and I met Grafton Burnwhite, and

from the way he was, I can tell that he didn't have a twin." He tossed Meesic back in the chair.

"I could have killed you, fool, I have a gun. I have two guns."

"I'm no liar," said Marshall.

"Maybe you're not. Maybe so. Maybe you did see Grafton Burnwhite, and maybe you were on the *Louisa*. But you can't expect me to believe somethin' like that."

"Stick it," said Marshall, already on his way out.

"Halt!" screamed Meesic. "You're touched, but you got a good temper. You'd make a superb train guard. Did you ever kill anyone?"

"No."

"Would you like to kill someone?"

"Yeah."

"Who?"

"You."

"Oh, I like that. I like that," said Meesic. "What would you do if you saw some son of a bitch hoppin' your freight?"

"Nothing."

"Nothin'?"

"That's right. I do it myself."

"Let me put it this way. What if some son of a bitch hopped the freight and was stealin' stuff?"

"I'd arrest him."

"What if he started shootin' at you?"

"I'd shoot back."

"To protect a lotta junk that doesn't belong to you?"

"Of course not."

"Then why?"

"Because if someone shot at me I'd be mad. I'd kill him."

"You're hired. Come back here in five days and pick up your stuff. I'll put you on the White Ox Special. That's one hell of a train. It winds all the way around the South—sometimes fast, sometimes slow. The women jump on 'cause they love to hear that White Ox moan. And in the winter it's the best place to be—comfortable, lotta landscape, nice slow pace. It's sort of a free agent."

"What do you mean, winter? It's only September."

"It's almost October, and the White Ox takes months till it gets to the East Coast."

"Where on the East Coast?"

"Depends on chance, on the lading. Could be Bangor. Could be Miami. You never know. Take the job. The women in the South love that White Ox Special. Only fifty cars: it's easy to get from the engine to the caboose. We gotta put the White Ox on line. Loses money, but it's a federal law. After the Civil War, the Yankees were upset 'cause we took their rollin' stock and derailed a lotta engines during our raids. You probably wouldn't know about that. Anyway, when Lincoln was shot, the Congress was hot-headed. They made a law said that, in perpetuity, the South has got to have a train movin' in and out of all the remote valleys and backwaters. They said it gotta be called the White Ox Special. I don't know why. But it's a great train. I swear, them women love to hear the White Ox moan. You'll see. They stand by the tracks and you can scoop 'em up in your arms as you go by; just grab a sweet little waist."

After a few days sleeping in a park, he boarded the White Ox Special. He was the train guard. They dressed him up in gray pants with a blue stripe; a blue shirt; a silver badge; a black garrison belt; and a pistol, which he put in the lockbox the first day out and did not ever see again.

It was an oven of dreams. As he traveled through the South his eyes opened on a great sphere of light green landscape and the skew lines of young trees, dry cabins with tin roofs the color of dark terra-cotta, quiet woods where he could breathe easy and fires burned a thick smoke, white houses sober on stilts at the edges of straight slow rivers, a catalog of small mountain scenes, log trains winding around bends, fragrant piles of pine branches on the outskirts of a lumber camp, unschooled children who could not stop moving, rolling over the countryside, driving back the evil eye, a land changed which should have been unchanged and which with the back of its hand punished transgression from its old ways and first sense—Indians, slaves, gray moss on ancient limbs, windows which did not slide right, cracks in the walls, shuffling engines, thin saplings amid the leaves in shadowy woods, lightning through a maze of dark, wet trees.

The White Ox was a steam train, probably the last of steam—exhalations, mist, hickory burning in a coffered steel box as warm and red as the red in the flag. Those white-bearded bastards who drove it through the snow, and through the green mountains in dark of night, made lamb stew cooked hot by the firebox. They drank whisky on the run, because they did not have to steer.

When day broke upon falling snow and snakelike curves cut through the bottom of Tennessee, there were the new cities. Seen from the fields they seemed to stand like islands in a sea, like crowns. They rose from the countryside like Alps or cathedrals; suddenly their countless noises muted into one constant sound like an underground river deep in a cave, a cool, anesthetizing sound.

Sometimes they halted in the wet snow beside camps of unimaginable people surviving on the quick leap of a rabbit. The train spit and drained as the train had done in Columbine. They mixed with the dark souls, and they went on—eastwards to summer and the seacoast. One lesson pounded through Marshall, burnt in by the boiler fires. He had to move on, and was by no means set to the job of laying net upon the land (as were classmates dull and Virginianized), but rather intended to move like a hopping animal.

So, he moved, through the calm and fragrant South, inhaling it and learning from its rapid lack of motion. This was a place in which were countless windows driving ever deeper than the flat-fielded views. Even in March, the sun was as hot as a pistol, and the sparse snow vaporized as if summer were chasing it around a predetermined course. The ground hissed and sucked with presumptuous March heat. Suddenly, it was spring. Suddenly, the train and the engineers saddled up by the engine (squinting ahead) ran over the sand of the coastal plain. Trees bowed low and small, and in reverence for the sea and its power the landscape ducked down flat and salty. At any moment they would find the moonlit waves.

It was night indeed. The spring was coiled and bright; birds were darting in and out of the clouds, or so it seemed. Norfolk struck in its random flatness, the wind from the sea blowing past dunes and houses. At the railyard, full of coal and deserted but for hoodlums themselves deserted, sea air blew translucent as pearl over the backs of the black coal cars. It was a nightclub for coal cars, and the moon shone over beaches and interfingerine bays.

Amazed that he was in Norfolk, Marshall walked to Virginia Beach and dashed to the ocean. After a quiet hour in the salt air, observing a round moon swallowed by fat clouds like an infectious billow, he sleepily made his way inland to lie beneath a winter palm.

16

Nearly fifty, Paul Levy was a full admiral in command of the Atlantic, the Mediterranean, the Caribbean—all the eastern approaches to the New World and a good deal more. His men and equipment might at any moment have been cruising under the ice cap, pushing across seas near the African coast, flying over Hatteras at unforgivable speeds, or stormbeaten in the Central Atlantic. The range of what they did dwarfed even this wide geography— boatmen knelt with the wind in their eyes; technicians dug deep into the innards of electronics full of colors and with more bent little legs than a termite nest; sailors scanned the sea; pastry cooks worked under the waves; boilermen lit their flaming torches; builders put up enormous bases; doctors delivered babies; lawyers tried cases; the Shore Patrol made arrests; warehousemen sweated in a world of stenciled objects; fat CPO's smoked cigars and slept peacefully at dinner tables; grooms took care of horses; bombloaders risked disintegration; theoreticians debated logicians; mathematicians tried their equations; prisoners rotted in jail; weathermen flew into the fists of hurricanes; and riders on gray ships bolted through running seas. It was early spring. Paul Levy wore a blue uniform covered with ribbon squares. For him, the Navy had been no work at all, and the only difficulty he had in his profession was when he froze in his tracks adoring it.

He sat at his desk relaxed and at ease, smoking a pipe with some sort of cherry or brandy stuff in the tobacco. A magnificent lighted map of the Atlantic covered one wall. The Norfolk naval complex was partly visible through the window. A great city of ships and gantrys, it was like another planet. Levy looked at Marshall straight on and said, "Why didn't you come sooner?"

"I had my own life," replied Marshall.

"And you don't now?"

"No."

"Why not?"

Marshall thought for a minute, and glanced at the swirling blue map before he answered. "Because the pretense of control has completely vanished. I knew first when light on the screen of the theater in Eagle Bay caused me to have a seizure. I tried to control it, but it kept after me and spoiled my plans. I couldn't get through college because I just couldn't sit still; I know I'll never go back. I can't stay in one place for very long. Doctors tried to tranquillize me, but I felt as if I were a tree they were felling. The long and short of it is that I have no real skills, no profession, no devotion. I'm not productive. In fact, I can't even make a steady living. All I can do is go from place to place exhausting myself as I see what there is to see."

"I'm partially responsible for that, you know. I insisted that they tell you who you really are, and since you have no way of being that other self of which you were robbed by shifts in history, you're sort of stuck. You don't really fit in anywhere. Where would you? You were born in the midst of a fierce naval battle off the coast of Palestine. You grew up in the Hudson Valley . . ."

"How do you know?"

Levy smiled. "I haven't really said anything yet. All I said was that you grew up in the Hudson Valley."

"But how do you know?"

"I know, because I've been following your progress since you were a year old. Not long after I returned to the United States I found out who had taken you. I went to Eagle Bay on several occasions, and knew you quite well until you were about two and a half. Then I was posted abroad, and after I returned I decided not to disturb you."

Marshall was too confused to be either astonished or angry.

"Then I began to raise my own family, but I kept in touch. We thought it best to wait until you decided on your own to seek me out. Now that you have, why don't you stay with us? That is, with my wife Susannah and our two children. Peter is ten. No one calls him anything but his nickname, which is Rollo. Amanda is four. There's plenty of room and we have much to discuss. Although I can't do much more than broach the subject now, I can tell you that I have been trying to discover the identity of your father."

There was a long silence as Marshall felt a surge of emotion working its way through him. Even though he had no idea of what he would find out, he felt that a certain resolution approached, that he was about to satisfy an overwhelming curiosity which, though unknown to him until this very moment, had directed his entire short life. He could not help himself, and he got all choked up. Paul Levy had expected that he would.

They spoke for the rest of the afternoon, interrupted by aides who came in with important matters to be discussed. Not used to sitting in an office, Marshall became extraordinarily fatigued and hungry, and could not wait to have dinner. He assumed that Levy's house was nearby. But Levy's position allowed him a great deal of flexibility. "I don't live in Norfolk," he said, as they walked into a small building by a huge tarmac, "but in Charleston."

"Charleston?"

"Yup."

"That's hundreds of miles away. Don't you work here every day?"

"Every weekday. I met my wife when I was CO in Charleston, and we bought the most beautiful house there, on the Battery. It's only three hundred and fifty miles south, and in an hour I can get from my desk here to my front door at home." They walked into a ready-room for combat pilots. "I ferry a different F-4 up and back every day. There's a maintenance schedule as sure as the tides. They used to have a man doing it as a full-time job. Now I do it instead—very efficient. An F-4 is a Mach 2.4 aircraft. Once we get off the ground, we'll be in Charleston in twenty minutes."

They lost some time as Levy explained to Marshall how to eject, and how to work the oxygen and the intercom. However, the plane had been ready on schedule and, with Marshall in the navigator's seat, they rolled to the end of the runway. At the moment of clearance they burst forward so certainly and with such terrifying speed that Marshall was pressed back in his seat as if he had been crushed by a bull, and couldn't understand how Levy could move his hands to work the controls. But they roared upward and shot through the clouds, leaving Norfolk behind as if it had been engraved on a plate. The whine of the engines was wilder than the whistle on a steam flier.

"It feels as if there's hardly anything except us and engines," screamed Marshall over the intercom.

"That's a good description," returned Levy. Then he banked, and swooped in a dive of several miles to show Marshall the delight of living on the border, close to absolute force, faster than sound, speeding in gravityless full-dimensional power flight. They traced the distant strip of Hatteras as if it were the white line on a highway—broken not symmetrically but only here and there by inlets around which the sea made sweeping circular patterns. Levy was an expert guide. "That," he said, gesturing out the canopy at a netted green treasure of fields, patches of blue forest, rounded and long-bodied lakes, and dark mountains behind which a revolving apricot-colored sun was vanishing, "is America." And when he said "America" he took the plane upward a half a mile, in an instant, so that if Marshall had not already been elated, he was sure to have been.

17

In a mild translucent dusk they approached Levy's house. Stars were beginning to shine. It was delightfully warmer than in Norfolk. The house was a subtle beige English neo-classical, with lines as restrained as those of the Parthenon, and immaculate white trim. Instead of a frieze, one round window cast its light from under the peak of the roof. Several stories of windows were lit and aglow. Through them Marshall could see colored walls, books, paintings, tall plants, and jewel-like lamps. The grounds were surrounded by a solid gray fence.

As they headed up a brick walk to the entrance, the front door flew open. First out was Rollo, who sailed from the porch and rushed to his father, only to stop short, glance at Marshall, and say, "What's that?"

Rollo had recently become a tough guy, and knowing this, Levy looked at him drily and said, "Shut up, Rollo."

"Make me," retorted Rollo.

"You want your allowance?"

"I can do without."

"You sure?"

"A hundred percent."

Then Levy leaned down and gave him a kiss, which he wiped from his face in great annoyance. Susannah Levy, a beautiful blond woman in her middle forties, came out with Amanda clutching at her dress. She took the child into her arms and gave her to Levy as he introduced Marshall.

"I'm Susannah Levy, and this is Amanda, and this is Peter."

"Rollo."

"Peter!"

"Rollo."

"All right then, Rollo, dumb Rollo, what a name." Then she kissed Marshall, which made him feel awfully good, and as he was about to be embarrassed, Levy handed him Amanda, who turned her head away in a fey movement which she then contradicted by resting against Marshall as if she had known him since she was born.

They passed through ranks of potted rhododendron and palmetto into the main hall, and into the kitchen, where they sat down to eat. The table was enormous, and all five of them filled only one end. A fireplace with a roaring fire made it necessary to fling open the windows. Spotlights and candles lit the room; there was a fine maritime painting on a far wall; the floor was of octagonal terra-cotta tile; two bulletin boards were filled with notes and invitations. As they sat down, a phone rang. Levy glanced in its direction and shook his head. "Let it ring," he said.

Marshall was surprised when Levy went to a cabinet and took from it four *kipōt* (Amanda would not be left out). Then Marshall realized that the candles were in front of Susannah Levy, and that on the table were silver cups and a *hallah*. "Not only that," said Susannah in response to Marshall's expression, "but the meal is *cashér*, and so is the Admiral—at least on Friday nights. He makes billions of exceptions. An odd bird, all in all." She began the ritual, which took twenty minutes, and then they feasted on roasted meat and potatoes, fresh vegetables, and the best red claret.

After dinner, when, with faces turned to the fire, the children leaned against their chairs, Levy lit up a Cuban cigar—"They pass through Guantanamo"—Marshall guessed that Levy was thinking about him, but it was impossible to tell. He might very well have been concentrating on a naval problem.

"Are you contemplating your naval problems?" asked Marshall.

"Oh, no. No no. I was thinking about something else."

"What? Marshall?" asked Susannah.

"Yes."

"And what did you think?"

"*Solvitur ambulando,* and I believe that it's so." He knew several thousand Latin phrases, and had her always running to the dictionary.

"What does that mean?" she asked. "I don't feel like getting up."

"It doesn't mean 'I don't feel like getting up.' "

"Paul."

"*Deo optimo maximo,*" he said.

"A high-quality cigar," added Marshall.

"*Dixit crescendo absoluta excudit in Regnum Paulus,*" he said. They dared not provoke him further.

He carried the sleeping children off to their rooms and put them to bed. Marshall watched Levy's face as he held the cigar between his teeth and maneuvered the nightclothes onto Amanda. He admired Levy, and was glad to be on his side.

The circular window was in the study, an enormous room under the roof, in which were five or six thousand books, several desks, an aquarium of unusual size, and the ever-present maritime paintings and brass instruments, as well as a fireplace in which Levy built and struck a birch fire faster than Marshall had ever seen it done. He went to a vault, neutralized a battery of coded alarms, opened it, and took out a slim looseleaf notebook.

"These are my researches into your origins. There are just a few pages, and they themselves are terribly inconclusive, but they took years to assemble. Would you like them now, or do you want to rest?"

"I'll tell you what. Why don't you put them back, until I have decided how I'm going to approach them—which might take a few days. Is that all right?"

"Sure, that's all right. I don't want to press."

"Okay."

"Tomorrow we're having a big party. All the brass on the East Coast is going to be there, and a bunch of big civilians. But I always invite my family and Susannah's, and lots of young officers—so you'll have people your age. These things aren't like real parties because they break up into knots of people talking shop. I know that you don't like parties. Livingston told me." Marshall nodded. "But do yourself a favor, *come to this one.*"

His room of white walls and dark hardwood flooring overlooked the rippling bay beating landward from the ocean. The wind was warm, the moon bright, and even in spring the palmettos and vines were as sweet as summer. It was good to be once again in a settled house, and to know that he might there begin to get his bearings. For many things had followed him and he wanted to confront them, so that he might turn in some of his ways and learn.

As he closed his eyes, listening to the rustling palms and the water lapping the Battery, he felt again as if he were in the navigator's cockpit of the F-4—spiraling upward at a blast; swinging through the sky in arcs as wide as half the state; hurtling forward and straight, high and clean; having left behind all slow-moving encumbrances; having surrendered himself to what he would find and feel, to the physics of that fighter's motion above America, Kitty Hawk, and Charleston in the Palmetto Country.

18

That Saturday was almost hot. Rollo and Amanda were home from school but not underfoot. Amanda was preoccupied with the discovery of flowers in the garden. First she approached the flower, walked around it to observe from all angles, peered over it, touched it, bent back the petals, and followed the stem down to the ground. Marshall watched a bee alight on a pure white geranium cupped in Amanda's hands. The bee arose and began to fly around her head. She closed her eyes and began to gasp, which meant that in little time she would break down completely. Marshall ran to the garden, took her from her footing of soft earth and, after a kiss, set her on the lawn, where she soon fell asleep.

Rollo was bent over a complex but childish mechanical drawing. "What's this?" asked Marshall, sitting down at Rollo's table.

"If I tell you, do you promise to keep it a secret until I get a patent?"

"I promise."

"All right. I noticed that when I went on my bicycle I could go five or six times faster than if I walked, with the same effort. I figured out it was because of the lack of friction in the wheels, and because of the gears. Anyway, it's a terrific machine, and it makes me able to go way over there without hardly trying.

"Now, Daddy took us riding. We went in Virginia. After we learned how, we went for ten miles in the forest and in the woods. The horses went as fast as a bicycle, and they weren't even tired." He looked extremely tense and serious, as if what he was going to say were the most important revelation in the history of all mankind.

"I invented a horse bicycle. It was obvious. It has four wheels, each of which has its own gears. The horse puts his feet in specially molded rubber buckets which attach to the pedals. The pedals are hydraulically mounted so that they will give enough resistance. Otherwise, he would break his legs. It's steered by a rack-and-pinion mechanism attached to the livers and then to ropes which go to the rider's hands." Marshall was speechless, but his face gave away his skepticism. Rollo became even more serious, knitting his brows as his father often did.

"The horse has to start when very young so he can learn how to do it. This is my third drawing. I make them better and better. With a horse bicycle, I could ride from here to Florida in five days, for only fifteen dollars."

Susannah sent Marshall and Rollo to the store to pick up a case of beer. They had plenty of champagne for the party but had forgotten to get beer. On the way and back along the Battery past piles of cannonballs and massive squat-looking mortars, Rollo gave away the secrets of the ages, in describing a vast catalog of inventions. He made Marshall swear a hundred times not to tell, or steal them. They were, in fact, often practicable and sometimes ingenious, and included a new design for a freight yard to facilitate easier switching; an optical anti-collision system for ships at sea; a means of transporting heavy loads over wilderness terrain with minimal effort; improvements for surveying and navigational instruments; apt and wonderful slogans for corporations and products; games; camping and survival equipment; new types of snacks; colas; food packaging; a record-keeping system for small businesses; the horse bicycle; clever kitchen and garden implements; and many different recipes for cakes and cookies—all of which sounded delicious. Marshall concluded that with a skilled and loyal support staff Rollo would become a corporate giant, and advised him to write down the ideas and have his father put them in the vault.

For the rest of the afternoon Marshall read outside and got as much sun as if he had been sailing in the harbor. He went to his room and slept in the cool shade, listening to the wind in the trees. When he awoke it was dark and the sky was bright silver from a moon which seemed twice its normal size and many times as dazzling. Marshall peered out the window into the moonlit garden. A rack of lamb turned above a hickory fire as the coals blinked with the turning. The veranda was filled with admirals looking over the water. Servants in white jackets ran back and forth with silver trays. From the livingroom came the sounds of a raucous and excellent rock band. No doubt this was why the admirals were outside.

He put on tie and jacket, and stood before a mirror. He was blond, lean, tanned, and (he thought) sort of handsome, especially in the light gray jacket and dark blue tie. He made his way downstairs past a group of women congregated on the second floor landing, and walked into a wild and elegant scene. The band was white-hot. He looked at the drum and saw their title— *Potato Za and his Band*. They were excellent, fast, disciplined, superbly electronic, artfully co-ordinated, and horribly ugly.

Rollo went speeding past, racing up the stairs as if he had wings, saying, "My aunt's here; she came from Virginia." The last thing Marshall wanted was Rollo's aunt, for aunts were, after all, dumpy and strange, with glasses which hung on black string. He wandered through the oscillating room. It was exciting. He had been to very few parties, shunning them in favor of sulking work, and sullen walks when it was always autumn and cold, even in June. But that night he mastered his fear and stood in a sea of music (Potato Za was singing "Call Me Up in Greenland"), naval uniforms, and French doors thrown open to the palmettos and the moonlit harbor run. Scintillations of percussion mixed with the light and dancing. The women with the young officers were, for the most part, extremely good-looking. They wore loose white dresses and danced with an elegant abandon which seemed to Marshall to be extraordinarily erotic, especially in an admiral's house. The floor was dark old wood. Paintings of frigates and major combatants, of white-maned sea storms, and of old clean coasts lined the walls. A grandfather clock with pale blue moons ticked brassily and independent in the bosom of the stairs.

Marshall stood by a table laden with cake and champagne. Glass in hand, he fixed his glance on the clock. He was thinking that the room was hot, and was nearly on his way out to eye the black bay, when he saw a woman descending the curved stairs, towed by Rollo, who let go and dashed into the kitchen. It was Rollo's aunt. She came to the bottom and stood still, staring at Marshall. It seemed to them that they were at the end of a long corridor. The music was like gold and silver pouring in an arch over the way between them—percussive stars and whitened sparks. They did not know how long they stood like that, oblivious of the comings and goings of others. Behind her was the brassy clock, behind him the bay. She had dark, chestnut-colored hair which was thick and soft. Her eyes were green. Her lips moved ever so slightly in astonishment. When finally she came close he was overtaken by the heady scents of good perfume, thin red Florentine leather, and the juniper and herbs of gin. And he was stunned by her high, perfectly formed shoulders. But he could see in her that which he had always loved. They looked in one another's eyes, transfixed. Marshall shuddered and would have been seized had she not brought him back as only she could, with characteristic love and tenderness, saying, "Are you seeing colors?" For it was Lydia.

Parting from her in Union Station fifteen years before he had seen the dark colors and the shafts of sunlight, the porters' red hats, and the black iron, and it had nearly broken him. But there on the Battery he found himself with her in a chamber of light and gold; she had become the most beautiful woman he had ever seen; and it was a clear spring night in South Carolina.

19

Far more luminous than the girls Marshall saw from a distance in the Saturday Regatta at Charleston, sunburnt in the sea's white clothes, Lydia Levy was graceful, warm, beguiling, brilliant, and lithe-limbed. She herself embodied the ravaging simplicity and beauty of static Charleston and its smoky wharves.

Upon his return from Palestine in 1947, an amazed Paul Levy had found his mother in an advanced state of pregnancy. His first trip to Eagle Bay had been to try to reclaim Marshall so that the new Levy baby would have a companion. But there had been no chance of that, and he had seen that the Livingstons were a fortunate choice, even if fortuitous. He had surveyed the splendid mass of Eagle Bay, the stables, the works of art, the discipline of the Livingston study, and decided that from a practical standpoint it would be better for Marshall to be nurtured alone and the center of attention. Then there was the issue of wealth. He did not know that Livingston would retire to his garden at a relatively early age, thus activating the stopcocks on a generous income and considerably reducing the family accounts. Still, the inheritance would not be divided, as would that of Levy senior. No one (including the Internal Revenue Service) knew exactly how much Livingston had squirreled away, because he lived simply almost to the point of fraud. Once, Marshall had cried because Otto Boar, the father of one of his classmates, had called him a pauper.

Lydia was born on a clear blue day in late September, 1947. Her brothers and sisters were much older than she was, and she grew up virtually alone.

She began her dancing in high school, during which time the beautiful child whom Marshall had known became a beautiful woman. When she graced herself with silver rings or just a velvet ribbon in her hair, she stopped hearts. At Berkeley, she had majored in history and spent all the time she could in the High Sierra—like Marshall, she wanted to live in a wilderness cabin. Like Marshall, she wanted to live high above the hills of San Francisco in one of the precarious flying towers there. Like Marshall, she wanted to farm in the mountains. They wanted so many things that it was impossible to choose. She was the only girl he had ever met who looked with favor upon his dreams of being in the Navy. She, too, liked to walk for miles and miles on punishing hikes, to climb obstacles and buildings, to listen to classical music as well as the music of Potato Za and his band. Like Marshall, she preferred to eat while walking, to have the kitchen clean while eating, to keep the windows open all the time. He hated coffee. She hated coffee. She hated drugs. He hated drugs. They loved to exercise, to read solid works of history. Scholarly books excited them. They liked country music, spotlights instead of round bulbs, dogs. They danced together to the music of Potato Za. They made perfect love.

Marshall lost track of time and forgot about the dossier that Levy had returned to the vault. Levy did not remind him. Since their parents had died in her adolescence, Levy had been like a father to Lydia, and he was delighted by what seemed to be an impending marriage, although he knew that Marshall had a task to fulfill. Marshall and Lydia together made the household shine like a jewel.

They recalled the last day on the train, thundering across the heartland. As soon as they tried to define what it had meant, to corner its undoubted importance, they forgot words and sense and drifted into one another's arms. "On the train," she would say, her lips numbing with desire and love, "when we rode for hours staring at the plains, the wheat . . . the mountains." By that time, he would be holding her tightly, kissing her shoulders, she with eyes closed and fingers spread. But nonetheless, they got the spirit of it.

They went to Atlantic Headquarters—the nerve center of seaward defense, a fortress of Levy's design. A great violet-colored room was crossed and circled by glowing translucent lines of red, blue, and green. Chunks of amber light representing the ships of the Second Fleet moved sluggishly across a black sea. A compass rose, projective lines, and the assurant grid of Mercator pulsed in high-frequency yellow. Twoscore men and women in white uniforms glowing ultraviolet worked faint consoles and followed the amber spots across empty seas. Aware that the plotters and trackers were young, Levy had had quiet electronic music piped in. They went about their jobs smoothly, as if they were in another world. The amber and the electronic tones were killing and rapacious to the senses. Intellect carried on there very well, affording its strange paralyzed joys in an advanced incursion of the future into a century still close to the land, the wood, and the salt of the sea.

They sought the light in a Charleston church full of little children tied in tight on a Sunday morning. Marshall and Lydia watched through long straight windows as boys and girls in knee socks and Jesus buttons squirmed on folding metal chairs. The palmettos bent in the wind outside. Wills were forced into ceremony and religion. Parents waited by the bay to retrieve their children, and vanished down a long water-bordered street into an uncertain distance—almost as if back into the interior of the Carolinas—to rest from codes and escape the law. Lydia said, "Those children will look back and remember the old light in their schoolroom, light long passed, and like us they'll see themselves stretched in a beautiful tension, always unknowing. Sometimes, I wish I had not been educated, and would be a fat old country woman indolent with fan and beer." And she easily achieved that homeward, lazy, rocking indolence—only to wake up with a dancer's body and a scholar's mind, gentle and true.

One day they went to the out islands. She was wearing white—white tennis shoes, a white skirt, a white blouse, and a white hat. Her arms were darkly tanned (it was already the end of April), as were her long and perfect hands. Her face was ruddy, and from her hat, bent in flowing curves like a flower, her energetic hair swept around her neck. They sat down on the side of a dune and she pulled her knees up to her chest, resting her head on the little platform which resulted. Marshall knew that he could spend the rest of his life with this woman—doing simple things like going to the beach and watching tankers and military ships beyond the shining ribbons of white and blue; driving into the country and sitting by a river; going to an outdoor restaurant; swimming in the salty estuary; holding her in his arms. She was the first woman with whom he felt entirely at ease (as he had known that he would), with no need to prove himself or to overwhelm, and no fear that she would go. He had often been afraid, combative, in pain. It dropped away.

They walked until they got to a road, following it until they reached a small shack outside of which was an old Coca-Cola machine. He took out some dimes and they found themselves with two icy bottles, which they carried along the heat-waved macadam road to a bridge, where Marshall opened the bottles on the girders. "I hate it," she said, "but I always end up drinking it." He almost fell off the bridge, because she was a thousand times more ideal than all the paintings on the back of all the *National Geographics* he had ever seen, when an American beauty takes the pause that refreshes. In her white hat, with hair shining, arm uplifted, and neck smoothly stretched, she drank. As her lips separated from the bottle and the remaining liquid fell back, there was a perfect sound, like a little bell.

"Hey," she said, "there're shrimp in this creek. Let's go get 'em. I'll use my hat. I can always wash it." In one move, she jumped into the water—landing almost knee-deep—swept off her hat, releasing a mass of buoyant hair, and began intently to skim the surface for shrimp, which ended their days at a roadside stand where, for a dollar, an old woman cleaned and cooked them, and served them up with fried potatoes. Marshall and Lydia slept in her barn.

When they awoke it was sweet and dark, with the light patterns of winter, and air as still and soft as silence. They drove inland, halted by a field, and watched for hours as the shade moved across it, a heavy weight receding and advancing on the pale new grass. They could hear hundreds of birds, and sweet smoke was slowly rising in a distant column.

They started back to Charleston in early evening. He went too fast because he was thinking of how it could be with her in New York, in the commercial districts and downtown where it was frenetic and violent. He imagined her standing by City Hall, the great ramps of the Brooklyn Bridge visible to her left, gray snow falling crystalline as if on the North Sea, diesel smoke from ships in the harbor, officials gliding up and down stone steps into halls bluer and finer than the shell of a robin's egg, heavy winter coats, men around bright fires in trash cans, and the penetrating cold. Looking into her face, framed by a fur collar and her hair, which glinted overpoweringly in the slanting sun, he heard a single tone like the sound of a shaking reed or a powerful note from Lucius's pipes beating over the mountainsides before the raid.

She stopped that vision completely when she turned on the radio and let out Elvis, who pulsated throughout the car and about the cool trees on the roadside. They agreed that Elvis was better old and crazy than young, that he fit into the landscape of the South best of all, and that he should never have left the South.

Having made a circuitous route inland, they drove past the warships in Charleston as one was lighting its boilers. Black diesel smoke poured from the stack. The ship was as strong, cutting, and gray as New York Harbor in winter. They sensed fire, and he looked past her, ravishingly beautiful in worn white, at the sailors doing their tasks inevitably and with directed energy. He loved her all the more when she understood why he shuddered with resolve at the sight of a warship. She moved her hands to the music and nearly danced in her seat as they drove by the water, and the sun finally started to set—round, driving, orange fire dipping into the back bays and branches of the sea.

20

They were married in the summer, after a quick and physical courtship. Queried about the wisdom of such a momentous step, Levy had said to Marshall, "I think it's a good idea. If you took time to look more carefully, you wouldn't know what to look for anyway. You might as well just jump into it, if the spirit moves you." And since the spirit did, one day in June Marshall became uncle to Rollo and Amanda, brother-in-law to Susannah and Paul Levy, and husband to Lydia Levy. Stunned, the Livingstons flew to Charleston. Suddenly Marshall was part of an enormous vital family. It was good that Levy knew the Livingstons, satisfying that there were children about, and amusing that dignitaries came from Washington to witness the union. Several tents and platforms were erected on the back lawn, and young women from the city worked behind linen-covered tables in a mist of beating sun. Palmettos had been fixed at the tops of the tent poles as if Marshall and Lydia were to be married near the Sixth Cataract of the Nile, and not in a Battery garden. The Livingstons brought engraved gemstones for Lydia. And that Saturday there was a harbor regatta—moving like magic on the summer inlet, pressing forward with grace and with courage.

Marshall was grateful, and not just because of the wedding. Some of Lydia's friends had flown in from Berkeley and arranged to meet her in a Charleston restaurant. Even at a distance Marshall heard over the phone as they specified in conspiratorial yet booming voices that he not be present. He asked Lydia why, and she replied that they had come to dissuade her from marriage. "They're feminists, and think that marriage is being a prisoner of war. They would rather spend their lives seeking out reflections of themselves in everything that exists. You see, if you are married to a man, he does not present you with a mirror-image. You have to look apart from yourself. They're afraid to do this, imagining that they would be subsumed, and per-haps *they* would be. But I do like them, or at least I used to."

"Are they against the family?"

"Sure."

"They would really rather see men and women apart?"

"Yes."

"And what about the children?"

"God help the children."

This was one area in which Marshall had not a defense in the world, and could not even begin to think clearly enough to argue. He could only feel, and it upset him very much. All his life, he had loved and been thank-ful for the Livingstons, and, lacking a real father and mother, did not understand how anyone could wish to rid himself of the true attachments for want of which he had been outcast and tormented. He was afraid that they would take Lydia away from him.

"Why?" she asked. "It doesn't make sense. How could they?" Then she realized that such things did not have to make sense—they just swooped down as hard and as surprising as falcons. Marshall was afraid because it had happened to him in a time that he could not even remember. She took him in her arms. "You don't know about these things," she said. "Of course you don't. Now what can I do? I know. Come to the Palm Restaurant and hide on the roof. It will be dark, and you can get up there. We'll sit in the court-yard, toward the water. It's a late supper, at ten."

He made his way to the restaurant and struggled two stories up a drain-pipe until he reached the roof. Just as he was clear, a Chinese chef brandish-ing a long knife rushed into the alleyway and, cursing in Mandarin with great ferocity, killed a slew of invisible swordsmen. Marshall groped along terra-cotta tiles until he caught sight of Lydia in the courtyard. As she had said, she was sitting at a table on the bayside. He perched on the roof unseen, squatting with chin in hand like a forgotten gargoyle. From above, he could see the full sweep of her hair. She was wearing a black shawl. He threw a pebble onto her plate. The china rang and everyone looked, but she calmly crossed her legs and scratched her nose.

Then the two young women arrived and embraced and kissed Lydia in a way that made Marshall bristle. He could hear every word of their conversa-tion. First they talked about women; women here and women there, women in literature, women in art. Then they talked about women; women in politics, women in society, women in sports. And then they talked about women; women in the cinema, women in history, women in agriculture.

At dessert they got to the heart of the palm. They wanted Lydia to come with them at that very moment and fly out of Charleston, without even going home to pack, without making a telephone call. They held up a ticket. "It's for you," they said. "It has your name on it. You can live in the co-operative. Come with us. Be our sister." With uncharacteristic softness, they looked into her eyes, waiting for her answer. Marshall was clenching his fists, swaying back and forth as if he were watching a boxing match. Lydia had listened silently. They thought they had her, and, for a moment, so did Marshall. What they said was powerful for the times, direct, and daring. There were two of them and only one Lydia, and they were skillful prosely-tizers, because they depended completely on making others believe what they believed.

"No," said Lydia. But they didn't take her seriously, and they started up again. She interrupted, saying, "Didn't you hear me? I said no, thank you." Again they began, as if what she thought meant nothing as long as it did not fit their expectations. This made her rather angry, for she was some-one who, most of the time, was taken very seriously.

"Lydia . . ." they oozed.

"Lydia, shmidia. Do you know what 'no' means, a nice, tough, assertive, no-nonsense 'no'?"

"She went soft," one of them said to the other, and they started to get up.

"Just one minute," shouted Lydia in rage. "If there's anything soft here, it's your mushy little brain."

"Where do you think you're going to get, with babies, and a house to run?" they screamed. "In a few years you'll come to us, you'll see, when you want to escape a dead, fascist institution which will rape the life out of you. Marriage is paid rape. There's no such thing as love, except between sisters."

"You are deranged. Don't tell *me* about getting along in the world. Who was *Summa*? Who won the History Prize? And what did you do? I happen to know what you did. You spent your time staring at your genitals in a mirror—four whole years!" They gasped.

"You could be a *pioneer*," they said, unable to escape a world of slogans.

"*You* be a pioneer," said Lydia. "Go out West. Beat off the Indians." They gasped again. "I'm going to have a family, and I will love them and be devoted to them. The rest will work itself out. And if that's a dangerous pronouncement in these times, then I choose to live dangerously. I can do it, even if I'm the last woman in the world who does. And you, you self-centered gherkins, keep on riding your endless corkscrew. But stay out of my life."

Marshall, who had been completely engrossed in the argument, lost his footing on the roof and began to slide. "Oh, no," he said, desperately clawing the smooth tile, but he continued to slide. "Oh, no," he said, hurtling off the edge of the roof, ripping his pants on a projection of drainpipe, and flying, as if aimed, right for Lydia's table. He landed on his back. The table broke in two and collapsed with a great clatter. A dozen old ladies began to scream uncontrollably, as if in a play when a woman sees a mouse. The two sisters assumed vicious self-defense positions. Marshall stood up quickly and began to hop around on one foot. In the sound of Lydia's laughter, his fear of feminism disappeared forever.

Among the hundred guests at the wedding were dozens of admirals and the Secretary of the Navy. The rabbi had forgotten to bring the canopy, so they improvised. They used a damask tablecloth as lustrous as snow, two rifles from the honor guard, and a rake and pitchfork from the garden shed. Levy and Livingston held the rifles, and Rollo and a young sailor held the pitchfork and rake, to make a tight canopy which glowed in the sharp morning sun.

Marshall and Lydia stood before the admirals in the garden as the tents were buffeted by the wind. The rabbi said, "They, who in the face of their mortality and in the decadence of their times, who with hearts gentle and true profess their love for one another, today have our blessing. Lord keep them safe." They smashed the glass. A jet climbed straight as an arrow against a blue and wistful horizon. They embraced, and champagne began once more to flow abundantly in the Levys' garden. Battered gently by the music, couples danced. A young man wrote something on the brim of a girl's hat. An officer held the collar of a woman's dress and talked at her determinedly as she looked down. A woman in salmon-pink satin had one hand on the table, and the other stretched out holding a champagne glass. The clouds sailed by as sure as the regatta, and Marshall and Lydia were taken up and beyond their control, lost in the music. They turned 'round and 'round on the dance platform oblivious once again of the admirals and the noise. Then they stopped and put their heads together like horses in the field, only to feel a flood of tenderness and love, and their courage tolling about them like a brass bell.

21

A collection of canopied launches had accumulated by the Battery wall. Sailors in garrison belts rested on piles of Civil War shot, and were brought one barrage after another of wedding food and champagne. At nightfall, the last of the launches pulled away into the smooth water and warm air.

The caterers folded their tents and retreated with the speed and finesse of the French Army. It took them no more than an hour to get everything in the trucks and restore house and garden to their original June splendor. Lydia and Marshall sat in the garden in familiar fashion—back to back. They seldom needed chairs, and were so expert at descent and ascent to and from this position that they operated in the smooth offhand way of acrobats. They looked in separate directions and thought independently, but returned to the same center, their backs warm and touching, and, sometimes, their hands entwined. It became almost an emblem for them, and they thought that if they were to have a coat of arms it would show Marshall and Lydia non-rampant, and a great symmetrical pine.

She gazed at the full darkness of a blossomed tree, listening to its lush spaces. She was thinking about her new name, and it tumbled on her lips as her old name had often done. Lydia Levy had by law and decree become Lydia Pearl. She said them over and over again: "Lydia Levy, Lydia Levy, Lydia Pearl, Lydia Levy Pearl, Marshall Pearl, Marshall Levy, Lydia Levy Marshall Pearl, Marshall Levy Lydia Pearl." She took yet another sip of champagne (they had decided to drink champagne all night), and the moon in the glass as flat as a quarter and as white as paint reminded her of her new name. It made the glass sparkle, she thought, like Lydia, and the moon was Pearl. There before her clear and reflecting was Lydia Pearl, and the confusion of names and refractions penetrated with her gaze into the softness of the tree, landing as if on a pillow.

Marshall stared at the whitened bay. Leaning against Lydia, he entertained visions of himself as a lustrous fighting fish piercing the waves of the Atlantic. He saw from afar the shimmer of a curved and muscular salmon rising in combat over the waves, and at the same time he felt the leap and the foaming white water, as if his eye had been in the fish, and his skin were smooth and glowing. He pushed against a fast river and went upstream jumping falls and resting in backwaters only to start again, against the water, which had once carried him downward. All around, the sound of breaking waves came rolling at him, and in his mind's eye he leaped another falls, flying in a great arc weightless and abstract.

Then Levy came silently down the path and invited them to his study. "It's a quiet night," he said. "Do you think you can make it up the stairs?"

In the airy room high above the bay, they sat in a triangular pattern—Levy at his desk, with a bunch of papers spread before him. Marshall felt momentarily perfect and fulfilled, and said, "You read it. So you do . . . too much champagne I say."

"I'll summarize, since they're partly in German."

"That's fine," said Marshall, "I couldn't read them in English."

Levy began, haltingly piecing them together, and then using them as the base for his own narrative. At first, Marshall's and Lydia's thoughts were elsewhere, but then they began to listen intently—if not soberly.

"From 'Report by Stabseinsatzführer Anton, Lodz, 11 February, 1943': 'This last Wednesday Bureau 17 received a group of prisoners from the detention camp temporarily set up at the station. All were members of the Polish underground. Several Jews were among them . . . two women and three men . . . Zelewski, Carnovski, etc. . . . and Katrina Perlé, a Jewess speaking Russian as native tongue . . . prisoners transferred . . . Jews given over to custody of SS Obersturmbannführer Rauf.'

"Strangely, here is an excerpt from the 'Report of the Commander, Group C, Kamentz-Podolsk, 23 September, 1943': 'Executions have taken place in the following categories: political officials, active communists, thieves and saboteurs, Jews with false papers, NKVD agents, denouncers of ethnic Germans, revengeful and sadistic Jews, undesirable elements, partisans, members of Russian bands, insurgents caught with arms in hand, rebels, agitators, young vagrants, and Jews in general. Appended is a list of those considered most vile and dangerous. They are no more.'

"Katrina Perlé is on this list, and on other lists, and it's always the same. She is captured. She is reported executed. She turns up again. When I was in Europe in the summer of 1950, I thought to see if others on the list were alive. It took several months, but the Red Cross found a man who had been on the roster of dead.

"He was in a hospital in Geneva, where I went to see him. His name was Metzner, and he was very sick. I was stupid, and I went in uniform. He didn't trust me. I came the next day in civilian clothes; he just looked at me and shook his head. He told me a little, but not much. Perhaps he knew nothing more.

"He said that he and Katrina Perlé had escaped, and that for the third or fourth time they had gone back with the partisans. They once came in contact with a dislocated band of the Red Army in Poland, far behind German lines.

"He said that when they first collided face to face deep in the mountains, Katrina fell to her knees on the snow, in amazement, and a tall Russian carrying arms and bandoliers of ammunition rushed to her through the mist and darkness. Evidently they had been in love before the war, and it seemed a miracle that both should be alive in the midst of winter, in a forest of high trees, behind the retreating Wehrmacht.

"I have his words here, as I took them down: 'On the first beautiful day, they were married. We had very little food and most of us were sick, but we paused for half an hour and the leader at that time, who later was killed, married them. They cut down some vines with berries and that is what they gave one another when they embraced. And they knelt in the snow as she had done when she had first seen him . . .' "

"And what of my father?" asked Marshall, unexpectedly drawn into a past with which he felt nearly as much intimacy as with his present.

"This is what I know of him, and this is all. His first name was Lev. He was from Leningrad. He was either an economist or an engineer, or both. He and Katrina Perlé said that after the war they would go to Jewish Palestine. He was tall, and Metzner said that his eyes were 'piercing.' That's it.

"But, Metzner is alive. He is a scientist. When I met him, I had no idea that he was anything other than a peasant. (He was a strange man.) In this folder I have a paper on glaciology, written by Hans Metzner. I know that it's the same one because of the picture. Look at it." Marshall saw an old man with white hair. The paper had been delivered in London, and Metzner was listed as Professor of Geology at the University of Lausanne.

Levy handed Marshall the dossier and headed for bed. Lydia could read German, and she and Marshall stayed up until the sun rose, going over the yellowed documents. In this way they spent their wedding night. Katrina Perlé and her husband had vanished from the memory of the world, and she had been cut down on a bright and beautiful day. Marshall and Lydia understood the rabbi's words about "the face of their mortality." They passed the night uncomfortable and upset. It was tense and sad, like the night of an assassination. The rabbi's words came clear to them, especially when a placid morning arose from the sea by Charleston as they read over and over the words that Levy had taken from the man in the hospital: "And they knelt in the snow as she had done when she had first seen him . . ."

VIII
The Sea
and the Alps

1

They rode in a boat-hulled helicopter with double-barreled jet engines and rotors that twitched like an insect's wings in a hovering staccato wheel. Wind and engines were deafening as the military craft faced to sea and ran a hundred miles in search of the British Merchant Navy motor vessel *Royal George*, upon which Lydia and Marshall would sail to Rotterdam.

A hurricane in the east raged undecided and alone over an empty patch of sea. Just west of the Gulf Stream, the *Royal George* steamed up and down waiting to see if clear passage would open and in which direction. They were short of crew when they put out of Norfolk with half a cargo of coal, and a man had been swept overboard in the gale. On his telex, Levy had received a full report, and offered to send a replacement for the voyage, to work passage. Thus Marshall was conscripted into the crew.

Though she was the Admiral's sister, Lydia had never ridden in a helicopter. Nor had Marshall, though he felt at times as if the noise of the rotors—like sudden rain beating on a tin roof—were entirely familiar. The helicopter crew had just returned from Vietnam, and were elated to be alive, frightened of themselves, and remarkably casual with their machine. Partly from habit, and partly for Lydia, the pilot guided his craft through cloud and rain as if he were a skier. He slid down a steep ramp of broken clouds and made a wide circle above the sea. He banked to nearly vertical and looked downward through the side window. He charged ahead and then veered into the soft ceiling. He put music on the communications system, and swayed the helicopter so that they felt as if they were inside a dancing elephant. Lydia loved this, and it showed in her face.

The boys from Dallas and Tucumcari, in fatigues and lifejackets, stared at her without letup. In the gulf off Vietnam, and shuttling inland over dappled plains and muted gunfire, they had wished for such a woman. She put her hand on the gun carriage and looked over the sea, watching the waves drive northeast. She felt that she held the helicopter and its lethal weapons in her hand, that it emanated from her like spokes in the wheel of visual lines made by the airmen in her regard, that by will alone she could direct and co-ordinate its flight, that in the slightest movement of her eye, she could turn it and make it sweep down. It *did* go where she willed, running smoothly over the sea, toying with the storm.

The Dallas gunner cried out, "I have a ship at two o'clock." They waited for a break in the clouds, and, as soon as they had locked in to a distant form tossing in the spirited sea, made for the ship. Dropping to twenty-five feet above the waves, they sped through mist and spray toward the high steel sides. The crew of the *Royal George* lined the bridge and forecastle, watching the helicopter approach over the water as if it would smash against the ship. The pilot increased speed and, only a few hundred feet from target, rose rapidly over the masts. Then he went over on his side and circled the *Royal George* for no reason other than to show that here were men on the sea and in the air, in steel machines knotted in the mane of a hurricane; that the engines were firing and hot; that they could go where they wanted; that in conjunction with the sudden winds and high waves, they were free.

The dazzling blades came so close that they nearly struck the ship. Like that of a muscular bird, a thickened quail, the body of the craft was streamlined with plenty of curved limb. The sound of engines shuddered down the decks like the rain, and coursed over the upturned faces of the sailors as the *Royal George* yawed, pitched, and rolled. Great waves lifted its bows, lurching along the sides like a flood in a gorge, and men in blue and yellow oilskins rushed to the main hatch cover as the helicopter hovered amidships.

The gunner threw aside nylon webbing at the door and swung out the winch, while the pilot followed precisely every sway of the ship, hand and eye usurping all his vital being. Marshall took the sling and pushed away. He was lowered into the rain, and a minute later he hit a slippery deck. Lydia followed, waving goodbye to Dallas and Tucumcari.

As Lydia slowly descended, the men of the *Royal George* were astounded—they had not expected a woman. She slipped out of the harness and swept her hands through her hair. So off balance had she rendered the sailors that they looked like prehistoric Britons. Open-mouthed, squat-faced, cliff-eyed, they rocked silently on yellow and blue sea legs like a chorus line of idiots. The officers saw Lydia and adjusted their tunics. Then a wave came unexpectedly from starboard and hit the ship with a ferocious hook. Grasping rails and lines as water poured from the deck into the sea, they rushed inside.

Marshall took Lydia's hand to help her through the companionway. As they looked back they saw the helicopter making a steady line to Hatteras and Virginia, where the sun would break through. In a confusion of oilskins and a dozen English dialects they looked at one another and realized that they hardly knew who they were. Suddenly they had come into the middle of the sea in hurricane season. The helicopter which had carried them was just a spot, cleaving its way to the coast. As the ship pitched into the storm they were shown down a long narrow corridor to their cabin.

They switched on a tiny light which did no more than accentuate the darkness, and they looked into their young faces dripping and windbeaten.

Touching their cheeks together, they embraced in the glare, surrounded by shadow which agitated as if with gnats or smoke. They held one another and moved to stay standing while the ship rolled and the sea broke above them. Though dark, the cabin seemed to open like a flower into a picture of Western landscape, a fountain of colorful images. Marshall did not know if the Lydia he held were the graceful young woman with long perfect hands and silver rings, or the little girl in a gingham dress, in a starry Rocky Mountain meadow. He loved her.

2

They started a tour of the ship in the engine room. The *Royal George* was brand-new and more automated than a Japanese toy. The engines were run by computers, and adjustments in speed, maintenance, and corrective repair were accomplished electromechanically. Several times a year in major ports an army of technicians boarded with packs of instruments for an overhaul. The regulars had nothing to do but stare at several stories of green enameled iron in the main well; and the catwalks might just as well have been for cats. However, the union was present, insisting that a complement of motormen remain in number sufficient to wipe and fire a sweating gargantuan sea engine of the type that had once swallowed whole the labor and attention of fifty men. Each watch of fifteen congregated inside a white glass-enclosed room suspended in the well, where the walls were filled with registers of lights. They were, to a man, old Scotsmen and Northerners, raised in steam. But they sat silently at consoles and read the *Illustrated London News*, while they listened to a recorded tattoo of bagpipes and reeds. They were old, white-haired, of deliberate gait and hard methodical breathing. Sunken eyes gazed before them with the expression of an animal brought from its den to a closed operating theater. It was as if they had been kidnapped from nineteenth-century ships. "Isn't it strange," said Lydia, when she and Marshall stepped off a ladder in a dim vibrating corridor, "that the future is always obvious when it first appears. That," she said, meaning the banks of LED and the silent running of the control room they had just visited, no less the passive men whose grace and skill had been prematurely cupped in brain and eye away from hand and body, "is the way it will be. So much intellect and so little else." They were alone in the dark corridor, on their way to the bridge and the kitchens. "Hold me," she said.

He reached into her dress, and with his other hand he felt her back and shoulders while they kissed sadly and almost wildly. They might have gone on that way forever, so rough and alive did it make them feel, had it not been for the sudden appearance of a young rating, who, upon seeing the voluptuous entanglement, perked up to say, "My goodness, in the passageways yet. Well done."

Whereas the engine room was a leap into the future, the galleys were a throwback to the twelfth century. Long-haired kitchen boys were jammed into corners and below tables, peeling potatoes and shelling eggs. Tremendous pots, cauldrons on tripods, hanging perforated untensils, and wooden boards laden with chopped onions, garlic, and beef were scattered about a cold slippery room filled with jets of vapor from leaky steam valves at the base of the ovens. There were two cooks, Dave and Harvey. Dave was tall and skinny, and resembled a prehistoric bird. Harvey was dark and inexact, and looked like the head of the Guatemalan Secret Police.

As stewards often do at sea, they sailed together in sin, battling for the attentions of the innocent young cookboys, despised by the randy deck force, ignored by the motormen, and cultivated by the officers for whom they cooked and served special meals. In the latter half of the voyage, Lydia was put to work in the galleys. At first Harvey and Dave resented her so intemperately that she moved in between them and took command, improving the cuisine ad infinitum and raising morale among the boys forever under tables peeling or slicing, forever subject to lascivious pinches from above. They came alive in Lydia's presence, turning from sallow candle-fleshed morons to bright apple-cheeked prodigies. Lydia lay with Marshall in their narrow bed, silvery clouds racing past the porthole on warm southern air, and delighted as he recounted her praise. At her table, the rough and insolent deck force was completely tame. "Tell me more," she said. "I feel like the daughter of the regiment."

And then Marshall would repeat what had been said: "This pudding's better than me mum's." "Does your missus give receipts?" "Hell's bells governor, I've never tasted such great lima beans." When she appeared in the mess one evening, they broke into spontaneous applause. And every night she would tell Marshall about her day in the "kitchen," as she insisted upon calling it.

Dave and Harvey were upset and did not speak for a week, except once when Dave was rustling a big basket of fried potatoes and Harvey was slicing cabbages. One of the cabbages rolled off the block and into Dave's cauldron of sizzling fat. Dave looked at Harvey for the first time in days, and said, "You little devil!"

To finish their tour of the 600-foot bulk carrier, Marshall and Lydia struggled across the deck to the forecastle. Clinging to handles on the anchor winches, they resolved to climb the mast. Marshall loved many things about Lydia apart from the indefinable main elements of their affection. One of these was her willingness to explore. Side by side they had swum raging inlets, roamed the mountains, and pushed through disgusting mush-footed swamps. And she had always remained ready to go. The crow's nest was sixty feet above the deck—no laughing matter in a hurricane. The spikes by which they ascended were short enough, it seemed, to be stubble on a beard. In wind and rain they went upward into darkness. Because the *Royal George* was a modern ship, its crow's nest was well appointed. Enclosed, heated, and carpeted, it was more like an apartment than an observation post. They were comfortable there, bobbing up and down high above a tumultuous killer sea. Swabbed with iodine-colored light and stretching from side to side, the bridge seemed like a wide rectangular eye. The sea was curly and white. Now and then a high part of it struck the ship, a storm within a storm. "This is just like *Die Fledermaus*," said Marshall, "in which a woman suddenly calls for music even though music has been playing for an hour. And when it begins, it's as if there has been silence." Every eighth or ninth wave covered the part of the ship they had crossed to reach the bows. They made note of this in regard to getting back, and realized that it had been only by chance that they hadn't been swept overboard on the way up.

3

Little love was lost between the crew and the Bosun, flown into Norfolk because his predecessor had vanished mysteriously somewhere off the Bahamas. The Bosun had one eye, wore a bright green hat, and was the toughest-looking bugger anyone on the ship had ever seen. "He beats up the plumbing at Dartmoor," they said. To show who was boss, he had eaten his glass, plate, and fork at the hurricane dinner. He hated the crew, and they hated him. He was a fearsome character, and they were a tough bunch. They hated him because he tried to make them work in the storm. He hated them because they were a unique set of work-shirking duds who hadn't done a day's labor in their lives. But they did have a case, because the ship was fully automated. A war smoldered in the spray of the hurricane.

At 3 A.M. the Captain sent an order to the helm. They were to steam south and loop around the storm—which seemed likely to hang about for weeks—traversing the Sargasso Sea in an unexpected penetration of tropical latitudes, during which the ship would stop at least once (against company policy, but the Captain was not a company man) for swimming and diving. When Marshall heard the Bosun at his door ("Get up, ye dirty little Yankee fucker"), he dressed, went to breakfast, and, with the rest of the crew, made his way to the main deck. There, a light rain beat steadily; like Charleston in late February it was cold without a hint of warmth but not as cold as the same rain in the North, even if only for the memory of recent balmy days and anticipation of those soon to come. It was a rain of the palms, promising somehow not to betray and kill them with a desertion into unremitting cold.

Twelve men lined up. The Bosun paced before them with a mean look in his eye. His fists were clenched and they beat against his thighs like drumsticks. "Who's the shop steward?" he asked the first man.

"Fuck you."

"Who's the shop steward?" he asked the second man.

"Fuck you."

He went to the third, fourth, and fifth men, and asked, "Who's the shop steward?"

"Fuck you."

"Fuck you."

"Fuck you," they answered.

The Bosun turned away for a moment, and then pivoted around, saying, "Okay boys, today we're going to paint the cross-buckle plates. You," he said, pointing to the first man, an enormous sailor named Roberts, "go get the paint."

"*You* get the paint," answered Roberts, "you silly one-eyed bastard."

The Bosun sizzled. "What's your name?" he demanded. Roberts was silent. "I'm going to dock your pay and put you off the ship. What's your name?" He took out a little notebook.

"Bellchicken."

"What?"

"Bellchicken's my name," said Roberts. "Wonderful Bellchicken."

"Bellchicken, eh. We'll see about that. What's his name?" he asked Marshall, who, because of a sudden adjustment in the line, was standing next in the row.

Marshall replied, "Bellchicken's his name, Wonderful Bellchicken."

"What's your name?" the Bosun asked Marshall. The next man jabbed Marshall in the ribs.

"Van Mushtif," answered Marshall. "Cock Van Mushtif." They twittered, and the Bosun felt as if he were beginning to lose control.

He said, "You British bastards! I'm putting every one of you on report. I don't know who you are, but I will. Give me your names!" He moved to the man next to Marshall, a Cardiff giant of nearly seven feet, with a frightening black beard and piercing eyes.

"Name!"

In a deep boomament of near-Welsh, the giant said, "My name is Weeny, Weeny Allison." He blew a kiss and mimed a curtsy.

The Bosun wrote in his book and moved on. "And you?" he inquired of the next man.

"Brutus, sir."

"And you?" he asked a frail buck-toothed Scotsman.

"Pale Horse."

"You bastard." The Bosun stepped to the next man. "And you?"

"Pale Rider."

At the point of giving up, the Bosun came to a middle-aged Londoner whose real name was Greylock Oceanard, and he did give up, throwing his notebook over the side and leaving the deck force until the afternoon, when he found them huddled on the hawsers in the forecastle, exchanging stories and shivering as the ship made for the south. Roberts was telling of the time when he was chased from a theater for yelling slogans, and in his dash to escape had not looked to check traffic. A bakery van loaded with dough had been barreling down the street, and had been forced to stop short at forty-five mph. The wet dough hurtled from the rear and pressed the driver against the windshield. He was all right, but when they pulled him out they discovered that he had cut quite a cookie, and people from miles around came to see.

The Bosun entered the forecastle. "To work, boys," he said, and they obliged only because they wanted exercise.

Lieutenant Buff-Wibbin came to direct the cleaning of Hold Two. Some of the men went single file down a set of steel rungs, while others slid down ropes to the floorplates sixty feet below (about twenty feet under the water line) and stood in an open-roofed steel cavern as big as a playing field. The sides sloped to nests of perforated beams and arches hidden in darkness, holding innumerable warrens, landings, and plateaus. Everything was covered with grain dry enough not to rot, and wet enough to smell like the first days in the creation of whisky. In addition to the grain, wooden beams and planks were scattered about, the remnants of dunnage placed to retard undo shifting of cargo.

Lieutenant Buff-Wibbin smoked a pipe and was regarded as a fool. He was lowered in the big iron vessel into which they would dump grain and planks. The chain was not quite long enough, leaving the vessel and Lieutenant Buff-Wibbin swaying to and fro several feet above the floor. He remained inside, surveying his crew of skeptics. Not only did they lack faith in him, but they had taken on the glazed, ward-of-the-state, vacant look they always had directly before the assignation of tasks. Buff-Wibbin was quite familiar with this. Swinging in his steel bucket, he began to throw out brushes and brooms, crying, "The thuds will wake the duds." They took the tools and ran up the steep sides, often as not sliding back. But after a dozen tries they all made it into the darkness, where they found comfortable places amid the beams.

"Aren't we going to work?" asked Marshall.

"We are working," someone replied, "and working bloody hard, I might add."

"Oh."

"Not only that, but we're getting danger pay."

"Danger pay?"

"That's right. It's dangerous here, especially in a storm. So, we get danger pay."

"Even if we don't move?"

"Who's to know?"

"If there's not a kernel of grain in the bucket, Buff-Wibbin will know."

"The bucket will be full in two hours."

"We *are* going to work."

"Certainly not. Buff-Wibbin will do it."

Sure enough, when Marshall peered out, there was Buff-Wibbin, shirt off, sweating, frantically throwing boards into the bucket, and sweeping great piles of grain. "Are you active up there?" he called out. "I know you're not working," he said. "I know it as surely as I know that Mozart was an Italian!" Eventually he visited each perch, where his men huddled like thatch-makers in a hay shortage.

"Our eyes are adjusting to the darkness," they said.

"Well, get on with it," snapped Buff-Wibbin, indignantly showing them how. They made token movements of their brushes and brooms, passing them back and forth in the air a few times as if to expel the curse of activity. Buff-Wibbin swept out all the grain in three minutes. Then he moved across a beam to another group, and Marshall heard the pitter-patter of wheat pouring over the rusted plates fronting the abyss.

When Buff-Wibbin had just about finished loading the bucket, an old Cockney stepped out of the shadows and bellowed, "It's tea toime! As union members, we demand our roite to tea toime! I've been on the sea for most of me loif. No upper-class fairy is going to take away my tea!"

"All right, all right," said Buff-Wibbin, "come down for tea."

But first they had to dump the grain overboard. When they came up on deck they saw that the weather had changed. The sea was high and white; waves crashed; but the sky was clear blue and no longer a jungle steambath. The bow wave of the *Royal George* was like an unloosed bale of pure white cotton. Near the horizon a destroyer took water over its decks as it plowed east on patrol. Tracers of foam covered even the deep troughs as the sea seemed to cast up energy.

They guided the bucket over the rail and watched as the golden grain flew in a shower down to the agitated waters. The heavy planks blew like chaff. Suddenly, Buff-Wibbin called out, "Cable!" as the bucket began to fall. Every man snatched the cable, and strained with bare hands to keep it from being lost. It was extremely heavy, and there was not enough slack for belaying. It gradually pulled them across the deck, until the lead man, Roberts (or Bellchicken), was pushed against the rail. Like a tug team at Darbydale Fair, they pulled rhythmically until their muscles seemed to be on fire. They succeeded in holding it. Sweating and inflamed in the middle of the line, Marshall heard the Captain on the P.A. system. Marshall had never seen the Captain, who must have been as quick as lightning, for in no time he had directed thirty men to the cable.

But just before they arrived, the bucket had touched the sea and taken on some water. The more water it took the more it closed on the waves and took water. The thirty of them cut their hands and smarted. For many minutes they held, dripping wet despite the cold wind, hearts beating like fast engines. The skin on the soles of their feet began to blister from tension against the deck. Breathless and white, Bellchicken was crushed on the rail, and the bucket was about to sink like a stone. But none thought to give up. Buff-Wibbin had rigged a splice, and calmly asked if they could move the cable a few feet so that he could join it to the broken end from the winch.

The Cockney counted to three, and they all pulled so hard that their faces got red and purple, and snakelike veins stood out at their temples. The bucket rose a few feet, Buff-Wibbin and the carpenter looped the ends and bolted them fast, and the Chief Officer started the winch. They hauled it up. It was half full of sparkling ice-cold sea water. They put their hands in it and some even tasted it. Then they started for the showers. Tired as athletes, their blood pounding and their muscles hard and taut from half an hour's agony, they went to change for tea—to which, as union members, they were indisputably entitled.

4

After a few days, they outran the storm's southern foot. No longer did they feel the lash of waves, roll between water cliffs, or take shocked coronets of spray. But hour by hour they went steadily into the tropics and motored over the pastel beauty of the sea.

As if they were on a cruising yacht, the officers opened bridge windows and stood in the light winds. Never quite used to such easy passage, sailors congregated on deck to enjoy the spring of it, the feeling of faraway fires in an island forest, the light blue of the sky south of Bermuda where the waters were not vexed. Lydia felt linked by her femininity to the quiet colors of the sea. Like a dog in a car approaching home, Marshall grew excited because something in him could feel the inner breezes and timeless clock of Jamaica. Just beyond the horizon, it seemed, were the island valleys. There, was a place where dying came painlessly, where heat and magic made even indifferent lives worthwhile. Marshall realized that he had never told Lydia about Jamaica. She thought that she knew, because of Charleston, where the sun also beat down, but there was a difference, which Marshall easily illustrated in his tale of Rica Vista—where time moved in an intoxicating circle. When Lydia closed her eyes and lay back in imagination of island ease, she saw the red earth, ice-cold streams, and an infinity of baking green. But Jamaica was too far southwest, and they gave themselves over to the pull of their voyage.

Ships are either living or dead. Those living seem to be as small and agile as ponies, linked with the wishes of their passengers, somewhat afraid of the night, alive for the first time. The *Royal George* moved toward the center of the sea. On the chart it was a wide blue belly. Even the Captain, experienced and disciplined as he was, lusted for the unmarked blue, trackless and magnetic, an open space in the cells of the world, as flat and easy as a savanna.

The pressure to continue an evasionary course was strong, moving upward from the ranks until the officers might have been crushed between the power of their Captain and the weight of their crew. But the Captain's eyes were clear, and (at the cost of $10,000 a day) he went considerably farther south of the storm than was necessary—not just for an excursion, but because he was always driven to explore silent places where no others went and from which merchants withheld the throb of their traffic. Lying off the trade routes, the center of the sea was not frequented. On old maps it held cherubim with faces and bodies reddened as if from tropical sun. It was an unnecessary place—caught with weed, slow, pointless, diversionary.

The *Royal George* pushed south by day, and by night as well when soft stars emerged brightening the velvet. The bow wave had become so smooth that it rolled like a geometrician's perfect wheel, or the exact traveling helix of Teferides. Marshall remembered how in their process across the sky starry nights were linked to the raucous geared lines of machines. Cosmas Indicopleustes had seen the perfect crystal box, and Marshall had a nagging and persistent vision of star tracks scratched parallel, forever, and completely, across its top. This etching cannot be described and far surpassed the deepest gravure on Achilles's silver shield; for it was not images, but the soft clear sticks of language arranged in magical pattern, which mind drew from eye like buckets from a well.

Late one afternoon the Captain strode onto the bridge. To his attentive officers he commanded: "Full stop." Then he said, "We shall halt until further notice. I want complete radio silence: the radio officer will disconnect his equipment, lock his doors, and neglect his log. Engines and auxiliary power will be shut down. No work of any kind will be done. The stewards will put up sandwiches and such for several days. No music will be played. Lock the beer locker. The smoking lamp will be out. Discord among the crew will be met with severe discipline. These are orders, gentlemen. Carry them out."

After half an hour the ship went dead in the water, and they discovered that the breeze and the waves had been their own creation. For without the ship's motion the sea was an endless smooth turquoise with only an occasional touch of wind. Though weakening, the sun was strong enough to burn, and the crew got all rosy. By order, there was no work.

Instead, the Captain sent out the boats to reconnoiter a circle of ten miles around the ship. Heavy launches and forty-foot lifeboats were lowered with great caution and ceremony. Lifejacketed, Marshall, Lydia, and the crew manned them with the intent to explore. In a near-nitrogen rapture, they pulled apart from the mother ship. The heat and the green met at the horizon in waves of air and light. In a motor launch with the stewards, who (except for Dave) were virtually midgets, Marshall and his bride skimmed over the sea until the *Royal George* was only a small block on the blue prairie.

Patches of weed, sometimes miles in circumference, covered the sea. Often, the mats were so dense and piled that it was possible to walk across the top. Dave and Harvey guided the launch and moored it to an island of sargassum. Though they thought it was all "silly," they did it for Lydia. She and Marshall jumped onto the dry crispy weed and ran across it as if on a giant mattress. The sun was hot, and as they ran they liberated perfume from sea berries crushed underfoot. Finally, at the base of a gray-green rill, out of sight of ship and launch, in the middle of deep ocean, they lay on the fragrant undulating mat and slept in the sunlight. After a few minutes they awakened filled with incredible desire and made love in the lee of the rill, in the open heart of nowhere.

Heading back, they peered over the gunwales through impossibly clear water. Far below, strange animals proceeded with their daily intercourse. There were the Great Slick Eels—150 feet long, as thick as trees, as sinuous as whippers' whips at carnivals, with heads larger than horses, and huge idiotic smiles. These Great Slick Eels hunted the foolish and fatuous Agrolian Fish—600 pounds, completely round, gaps in its front teeth, and scores of useless little legs. They saw the fabulous Shmata Ray, as lithe as linen in the wash, as colorful as a Third World flag, moving in the deep with short repulsive jerks. Then there was the Noiseless Laughing Dill, a huge columnar Coelacanth which Lydia swore was wearing opera glasses. Harvey and Dave thrust their heads into the salt water and observed with wonder the Honey Fish, the Water Bat, the Decapus, and the Optamoovulgian.

Speechless from what they had seen, flushed and burnt from the sun, the crew hoisted up the boats and went to fetch their mattresses. Then they lay on top of the hold covers as afternoon turned into evening, when the stewards brought around sandwiches and bottles of tea. When darkness came they looked at its starred walls as the Christians must have done on the first night that they had driven the Moors from Granada. Then the Scottish cabinboys discovered that the fish were luminous and blinking, coiling in the waters like Broadway. The mats too were lighted by organic phosphorescence, and as night proceeded they grew brighter and brighter. When everyone was nearly asleep and only the Captain stood, staring from the bridge to the sky, they were awakened and energized by the rising moon, which danced self-contained on the horizon and twisted in distant sea vapor as hot as a flame in a cup.

They were resting on a deluge of bioluminescence. Planetary groups lit the ship's sides and were visible on the horizon for 360 degrees. Their pulsations and patterned telegraphy, as some slipped out of sight in the curve of a wave and then returned, were like the winking lights of a computer panel or the blackened mantle of a glittering city seen from the air. What shakings and awe must the first navigators have had when becalmed perhaps forever in the center of an infinite half-sphere, the sky and floor of which ticked clear celestial and diffuse animal light. The *Royal George* was surrounded by glassy glowing waves—an evening of silence for the assembled crew.

Then they started from fright, for the Captain had arrived with the grace of a ghost, and stood tall in his white uniform amid the reclining men. Seldom did he move among them. Close to seventy, he had been an admiral of the Royal Navy, who, upon retirement, could not stand to part from the sea. When the water was as smooth as a mirror, pastel by day, rich and blue-hearted by night, he grew restless.

"For those of you who would wonder," he said, largely in pretext, "we are at the center of the sea, off the trade routes, where few have seen fit to travel. To the northwest is North America"—he pivoted and faced the various directions as he spoke, as accurately as a compass—"to the southwest, Brazil with its jutting northern chin, and then the Amazon and the white Andes; to the southeast, Africa, being worth three or four continents; to the northeast, Europe, the clockmade heart of a mechanical world. We are roped between the four, nearest the dry shelf of Spain.

"Half a thousand years ago the Spaniards, as if sprung from seed, burst in virility upon the sea and passed this point in little ships to find and conquer a new world. Since that time we have been retracing and elaborating their routes, but have none of our own. Since that time we have become as immobile as whales upon the beach—fat, shoddy, recreant, dissolving. For there is only one condition in which a man's soul and flesh become as lean and pure as his armor; in which he finds in the art of his language and the awe of his music, unification with his own mobile limbs; in which he can find entertainment so intense as to draw him without a twitch into complete abandonment of the things of the world; in which he gathers speed and rises to his natural task as if he were an eagle destined for flight or a porpoise propelled in arcs across the water.

"Do you doubt me? Doubt not. I learned in Algeciras what this was, as I looked upon the Spanish walls which are not walls, as the lines of earth and sea were solid in one piece inviting passage, as the poverty appeared infinitely rich. I learned in the blink of an eye. I learned as the thin slapping music beat to ceilings and beams, as the percussion of dancers' feet seemed to exhort going out beyond the harbor and into the straits—beyond the straits.

"Doubt me not. A pair of dancers was dancing twenty years ago when I thought that I had settled in. We touched at Algeciras for only a day. The secret was that they moved when they did not, and did not move when they did. They wore black, and were as concentrated as birds startled upon alarm. Their dance was like that of the bees, for God in heaven they retracted and they turned and they jugged and they jiggled, and her back was as smooth as the gust from a fan, a sweep of vanilla, and in their movements unknown to them they pointed always west and to the sea. Though they moved up and down and to right and left, the lay of their furious dance pointed west and to the sea.

"It was that way too, five hundred years ago, when from Spain's jutting shelf they moved to fulfill the neglected task, their dancers doubtless pointing them. They found a new world with twenty-thousand miles of spine, peaks we have yet to climb, plains like seas, plants and animals humorous, terrifying, and new. Like bees, their passionate dancers had pointed them. I fear that I will die before I see such dancing anew, directing us after half a thousand years outward and to the heavens, where we must go if we are to be men.

"For we are on the brink of new worlds, of infinite space curtains drawn and colored like silks, luminous and silent, moving slowly and with grace. We have come to the edge. Our children will view a terrible openness, and the vastness will change us forever and for good. I will never see it. I am seventy and I wish only to see dancers who will arise to set the right course.

"In my heart of hearts at seventy on this ship stalled in the middle of the sea and stars, I wish for the dancers who will arise as did their predecessors in one wave linked with the past, moving when they do not move, not moving when they move. When I had passed half a century, I was awakened in the fury of a dance in Algeciras. Though a captain for many years, it was that day by the curve of her back that I became a Captain and a man—when I watched history artfully running its gates with iron grasp and steel-clad direction."

5

Rotterdam is approached rapidly from the sea through sand-flanked jetties. On the beaches, tents stood for the last of the holidays. The light was dimming as the *Royal George* dashed in past the Hook of Holland, and, when finally it was moored in a forest of tanks and spires, darkness spread across the flat as if a Flemish devil had sucked away the light through a crunchy reed.

Marshall did not like it when Lydia kissed the crew goodbye. He resented that she pecked in affection at Wonderful Bellchicken and Greylock

Oceanard, though he knew that as she kissed the bashful bastards of the deck force, she was extending as well his deep fraternity caught behind the proper ice of manhood.

Then in a taxi to the city he ravished her and she ravished back. Hegenbuckle, the Dutch taxi driver, nearly crashed into a limestone mile post, a bus stand with a soup advertisement, and a group of sweet daisylike schoolgirls on bicycles, because he was glued to the mirror in which Marshall and Lydia kissed with such verve that the glass fogged.

As they rode through the flats of Rotterdam they paused momentarily to see great constructions of flame and spidery steel spreading for mile upon mile around them. Sparkling refineries beat against the clouds with bright ventilations of pulsing fire, drawn and tenuous like cotton candy, orange and upward in an explosion of the new virtues, an exposition of a new lifeblood. Certain fools thought that this was chemical engineering, a studious necessity, an obvious alacrity, a logical linkage. It was nothing of the kind, but rather a portrait by complications, an abstract of humor from above as impennous necessities were snared by thematic joking.

Rather than lose his mind, Hegenbuckle spoke. "I have noticed," he said, "that you are Americans. I told from her chestnut hair, her green eyes, her face worthy of a princess, and her long and articulate fingers—a very Dutch attribute. She is undoubtedly of the South, of Virginia, and a Jewess."

"Yes," said Lydia.

"I have been learning English. Since the time of Erasmus we Dutch have envied English. What an ecstatic language, a language to fill the boots of the greatest dream, a language of milk, a language of jewels. In itself it is worth more than nations. It strives and it loves, in words and phrase. Needless to say, like the waterbug, or the needle, we too love it and respect it as our king."

"It is everyone's king," said Lydia, squinting through the windshield as rain came down and wet the fields as green as watermelons.

"He's mad, isn't he?" asked Marshall.

"No, he's not mad—just a little confused," answered Lydia.

At the train station, Hegenbuckle refused payment, saying, "It is not necessary. I never accept fares from Captain Keslake or his men. I am delighted to serve him, for I too have memories, of the flaming places of Djakarta and unkindled Curaçao. Throughout the Netherlands and throughout the world, they are quiescent and self-serving, dwellers on the human condition, lookers to the self, incapables of independence, living shanties of bastardized language, mechanicals who draw downward. But some day," he said, lifting hands and eyes gradually in imitation of ascension, "we will rise. Rotterdam will be an old city like old wood. We will breathe easily as the universe opens to us. And the world will cease to agitate and boil."

6

There was a train to Paris, which took many wonderful hours. On board were hundreds of musicians from New Orleans completing a vast worldwide tour. They played continuously as the train crossed Belgium and northern France. They were not practicing, but rather they played because they could not stop.

Fat, brown, and bullet-shaped, Malcolm Tucker led his band in Marshall and Lydia's car, and made his drummer base the tempo on the knocking of the tracks. Across heavily breathing countryside the train traced a steady line like ink from a mechanical pen. Malcolm Tucker had an uncanny resemblance to Monroe, but Marshall never had a chance to ask about it, for he and Lydia were held in their seats by the internal combustion of the music. When Malcolm Tucker played "Blue'n the Blues" over and over again, they were pushed against the furry backs of their chairs as if by a wave. New Orleans appeared before them hot and gleaming near the lapping Gulf.

"I know this music," said Lydia. "I grew up with it. It's the music of the South, a distillation of war, slavery, and death, the unleashed human spirit cavorting in mathematics without symbols, flowing from weighted souls. Malcolm Tucker sure can play."

They reached Paris in the middle of the night. As if summer had come again, fiery music resounded through the train shed. Marshall and Lydia went with the herd of musicians through dark and silent streets lined with trees which had just begun to lose their leaves. In the attic of the Hotel Scribe, among giant drums pulling elevator cables, overlooking the arched and bow-shaped roofs of Paris, the musicians continued to play—slowly, slurring, half-dead. They played as they lay in their beds, as they ate, as they shaved. The roof vibrated. The sky was confused, having once looked down upon the ground of the Scribe when a farm had been there, and, before that, when it was green and waxy, a wolf-filled wood.

Lydia took off her dress and washed at a pink lavabo by the bed. She lay back against Marshall, and he kissed her on the long, straight side of her face. As his forehead brushed against the soft hair of her temple, he tasted cold water. She told him to wash, and after he did and the blood had stopped beating in his eyes, when it was mild and soft, they lay back and listened to the arrogant strutting music. The warm autumn was soon to be cold and clear.

In the morning, the musicians got each other up like a row of rising mah-jongg pieces. Malcolm Tucker lay in his undershirt, bunched-up on the bouncy bed. The pianist ran into the room.

"Hey Malcolm. Hey Malcolm. Wake up. Those white kids is gone."

"Gone? Let's see." The two of them went to look. They stood in their underwear, exhausted but itching to play, and their faces had furrowed looks.

"They sure move fast, Malcolm. They gone."

"That's right, but we're always around, travelin' from place to place, crossin' paths and such. It's hot, Lewando. Why don't you go down and see if you can get us a pitcher of ice-cold tomato juice with vanilla."

"You bet," said Lewando, pulling on his shirt.

Marshall and Lydia were bleary-eyed, on yet another train, rushing to the cool of the Alps and the sea-green of Chamonix. Lydia was pale, but she looked magnificent. Marshall watched her as she slept, alarmed that his all-too-active eye had seen her as purer than alabaster. But then, far above misty rows of pine the mountains appeared in sunlight, white ice reflecting in seething bursts like cannon fire in a battle. Lydia awoke and peered through the glass at the ice ramparts. Her face was indeed as smooth as alabaster, and she had magic in her eye.

When they arrived in Chamonix they were extremely tired, but Marshall had a certain affection for viewing recurrent images from exhaustion. In the same way that the static and scratches on an old record can make it more hypnotic than if it were clear, so too the veil of fatigue can enhance the always incomprehensible greatness of mountains. They found that when they were tired there arose within them a driving power seldom utterly allayed, an imagination by which they could effortlessly travel the peaks, catapulted by self-generative vigor.

Many a traveler has arrived in Chamonix late in the day and ignorantly wandered off to climb the mountains, as if they would succumb to so casual an assault. Marshall and Lydia saw from the unparalleled height and distance of the white world spread before them that they had to approach slowly. After they left their knapsacks at a little pension, they walked until the streets began to fade and clean meadows overtook them. They wound on an earthen path to the top of the hill which in that valley is such a nuisance to roads and railways. It allowed a long uninterrupted view of high fields, mountain walls, and mute bays of ice stopped still as if the world were only a photograph of itself. The great glaciers called out with cold Alpine names— Miage, Bionassay, Tacconaz, Bossons, Tour, Argentière, and the Mer de Glace. But for the few thin lines of the téléphériques, and a hut or two amid the mountains the great space before them was as uninhabited as the sea. It took such mighty leaps, and its spires thrust so high, that to look upon the depth and distance of it shocked and beat upon one's insides as if a shell had exploded nearby.

Somewhere at the junction of the Vallée Blanche (a great white wave which came tumbling in stillness from Mont Blanc) and the Mer de Glace (an enormous river of ice), Metzner lived in a wooden hut. He stayed on the glacier for months, despite the chance of being buried in an avalanche from the Vallée Blanche or swallowed in a crevass of the Bergschrund—where, in sharp and fickle disorganization, the glacier began.

"I know from men like that whom I've met in the Sierras, that they don't like to talk. Complete isolation stops the tongue. They become entrapped in their own silence," said Lydia, gazing at the dance of clouds above the timberline. She knew almost surely that he would then contradict her, for she could sense the tension to which he was often subjected because he didn't really know who he was, because his mother (and possibly his father) had died by violence—and because he was, perhaps, a bastard. In these times, he drew away from her and became cold, possessed, and tormented. He had told her that more than anything in the world he hated hardening to her, but that he found a certain satisfaction at being driven, at being the agent of inevitability, at suffering the pleasurable siege of determination. She hoped for him someday to rid himself of those driven strengths which took him from her. They were, after all, about to venture onto the glacier in fulfillment of the first steps. As if he had not heard her, Marshall stared at the path leading to the mountains. "Marshall," she said, "I think that men like Metzner become too embittered to remember anything reliably . . ."

"That's so," replied Marshall. "But I know myself from complete isolation, that memory sharpens until it is a scalpel which cuts out the heart. Every detail has an edge, and the details swarm at you like gnats. I believe that the keenness of his memory will compensate for his reticence. First, though, we have to find him." He motioned at the array of distances before and above them. "Look."

As they made downward, the city began to light up softly. They saw cows plodding through a gate, directed by a little boy with a switch in his hand. The copper-colored bells made them remember that one cow in Columbine had been given a bell, and that at night in their separate cabins they had heard it. They would rest on Sunday, outfit themselves the next day, and begin practice climbs to break in boots, clothing, and equipment. They were both fairly competent mountaineers, experienced on rock and ice.

Marshall flung open the wooden shutters and a world of mountains flooded into their room—thousand-foot pitches covered in ice, vertical faces of a half a mile, white massifs in direct moonlight. They slept as one can sleep only high in the mountains, after a hard day, in pure air, in a country at peace.

7

Closing a curtained door behind them, they called at the Compagnie des Guides de Chamonix. Because it was the beginning of an unheralded holi-day about which they had heard only vague rumors in too rapid French, one man alone was in the office. He was an old veteran who observed the moun-tains but did not climb. He looked like a kindly baker with silver-gray hair, and would have been easily believable in a white apron instead of his dark blue suit with several enameled pins on the lapels.

They told him their needs, and he responded with the care of someone who has spent decades climbing rock walls thousands of feet above nothing. His accent was so French that it had a life of its own, and it seemed as if there were four people in the room.

"I am aware of Professor Metzner, and I can tell you that if you wait two weeks or perhaps three you can find him then in less than a day. The téléphérique goes to a point relatively near the Bergschrund. Or, if you wish, you may take a helicopter and the process will demand only an hour or two. But you will have to wait two weeks or more."

"We can't afford to stay for that long. Why two weeks? Are your guides that busy?"

"To the contrary, they have practically all returned to their winter professions. The season is over. You could get a dozen in no time if it were not for the *Vent du Souverain*. No one will go up, no one can go up, in the *Souverain*. The téléphériques cannot function, and conditions become ab-surdly dangerous, worse than the most savage day in winter. No one, except perhaps Gaston Reynelle. But I would not advise it. It is too dangerous, and though he is the greatest Alpinist in the world, he has never seen the *Vent du Souverain*, for the last one occurred just before the First World War. I was merely a child. Gaston was not even born. No, no, yes, yes, even his father was not born!" he said, holding up his finger, allowing Marshall to see how the sign for exclamation had originated.

"Monsieur," said Lydia with an elevated dignity reminding the old guide of days when he had assisted on royal climbs, "please tell us about the *Vent du Souverain*. It is something of which we do not know."

"They have felt it already in Zermatt and Argentière, which means that it will entrap the valley within a day. It is something from ancient times, and it arrives without much warning every half century or so. It is . . . it is a rare and miraculous condition brought about by the conjunction of Arctic and African winds. They meet in the Alps, twist above the mountains, and . . . *lutter*."

"Struggle."

"No, more precisely . . ."

"Wrestle?"

"Yes, wrestle. *Le combat entre les vents.* (The French language is the most magnificent. It is our king. Its sounds are so beautiful that they are better than most nations, and thus synonymous with France.)

"The northern wind always subdues the one from the south. When they have stopped winding about the summits, they fall to the valley, the hot wind underneath. In the valley it becomes like summer. The fields are dry and everything is hot, as hot as the Sahara. One can hardly move . . . *im-mobilité.* But above!" He became excited, and, as old Frenchmen often do, proceeded to publicly amaze himself. "But above! It is unbelievably cold. Avalanches tumble into the valley and turn into rivers which boil and vaporize before they can put even a drop into the dry bed of the Arve. While the air above is clear and dense, the air below is thin and molten hot.

"Thus at night it curves into a mirror which gathers or rejects the light. Sometimes the moon appears blindingly—a hundred times its natural size—and the mountains are roofed with white. We watch then the mountains of the moon itself. Sometimes the stars shower upon us and each man and woman shudders and fears. And sometimes it is absolutely and completely black—a void.

"This occurs once in a half century, for two weeks or more. No one can come or go because of the cold in the passes. Everyone must sleep in tents. Forests of them spring up in the high meadows where the people try to catch some cool air—always to no avail. The populace is alternately gay and deeply sad. In the last *Vent du Souverain* my grandfather lost his life. Whereas the Swiss remain perfectly safe, the French are drawn by passion. From our meadow we saw a sphere of ruby-red fire at the summit of the Drus. My grandfather believed that it was God, and he set off at midnight across the Mer de Glace; foolish old man. He died within a wave of ice and forty years later his remains were spewed by the glacier. On his face was still an expression of wonder.

"I know of this professor of yours. He is not wise. In the *Souverain*, the glacier undergoes violent contractions, and becomes most dangerous."

"And no guide will work except Gaston Reynelle?" asked Marshall.

"Perhaps not even he, though his will and determination have won him many triumphs. He has gone alone to rescue the rescue party. When just a boy, he climbed the Southwest Pillar of the Drus—the Col Bonatti—alone, at night, in winter! The other guides cannot speak to him because they become paralyzed with envy. He has no friends. When he is not in the mountains, he works in his father's blacksmith shop—Reynelle et Fils, Rue Rebuffat, 24. Perhaps he will listen to you and, more than likely, he will venture into the *Souverain*, for it is his nature to be arrogant."

Gaston Reynelle was dark and thin. His expression was so intense that his eyes burned like rays. Marshall and Lydia looked through the window of 24 Rue Rebuffat and saw Gaston in an enormous room, striking hot metal on the strong absurd face of an anvil. He sweated, and his concentration was a marvel to behold as every sinew in his body struck at the red, and sharp metallic sounds rang out amid the darkness. His face was leathern and angular, his hair curly and black. One could see by the sheer musculature of his chest and arms that he drove himself beyond his own limits.

It was stirring and pitiful to see him pounding life into the metal. They knew that he was using up his mortality rapidly and without reward. But the metal glowed before him, his brow was furrowed, and the arm wielding the flying hammer flew. At times he would sigh and breathe deeply, unaware that he was being watched. He threw out his lean arms like a ballet dancer and stretched his neck. He seemed then to be caressed by an abstract spirit.

Embarrassed to watch, they knocked on his door and went inside. He looked at them with a fiery clasping eye. His strength circled them on a beam.

"Yes? May I help you? At your service," he said, abandoning his ecstasy at banding the expansion of metal.

"Are you Gaston Reynelle?"

"I am Gaston Reynelle. In all of France and all the world there is none better in the mountains."

"Then we have come to the right place, for we need a guide to lead us in the Bergschrund of the Mer de Glace."

Gaston smiled. The fire beat and echoed behind him. "*Certainement!*" he said. "But in no circumstances for any reason will I take such a beautiful woman into the mountains during the *Souverain*."

"She can climb."

"I will not."

"She is skilled."

"I will not." He struck his iron hammer against glowing steel and sparks flew as if to underline his determination. "I will not. Women are too beautiful. I will not!"

8

Lydia sat sadly on the balcony of their room as Marshall and Gaston made their way toward the summit of Mont Blanc, over which they would pass to descend through the Vallée Blanche and the Bergschrund. She cried like a leaf. Even though she had urged Marshall to go without her, she disliked breaking with their practice of sharing. But it was done, and she was left to see the *Vent du Souverain* in the valley, while they climbed.

Chamonix was broiling and dry. Above, the snow raged and the cold air was blue. She took off her sunglasses and turned her clear face to the distant round dome of Mont Blanc. With a sweet nearsighted stare, she gazed at it, and then rested her cheek against her bare shoulder, feeling that Marshall had left her when she loved him most. Determined to see the valley and its pastel tents in the heat of the *Souverain,* she wept nevertheless for being left.

Though not too well versed in technical climbing, Marshall exceeded himself early on, and Gaston was pleased as they crossed the lower glaciers and wound among the hills of ice. They traversed snowfields, pushing against the cold. They made their first camp as night fell and the stars battled above them. Lydia lay sweating in her bed, her arms outstretched for Marshall. Marshall held his own body to fend off the cold, and hallucinated images of terror and madness. Gaston, the brave one, screamed in his sleep.

When morning arose in a blaze, Marshall and Gaston, entranced and enraptured, progressed upward amid swirls of ice and fresh snow. Between them was Gaston's dark purple rope. Four times, Gaston fell into newly covered crevasses. Marshall was pulled to the edge as if by a team of panicked horses, but he always dug his crampons into the singing ice and arched himself over his ice axe, digging deep into the pure white until he ground to a stop while Gaston hung tensely in the middle of the crevass, slowly spinning, looking above to see if Marshall would hurtle over the blue edge into a shared death. Then Marshall would belay Gaston and rig a Bilgiri, pulling him up rapidly. Gaston was so rugged that he insisted on forging ahead despite the falls. They traveled thin cornices in slow-paced agony, chests aching, mouths burnt by subzero air. Sometimes a hundred yards took an hour. The atmosphere was in attack and warred to break their momentum. But they continued past delicate white edges and over brittle constructions of ice, until they reached the summit of Mont Blanc. After a circling and dizzy look at the green world gone afire below them, they started for the Vallée Blanche.

They had to cross a spine of ice so thin that it was necessary to cut not the customary steps but handholds, so that they could hang on either side. Marshall suggested that if they both fell, they would balance out. "Don't be a fool," said Gaston, indicating the thin ice wall between them. "The rope would be severed immediately. We are moving across a knife." But they managed to negotiate even this upturned blade of ice and arrive at the Vallée Blanche.

They commenced their glissade, perhaps the longest ever, for the extreme and sudden cold had flattened the rills and laced over the gaps of the valley, into which they slid as fast as skiers, leaving two three-line tracks. Balanced on ice axes and heels, they fell through couloirs of virgin snow. Curtains of white leaped up behind them. They willingly flew off cliffs, landing in the snow, getting up again, sliding downward until their great hour was finished and they slammed into the forest of ice in the Bergschrund. Somewhere in the upright glittering mass, Metzner had his hut.

In the valley, Lydia made the rounds of pastel tents and documented with her Leica the gentle goings-on of the *Souverain*. Then she threw away her film and joined a group of red-collared Savoyards on a trout hunt in the stopped pools of the river's upper tributaries. They dashed and splashed about, catching the trout in their hands with great glee. At night tents glowed from the braziers within. Lydia found a family with whom she took up residence. They made punches of purple wine and mountain flowers in ice. Only when the moon covered the valley like a bright inner lid of a sarcophagus did she glance at the mountain walls where Marshall was making his way.

After days of searching the Bergschrund, Marshall and Gaston had run out of food. They gnawed the ice for water. At night in their frail one-man tents they nearly froze, and they spent the cold days in fear and trances. The air slit their lungs like a sword as they climbed with crampons, ice axes, and ice screws, up and down the Bergschrund, finding not a trace of Metzner or his camp. There had been much shifting of the glacier. Gaston said that he had undoubtedly been buried.

"In fifty years his body will be thrown out at the base of the Mer de Glace, and they will say, 'Here is the professor who perished in the *Souverain* half a century ago.'"

They started the descent. Gaston kept falling into hidden crevasses, but Marshall had become so experienced at rapid belaying that he allowed Gaston to drop only a foot or so. He was shocked beyond speech when Gaston angrily ordered him to be less efficient, saying, "Let me fall five or ten meters without interruption. I like it." Because Gaston had to work with his hands to place ice screws when they went up steep walls in the undulating surface, the tips of his fingers began to turn black. Both he and Marshall worried about their feet, which they had not felt in a long time, but Gaston said that if there were no pain, there was probably some hope—a paradox which startled Marshall from an icy reverie in which he had concluded that his life was not quite his own, his history was growing suspiciously powerful in its influence on his present, and coincidences were too many. His origins pulled hard, and he wondered if he were caught in an elaborate bittersweet play, the esthetics of which were formed around inevitability.

Halfway down and halfway through his thoughts he bumped hard up against Gaston. Preoccupied, he had been following the rope like a Chard Ox. His face stung, and he had nearly knocked Gaston into a deep crevass. Gaston neither reprimanded nor thanked him, but simply stared down. Marshall saw too, and even in the cold a chill ran along his spine. Hanging on a climbing rope 150 feet down from the lip of the chasm and 500 feet from the almost imperceptible ice-blue plates at the bottom was a dead man. His hands were frozen onto the rope, which he had gripped just above his head so that his arms were arched symmetrically. His face was upturned toward the light. He spun around gently.

Gaston retreated about twenty feet and hammered both his and Marshall's axes into the snow until the heads were a few inches above the surface and a foot apart. He took the rope and secured its center with an ice piton in back of the axes. He passed the ends through the carabiner hole at the top of each axe, and threw them over the crevass edge. He fixed one end of an auxiliary rope to an ice screw, and threw it over the edge next to the other ropes. He then rigged a bunch of slings, dropped his pack, and linked onto the two ropes. "Bilgiri," he said to Marshall, who nodded. "It was easy before, but here it will be fifty meters—not so easy. You will have to read the ropes carefully."

Gaston rappelled off the ice walls until he was deep in a world as blue as the sides of a high barrier reef. In a short time he was close to the body. Certainly Metzner, it was an old man clad in bright orange. His hair was white, and his wide-open eyes were blue.

IX
Settlement
of the Dove

1

The rivers ran wild in his last summer before university in Leningrad. Even in late July one could feel the autumn, though the heat continued tenaciously. Trout and wild ducks shared deep circuitous pools caught behind white frothing falls. Pines and firs of green and blue-green waved in the wind as clouds passed above. Woodsmen drank wine that they had hidden, and lay on the steep pine-needled banks, faces to the sun.

Several hundred miles south, beyond her father's massive forests, Katrina Perlé was beginning her walks to a cathedral full of wheat. And in the forests themselves, in a small village of exiles, Lev dreamed of women, or rather, of one. He did not yet know her, but she was sandy-haired and blue-eyed, and looked as though her coloring were perpetually of the beaches in August. Though the village of malcontents was only a bitter speck amid an ocean of forests, he carelessly envisioned deeds of heroism for the sake of this woman whom he loved. He was young enough not to know that sometimes heroes live while those that they would protect die.

His father was a doctor, in whose view Lev's unrelenting patriotism and romanticism were wild idiocies bred by isolation in the forests and rebellion against the cynical dissidents there suffering at manual labor, against the disaffection of the father himself. He did not know that the enthusiasm of his son, and of countless other sons, would be necessary for survival in the years to come, and that the collective senses of a whole nation are always infinitely better attuned to the future than the senses of any individual—this in itself a strong argument against the dictator he detested.

Deep in nature, they thought feverish political thoughts—which was especially foolish in light of their ineffectual histories; they were (as was everyone in Russia at the time) failures. One reason for Lev's painfully naïve political raptures was that he was not really political. He preferred, for example, to ride logs down the river.

He would go to the chutes in morning, and when the loggers had put together a raft of ten or twenty bound logs he would leap on and ride faster and faster until he was dancing with the rolling wood, holding the chains as he was dipped into the cold current a dozen times a minute. In the baylet below his house he would fly clear of the logs, swim quickly to the bank, and make his way homeward through the green bushes, his clothes steaming as he took berries on the run.

But one day in the beginning of September he had to leave for Leningrad. That morning he bathed outside in the shower they had made by hanging a canvas bucket from a pine branch. He was eighteen, and thought that he was a fully grown man. Quietly resigned, his mother knew better.

She fixed his breakfast. The father too was about to leave, for the little hospital. Lev glanced at a suitcase he had packed the night before. He was so frightened that he almost shook. Then they stood at the doorway; his father embraced him; his mother embraced him; and their incipient tears vanished in laughter when they discovered that he had forgotten to put on his boots.

He did not know it, but he would never see them again, and the woods were to become so lost and far-away in time and geography that they would seem like a fairy tale.

He came to the wooden steps, with the newly polished boots. His mother bent down to kiss him as he put them on. His father said, "I have to go now. I'll be late," and touched him on the head.

His mother said, "We'll see you at Christmas. It's only three months or so." She had been wearing a gray dress with a gold clasp—things from the city. The flies beat against the screen; his father disappeared down a pine-clad path; and he pulled on the boots.

2

Thirty-five years later, a lean man with silver hair bent down to remove his boots. A life of war had engulfed him completely, made him a soldier, brought him to Palestine, given him the rank of general. He had seen many wars and many campaigns—the Russian Army; a transfer to the Naval Infantry riding horses and fighting across the forests; capture; escape; the partisans; and then the search for Katrina, which had led him to Palestine. There he fought the British until '48; the Egyptians, Jordanians, and Syrians in '48; the Egyptians in '56; all three again in '67; and then for years and years in the War of Attrition he had divided his attentions between his command and general staff work.

He had never remarried. Nor had he fathered any children, and as if to underscore the waste, his mistress had left when he retired from the regular Army. But many things kept him busy. Half of the time he looked after a brigade on the Northern Front, and in the other half he worked with the foresters, also in the North, as they tended the miraculous plantations of pine which had reforested Galilee and the foothills of the Lebanon. They traversed the valleys, armed not only with axes and saws but with rifles and machine guns, and they trimmed and cut silently, as perhaps he would have done in Russia had he not sought out Katrina.

He was a strange man—devoted, cynical, terribly strong despite the

grave fault which split him apart from real life, usually cheerful, but sometimes deeply sad, and forever refreshed by the sight of even little forests and
young trees in their second and third decades. He knew the terrain in the
North as well or better than any man. While coursing the forests there as a
soldier or woodsman, he frequently thought of Katrina Perlé.

How perfect it had been in Leningrad, discovering that they both were
provincial and that they were always drawn softly outside themselves to the
world of green. They fell in love and rambled about the gardens and the
dirty railway sidings—where they found several things to their liking. It was
quiet when there was no work. Small pine seedlings had sprung up in the
cinder bed. Amassed ties in great resinous piles were sweet and fragrant.
Blue sky was visible down the line. The tracks formed a continuous ribbon
which they knew touched at the heart of their province. And the heart of
their province was light green, as the wind passed over it flawlessly.

For Lev it was hard and purifying to stay in tents or shacks below Har
Meron, lost in the trees with old and speechless Moroccans beaten down
since birth, who wore soft slippers of carpet, and rags about their heads as
they silently padded through the forests. They looked like Chinese; their
faces were windswept brown; their eyes sparkled and said that they had survived: nothing else. In fourteen-hour days they cut and trimmed and burnt—
the volume of their work monumental, their feel for the terrain equally
startling.

At night when they returned in dim light to cabins or army tents, it
was most difficult. Lev's hands were at rest and he had nothing to do but
stare past the blinding lantern at trees which ringed the camp. These trees
were as perfect and beautiful as always, these tall squeaking cedars, and the
pines which had a white sound in the wind. The Moroccans and Turcomans
and Kurds plucked their stringed instruments while the tea was allowed to
boil in battered aluminum kettles as thin and delicate as foil.

Beyond, in the trees, her memory took shape. A passionate, genuine,
loyal love was minted one day in a Polish forest on the side of a mountain,
when the world was white and snow had begun to fall, and they could hear
the continuous rumble of artillery a hundred miles away like summer
thunder speaking to them in their shelter amid the pines and cedars. In the
trees, in the trees the two bands had moved together silently in cautious
recognition, and then Katrina had knelt as the snow came down and war-
weary faces peered from aside the brown trunks.

And sometimes he thought that he was dreaming, and then he did
dream. In the forests of Northern Galilee, the faces of the other woodsmen,
the slightly oriental cast of their eyes, the dry orange fire, the weapons on
the ground or over shoulders, the black tea, the dark vaults above the flames
ending in ravishing unseen stars, the alertness for terror in the woods, the
sound of artillery on the Golan constant and like the sea, and the clear colors
and perfect air which enwrapped them as if in crystal were part of the con-

tinuing wave of men at war in the primal forests, fighting over the earth's
surface from beginning to end.

This was what he had known. Who was to fathom what the Moroccans
and old Turcomans and Kurds were thinking exactly—but they too were
dreaming of home in a golden age, as they, without knowing it, were in the
thick of yet another golden age. Though Lev would have preferred a living
Katrina Perlé, there is little more exquisite and taxing than devotion to a lost
love. For it is one of the ways in the world to confront and beat mortality,
like standing on a platform above time and earth and compassing everything
in an eye, commanding time, inviting all images to circle and concentrate
until they sear the cup of the eye like fire. Lev had lived a hundred battered
lives—it was his choice. Some men are like that. They halt time by intent
and determined recollection. If it were not for them we would know no value,
and our lives would slip through our hands like a wet rope. But they slow
it in their self-destroying grip.

Before he had time to unlace the heavy boots one of his men came to
him and said, "Don't bother. They say on the radio that there are going to
be big thunderstorms, and that this is it." He meant the beginning of the
rainy season. Their work would be curtailed. Since on this tour they had only
three days left, it was up to Lev to do the obvious. "Well?" asked the old
Moroccan.

"Okay," he said. "Let's go now, but make it quick or we won't get to
Haifa in time for dinner."

They extinguished the lunch fires, gathered weapons and tools, and
nearly ran through the woods to the truck. Lev rode in the cab—a lucky
circumstance, for the men in the back were punching, screaming, and throwing food at each other in their mysterious enthusiasm. They gathered speed,
passing valleys in the forest that they knew so well, and they came over a
ridge and saw Haifa standing like a white mirage, many miles beyond them,
across the land and the bay, perched on Mt. Carmel, a perfect city for which
they had great affection.

Lev would once more be a general; it would soon be time to rejoin his
brigade. The gap between him and the others in the truck became more and
more apparent as they approached Haifa. He would go to an apartment in
a tower high on the mountain, from which the sea spread out visually for a
hundred miles in three directions. They would home to burrows in the
Hadar.

Having gone against traffic, they arrived in Haifa at dinnertime. He
paused at the name on his mailbox, feeling, as always, like a thief. The core
of his life was cast around a time when he was called Lev, and he would
always be that in his own mind and heart. But after some years in Israel he
had Hebraized his name, and to everyone else in the world he was Arieh,
one of the minor generals.

He entered his apartment and walked across the livingroom to a wide balcony from which he could see the city, the sea, and the dunes of the North Coast. Without taking his eyes off the sparkling lights he stepped back and cast his handful of mail onto a table where the maid had left fresh roses. Then he went out to the balcony and watched until it became completely dark. The clouds were steep and forbiddingly purple. But to the west the weather over the Mediterranean was still and perfect. For just an instant before he went inside and turned on every light in the house, he had cast a practiced glance southward to a dark feature of the coast he knew well, where waves and spray were dashing coldly over sandbars and beaches, a wild spot on the coast, covered with pine and palm.

3

It was December, but in Tel Aviv some people bathed in the sea. The gardens were sleepy and the bees flew very slowly because it was so cold at night that they became punchy. By the time they had fully awakened and regained their legendary efficiency, the sun was already going down and they had to start back for various hives in the orange groves circling the city. They do not fly more than several stories up, and so had to follow the plan of the streets—an exhausting process which some of them seemed to avoid by taking the bus, a risky endeavor because Jews on a bus panic if they see a bee or a mosquito, and will not rest until they have forced it out the window or crushed it in a day-old copy of *Ma'ariv*. But the bees were skilled at hiding in boxes of vegetables, perching silently on top of a hat, or riding in neat organized rows on the roof of the bus.

The Jews of Israel loved winter more than other seasons because in most parts of the country winter was like spring. Whereas in summer the heat was intense and the colors furious, in winter the air, the sea, the reflections, the flowers, and the light were tranquil. Except when the Mediterranean went wild in storm, it was a time of healing in a weak but warm sun, in the sometimes cool breeze over the deserted Yarkon and its puntlike boats, and in the quiet shadows of silent flower-edged verandas.

To begin their life in the East, Marshall and Lydia had found a tiny whitewashed room in the old Sea Quarter of Tel Aviv. Most of their neighborhood had been leveled by time and bulldozers. It was ridiculously poor there. They paid eight dollars a week for one room, two cots, a table, a chair, and a sink; with ten dollars a week for food, they ate quite well. They shopped only in the great market at closing time, when vendors were tired and wanted to empty their stalls and go back to Petach Tikvah. The old Moroccan granddaddies who traded tomatoes and cucumbers all day were quickly infatuated with Lydia. She was sunburnt and tall, green-eyed and auburn-haired, with a radiant white smile. They thought that she was an angel, and, since they did not want to carry their wares back with them, she often fetched great bargains—a dozen grapefruit for 25¢, a kilo of rice for 30¢, five enormous tomatoes for a dime. Marshall, for his part, would stare down the chicken vendors and come away with a fresh-killed hen for half a dollar, or eggs at 2¢ apiece. Sometimes they dealt so well in the frantic market (where thousands of shrewd traders bluffed and lied and counter-bluffed, but Marshall and Lydia were just honest, naïve, and cheap) that they had enough left to buy a bunch of daffodils, a potted geranium, or a chunk of halvah—Lydia's favorite candy. And each day they would sit by the sea from eleven until three, with four fishing lines out. Often they caught nothing, but when schools of sea bass and other plump Mediterranean fish were running they had to quit early and sell their surplus to a nearby hotel for soldiers with nervous breakdowns.

Though choked with rampant Western institutions, Israel was built upon the East, and Marshall and Lydia could not escape its singular signs. The sea surged not far away and the light in their room changed through an infinity of degrees as day progressed, diffusing a thousand colors of cream, orange, and red against the bare white walls. In what they assumed was not a rare practice, they learned to contemplate an object—such as a pitcher of flowers—while the light played across it. This they could do for hours as it became cooler or warmer and shadows swelled to the full or retreated. They felt the life of the air as it moved unseen about the room. What a great event when an old white horse drawing a lumber cart would clop down the street, shattering the rhythm of the waves with the complex reports of its hooves. They saw that insects in the garden flew in ellipses, and that the flowers were full of motion.

They became extraordinarily thin and bright-eyed, and their senses were so sharpened that when they went to a movie and it flooded onto the screen they felt as if they had been knocked over by a wave. Marshall was per-petually at the edge of seizures, but taught himself how to control them by concentration. Once, they were riding on a bus down Allenby Road where many trees fleck the light and make it green and mottled on the masonry. It was unusually quiet; the bus went steadily along, its wheels rolling hypnotically. Marshall was pulled by the light which burst through the trees in glorious flashes. But then he looked at the gardens within the arcades, and down the disappearing perspectives of the quiet side streets. He clenched his fists and, by power of will, brought himself equanimity. In winter there was as much fog and mist as sun, and in storms the rain and waves threatened to drown the road by the sea.

Especially on the gray days, they exhausted themselves in the mill of the semi-feudal, part Eastern European, part Ottoman, part Moroccan, and entirely Jewish bureaucracy, the likes of which have never been seen in the world and will not be in any worlds yet to be discovered. But somehow (as if there were workers in hidden underground cities) the country grew and prospered despite its civil service, while fighting off a breathtaking coalition of enemies, teaching itself its own language, parleying with the great powers, and attending the cinema five times a week. How this was done, no one knew.

Trained in the Sudan or rural Mexico, the syrup-blooded bankers required twenty visits, fifty coffees, and a dozen stamps and seals to cash one check for five hundred dollars. The back of the check had so many signatures and imprints that it looked like a micro-edition of the Rosetta Stone. At each visit, Marshall would wait for several hours in several anterooms, where Arabian rugs had upon them leather cushions, which in turn had upon them elaborately tooled Eastern trays, which had upon them in turn piping hot strudel, which had upon it in turn indestructible flies the size of grasshoppers.

Marshall had to explain why he (an Israeli citizen) could speak practically no Hebrew, and was trying to cash a foreign check into dollars. Having been born in Haifa, Palestine, as his passport said, he was upon entry to Israel issued a set of many documents which he and Lydia were translating over the weeks. He was liable for military service, income taxes—everything. By virtue of being his wife, Lydia too had become an Israeli. Suddenly they found themselves subject to a comprehensive set of Levantine responsibilities, most of which seemed to derive from the Mamluk Interlude, and some of which were strikingly contemporary—notably, Marshall's imminent conscription into a modern mechanized army. They became professional office-sitters, official stamp-purchasers, rushers to the post office, waiters on line, and explainers to fat little men who looked like East German woodchucks and sat behind barred enclosures sipping tea and eating sesame cakes.

Only after they learned the language would they begin to search for Marshall's father. Without further knowledge of Hebrew, it would be a hopeless task to wade into the most complex and heartbreaking cell of the bureaucracy—the Bureau of the Missing. They knew (from Metzner's narrative) that he was tall, with blond hair and brown eyes, that he was Russian, and that with his intimate knowledge of the land he had enabled his fighting group to survive in the forests.

So Marshall and Lydia went on their forays in the mornings and early evenings, or rested quite happily amid the palms, green gardens, and quiet streets. And when the storms stopped and spring began to blacksmith the fields with a burning Middle Eastern sun, they moved up the coast to Haifa, where they were to study in a language school in the Bat Gallim Quarter.

4

Haifa lies on the north face of Mt. Carmel. Air Force pilots cannot resist flying down the ridge until, on a great thermal, they come over the top of the
mountain and the world opens to them. The city beneath is white and
breathless—full of gardens and eye-intoxicating rows of stairs spread out and
falling like charts of optical illusion. The steps on the mountainside go up at
some points until they reach so far that their lines fuse in a dot. And often
they wind lasciviously through arches and iron gates and by walls on which
vines themselves are winding.

Marshall and Lydia went up the mountain on a day late in July. They
saw the city and a hundred thousand roses. In the distance over the bay
were great beaches and walking dunes. Beyond these were green hills of
sandstone and thorns, and beyond the low hills were small mountains high
enough for sweet valleys, and finally (as if in another world) the mountains
of the northeast, in Syria and Lebanon.

Out to sea a submarine was rising in a ring of white. It was headed for
the Navy base in the harbor, where dozens of swift heavily armed boats lay
in electrified enclosures. In their gray rows they looked from above like
sharks in a stable. Grenades were often tossed into the harbor from a speeding launch and, like an invasion fleet, a hundred ships rode at anchor in the
bay, but they were there for oranges, electronics, cement, and oil.

Haifa is as airy and peaceful as a stranded bank of clouds. But they
had lived there for some months, and they remembered several hundred
fully armed soldiers rushing from their assembly place in a square to a line
of waiting trucks—the violent mountings, the black twin 40's on halftracks,
the diesel engines starting one after another until the convoy moved east
and captured the commercial streets.

Their hearts went out to these people with whom by law they had
become one. For they were engaged in a grip against massacres and, to be
honest in a way they have never been, they expected to die at the hands of
their enemies as if in continuation of an inevitable pattern. The Sfardim were
delighted to confront the enemy on his own terms. But the Ashkenazim bled
with European ambiguities. The Sfardim were great fighters, a shock to all, a
vitality untutored. They stormed enemy redoubts, with the mountains of
Morocco and a host of devils in their eyes, and the enemy melted away like
clarified butter. Dark of skin and quick as insects, the Sfardim were the spark.
But the Ashkenazim—refugees from slaughter, full of bitterness, not afraid
to die—were the ones with the staying power, and stay they would.
Assembled on the square, they had been an essay in victory.

Marshall was drawn to the convoys, sensing that his place was with the nervous barbaric soldiers and the potent weapons. He loved Lydia so much, and yet he wanted to go north and fight. He valued her above all, and yet he was drawn to the Army, to the very words for it. When he thought of how it would be, he imagined Gaston Reynelle's forge, and he saw hot iron as it was struck, moving inside itself in crimson planes and rosy swirls like sunspots coding out a message of leanness and war. The name of war spread across the Galilee and caught him up as surely as the closing of a steel lock or the crack of a breach.

At dusk, they felt the vitality of the city as its lights snapped on by the thousands and gleamed over the ship-studded bay. Back down they went, passing Stella Maris and the naval headquarters from which, a lifetime before, Keslake had been summoned to intercept the *Lindos Transit*.

In the palm-filled courtyard of the language compound, scores of Russians sat on benches, smoking cigarettes—the red dots of which spotted the darkness like socialist fireflies. Everyone was going to dinner, and Lydia put up her hair. The Russians—mainly chemists and chess players—were surprisingly formal at evening meals. Perhaps they thought that they were someplace else.

Marshall considered his wife, her arms up like the arch on a wedding cake, her tanned face aglow in fluorescent light, her green eyes as lovely as tiny sea turtles. A cool breeze flooded the room; it was incomparably peaceful, until a long train of flatcars carrying tanks and halftracks passed outside their window. The fiberboard walls and plastic louvers shook as munitions cars raced by twenty or thirty feet away. Soldiers in battledress came out of the darkness into the flash of security lights and then disappeared in a tunnel of black. They had neutral, expressionless faces, and they lived in a different world.

After the train had passed and Lydia was ready to go to dinner, Marshall thought that she had not noticed how it had affected him. But she had, and she came over and sat on the bed. "What kind of train was that?" she asked, knowing painfully well exactly what it was. As Marshall explained, she closed her eyes and embraced him.

5

By custom, Marshall and Lydia strolled after dinner on the promenade near the sea's edge in Bat Gallim. Whereas thousands of feet above on Rehov HaNassi there were groves of pine, by the sea on Quai Pinchas Margolin there were bent and humid palms among which at some time German immigrants had built chalets unsuited to the leveling wet sea winds.

Killing time before he went on duty, the night watchman of the language compound came down the promenade as squadrons of breakers beat against the old sea wall. They had seen him often, sitting in a corner near the gate, surrounded by stark rays from a naked bulb above him, nearly en-wrapped by vine tendrils, reading Egyptian paperback books. He wore a peaked desert-colored cap with a shiny black visor and a green band, and an ancient double-breasted brown suit. Even in the light of the moon or burn-ing tungsten, his skin was Alexandrine and dark; but his face was European.

He sat down next to them on the bench where they had settled to be alone. Soon to die, he said, he paid more attention to chance contacts, con-vinced that his life had been too complex and varied just to slam shut like a wooden case. There had to be continuity, and before he died he had to con-nect, even if it meant intruding upon Marshall and Lydia with the accept-able tyranny of the aged. His name was Lamarel Foa.

"That's Italian, isn't it?" asked Marshall. Both he and Lydia spoke an extraordinarily archaic and mellifluous Italian, one of their best shared assets.

"It is one o half Italian, and one o half French. My father was o ho Italian, and my mother o ho French."

"Oh."

"Oh ho. But as an little baby of o four, I was removed from the city of my birth, beautiful ancient Marseilles, and taken to Alexandria in Egypt. There for o fifty years I lived a life both wondrous and strange. In o nineteen o fifty-four I was exiled, and fled to Johannesburg, but then in o nineteen o sixty I came here, because I did not wish to be o ho South African. Would you like to hear the story of my life, a life of o eighty years?"

"Sure," said Marshall. "But listen, Lamarel, you don't have to say 'o' before numbers, or 'o ho' before adjectives of nationality."

"Oh no?"

"No."

"Oh ho. That will be useful, and save precious time, though time matters no more. But I do wish to improve my English."

"And I," said Marshall, in Arabic, "would like to practice Arabic."

Lamarel was stunned. "It is a miracle that you speak Arabic," he said. "We can help one another."

And then he spoke of his life, and at times of passionate memory he glided swiftly and irrevocably into Arabic. Speaking Arabic is like drowning upside down in a well, gasping for air and writhing. It soon tires the speaker and lays him out flat, exhausted, and wall-eyed. This, unknown to scholars, is the reason for the Arabs' fatalism—their language is like a beautiful prison complete with guards who beat them.

He told a tale of endurance—charming Lydia, stirring Marshall. The moon rose and made a perfectly smooth arc; the west wind came in from Egypt and the Delta; the soft lights of Stella Maris glowed from the moun-tain; and in a slow dipping rhythm, the lighthouse flashed its untiring beam.

The eldest of his sons had died in a fall from Table Mountain in South Africa. "I said, 'If you go there, you will die. Why climb steep walls?' I asked him. I told him. But . . . I know myself what it is to go where no one has gone. After all, I had lived through such a time. So I did not tell him, hoping that he would be strong and lucky, as I have always been. But he was not."

"But you did tell him."

"Only not to go, not what I myself had seen."

"What had you seen?"

"How do you think I would feel if I were to tell you, strangers, when I did not tell my son, and he died?"

"I see."

"I must go. It is time to take up my post."

Lamarel plodded away to meet the rigors of a soft hot night. Marshall and Lydia returned to their room overlooking the railroad tracks and Kiryat Eliezer, behind which the hillside rose sharp and sudden in the moonlight all the way to Stella Maris, awash in silver blue.

6

The Israeli Army is run by an elite corps of overweight teenage girls who are recruited to fill out forms and type orders. Every single one of them has red freckles. Sometimes they are not overweight, but slim and tall, and in that case their offices are crowded with soldiers and those begging to enlist. Summoned frequently to the yards of various commands for physicals and interviews, Marshall quickly made friends with a score of these girls, and what they said was always the same. They looked up, honestly hopeful, and said, "Your notice of when to report should come through in a week, maybe two weeks, maybe three . . . okay, a month, but no more than two months . . . four at the worst," which meant six months. Marshall had the strongest impression that, save a few, these girls cared deeply for the tormented soldiers and reservists whose papers never came through, and he wondered how they could have enough tenderness to be genuinely concerned for the men behind the numbers, waiting outside their tiny offices in the long corridors of cool stone fortresses. In transit from the north to the south, or from the south to the north, with submachine guns slung from their shoulders and ammunition pouches at their waists, the thin, tough, and resigned soldiers, who looked as beaten as anvils, called the girls "angels."

To get from the language academy to the mobilization office, Marshall had to make his way through the waterfront, and he could not move an inch in Haifa port without attracting black marketeers, con men, pickpockets, and pimps, who thought that he was a Scandinavian sailor. If a ship from Northern Europe were in, Marshall had rough going amid the acres of vegetable carts, the placid sacks of coffee, and the roaring diesel trucks on Jaffa Road.

Old men in blue serge suits came up to him and opened their jackets to display radios, watches, pistols, drugs, pornography, and (once) sandwiches. "You buy sandwich? Half price. Meat sandwich. Cheese sandwich. Pizza pie."

"No thank you," said Marshall.

"Wait! Buy meat sandwich, I give you pizza pie! Four pounds. Cheap." He opened his coat, and Marshall saw slices of pizza pinned to the silk lining.

"*Atah meshuga*," said Marshall. "Completely nuts."

"Buy watch." He opened the other side of his coat, and a chorus line of watches flashed in the sun.

"No."

"Onions! Cheap! You buy onions. Make delicious soup."

An Arab bus from the West Bank was parked on a hill. Suddenly the brakes gave way, and the bus, empty but for the astonished driver, began to tear down the sidewalk, knocking over trash barrels and street signs, scattering the vendors and crushing their wares. A sea of hot cooking oil from a smashed felafel stand poured onto the street. Several cars went out of control and smashed head on, and a tank truck jackknifed. A tandem trailer carrying half a million oranges disintegrated, and the oranges exploded through the street like shrapnel. The old man bent and picked up half a dozen of them. Stumbling backward over hundreds of oranges, he said to Marshall, "Buy Israel oranges. Sweet, juicy, one pound! Half a pound. Twenty-five agorot. Ten agorot. Five. One. You drive a hard bargain."

"No," said Marshall. "That's not it!" He ducked up a side street toward the mobilization office, which was called the Lishcat HaGiyoos. On his way across the Municipal Park he noticed through the fountain that Lamarel sat quietly on the other side, studying his shoes.

Poor Lamarel, thought Marshall. Lamarel had come early for weeks just to watch the Jordanian news and discuss it with Marshall in Arabic. When it got dark, Marshall would leave to go to the sea with Lydia, and Lamarel would sit on the porch and put in an extra hour or two in his peaked desert cap, guarding the language compound. Many times he had begged Marshall to come with him to the port and have a coffee, as he said, but Marshall had never had time. He knew that Lamarel wanted to dissuade him from joining the Army.

Lamarel believed that Marshall could only come to ruin in the Levant, where one had to surrender, pay out, lie back, and live. He had seen too many like Marshall give up everything they had, and their lives, because they did not know the lax requisite submission of the East—simple rules of conduct written in the architecture of the cities, in the faces of the old, in the bold horizontal lines of Arabic, and in the olive-cluttered terraces on the hills. Even the illiterate knew, and could move in the right ways. But Marshall was unaware.

As Marshall rounded the fountain, he saw that Lamarel was crying. But Lamarel caught sight of him, wiped his eyes, and took him by the arm. Marshall forgot the angels, and went instead with Lamarel down into the chaos of the port. There, on Jaffa Road, they were swept up in a confusion of smoke and rays inside a bar for Indian sailors. A jukebox played raga after raga after raga. Slight dark sailors in white cotton suits sat and lay under columns of sun streaming from a dirty glass window. Otherwise, it was nearly dark. Whores moved about, always sitting on the edges of the tables when they pulled up to a group of sailors, who seemed too frail and childlike for these elephant-legged Moroccan girls. Lamarel was known there. Immediately, a woman brought them beer and a tray of brownish-yellow hardboiled eggs, peppers, and white cheese. She bent down low to show her breasts. Marshall felt imprisoned by the beams and ragas, lifted, turned slowly on his head around and around. He had either to grasp the table, or float.

Then Lamarel forced beer after beer into himself. "Have an egg," he said to Marshall. Disgusted by the sulfurous egg, Marshall did not want to be rude, and ate it, after drowning it in salt. Soon he was at the beer. The more eggs, the more beer. The more beer, the more eggs. Finally he realized that the thick smoke weaving in the white rays was some sort of drug. He felt distended. He gave up for the afternoon on his perfect diet and perfect body —he was so strong that he could butterfly for an hour or more in the warm buoyant sea—and held fast to the table, trying not to fall down. Dravidian and dark, the sailors chirped all around him, their forever optimistic Indian speech making the room into a bazaar. All Marshall wanted was to go with Lydia to the wave-beaten sands south of Haifa, and dash himself in the sea. Then, in drunkenness and who knew what else, Lamarel began.

"I was born," and when he said "born," he slammed his fist on the table as old men of the city often did, "in Marseilles. In the summer of 1899 my father and mother left on a coal wheeler and crossed the Mediterranean to Alexandria. Marseilles, though I hardly remember it, was the apron of civilization; upon it the winds of Africa cast themselves upwelling and hot. It was a silent pocket, forgotten, heated, erotic; but I must be speaking of Alexandria and Cairo, for I did not know Marseilles.

"It comes before me very often, and those are the times when I think I am again about to die. Let me drink, and I will tell you of the Mediterranean peoples, defeated peoples unlike those you know, cast about and weakened until they found that the greatest power lay in acceptance of worshipped acts. I say as a beaten Jew that we were a parody of the condition put upon us, and that in our fall we were driven like dust in the afternoon air. We moved together in the heat like pine needles on the trees in the shadows of Meron. We were made ridiculous, laughable, sweaty, drained, even ugly, and all the time we held the amber light for which we fell. We were, all of us here—the Muslims, the Jews, the Christian ladies—parodies of flesh, a quarter of the globe orchestrated to amuse the Divinity, made to dance the falling dance, wills receding before the touch of God, dear God, ever so gently, and yet our lives continued. By our complete acceptance and belief, we have defied Him beyond measure.

"But I have learned a trick of His. He will not let you speak of Him for more than an instant without seeming like a fool. Therefore, you can throw out any whose profession is to be a man of God. These are the worst imposters, devils who belong at best in a carnival. They are lower than normal men, for what they pretend to be. I once punched a rabbi."

"What happened?" asked Marshall, gripping the table to stay afloat.

"He beat me over the head with a candlestick until I fell unconscious. But what does this have to do with you? Nothing. However, I can tell you that as sure as my name is Lamarel Foa, everyone in Bat Gallim thinks that I am mad."

"I know," said Marshall. "The baker's wife told me never to speak to you because you are possessed."

"Ah, those horrible peasants! They are superstitious and they know nothing. I cannot even buy stamps or a newspaper in Bat Gallim, for they fear to look me in the eye. All because of the flies in my room. And who do you think sent me those flies?"

"Flies?"

"Yes. One night about ten years ago there were hundreds of flies in my room. I had no screens, and there were so many that I breathed them. I had nothing—no newspaper, stick, or broom—with which to drive them away. So I picked up my chair and used it. The chair was heavy, and not very accurate. I broke most of the things in my room. I smashed pictures, plates, light bulbs, everything, and only managed to kill one or two flies. It was so frustrating that I began to scream. When I stopped, covered with sweat, I looked up, and saw two hundred people watching me from the street. Boys had climbed trees for a better view. Just then the fire brigade arrived and, as is the custom with lunatics, sprayed me with cold water. I was so humiliated that I did not leave my house for two years. During that time, there was no reason to shave. When I came out on the street for the air raid sirens in the June War, my beard was five feet long and my hair came down to my waist. The people of Bat Gallim will not forget that. They have their own reputation and need someone to whom they can feel superior.

"You see, in 1957, a certain butcher named Shlomo had calendars printed and distributed throughout the quarter to every household. They had a beautiful color photograph of the Bat Gallim Casino, and everyone was so proud that they hung these calendars and used them to determine the dates of festivals and holidays.

"Everything was fine except for two mistakes. The printer had put that Carnival and Purim came together on the same day, and not only was there that mistake but that day was also listed as Fool's Day. Joke and costume shops in Haifa had to stay open at night for weeks as everyone in Bat Gallim decided to burn both candles in this triple holiday of madness, which, of course, did not really exist. In addition, the Moroccan and Bulgarian immigrants (who did not know of such things) wanted desperately to excel in the ways of their new homeland, and competed ferociously in devising practical jokes and nonsensical schemes. Even I, with no taste at all for buffoonery, bought plastic fangs and goggle eyes—they were popular at the time.

"Then a report appeared in the paper that a government delegation was coming on the day of madness. It was to consist of the Minister of Immigrant Absorption, the head of the Jewish Agency, the Prime Minister, the two Chief Rabbis, the President, and, for good measure, the Chief Rabbi of Brazil. The purpose of the visit was for them to be shown how well the new immigrants had adapted to national customs. 'They can't fool us,' said the people of Bat Gallim. 'We know what to do.'

"On the appointed evening, a long official motorcade crossed the tracks and entered Bat Gallim. To their surprise, not a soul was to be seen on Rehov HaAliyah. But when they turned down Bat Gallim Avenue and made for the sea, they saw the entire population assembled on the sidewalks. Every man, woman, and child wore a disguise—fake beards, buck teeth, crossed eyes, wigs, and costumes made of skins, aluminum, paper, whatever. Women dusted the palm trees, and the children had been instructed to bend down and break wind at the visitors—a mission which they carried out with great gusto.

"The high officials and their staffs were stunned. They got out of their cars and looked around them in astonishment. The people of Bat Gallim are not stupid, and immediately recognized that something was wrong. Not daring to reverse themselves, they became very serious and embarrassed, and, with their costumes on, they proceeded to carry out their plans.

"A wretched Bulgarian woman with goggle eyes, a fish tied on her head, and frogman's flippers, approached the dignitaries, gave them bunches of weed, and recited Slavic palindromes. In tears, the mayor rode up to the motorcade, facing backward on a jackass. He was supposed to have given a welcoming speech, but all he could do was weep. And this fellow had had his eye on a seat in the Knesset. Politics are fickle.

"The officials jumped in the cars and fled. Of course, Israel is a small country—beautiful, but small. Everyone knew within an hour.

"But it is past noon and I must soon see my mistress. I asked you here for one reason. You must not go into the Army. This I know. You will be killed."

"How do you know?"

"I know," Lamarel screamed, "because I have ridden with the god of war."

"Was it a nice ride?" asked Marshall. "I may be drunk, you may be drunk . . ."

"And you may not realize it," said Lamarel as he began to slip into the past, "but I am the same fool as you, or at least I was, until I learned.

"In Egypt, we continued to regard ourselves as French. Though I was as Egyptian as I could have been, there was a touchstone in my heart for France, which I loved as a man loves a woman. I was loyal in absentia, and, in walking the streets of Cairo and Alexandria, I put my feet down on the plan of Paris. Little did I know that had I stayed in Cairo and continued to imagine Paris I could have lived richly in my imagination forever. It was only when I proudly decided to fuse my life with my dreams that I came in for trouble. Dreams are stronger. How could I not have known that, in Alexandria—lost in layered light.

"At the beginning of the First War, I went to Paris and volunteered for the Army. Can you understand how stupid that was? I crossed the Mediterranean from corner to corner and traveled hundreds of kilometers so that I could be put in a dead man's coat and be made to live in the mud like a cold damp pig—and what is worse about the Army, we were totally forgotten, as if we had fallen into hell.

"We went on a boat in a river, about a hundred of us, in the heavy coats from the dead, and we lay on the metal deck in a ring like a necklace of men and arms. Though it was raining, there was a slight overhang and only our legs and boots were wet. Dry from the knees up, we tried to sleep. It was daylight, and we were quite warm, even hot, in those heavy coats. I was leaning against a wall, my hand on my rifle (if it were stolen, a month in prison). We moved through a light mist; the steam pistons echoed off the banks; and then a German plane came from over the trees like a kite or a bird.

"Most of us had never seen a plane. It left and came back, shooting its machine guns. There was nothing to hide behind and we didn't want to go in the water, so we sat there and loaded our rifles, and when I say 'we,' it is with a sense of remembered *fraternité*, although I hated them and they hated me.

"The plane would go away, and come back again shooting. But there were a hundred of us firing at it. I was terrified, but paralyzed with laughter; no sound, but my legs and lungs were numb. Weak with this silent laughter, I had great difficulty loading my rifle. But I was pleased by the copper cartridges and the sound they made as I put them in the magazine, when I snapped the bolt, and when they were ejected to the deck.

"I aimed at the plane and shot. We all did. Not one stood or changed position. There was no talk. This went on for at least an hour. We saw the paths of bullets in the water, which sometimes looked as if it were boiling. The bullets hit the plates of the ship, but they never hit us.

"The Captain sat in a glass wheelhouse, and was drinking from a mug. Every few minutes he turned and looked at us, smiling in slow motion, his face glowing from behind a blue jacket and cap. The sky cleared; cold winds arose; and the plane kept returning. It was freezing outside, but a current of heat came from the wheelhouse and we were warm and happy, conscious of the clicking of the brass, the closing of the barrels, the cavitousness of a cartridge once it has been fired, and the sound of it empty falling to the deck.

"The Captain's wheelhouse continued to grow lighter and lighter until the glass was like a construction of clear rainbows. The plane had gone, never to return. Our rifles lay by our sides, and we were frozen into one position staring at the wheelhouse, from which a higher and higher heat was coming— rushing air warming just the tops of our bodies; our legs in our boots were frozen. It was painful and yet pleasant. Our eyes riveted upon the Captain, we saw that the blue wool of his suit and cap contained glowing waves which moved up and down as if in molten metal.

"When he turned and smiled, his teeth were so white that they stretched our necks even farther forward. We were paralyzed in pain and pleasure for hours. Darkness fell and beams of white came from the pilot house, as solid and massive as the blackest of any beams on a great iron bridge. We moved through the night, and the next thing we knew, we had arrived at our desti-nation. We were cold and wet, surrounded by spent cartridges. The wheel-house was dark, and as we marched off the boat, over rain-soaked boards which did not bend under our weight, we said nothing. It was never men-tioned, not even once. There was nothing to say. We had been plumbed to our depths, and we went through the war like dead men . . . like dead men. Do you understand?"

Marshall could hardly keep his wits about him. His hands were pale and bloodless, so hard did he grip the wooden table. Swaying to and fro, he looked around him. The sulfurous smoke from the charcoal cooking pits was thick and intolerable. Most of the Indians had taken off their shirts. Their eyes glowed, and their skin was leathern. Marshall surveyed them in many-tiered balconies above him, perched with their chins resting on their hands. They seemed to ascend into the blackness and smoke as far as the eye could see. "Lamarel Foa! Lamarel Foa!" Marshall said before he fainted. "This is only a one-story building! Who are you?"

Lamarel Foa laughed in a terrible, dreadful, hideous, frightening way, and Marshall dropped to the floor like a rock.

7

One October morning three days before the conclusion of the language program, a military messenger on a quicksand-colored motorcycle roared into the compound. There does not exist in the world of men a creature more alarming than the military messenger. The *ne plus ultra* of bad news and excitement, he carries in his locked leather pouch ordinations of life and death, sentences of power, the fate of armies, the future of civil populations. His arrival at camp is an electrification.

This one had rushed down from Northern Command at seventy miles an hour through choked streets, by jumping sidewalks and driving his old British military motorcycle down steps, through gardens, and along the track bed—in a race with the Tel Aviv train. He had sergeant's stripes, a sidearm, dust goggles pushed onto his brow, and a military police armband. The license tag on the motorcycle was white with red numbers. He had a siren and a guidon flag, and the civilian police wouldn't touch him.

Upon arrival of this fire-hot moon calf, the language students exited their classes and pressed to the rails of promenades, galleries, and porches. The Russians in particular were concerned and alarmed: they were always overly impressed by anything to do with the state. The messenger checked out the girls as he unlocked his pouch and removed several envelopes, which he scanned and shuffled. In a practiced manner, he faced ahead and shouted above the sound of his idling motorcycle, "Pearl! Marshall! Forward!"

Marshall ran down the steps. The messenger collected his signature, gave him an envelope, put on the dust glasses, and mounted his motorcycle, driving it right through the shallow duck pond and scattering the ducks. His acceleration was heard until he hit the South Road and buzzed away at 120 mph.

Marshall went upstairs and handed the envelope to Leah, their teacher, the dark-eyed daughter of a Greek stevedore. The intermediate class of nurses, engineers, liberal arts graduates, girls who wanted husbands, and boys with serious character flaws which led them to gain weight and speculate in West Bank real estate, settled back to hear the communication. Leah read it in Hebrew, explaining in Hebrew the words that the students did not know.

"It says: 'Northern Command, Second Mountain Brigade, Headquarters Detachment, Haifa.'" Like a stewardess demonstrating a lifejacket, she held the envelope before her. Then she opened it and read. "H.Q./Class four order/Direct/8 October, 1972/Z.H.L. 191–4372. Pearl, Marshall: HaAliyah 71, Haifa. Notice of conscription. Report to Lishcat HaGiyoos, 22 October, 1972, for assignment to training prior to service in Second Mountain

Brigade active cadre. General Arieh Ben Barak, Commander, Second Mountain Brigade."

Knowing that in two weeks Marshall would leave for the Army, they moved on, this time to the Emek Bet Shan, a valley of the Mountains of Gilboa—hills which flanked the midlands of the desert before the Jordan escarpment. During Marshall's year in the Army, Lydia would stay at Kfar Yona. With luck, he would come home to her at least five days a month, and she would farm, work in the kitchen, or teach in the school—there was no way to tell. The kibbutz was famous for the many officers it had sent to the Army, and for the dates, wheat, and olives it grew on the bone-white floor of the valley. Half of the time, this valley was so hot and dry that it seemed to be the intercross of hell and terrycloth. But sometimes, it was said, the humidity was very great and the farmers went fishing in the air through which swam lost and startled prawns and other smallish crustaceans. (In the very beginning, the pioneers had thought that these were flying scorpions.)

Marshall and Lydia arrived at sunset and walked east from Bet Shan through the groves of olives and dates, past abandoned fortresses, down a narrow road which led through fields carpeted with crops as white and smooth as linen. New stone walls had just been completed at the road's edge, and the master masons had carefully smeared the joints with potted gallium and limonite. A linesman with a rifle worked alone near the top of a pole. It was quiet enough for the crickets and frogs to sound like a human multitude, and the high royal palms were no less elegant than their counterparts on the Riviera. But here were vultures, and great distances, and hawks which crossed from the Jordanian mountains to prey on creatures of the field. Israel sent back its own hawks, made of metal. In their approaches to the Golan, flying low by the Jordan to evade enemy radar, the Phantoms, Skyhawks, and Mirages from Ramat David often passed over Kfar Yona and other settlements in the valley. They came within twenty feet of the lookout towers and they scared the animals. The secretaries of the kibbutzim complained to the Air Force, but not very vigorously. Though the fighters spooked the cattle and the chickens, the people of the kibbutzim felt their hearts shake with pride as the planes ripped about.

Marshall and Lydia walked toward the ring of towers which marked the kibbutz—a grove of tall trees among which some red roofs glowed in the setting sun. As it darkened, crows lifted above the date palms; a cold wind pressed down the sine of the mountains; and the perimeter lights of Kfar Yona came on like a string of shining porcelains.

"It's beautiful," said Lydia.

"It is beautiful," answered Marshall, "especially in light of the fact that it's an armed settlement."

Lydia looked puzzled. "Who said it was an armed settlement? It doesn't look armed to me."

"It is."

"Oh it is not. Ever since you found out that you're due for the Army, you've become a general. But you're only going to be in for one year; you'll be a private; you'll be home for five days a month; and there's not likely to be a big war."

"What does that have to do with Kfar Yona?"

"A lot."

"What?"

"Just don't take any chances, if you don't have to. You're not going to find your father by being in the Army, but by looking after you get out, and to get out, you have to stay alive."

"Do you know what logic is, Lydia?"

"Certainly."

"Then why don't you ever resort to it?"

"I do."

"Stop." He walked behind her, put his hands up against the sides of her head, and directed her sight like a mounted searchlight. "Look," he said, pointing toward the settlement, "guard towers . . ."

"Oh, is that what those are?"

". . . deep perimeter fencing, fire fields, arc lights." The lights had just begun to sweep over the crops, like dancing stilts. "Look." He turned her head, touching her gently, so that she could feel his compensatory surrender for each point that he won—their custom in disputes.

"A halftrack, see? I count five soldiers inside."

"Oh! I thought it was a storage tank."

He wheeled her around until she stared into the darkness between the date palms. "There."

"What?"

"Look hard." Then she saw three soldiers standing in the trees. They were armed to the teeth, and, perhaps appropriately, they were smiling. They were the archetypal soldiers who need almost not be described, except that they were very dark of skin, and they had vacuum bottles slung over their shoulders for the night of patrol among the trees.

A corporal approached without a sound, for despite his rank he was practiced at being bodiless in the silent groves. "Good night, friends," he said in English. "Where you going?"

"Kfar Yona."

"Kfar Yona is there." He pointed. "Just a kilometer. On the right. On the left is other kibbutz. He is Kfar Tsofar. Kfar Yona is better, better food, very pretty, more peoples. There are in the Army, many peoples from there. His name is like . . . a dove."

X
Refiner's Fire

1

The courtyard of the Lishcat HaGiyoos was filled with several hundred new recruits, who stood in groups according to the unit for which they were destined. Each group was addressed by officers from its future command, and then ushered out to waiting trucks. Finally, only those hundred and fifty or two hundred attached to the First, Second, and Third Mountain Brigades were left. Marshall had found two other Americans, with whom he sat on hard benches freed by the departure of an elite armor unit's new men.

One of the Americans was named Robert. He was a physical education instructor from Brooklyn, six feet seven inches tall, perhaps the strongest man in the world. The other was named Lenny; he had been a washing machine repairman in Los Angeles; he was very handsome, and he had a trim beard. They consulted, quickly discovering that they had a limited command of Hebrew and that Robert and Lenny were veterans of the American Army—where Robert had been an instructor in hand-to-hand combat, and Lenny had been a weapons specialist and sharpshooter. Robert was married. He often looked in his wallet at a picture of his wife. Lenny had never had a wife.

They immediately sensed a strong affinity, communicated in a certain nervous irony common to those with similar backgrounds together in a strange place. Though in America they would have been strikingly diverse, in Israel, by virtue of being Americans, they were practically clones.

They speculated on the character of the training, but their primary concern was where they would be stationed. All three were from kibbutzim, and dreamed of being sent to a base near home. This often happened, and it was said that the assignment officers did what they could for older and married men. They discovered that they were only-sons, which meant that, excepting all-out war, they would be held back from combat zones as much as possible. There was fighting on the Golan and on the Lebanese border, and they surmised that the only-sons of Northern Command would fall to the bottom, on a line running roughly from Haifa to Bet Shan—a line near which they lived. They would have speculated themselves into generalships and Mercedes limousines driven by buxom girl privates, had not an officious captain screamed, *"Le kol ahshev!"* which means, roughly, "Attention!"

They did not know how to come to attention properly. Instead, they stiffened and blinked, and their hearts beat faster. Most of the recruits were young and very frightened. Some were peasant farmboys; a few were Druse Arabs; many wore gaudy flared clothing—tight pants, jewelry, pimps' shirts with pictures of pineapples and fish. But they all became completely silent when a general walked in and stood on a raised platform before them. He spoke as if he were subjecting his words to a critique at the very moment they sounded, trying not to say the unnecessary, to compress his message, to be uninfluenced by the great gap of power and experience which lay between him and the new soldiers. He knew well that a few of them might eventually rise far above him, and that more than a few were already happy and had loving families—something which had eluded him. Though he spoke with great dignity and authority, he spoke with respect for those he addressed.

"Good morning," he said. "I am Arieh Ben Barak, Commander of the Second Mountain Brigade. Today, you enter the Army of Israel. I cannot remember the day I did so myself. It is surrounded in confusion, for in those times everyone was in the Army and no one was in the Army. But anyway, you will soon be joining me in my command, or in the neighboring commands of the First and Third.

"Our job is to protect the northern approaches to the heart of Israel. There are far too many Syrian soldiers, and they are well armed. But, as you will see, the terrain is on our side, and the Air Force helps us immeasurably. You may ask: 'Which Air Force?' I can tell you: our Air Force, because it is so good; and their Air Force, because it is so bad. Though many of you will be with us for only a year, you will always return to the Mountain Brigades for your reserve duty. Now you are to be given infantry training. Pay close attention. We run tight brigades, and you must know what you are doing at every moment. Though it is difficult to live in this way—you will see what I mean—it is not unpleasant; especially in that time goes very fast for a man who does his job well. I guarantee you this. I know, because I have become an immodest old man in the snap" (he snapped his fingers) "of my fingers."

They laughed.

"Now go and learn, and when you come back, you will learn more. *Shalom.*" He walked off the platform and vanished into the corridors of the fortress.

The General had a quick sensitive face; they had been impressed by the way in which he carried himself, and by the intelligence of his voice. Already, he had begun to build their morale—because they sensed that he would guide them properly and well.

They raced in an Army truck down the Haifa–Tel Aviv highway, often sighting the sea, rolling past a thick green belt of canefields and groves, heading for the induction center at Tel HaShomer—a place called Bakum. Whenever Marshall had passed beautiful landscape, or ridden fast in a half-open truck, or seen the sea vanish and appear from behind dunes and hills, his soul had arisen. But despite the scent of new-fallen cane, of oranges, despite the excitement of the moment and the passage of October sun across the beginning of his first day in a crack army besieged on all sides, in a small country in Asia, despite his natural fear, he was quiet and calm, and unafraid, and happy. He felt like a man-angel, as if nothing in the world could upset him, as if his heart—usually exposed and alert—were safe within a fortress. He was surprised to feel for the first time in his life just like everyone else.

When the Commander of the Second Mountain Brigade had walked into the courtyard of waiting recruits, the forces driving Marshall were temporarily stilled and quieted. It was as if he had always been in pain, and then the pain had stopped. He was puzzled and did not understand. He did not realize that the Commander of the Second Mountain Brigade was his father.

2

Tel HaShomer, or Bakum, had about it the air of a navel, being the center of gravity for military affairs, in almost the exact middle of the country, and where regular soldiers like Marshall, Robert, and Lenny were inducted and released. It was the busiest place Marshall had ever seen, a hive of soldiers and equipment. It looked like a staging area for an invasion, an Italian opera during a martial finale, or a Roman farce, and Marshall and his friends could hardly move a step without being cut off by a tight column of armed troops, hurrying down one road or another.

Once, six infantry battalions intersected at a crossroads, where an MP in the center directed them like traffic, motioning through the shortest columns first. The last group was half a mile long. Soldiers not in formation were running heatedly from place to place, beads of sweat on their red faces, equipment jangling from them like the pots and pans of peddlers. And mechanized equipment—either singly, in platoons of half a dozen, or in armored columns of staggering size—was moving everywhere else. Marshall, Robert, and Lenny stood open-mouthed at a corner as two hundred tanks drove past them no more than ten feet apart. The motors of one tank are as concussive as all the drums in a symphony orchestra resounding in unison. The sound of two hundred tanks shakes the earth and vibrates buildings as if they were hollow reeds.

The recruits of the Mountain Brigades walked a few miles past unending supply dumps, vehicle parks, tank depots, arsenals, armories, hospitals, and fortifications. They were headed for the Identification Division, where they would be photographed and issued documents, and where a record would be made of their teeth. If a body were too mutilated or burnt to identify, some-one would resort to reading its cavities and crowns. On the way, they saw a distant hill covered with dark green vegetation. "That's funny," said Lenny. "Every inch of this place is taken up with military stuff. Why do you think they left that hill there?" As they closed on it they discovered that, though a hill, it was covered not with vegetation but rather with an infantry brigade of nearly 2,000 soldiers in drab green battle regalia, who were all looking in-tently into a small canvas booth. Marshall assumed that a general was addressing his command. What else could hold the attention of 2,000 armed men sitting under the hot sun? But as the recruits passed they were able to see inside the booth. There was no general lecturing on the fine points of war, and no tactician explaining the capabilities of a newly acquired weapon. It was a puppet show—little Hebrew-speaking puppets bouncing up and down on a stage surrounded by flowers.

After bored dentists had called out the peculiarities of their teeth, they were marched into a dining hall and given a class-2 Army meal. Marshall and his companions were used to this fare, the sustenance of every kibbutz. It can be described in three words—Polish Oasis Cuisine. However, they noticed that the boiled potatoes were covered with blue stains. Marshall summoned the dining hall officer on duty. By custom, he was armed.

"What's this?" asked Marshall, pointing at the blue potatoes.

"What's what?"

"This," he said, indicating the potatoes more fervently by moving his hand back and forth in accusation. The officer looked.

"Potatoes," he said.

"Oh yeah."

"Don't you eat potatoes in America?"

"They're blue!"

"The potatoes in America are blue?"

"No! These potatoes are blue."

"Oh yes. These potatoes are blue. So?"

"Why?"

"Why? I don't know why. Who am I, Sherlock Holmes?" The officer started to walk away, but pivoted around. "As it happens," he said, "I do know. I just remembered. The soldiers who peeled the potatoes have just come back from testing fountain pens."

Marshall was speechless. Then he said quietly, "Didn't they wash their hands?"

"Why?" asked the officer, departing. "Ink is clean. It comes from rocks."

After the magical point at which the recruits were issued their equip-ment and uniforms, and suddenly became indistinguishable from battle-worn veterans, the dining hall officer approached, towing a higher-ranking, pasha-like, Egyptian-looking fatso who carried a swagger stick. "This is the one," said the officer. With fire in his eyes, the "Egyptian" approached Marshall. Marshall could hardly believe what followed, but it did.

"You say," said the fat pasha, "that it isn't *cashér* for kitchen troops to test fountain pens. You say, that we don't know how to run a *cashér* kitchen. You say, that I don't know my job. You say, that I am guilty of violating the commandments. You say, that ink does not come from rocks. You say, that I should be reprimanded by the rabbis. You say, that I should be thrown from the Army like garbage and cast out on the street to beg and die."

Marshall was at a loss for English words, much less Hebrew.

"Who were your confederates?"

"These two," said the other officer.

"All right then, the three of you, come with me."

They protested, but the pasha screamed, saying that he was a major and they were hardly even privates. How dare they not follow his orders immediately? He made them stand at attention, sticking out their chests and chins. Then he marched them off, kitbags on their shoulders, away from the others in the Second Mountain Brigade. A week later and they would have told him to go to hell. But they didn't know, and they ended up in a vast supply hall. It was cool inside and the whitewashed ceiling was very high; its white and off-white color currents mixed like the visual acoustics of an eggshell.

Stacked against one wall were a dozen cartons. In the middle of the room a long black table was covered with pads of paper and big bottles of ink.

"Oh no," said Lenny.

That night they tested a thousand fountain pens. They were shown how, and left alone. None of them had slept the night before. Marshall had been so keyed up that he had stared at Lydia until dawn, drumming his fingers on the sheet as he contemplated her sleeping face.

So it was difficult indeed to fill, test, and empty all those pens, especially since they worked in the light of only one forty-watt bulb. In a fit of remorse, the dining hall officer came at midnight and gave them chocolate bars and cold water. They worked in a stupor until the sun rose. Of one thousand pens, twenty were defective.

At seven the pasha arrived and threw them out. They walked in a daze to an empty assembly point, with no idea of how to join the rest of their Brigade Group. An officer passed, and they asked him what to do. With the greatest confidence, he told them to stay where they were. Soon, another contingent would be along and they could ride down with it to the big training base in the Negev, where they could rejoin their unit.

Within half an hour they were surrounded by fresh troops. In another four or five hours, the trucks came and they embarked. These troops were much rougher than any Marshall had ever seen. He thought that it was because they were battle-hardened. Like a crazed mob, they rushed for the best seats in the truck, and, as he was climbing in, he was kicked in the face.

Finally, the three Americans sat deep inside, and the trucks started rolling. They could see minute spangles of sun coming through pinholes in the dark canvas. The teeth and eyes of the other soldiers shone—they seemed to be very unusual.

3

It was a convoy of six trucks escorted by four jeeploads of military police. Soon the three Americans realized that the troops with whom they rode had special qualities. For example, five or six of them screamed continually, as if they were trying to say something and knew no language. But these few created only one point in a trident of noise. Another point was the irresponsible gunning of the motor by the truck's driver, and his habit of traveling at high speeds in low gear. Point three was the conversation of the remaining soldiers, who seemed one and all to have hearing defects. Their shouts were repugnant and damaging. And, a soldier in the back near Marshall had his hand in his pants and was busily masturbating. They tried to ignore him, but he just went on and on.

Someone had cut a hole in Lenny's kitbag and was in the process of removing a winter jacket when Robert lifted him bodily and cast him to the other side of the truck, near a man who was ugly, mean-looking, and rather large. Though the truck was crowded and people were pressed together, he enjoyed several feet of bench all his own.

Most of the soldiers had a crazed demented look which caused their eyes to seem like the windows of a slot machine in which were visible not the symbols of apples, diamonds, or bells, but rather a high-speed shuffling of evil thoughts, remembrances and anticipations of evil deeds, and the singular electrical flashes of the evil mind. Except for the kingpin, they were horrendously slight, scarred, undernourished, and nervous. As if each one had just finished sixteen cups of espresso, they couldn't sit still; they shook; they trembled; they chattered; they and their faces erupted into hideous smiles and wide-eyed laughter. Their teeth were rotten, and projected at a universe of angles within the various mouths, but those teeth not gone were white and sparkling.

Ten miles from Bakum, one of them went to the back of the truck, hung off the side, and threw himself into a ditch. The convoy stopped short and two military policemen chased after the jumper, who had a limping head start of about a hundred feet. The soldiers cheered for him and went wild when he climbed into the curly fork of an olive tree and kicked at the MPs. He was screaming: "I want to go home! I want to go home!" Finally, the

MPs grabbed his feet and started to pull him, but he held on and screeched like a cat. They pulled, and pulled, and seemed only to shake the tree.

A young lieutenant approached the scene and yelled an order. Another MP who was sitting in a police jeep, gun trained at the knot of heads protruding from the back of Marshall's truck, rushed forward, his weapon at the ready.

"Put that down, you fool!" shouted the lieutenant.

"Yes, Commander!" answered the MP. Then the lieutenant said something to him, and he ran to the tree, where the two other MP's were in a sweat trying to break the jumper's grip. The jumper was stretched as straight as a ruler and the tree shook as if it were in a fit. The third MP looked tentatively at the lieutenant.

"Go ahead, idiot," said the lieutenant.

The third MP walked carefully under the jumper and looked up at his exposed belly. Then he turned briefly and flashed a foolish smile at the convoy, after which he reached with one finger and gently touched the jumper's stomach, saying, *"Kitchee-kitchee-coo!"*

The jumper bent double so convulsively that he caught the MP between the two halves of him as if the MP had sprung a bear trap. The more the MP struggled to free himself, the more he tickled the jumper, and the tighter the jumper closed, shrieking hysterically all the while. Finally, like an umbrella in a storm, the jumper sprang the other way, and the dazed MP got up and staggered about.

After the jumper had been thrown back in the truck, Marshall heard the lieutenant mumbling to himself, "These bastard madmen are all incredibly ticklish." Marshall remembered the many times Lydia had reached out to him at night and caused him to jump two feet in the air, prone, with just a gentle loving touch to do it. *He* was incredibly ticklish, the most ticklish boy in Eagle Bay. Perhaps, then, *he* was a madman. He seemed, after all, to be riding in a caravan of lunatics.

The jumper was unbelievably frail and looked like a wooden puppet. There was no muscle or flesh on him, as if he had been ravished by polio. The kingpin picked him up and put him on his lap like a ventriloquist's dummy. He stroked the little fellow's head in affection. "What's your name?" he asked.

"I am Yakov," said the marionette, terrified, squirming to get away. But the kingpin held him in a tight grip and would not let go.

"I am Ashkenazi," said the kingpin (most certainly a Moroccan). "Yakov, you will be my servant."

The soldiers burst into laughter. Yakov did not dare laugh, but his eyes searched back and forth in terror. Occasionally he would have a fit of squirming, but Ashkenazi held him tighter and tighter, as if Yakov were a bird that Ashkenazi had just trapped and wanted to observe before roasting. All

Yakov's hysteria and weakness showed in his darting liquid eyes. He seemed to be looking for a way out, but he saw only the darkening canvas and the hills in dusk.

4

They approached Jerusalem in half-darkness. Its walls were as white as the moon. The city lay across hills between which were stands of pine, and the air was clear and touching. Marshall strained to see out the back of the truck and saw mainly a darkening blue space framed in a vault of overstretched canvas. There was a certain rhythm to the way the convoy moved through the outskirts of the city—up and down hills, around corners, stopping for a moment at crossroads—and it was sad to see warm lights shining from the lovely red-roofed houses of Jerusalem stone.

They knew something had gone very wrong, and that having come so far they might never reach the Negev. Through cautious questioning, they discovered that they were in a convoy of prisoners experimentally released for service in the Army to help alleviate the critical manpower shortage. Ashkenazi was a murderer. Others were rapists, muggers, burglars, drug peddlers, pimps, male prostitutes—there was even a bookie, who seemed likely to explode from frustration because he was convinced that he was a white-collar criminal improperly confined with cutthroats.

But not all were criminals. In a stroke of genius, the Army had leavened the brew with a choice selection of terminal idiots, cretins, and the several alingual lunatics who—as if their noise were necessary to power the truck— had never stopped screaming. There were as well many innocents; terrified fat boys who had failed the lenient selection tests both physically and mentally and then found themselves inducted into the Army in the company of in- corrigibles; maniacs with no apparent defects except that they had gone to mobilization offices and begged to be conscripted (the harried clerks had a system with which to skewer these irregulars, and skewered they were); and normal soldiers in transit kidnapped by the guards because a few convicts had escaped and had to be replaced.

The kidnapped normal soldiers gravitated together as soon as they could recognize each other. They cursed and clenched their fists. It was refreshing to see genuine undisturbed anger, to sense a yeoman's indignation amid the rocking and screaming of bedlam.

One of the normal soldiers was a Kurd named Baruch. Just nineteen, he had already seen a year's service in a demolition platoon. Sensing that Marshall, Robert, and Lenny were civil, he cut a path through the lunatics. As darkness settled completely and they forged steadily north toward what they guessed was Ramallah, Baruch conferred with them conspiratorially. They exchanged information and formulated a plan. At their destination, which Baruch said was likely to be a camp called the Fourth Daughter, they would band together and insist on seeing the base commander. Baruch would speak for them. This seemed reasonable and likely to work.

They rumbled through the green and yellow steel gates of the Fourth Daughter and drove up a hill to a vast concrete field where the trucks formed a line and the incorrigibles scrambled out into the cold. Though they had sweated in Tel HaShomer, in the Fourth Daughter the high mountain air was clear and frigid. Beyond a hazy ring made by the security lights Marshall could see massive sharp blue shapes—mountains and hills—while above, the stars burned and trembled like blazing phosphorus.

The cold silenced even the worst of the criminals. They shivered and clutched themselves in the light of two spotlights on the MP jeeps. Young officers and sergeants from the camp counted them. Then the MPs switched off their floodlights and drove away. This produced a chorus of whistles and cheers from the prisoners, but a strong hoarse voice came out of the darkness: "Silence! Beasts!" Even the prisoners, used to terror in the bottom of the worst jails, became frightened.

A major had spoken. They could barely see him. Only his silhouette was visible and it comprised a sharp peaked cap, a swagger stick, and a frame as upright as iron. Baruch swallowed and was moved to reassess his plan. But he stepped forward courageously, the three Americans directly behind. He approached the Major, who was only a high-angled shadow.

Baruch was so short, stocky, and muscular—no army shirt could close on his neck—that it seemed at first as if something were terribly wrong with him. He had a thin pencil mustache, and one of his front teeth was chipped. To supply a great mass of chunky muscles with decent amounts of oxygen, he was obliged to breathe hard through an open mouth. He had a lisp, and the continual passage of air past the chipped tooth added a high-pitched whistle to his labored respiration. Standing at attention before the Major, he appeared to be a prize example of the flotsam trucked in for a lesson in the sternness of an army always embarrassed because it was not stern. Baruch had that certain Syrian woodchuck look, as opposed to the coffee-colored frailty and gray lips of the North Africans. The Major detested both types.

"Thir!" Baruch said. "I reqetht permithon to thpeak." He saluted smartly, eyes straight, like a trooper.

"You shut up, you fat little Turkish bastard, and get back in line," said the Major, with great hatred. Baruch stepped back, the others with him.

It was nearly midnight and they were very cold by the time they were divided into platoons of fifty and marched up a hill past dozens of white-washed rectangular buildings which shone in the moonlight. In front of each building, guards stood in fatigues, caps, and blankets, automatic rifles slung over their shoulders.

They passed a group of fully armed shock troops who were eating a late meal after a night exercise. The shock troops began to insult them; Marshall felt pieces of food hitting him; and he passed on amid curses that he did not understand. In his third night without sleep all he wanted was a blanket and a chance to lie down.

Because they were marching in a maze of barracks, he assumed that they would soon reach one of their own, and that there he would find a clean, simple bed. Perhaps, he thought, there might even be a campfire, something to eat, or hot showers.

In his platoon were three little Bengalis in whose eyes were stars of suffering, like those Marshall had seen in the liquid gaze of the Moroccan criminals. The Bengalis were so practiced upon resignation that, despite their adoption of Marshall and the other two Americans as protectors (the biggest Bengali was four foot eight, and he weighed a crushing seventy-nine pounds), they were able to give Marshall and the others great comfort. They said gentle things in chirping gentle voices. They were used to sickness and starvation, and fed on winds and constellations as if they had been mariners in the Bay of Bengal, or pearl fishermen.

"What do you care," they said to Marshall, as the dark grouping of men marched upward on a star-shattered hill, "if you die? To die is tranquil. You see the fine clear light. It is heaven, ecstatic, perfect."

"Are you Jews?" he asked.

"Yes. We are Jews," one of them answered.

They halted before beds of straw in an enormous room illuminated by four candles. The whitewash was like rising smoke, and through broken windows soon closed by those who preferred to breathe their own foul breath, Marshall could see Rigel, Aldebaran, and the Pleiades. His pupils were immobile and he felt that he had fallen irreparably into the East. Though he smarted, he stayed still. As images of these battered Moroccans raked by centuries of absolutes began to assault him, he learned to daven. He had already been assaulted. The robbers thought he was rich. The homosexuals desired him. The rest were mesmerized by his coloring and the gold in his glasses. His mouth was dry. His vision swam. Sergeants paraded them in a circle around and around the barracks, handing them equipment—packs, grenades, rifles, bandoliers, helmets, bandages, cutlery, aluminum bowls, blankets, and shovels. The sun began to rise. Marshall found himself swaying back and forth, davening, moved by waves of energy which swept past the dawn in a great crackling storm.

They did not sleep. As the light flooded in the small windows, Marshall discovered that half of the things he had been issued just a few hours before, and all of his money, had been stolen. "Where do they keep it?" he asked Lenny, who also had been fleeced.

"Look," said Lenny, "if they can steal it that fast, they can probably sell it that fast."

"But the sun hasn't even come up!"

"It doesn't have anything to do with the sun."

In bright dawn, fully equipped, they began a long march. "Fifty kilometers," the sergeants (new ones were delivered by jeep every four or five hours) would say. "Fifty kilometers. The Army will teach you how to behave." They marched carrying unloaded weapons across the dustiest, airiest series of whitened hills that can be imagined. Each ridge of bleached rock was immersed in bright sun and shadow. Their spirits were lying prone, but they continued until they enjoyed the waterlessness, the dryness, the pain, and the burning sun circle. A sweet perfumed smell arose from the bright eyes of the Bengalis. Marshall struggled to look back at them, sighting their slight forms over the kingdoms of hallucinated green which his bloody mind had set all about him. "That is history. That is history," they said, and smiled.

They walked, and they walked, and they continued to walk, and they made twenty dazed circles around Ramallah, the white towers of which arose in front of them like ice. When soldiers collapsed, others carried them. The water was restricted until the column of one hundred and fifty struggling men, twenty on stretchers, began to imagine a world of bone, which they deduced from the link they made between their innards and the never-ending dry rock and dust. They marched on, as if they were ascending.

The soldiers began to foul their own clothing as they walked. They marched about the hills in circles as if they were climbing a ziggurat. Marshall had several spasms of inchoate joy. For a moment of perhaps minutes or hours, he loved the dust, exploding in love of the dust. He let the sun in past his eyes. Soon he fell, but was taken up, and he was kept moving as if on a tide, and, in near-unconsciousness, he walked again. Then, with the suddenness of a door slamming shut, they arrived at their barracks and collapsed on the beds of straw.

"Three hours," said the sergeants. "Three hours, and then you will arise and work in the kitchen."

In full battle gear, his mouth full of straw, someone's foot across his back, Marshall slept for three hours. In those hours, the stars swept by him. They were cold and they spoke directly from darkened faces. "You have died," they said. "You have died, and are with us. Finally and forever, you have died."

"I have not died," he answered back, laughing at them. "I have not died. I am just sleeping, and dreaming of sweeping starlight." The little crying faces could not lead him beyond. In his sleep, he reckoned the breathing of the fifty. He was seized. He doubled over. He tightened harder than steel, as sparks and light and lingual noises fled past on a wave of stars. The gold burned. The silver was white fire.

5

At three in the morning two sergeants in sunglasses kicked open the steel barracks doors and strutted up and down the urine-stained aisle, bending over sleeping forms and screaming savagely, "Arise! Arise!" It was great pain to be wrested from deep sleep and dreams, and the soldiers would not move until they were kicked. The worst criminals began to follow the sergeants, imitating them. They not only kicked the stomachs of sleeping men and ripped off their blankets, but they grabbed their genitals, stuck fingers in their eyes, and pulled their hair. The sergeants took note, and immediately promoted their imitators to the position of "drill leader."

Lenny smiled bravely as a fleet of devils rampaged above them in the stinking darkness, dressing, fighting, stealing. Everyone was subject to human touch at any moment, and explosive voices detonated ceaselessly. When the criminals spoke, Marshall could always smell their horrible breath, and they sprayed him with saliva, barking like mad dogs. If he turned away, they became offended, and threatened or manifested violence.

The sergeants screamed, "Shave!" and there was a rush for the doors. Everyone wanted to be first at the cold water taps a little way up the hill. After he had pulled on his boots, Marshall groped in his kitbag for his razor, toothpaste, and shaving cream, which were gone.

"Did you have American toothpaste?" Robert asked.

"Yes. I did. Why?"

"Last night before the candles burned out, I saw one of them eating it. If I'd known it was yours, I woulda got it for you."

"Thank you," said Marshall dazedly. "I appreciate that."

They told the sergeants that their razors had been stolen. The sergeants looked at them and said one word: "Shave!"

They found some rusty razor blades, and, after splashing their faces with freezing cold water, they scraped off beard and skin until their cheeks burned.

"Let's try to stay together in the kitchen," said Robert. "We can help each other, and maybe we'll have some quiet. Let those bastards kill themselves off. If we conserve energy and spot for each other, we'll have a great advantage. Also, we've grown up on high-protein diets. We're stronger than they are."

"Where do they get all that energy?"

"I don't know. I think it's because they're crazy."

"We're smarter than they are, too."

"But they have street wisdom."

"Bullshit. They're morons. The only advantage they have is that they're immoral. That's a short-term advantage."

"We're only going to be here for a month."

"A month for those guys is like a decade for us. If we keep our heads, we'll be all right. We've got to remember a couple of things. One: when you're in the kitchen, steal as much protein as you can. They haven't fed us yet, but I have a feeling that it'll be swill. Eat raw eggs, raw chicken, cheese— anything except raw meat, because of trichinosis. But if you see some good lean beef, hell, eat that as well.

"Two: don't let them push you an inch. If there's a threat, we'll group together. I think the three of us plus the three Bengalis can hold off anything they can give, and there will doubtless be others who will come to our side."

"The Bengalis are terrified. They've already been beaten."

"What do you expect? They only weigh seventy pounds. Three: be inventive. I'm sure ways will turn up in which we can avoid what they plan to do—which is to pound these vermin into the ground until they're worn out and quiet enough to post to various commands, where they'll wash dishes and clean garbage cans. I saw it in the American Army. First they take them in together and knock the crap out of them. Then they isolate them and keep them down by making them clean latrines all day. We can beat the criminals *and* the guards. We're older. We're stronger. We're smarter."

They went to the barracks, where the others were formed up in rows of three, and formed their own row of three. The platoon was counted and marched double-time through the dark to the kitchens. Marshall's hair had been cut short; he was cold and hungry; he was lost in the resounding boot-steps of fifty men; he breathed the fresh night air, as clear up there in the mountains above Jerusalem as winter amber.

In the officers' kitchen they were mustered into various detachments. A dozen unfortunates were given refrigerator duty stacking cheese and counting celery sticks. Some sat around huge vats of hardboiled eggs and took off the shells. Some swept the floors or cleaned ranges and cutlery. Some set table. The three Americans were ushered into a great room in which were a dozen stainless-steel carts each loaded with filthy dishes from dinner the previous night.

"Wash those dishes," the sergeant ordered. "It's three forty-five. I'll be back when the sun comes up. You should be finished by then."

"Two hours?"

"Two hours, and maybe fifteen minutes. I'll come back at six. I want every dish clean, the floor clean, the walls washed. Understand?"

The minute he left they bolted the door and went to work at triple speed. It was a three-hour job, but they had plans. First they organized their approach. Then they attacked the trolleys, clearing off all the dishes, scraping the food into garbage cans, etc. They consolidated everything into neat stacks on two trolleys and started to draw the hot water. Working the way Americans can when they want to—in speed, enjoyment, and rhythm—they didn't rest for a second. As they drew the water they washed the ten empty trolleys and arranged them in a corner. Then they attacked the dishes in assembly-line fashion. Marshall supplied Robert with stacks of dishes. Robert scrubbed them clean and flipped them into the next sink, where Lenny rinsed them and stacked them on the workboard. Marshall then emptied them of excess water and placed them on a clean cart.

"You guys like country music?" asked Lenny, his hands rinsing and stacking so fast that they looked like an automatic loom.

"I do," answered Marshall.

"Sort of," said Robert.

"Want me to sing some?"

"Go ahead."

As Lenny sped through the rinsing he sang beautifully, and the room echoed with lyrical music.

"Where'd you learn to sing like that, Lenny?"

"I don't know. L.A."

They loved it. They really loved it, and they washed so fast and so well that all the dishes were done by 4:30. They hosed down the remaining carts at the same pace, scrubbed the stainless-steel sinks and counters until they sparkled, washed the walls and windows, cleaned behind the window bars, washed the floor, and put everything in perfect order. By ten of five they were completely finished, had drawn the two big sinks full of steaming clear water, and stacked all the trolleys in front of the door.

They took off their clothes and put them down in the order in which they would pull them on again. Marshall spread himself over the carts and went to sleep. Robert and Lenny climbed into the sinks and eased them-selves into the wonderful water. With just their heads showing, they broke into clean sweats and strings of pleasant exclamations. Soon, Robert got out and drew fresh water for Marshall. They alternated sleeping on the carts or in the baths. Bathed, warm, and relaxed, they dressed at five of six, let out the water, and stood waiting for the sergeant.

He came in exactly at six and saw them pretending just to have finished. He thought that they were suffering. "Now you come with me," he said. "You will do the breakfast, lunch, and dinner dishes. But in between, you keep busy." The sun was climbing over the rocky hills, bright and sharp. He led them into a shadowy room where the three exhausted Bengalis were standing next to what seemed like twenty million cans of sardines. The Bengalis were in tears.

"Why are you weeping?" asked Marshall.

Wilson (their spokesman) answered. "That man," he said in the hypno-tizing gait of subcontinent English, "told us to open all these sardines!"

"So?"

"There are too many. For there is only one machine to open the cans. Oh God in heaven, how we open a thousand cans in two hours, good God, with one dam-ned little machine!" He stamped his foot in rage and frustration. They had been taking turns, going through every step of the process individually.

"Look," said Marshall. "We'll set up an assembly line."

"What is that?"

Soon they had a little sardine factory humming along at an astounding pace. Robert turned the big crank to power the machine. Lenny placed the cans in position. One Bengali handed him cans. Another Bengali received the cans. Marshall arranged them on trays, stacked the trays, and put full cartons next to the supplier Bengali. The third Bengali rested, relieving the other two at turns. They took sardine breaks, during which the Americans would eat. "Eat up," said Robert to the Bengalis. "It's good protein."

"Protein?"

"Jesus," said Robert. "No wonder you guys are shrimps. You don't even know what protein is."

"Shrimps?" said Wilson, looking at himself, highly amused. "You call us shrimps? Why? Shrimps are animals that live in the sea. Many legs." He looked at his own legs and held up two fingers. "Just two."

"I mean that you are so little, because you never had any protein."

"We are not little," said the littlest one with evident sincerity. "You, though, are ab-nor*mally* large."

"Then why is it that it takes two of you to carry a rifle; you can't get over walls and big rocks unless we throw you; your uniforms are four sizes too big; and your heads fit inside your helmets like bell clappers? It must be dark in there. Maybe we should drill holes near the top so you can see out."

"It is not our fault," answered Wilson, "if the Army makes all these stupid things for great big giants." They went back to opening cans, and devised a plan whereby the Bengalis could take a bath.

"You foolish Americans!" said Wilson as Marshall and the other two Americans were ordered back to the kitchen. "You are a great imperial power, but God makes you wash dishes. Good. Good good good!"

It worked. The sergeant did as expected and ordered the Bengalis into the dishroom. But in twenty minutes the Americans heard shouts and high-pitched screams. Then they saw the Bengalis being marched down a corridor, naked, crying, their clothes in their hands. The worst criminals—who had been given the better jobs of setting table and sweeping the dining room—clustered about and derided the Bengalis. Then Marshall, Robert, and Lenny were taken back to the dishes. The sergeant propped open the door and said, "I look in every ten minutes, criminals."

Lenny slipped out and spoke to an egg peeler. "It seems," he reported, "that the Bengalis decided to take a bath *first*, and jumped in the sink immediately. The sergeant came back to give them fresh scour sand, and there they were, the three of them, naked as the day they were born, curled up in one steaming sink, fast asleep."

"What happened to them? It looked as if they were being marched out to be shot."

"There was some sort of a mini-trial in which an officer sat on an upside-down cooking cauldron. They have to work in the refrigerator, stacking cheese. They're completely unaccustomed to cold, and the blocks of cheese are much too heavy for them. The stacks have to be seven feet high. How are they going to lift a thirty-pound block of cheese seven feet in the air?"

Marshall began to feel all his days without sleep. His body ached, and time seemed to have fashioned itself after infinity.

6

The first day in the kitchen they worked from 3:45 in the morning until 10:30 the next night. They helped the Bengalis stack the cheese, and washed walls between rounds of dishes. When there was nothing to do, a sergeant dumped garbage on the floor and made them pick it up. When that was done, he took them outside in the rain and ordered them to sweep the mud. Staggering as he served dinner, Marshall thought that perhaps he was dreaming when officers overturned plates of food and demanded that the company of misfits clean up the mess.

The dining hall smelled like wet wool, and the rain poured down outside in the dark. Officers and drill sergeants shouted as they ate; they had wet, shiny black hair; they seemed to hold all the power in the world. It was they, after all, who had denied Marshall sleep for four days. Reeling from table to kitchen for food, retching as he cleared off plates, tripping over deliberately outstretched feet and then being forced to apologize, Marshall began to conceive an active dislike for nearly everyone around him.

Being what they were, the criminals could not help each other. In trial, they turned against their companions, making any ordeal worse. One went on a brief rampage with a kitchen knife. Others threw food, carried on petty feuds, or told the officers when someone had found a comfortable hiding place in a dark storeroom.

Marshall kept falling. A captain told him to bring a lemon. When, in confusion, he brought an orange instead, the captain screamed at him as if he were going to kill him. The more Marshall fell, the more they thought it funny to trip him. Finally, he hit his head on a boot, and blood streamed down his face. He felt a fluttering inside, and couldn't get up. Everything above him seemed like men and devils and sounds and smoke moving in hostile whirlwinds. He crawled forward, trying to reach the kitchen, but Robert and Lenny picked him up and brought him into the bakery, where they gave him some tea, and meat they had stolen from the Major's table. Marshall ate for strength, crying all the while like a drunk. He thanked them and thanked them and would not stop thanking them.

"That's all right, Marshall," they said. "You can do the same for us."

Baruch came by, with a broom in his hand and a tentlike apron draped across his middle. "It hurths," he said. "I know. Insthide."

"I'm married," said Marshall, his heart racing yet weak, his eyes glassy and acid. "I have a wife, and I left her out there in the rain and darkness."

"Not tho," said Baruch. "Not in the dark or the rain."

"Yes, she is," Marshall said, shaking. "Yes, she is. I left her alone there."

"Not alone, in the kibbutths, with friendths. It'th warm and thafe there."

A sergeant burst in and dragged Marshall to the pot room, a freezing cold cockpit lighted by a flickering candle. Wind whistled through the cracks and sometimes brought in rain. Marshall and a tea-colored Libyan who chanted again and again, "The moon, the moon, the moon," had to wash five-foot-high cauldrons which came to them full of slop and caked food. The storm had knocked out the hot water. Their arms grew numb and blue. Because they had to crawl inside the cauldrons, their clothes and hair were soaking wet and covered with stinking garbage. Marshall wondered how long he could keep going. After two hours, the Major walked in, flanked by two younger officers whom he was trying to impress.

Perhaps they had just finished a long conversation over hot coffee and pastry brought by the animals in Marshall's platoon. The angles of the Major's jaw matched perfectly the brim of his peaked cap, and his face was cruelly symmetrical. The other officers screamed at Marshall and the Libyan to stand to attention.

Holding his breath, the Libyan stood with fists clenched and a crazed smile. Marshall didn't strain very hard to stand straight, and brushed something wet and soft from his forehead. Dirty water streamed down his neck. The wind howled darkness like a dog, and the candle nearly blew out. Marshall felt feverish. He saw the Major's stick, held under his arm like a riding crop. He remembered the Major's pompous gait and his vanity at table.

"I hope you do a good job," said the Major, barely concealing his disgust at having to address two such repulsive creatures. "I want you to scour these pots perfectly. There's been a cholera epidemic recently in Ramallah and we've had a few cases here. I don't want to get cholera. So be clean. Make them shine. Is that understood?"

Marshall was so enraged that he felt as if he were going to float into the air.

"Yes, Commander," answered the Libyan, but Marshall was trembling like a lunatic. He bared his teeth. The Major stepped back and took a tight hold on the stick. He too was mad.

"Soldier! I asked you a question!"

"You take your question . . ." answered Marshall, saying each word roundly and making it vibrate. "You take your question, and shove it, you stinking son of a bitch baboon-faced faggot bastard!"

The Major turned to his aides. They shrugged their shoulders. "In Hebrew please," asked one of them.

"Oh," said Marshall. "Yes, Commander!" After the Major left, one of the officers stuck his head back through the doorway and said quickly into the dim light, "It's lucky for you that I agree with what you said. *Shalom.*"

They were marched back in the rain. In the barracks, Ashkenazi sat surrounded by three candles, reading a pornographic magazine from Turkey. Yakov held it and obediently turned the pages. Everyone threw himself down and slept straight away, but several hours later, when the storm had passed, a fresh batch of sergeants circulated in the freezing darkness, waking the men. "Arise!" they said. "Arise!" Once again there was to be a night march around Ramallah.

Marshall awoke freezing cold and in pain, but when he got up and pulled on his battle gear he felt excited and happy. A great surge of energy passed through him, and everyone seemed to share in a feeling of well-being. Sleep had at last become irrelevant. He made his way to the cold-water tap. Nearby, people were urinating and it sounded like horses. Nonetheless, the air was fresh, and though it had been cold in the barracks, the night was filled with currents of warm air. The storm had vanished completely, and the stars and shooting stars (of which there are always many in the mountains near Jerusalem) seemed like a soft meadow of light.

As they marched on the road to Ramallah it was deathly quiet. Just a few bulbs sparkled low and yellow from the houses and the minaret towers, past which the air flew and wound and doubled over. Marshall thought of Lydia, and his love for her lifted him. It was only the fifth day and he had already learned their tricks. Though he might have seizures, fall to the ground, and bleed; though he might be taken for a criminal; though his face be cut and infected, his body sore and starving, his clothes greasy and malodorous; though he might break and weep and be driven somewhat mad; though he was at last and finally completely out of control—he would survive and make it through. Or perhaps he would die, but he would fight them at every turn.

If he could awaken in the middle of the night and find himself lost in a hundred million stars, if he could walk down a road in a tranquil bath of sweet air, and if things were so apt to be turned upside-down despite the designs of men, he could not lose in the end, for the will of the world was a most marvelous and independent thing.

That night they walked around Ramallah nine times until the sun came up and the wind rattled everything that could be moved.

7

They had marched out of the Fourth Daughter in a great column of two thousand armed men, of which they had been able to see neither the beginning nor the end but just a powered line weaving the road. The three platoons of criminals had been shunted off in different directions after about four miles. Marshall remembered the featureless expressions of the peasant soldiers in back of him who had rushed, weapons in hand, to take up slack in the line. "Where are they going?" one of the criminals had asked a lieutenant.

"They are going to conquer Tulqarm."

"Excuse me, sir, but didn't we already conquer that, in 1967?"

"It's an exercise, idiot."

"Why aren't we going?"

The lieutenant looked them over. "Because you lice couldn't conquer a post office box, that's why."

He was not entirely correct. Despite their seventeen languages (Hebrew, Arabic, Moghrabi, French, Italian, English, Russian, Turkish, Greek, Kurdish, Farsi, Hindi, Amharic, Spanish, Tuareg, Bulgarian, Rumanian), their communications were superb. They were so nervous and overactive that even innuendos traveled throughout the group like lightning along a well-watered synaptic pathway. Despite their ignorance and insanity, they were resourceful. In two weeks they had stolen everything halfway valuable in the camp, even if it had been bolted down and guarded. Despite their physical weakness, they were brawlers and dirty fighters, and they had terrible tempers. Easily a third of the criminals were epileptics, like Marshall, but in their seizures they grew terrifically violent, manifesting the strength of ten men. Marshall knew that in a battle, instead of pitching and whirling about like crazed trance dancers, Sufis, they would hold still and turn the world about them in fury. That, in fact, was why they were criminals. There was a tempest in them. Only when they applied it to others and the world beyond could they be still. Despite their poor marksmanship, lack of comprehension in regard to automatic weapons and specialized equipment, and absolutely maddening casualness about hand grenades—they kicked them around like soccer balls—they were just good enough with weapons to conquer a post office box, possibly even the post office itself, and maybe even a poorly defended small town.

Strung out along a stone wall, they were resting in a field, prior to an exercise of their own in which the fifty of them were supposed to take a distant hill defended by another platoon. About a thousand feet high, the hill was covered with rocky terraces and redoubts, and the sun shone from behind it, blinding the attackers. At various points officers were posted as judges, their field glasses sometimes glinting as they scanned the game board.

Marshall studied the hill. It was impossible to get to the summit alive via the light-lacquered west face, and he assumed that they would use an indirect approach. F-4 Phantoms and Mirages flew across the sun on runs in support of the troops taking Tulqarm, and the criminals were denuding a nearby fig orchard as three Arab women looked on gravely and impassively from the roof of their house. Marshall had learned not to interfere as his barracks mates stole. This was for them the holiest of activities, and, if interrupted, they would rage like jackals pulled away from meat. But he was angry and disgusted that they made off with half the crop of an innocent kitchen garden.

"Criminals will be criminals," said Lenny.

"But they don't have to be taken into the Army."

"If it's a little army fighting big armies, yes they do. More than half a million Egyptians, half a million others, and a few hundred thousand us."

"That's not so. Numbers are not decisive in the case of war," said Marshall. "For example, the two of us could take that hill and be waiting for the judges when they come to the summit to report to the citadel commander that all of us have been killed."

Lenny looked at the blue flag waving from atop the seemingly unconquerable hill, and shook his head. "Ha!" he said.

"I'll show you," said Marshall. "Just wait until the orders come through."

They rested. Yakov loaded figs into Ashkenazi's knapsack. Some soldiers drank water and ate sunflower seeds, but most slept, their rifles and machine guns leaning against the wall. The Arab women continued to stare at the half-naked trees, thin from lives on rocky soil.

Marshall was half asleep, thinking about the beach at Amagansett. He saw Livingston, a younger, dark-haired man, showing him how to dive through the waves. "Like this," he said, and dived into an eight-foot breaker, disappearing as if into another dimension. Livingston was forever puzzled because Marshall refused to do as he had done—taking instead the full force of the wave, being knocked down, pulled under, and swept along upside-down and backward thudding against the bottom, only to emerge fifty yards away choking with foam, sand, and salt. "Marshall. Dive *through* the waves," Livingston said to the six-year-old. "You can dive into the pools of the Croton River. Go *through*. That way, you won't get battered each time."

Marshall had looked at the breaking surf for a long while, as if he were judging something. At last he turned to Livingston, who delighted in seeing the little face with a missing tooth. "Well? Are you going to go *through* the waves?"

"No," Marshall had said.

The lieutenant's voice broke all reveries, and he had them stand to as he explained his completely idiotic plan for a direct frontal attack. They would all be killed. "Robert, do you want to come with us?" asked Marshall.

"Yes."

"Help me make a diversion." Marshall picked up a rock, and, when no one was looking, threw it at Ashkenazi. At the same time, Robert pushed the son of a Rumanian butcher into a Hungarian second-story man. The second-story man attacked the butcher's son, and Ashkenazi, who thought that he had been a victim of their fallout, proceeded to demolish them both. The uproar was tremendous and groups formed around the fighters.

Marshall, Lenny, and Robert flipped themselves backward over the stone wall. As the fight played itself out after the lieutenant fired a shot in the air, they dropped down a hill and ran past the Arab house onto a road.

From the road, they could see the rest of the platoon sneaking like thieves amid rocks and bent trees. "They're crazy. They'll all be dead before they reach the second kilometer on the flats."

"And what about us?" asked Robert. "Where are we that's so special?"

"Don't worry," said Marshall. "We'll have that flag in our hands in an hour and a half. We might have to wait here for a while, but probably not for long."

They thought he was crazy, but in ten minutes they saw a truck coming down the narrow road. Marshall stuck out his hand pompously. The Arabs in the truck looked at them in deferential hostility. "Oh sirs," said Marshall. "Would it be your pleasure to provide small transportations?"

"Surely, oh my sir," said the driver, hardly able to refuse three armed soldiers.

"Why do you ride with us?" asked one of them. "You have many tanks and trucks."

"Reasons of state and developmental prerogatives of the littoral republics in the Arab League," answered Marshall, lifting a phrase from many winters past in the language laboratory at Boylston Hall.

"You are not Israelis, are you?"

"We are of all nations and all beliefs," answered Marshall, "and we have come to Algiers to affirm the solidarity of the Third World in the price evaluation of basic commodities essential to Western manufacture."

"Oh," said the Arab. He laughed nervously and was silent for the rest of the trip.

"Why did you say that to them?" asked Lenny, afterward, when Marshall had translated the conversation.

"Because I don't know how to say anything else," answered Marshall.

"All they ever taught us was political stuff, the Koran, and medieval anatomy texts."

They hid their packs, shovels, helmets, and jackets. Short-sleeved and draped with weapons and ammunition, they began the ascent, taking little care, intent upon reaching the top quickly. The cliffs were steep, and there were places where Marshall normally would have used pitons and etriers. But they moved along smoothly, and the sun reflected from the bronze rock, hot and hale even in November.

Their weapons sometimes clattered against the stone, but it didn't matter. The sound could not arch over the summit, and the wind was coming from the other side. They climbed using hand-jambs and chimneying cracks the way Marshall showed them, and every once in a while they would look out into the blue spaces where gulls wheeled and turned after inland flights from the sea.

As they got higher, they saw Ramallah past a low hill, rising in white patches and artful spires. They thought that in a hundred feet or so they would be able to see Jerusalem, and they were right. It was a series of quiet terraces sitting in the static mist which even clear light sets between distance and the eye. Al Aqsa glowed and winked a gold fleck. They wondered what the gulls could see from thousands of feet above and what the pilots could see from planes so far up that they seemed silent and weightless.

From a distance the three climbers looked like mites on the rock walls. Finally they reached a spot just under the lip of the summit. Marshall peeked over. "They're all there, looking the other way. Ten soldiers and three judges. There's a sentry post between us and them, but the sentry is a Bengali and he's also looking the other way. They're downhill from us."

Staying in position, Lenny silently lifted his automatic rifle over the ledge and trained it on a group near the flag. He put two extra clips of ammunition on the rock, and took a bead. Marshall and Robert crept over the ledge and hid. Marshall had a knife in hand, and three grenades hooked to his belt. Robert held a submachine gun, and carried an extra magazine in his teeth. They moved forward while Robert kept his gun trained on some soldiers who had a light machine gun on a tripod, and who were reclining in a sandbagged pit.

Marshall and Robert stopped at a flat rock. Robert took position, well within comfortable range. They looked back at Lenny and saw him staring quietly down the barrel of his rifle. The soldiers at the citadel took occasional long-distance shots at those in the platoon who were unfortunate enough to be trapped near the base of the hill. Marshall heard a captain say, "He's dead," as he put down his binoculars and checked off a figure on a clipboard.

Marshall removed his shirt and crawled toward the sentry, who was combing his hair and facing the opposite way. Marshall had to remember not to kill him, but just to pretend. Grabbing him violently from behind, he put his hand over the poor Bengali's mouth, and pulled him instantly backward beyond the few sandbags. Marshall held the knife at the terrified sentry's throat. "You're dead. Understand? Dead. Shut up. Okay?" The Bengali nodded. Then Marshall hopped into the sandbag redoubt and lay flat.

He placed the grenades in front of him, pulled their pins, and tossed them. They exploded quite loudly even though they were not real. Lenny and Robert opened fire, emptying four clips before the amazed victims could even see what was happening. Had the grenades been real and the bullets not blanks, the citadel troops would have been dead. They had not even turned their machine gun, or lifted a weapon against their attackers.

Robert and Lenny ran up, holding their freshly loaded weapons on the troops and officers. Marshall was already there.

"You see," he screamed, ripping down the signal flag. "The best army in the world." He couldn't stay still, and had the knife in one hand, and the flag in the other. "You treat us like criminals. You treat us like idiots. But we're not the idiots. You are. And we just proved it, because we killed you in your own game."

8

A certain equanimity prevailed during a two-day storm when sheets of rain were thrown on the hillsides in sporadic bursts and clouds brushed against the rattling windows. Marshall, Lenny, Robert, Baruch, and the three Bengalis (Wilson, Prithvi, and Chobandresh) sat on upturned wooden crates arranged in a circle around an enormous cauldron in one of the enlisted men's kitchens. The floor was red terra-cotta tile. Several poorly joined windows gave out on wet rock ledges and water-battered bushes. Steel shelves covered the walls and were piled high with canned goods and sacks of flour. It was the afternoon of the fifth eighteen-hour kitchen day since the Americans had been released from the stockade.

The officers on the mountaintop had understood English perfectly, and had not taken kindly to Marshall's remarks. Therefore, instead of being rewarded for their spectacular victory they were charged with absence from a training area; abandoning equipment; being out of uniform; abuse of officers; and getting from point A to point B faster than is humanly possible without giving explanation. Of all the accusations, this was the gravest. At the trial, the Major presided in splendor, directing a frightening ritual of salutes, attentions, and formulaic greetings.

Baruch had volunteered to be counsel for the defense, and Marshall discovered to his dismay that Baruch not only lisped and whistled, but stuttered painfully when speaking in public. The Major had no patience with this, and kept interrupting him, saying, "State your case or shut up." Heavily laced with constructive self-interest, Baruch's case was that neither the accused nor their attorney should have been in the punishment company in the first place.

"That is completely irrelevant," the Major responded. "At issue here is a set of specific charges, to which you will confine your discussion. Is that clear, you fat little Turkish bastard?" The Major's troop of pompous lieutenants thought that this was very funny.

When it came time for sentencing, Lenny was first up. "State your full name for the record."

"Leonard Schnaiper. They also call me the Delaware Funny Boy." Laughter came this time from the accused.

"Trainee Schnaiper, you will forfeit a month's pay and spend two days in the stockade. Next, state your full name for the record."

"Robert Stein. They also call me Mr. Jive," he said in appropriate dialect. He received a duplicate of Lenny's sentence.

The Major tensed when Marshall stepped before him and saluted. Marshall comforted himself by thinking that the more punishment he got, the better.

"State your full name for the record."

"Marshall Pearl," said Marshall.

"What kind of name is that?"

"Half Anglo-Saxon, and half Pearl, Major."

"Is Pearl a name for Jews?"

"Yes, Major."

"Is it your father's name?"

"No, Major."

"Do you know who your father is?" asked the Major, delighted to have found so quickly what seemed to be a very weak spot.

"Yes, Major. I do."

"He is not named Pearl?"

"No, Major."

"Who is he?"

"He is Anwar Sadat, President of the Arab Republic of Egypt, Major."

"Trainee Pearl, you will forfeit two months' pay and stay three days in the stockade."

"That's not enough."

"That's what?"

"Not enough, not enough. How about three months' pay and four days in the stockade?"

"Very well. You have it."

"Major."

"Yes?"

"I'll take five and five."

"Are you mad?"

"No, Major, but you can't do anything to me that I don't want you to do. Do you understand, Major?"

"Would you like thirty days in the stockade?"

"I would be truly grateful, Major." They could see in his face that he would have been truly pleased to spend thirty days in the stockade.

"You will serve the same sentence as the others."

"Thank you, Major. It is just what I want, Major."

"Get him out of here," said the Major. "Just get him out!"

Being in the stockade was not so terrible. They ate the same food, didn't have to work, and only one other prisoner shared the little stucco building. He was a rotund Egyptian with two front teeth absent, and he had the rather distressing habit of ripping up his clothes, banging his head against the wall, and saying, *"Ani meshugah, Ani meshugah"* (I am crazy, I am crazy), over and over again. At first they were frightened by this fat fellow Safran, but when the guards went to dinner he stopped and turned to them with a sigh. "I'm not crazy," he said. "I'm just trying to get out of the Army."

Marshall recalled the Major's summation before sentencing: "If, as you allege, you should not have been assigned to Company T, it does not make the slightest bit of difference. You have found the right place, as your actions show. It may have been out of order to begin with, but it has proved correct. As I have always said, a great army makes great mistakes."

It rained all the time. The big cauldron was filled with an infinite number of hardboiled eggs to shell (there were so many that once in a while they came upon a chick). To heat the room, they had six burners on an open-frame gas range burning green and blue in double rows. By their fourth day they were allowed to stay together in their anteroom as long as they were continually engaged at various tasks. Lenny sang, or the Bengalis hummed and drummed exquisite ragas which blended resolutely with the rain and green fire and drafts of wet mountain wind. They were even allowed to make a kettle of tea, and they would have been happy, were it not for each man's freshly kindled passion for home. And they were always tired—so tired that their eyes sagged like horse collars.

As they shelled the eggs they spoke about their condition. They were disgusted by the uncivil behavior of the criminals, especially since Ashkenazi had organized a ring to extort money and unmentionable services. Were it not for the three Americans, the Bengalis would have been done for, and had it not been for a magnificent and heroic Rumanian boxer named Mush, a few unfortunate Russians and Czechs would also have been done for. As it was, the entente of three Americans, three Bengalis, Baruch, four Russians, four Israelis, and the boxer—sixteen in all—was more than enough to protect against Ashkenazi and his subalterns. Quickly coalescing into an alliance, the sixteen wielded immense power and rose above extortion and attack. The rest were suicidal or evil—except for little Yakov, who was good, and had fallen irreparably into the hands of Ashkenazi. But even Yakov survived continued indignities. The protected ones saw him tossed about in the storm, and loved him not only for his suffering, but because he seemed to be a just man caught in the body of a broken toy.

"What would you do then?" asked Baruch. "How can you control thuch awful criminalths?"

"Beats me," said Lenny.

"Oh oh oh. Nothing can be done. Nothing can be done," chirruped Chobandresh.

"Now that I've lived a few weeks with these maniacs," said Marshall, "I know exactly what to do."

"What?" said Wilson.

"The Code of Hammurabi."

"You must be kidding," said Robert.

"Must I? Apart from minor imperfections, it was a good code. It said an eye for an eye, no more, no less. If a man kills, I believe that he should be killed. Is he not a man? Is he not responsible for what he does? And if he is not, who is? And if we are prideful enough to attempt forgiveness for one who has taken a human life, are we not stepping beyond our competence? Let me tell you, if someone killed Lydia, he wouldn't live long."

"What about rape? Should the rapist be castrated?"

"No. If you castrate him, you deprive him of his sex for life, whereas he has probably not done that to his victim. He should instead be raped by a sex-crazed hog—twice. That would be just punishment, and would rehabilitate, in that it would educate. I would save castration for those who molest children, for the terror and permanence of effect call for similar terror and permanence."

"What is a hog?" asked Chobandresh. "Is it like a dog? It sounds like a dog." Marshall explained.

"What about the menu of criminals on a lower scale; the burglars, the pimps, and all the rest that we have to live with here?"

"Again, an eye for an eye. A burglar would do hard labor to pay back what he has stolen. One who robbed and beat his victim would be beaten and committed to hard labor."

"That's barbaric."

"It isn't barbaric. It's ultimately civilized; just. Those who attempted crimes would know that they themselves would suffer exactly what they imposed, no more, and no less. If this were not a deterrent, it might at least serve as moderation. Killers would be killed. Rapists would be raped. I say that it's barbaric not to impose upon these murderous beasts what they impose upon others. Nothing else will stop them save a perfect world. I have compassion for the victims. My civilized mind carries the image and feeling of their pain long enough to insist upon retribution. Those who have compassion only for criminals are compassionless, and themselves criminal.

"Think. If Ashkenazi had been hanged, there would be an equality of souls in the world of the dead, and Yakov would not now be suffering. Justice should be a blind weighmaster, mechanical, as in the statues. Criminals should be stopped in their tracks, one way or another."

"In my country," said Wilson, "many, many good people die. Oh, they die in floods; they die by the horrible sicknesses; they die when there is no food. I have often seen a mother and child lying by the side of the road, soon to be corpses, the flies on them already, the crows walking to and fro nearby. It seems to me that you in the West do not realize that to live is a great privilege. Mercy should not be wasted on the likes of Ashkenazi, Lord God no. Oh no by great God. Why, if a sweet child must die for lack of food . . . why should a man who *takes* a life be allowed to live? You say that we do not hold life dear. Quite to the contrary. You do not hold life dear. If you Westerners loved, if you knew how to love, you would not let killers go free." Wilson had never understood why in Israel there was no death penalty. Even terrorists who came from abroad and massacred the children in schools were allowed to live. "That is wrong," said Wilson. "So help me, that is most wrong."

A lieutenant burst into the room. He surveyed the comfortable salamandrine flames, the cauldron of a thousand eggs, the dancing shadows, the unfamiliar foreign faces. Then he spoke. "Abandon this work, return to barracks, don your battle gear, and assemble in threes for night drill."

"Jesus!" said Lenny. "It's raining a flood. Look at all the lightning. We've been working a thousand goddamned hours. We can hardly stand or see, and now we have to go on night drill."

"Too many lieutenants," answered Marshall. "Too many officers, too many criminals, too many pogrebins, too many eggs." Then he popped an egg into his mouth, swallowed it whole, and smiled.

In the hypnopiasis of fatigue, they marched to the drill field in the pouring rain. It was as if stagehands on scaffolds were throwing buckets of water at them. A thousand men assembled on the concrete square to be tested in disassembly and assembly of their Uzi submachine guns, in total darkness. The Uzi is a simple weapon. Marshall could take it apart and put it back together again in a flash—with one hand. The Major sat on a shielded platform. His contribution to the exercise was to declare that they would wait until the lightning stopped, for its illumination gave unfair advantage. They waited in the rain for two hours. Marshall saw endless rows of soaked men—grave-looking, snarling soldiers who appeared suddenly in a stroke of daylight, and then vanished into complete darkness. Minutes later they would appear again in unchanged, unflinching ranks, all thousand souls standing

still. It was revealing and somehow touching to see the rain pouring off
those stubby upright forms, and to see how patient they were—even the
criminals.

When the lightning stopped, they were tested group by group. As the
gun parts spilled onto the pavement they chimed like the bells of a Vermont
town. Marshall, Robert, and Lenny passed splendidly and worried for the
sake of the amechanical Bengalis. But the Bengalis did beautifully. They put
the guns together perfectly and rapidly—because they could see in the dark.
"Of course we can see in the dark," said Wilson, his eyes flashing white.
Lenny nearly collapsed.

"I knew that," said Robert, lying through his teeth. "It's common
knowledge that, under stress, Bengalis can see in the dark."

Then one of those high-spirited old Iraqi sergeants danced out into the
middle of the battalions and began to tremolo. "Line up! One two, one two!
Line up! In threes! One two, one two! Sing out! Sing out! Morning's come!
Sing out! Sing out!"

The thousand soldiers and several hundred criminals, who had been
standing in the rain until three o'clock in the morning, buried him in a flood
of curses which resounded off the drenched hillsides. He did not understand
their lack of enthusiasm. After all, he was marching them to a great hall,
where, in the middle of the night, in their wet clothing, weighed down by
submachine guns, helmets, and shovels, they were to enjoy a talent show.

As they filed into the hall, Marshall wondered quite wearily what kind of
talent would be abroad in an army prison camp at three in the morning in a
lightning storm on the West Bank of the Jordan. Would they be professionals? If so, they probably would not be very well known.

Rain came through two dozen places in the corrugated roof. They sat
on hard benches. The thickness was intense, a sea of bodies and steel
helmets—all olive, all drab, and all wet. The hall was lit by rows of smudge
pots. Oily smoke banished their hunger and added to their fatigue. Then two
soldiers lit candles and carefully placed them about the stage. The flickering
light was as rich as alabaster or mother-of-pearl, and the rain beating on the
roof—like a heartbeat—stilled even the criminals. A thousand men half-
closed their eyes and stared at the altarlike stage in shadows and smoke.

As if from nowhere, a stupendously tall captain vaulted over the candles
onto the stage. "Yossi! Yossi! Yossi!" screamed the several hundred soldiers
of his company. He was much loved. Thin as a rail, with a sad pioneer-type
mustache, he resembled the classic painting of "a soldier in war, speaking to
troops by candle light in a dimly lighted barracks."

His elegant Hebrew was far beyond Marshall's understanding, and he
spoke for an hour. Few of the criminals understood what he said, but they
remained silent because they were tired. At about four o'clock, when it
started to rain so heavily that water rose in the lower part of the hall, he said,
"Okay. Now for the talent show. Who has talent?" Utter silence. "There are

a thousand men here. Someone must have a theatrical skill." They were so tired that every once in a while a sharp thud signified that one had fallen asleep and toppled off his bench. "Come now. Statistically, there must be an acrobat here." A hand went up. "You, are you an acrobat?"

"I am not only an acrobat, I am an acrobat's acrobat," he said, and as he pushed his way to the stage the soldiers awoke into cheers and whistles. Yossi stepped back. The acrobat took off his weapons and equipment and faced the expectant audience. "I will stand on my hands," he announced. They applauded. He bent down, put his hands against the floor, kicked up his legs, and collapsed onto the stage with a cry of pain. The audience tried to control its laughter, but was no more successful than the acrobat had been in carrying out his promise.

He blushed. "I will stand on *one* hand," he said breathlessly. They broke out into guffaws. He tried to stand on his hand, and immediately keeled over onto the boards, smashing his ankle. He hopped about the stage, cursing. The audience could not control itself.

"All right then. Wait a minute. I knew it would come to this," he said. "What would you say if I told you that I would stand on one finger?"

"Idiot! Beast! King of the chickens!" they yelled.

He took his helmet and placed it at center stage. But instead of standing on his finger with the helmet as a base, he began to do a strange undulating dance, weaving his hands and rolling his eyes. "Snake dance! Snake dance! Snake dance!" they screamed. At the edge of the stage, Yossi wondered how this lunatic had emerged, and then he realized that he had come from the mad platoon.

The acrobat twirled and gyrated, stuck out his tongue, crossed his eyes, and waved his arms. The audience loved him, because he was obviously completely out of his mind. They cheered and stamped their feet, screaming out, "Snake dance! Snake dance!" until, amidst thunderous applause, he snatched up his things and disappeared into the crowd.

Ashkenazi stood up and looked about. At first everyone was scared. But when Ashkenazi, making his way through them like a man who is waist-deep in the surf, asked with hungry anticipation, "Where is Yakov?" they lost their fear and began to chant: "Yakov! Yakov! Yakov! Yakov!" Encouraged, Ashkenazi ran through the waves, scanning the soldiers. "Yakov! Yakov! Yakov!" they chanted, stamping their feet.

Yakov had hidden in a fire sand box. After cruising the hall, Ashkenazi stopped and thought. He saw the sand box and pranced over to it. He laughed evilly and said, "Yakov . . . oh Yakov." Nothing happened. But then with extraordinary suddenness the lid of the box exploded open and Yakov jumped out. He ran down the aisle squealing shrill high-pitched whistles, and Ashkenazi pursued.

After three circuits of the hall, Yakov was lifted into the air, his limbs flailing, a cry of despair coming from his lungs. The soldiers were giddy with laughter. They expected to laugh more, and looked eagerly as Ashkenazi dragged Yakov to the stage, took a chair, and put Yakov on his knee. Ashkenazi held Yakov's head like a knuckleball. Yakov was powerless. Tears began to stream down his cheeks.

"Who are you?' asked Ashkenazi.

"I am Yakov!" said Yakov, enraged.

"What is your profession?"

"I am a soldier." Though the soldiers had quieted, they laughed again.

"No," said Ashkenazi. "Tell the soldiers what your profession is."

"I am a soldier," said Yakov. But Ashkenazi began to squeeze his head. He pressed harder and harder. The others were now silent. In the beat of the rain, they were saddened and horrified. New tears welled up in Yakov's eyes. The tendons in Ashkenazi's arm stood out. But Yakov would not give in.

"Tell them that you are my servant. Tell them that you are my servant." Still, Yakov said nothing. The soldiers began to wince. Ashkenazi himself was in agony from squeezing Yakov's head. The soldiers did not breathe. They waited for Yakov's skull to be crushed.

With magnificent force, a rifle butt swung from the darkness and hit Ashkenazi like a crack of thunder, propelling him across the stage ahead of a trail of his own blood. He landed in a bent heap in the corner, and began to twist out of it. Yossi threw down the rifle, bounded to Ashkenazi, took him by his ammunition harness, and stared at him with fire. Yossi's teeth were clenched and his mustache twitched as it rode high above the taut corner of his mouth. "Who do you think you are!" Yossi screamed.

"He's a murderer," yelled someone in the crowd.

Yossi drew his pistol and forced it deep into Ashkenazi's mouth, so deep that Ashkenazi retched and moved his whole body. Yossi cocked the hammer. His eyes flashed. "Murderer," he said, "if I see you within ten meters of that little puppet, I'm going to blow your brain apart. Is that clear to you?"

Even with the pistol pushed into the back of his throat, Ashkenazi tried to beg. After Yossi holstered the gun, Ashkenazi went to kiss his feet, but when he saw all the soldiers staring at him in complete silence he ran out into the rain. Yakov began to posture and strut.

It was five o'clock in the morning when the Hasidim rushed onto the stage to sing and dance. Though the room was dark and no one had slept, the twist they had seen had enlivened them, and the dances of the Hasidim— slow, Eastern, almost melancholy, but full of satisfaction and joy—seemed to be a celebration of justice. When they were exhausted and had to rest, a small, deft soldier hopped over the candles onto the stage.

He, it seemed, was a true performer and had been a professional in Buenos Aires. His name was Hector Encaminar. He was a Flamenco dancer. "I am a dancer," he said, "the greatest dancer in all of Argentina. I came here on a ship. I was crazy."

They thought that he was going to be like the acrobat, and they booed him. But he approached the panting Hasidim and assigned them hand-clapping parts and wailing moans—which they did very well. The soldiers saw by this alone that he was a genius.

Then he began to sing. His song reached through the rafters and stretched the roof. It was strong; it turned on a hundred lights; it transported them; it dried the rain; it was as if Hector Encaminar were standing on the greatest stage in South America in front of a thousand women in lace and roses. His voice rang out and it was piercing; it was like water; it was like having slept.

Then the soldiers' hearts flew. For Hector Encaminar did a few teasing steps in his heavy boots, and the stage became like the diaphragm of a timpani. He threw his head back, and danced more and more rapidly. They cheered. They were elated. His song grew stronger, his eyes closed, and the reports against the floor were as loud as the cracks of rifles and as fast as two machine guns firing simultaneously. The percussions cleaned the room. His boots sailed in flashing circles, beating in sustained series, reversing like the illusion of spokes, spinning, disappearing. The hall was filled with the refreshment of machine gun reports and his shouted Spanish song was clear at every note.

He danced that way for half an hour, until light began to blot through the heavy rain. It was morning and time to go back to barracks. But they were lost in Spain. The smudge pots swayed as a thousand soldiers stamped their feet and clapped their hands. The Hasidim had turned into passable Spanish Gypsies, moaning enthusiastically. Hector was dazzling. Deep in ecstasy, he pounded the floor harder and harder.

Then Yossi threw open the door and wet gray mist flooded in. As it covered the soldiers they stopped their accompaniment. Finally, only Hector was not in the mist. As it rolled to his feet he spun around and stamped the floor boards one last time. He actually said, *"Olé!"* And then he bowed. It brought down the house.

As the soldiers filed out into the rain and fog they were charged with an energy that they did not understand. All feuding groups had united. They were ready to do anything or go anywhere. Having been lost in Spain, having cleared their souls in the dancing of Hector Encaminar, and having felt as if the lightning of that night had run up and down their backs, they looked at the chill mist and they laughed.

9

Perhaps long before, in the dim time, the Jordanians had had hot showers. But they must have taken the hot water with them when they retreated in 1967. A greater advocate of cleanliness and purity of body than either of his friends, Lenny sat beneath a numbing stream, legs enfolded lotusly, eyes closed, chanting some nonsense he had learned in Los Angeles. Soon he was blue.

"Hey Lenny," Robert said. "You've been under there for five minutes. It's not good for you."

"I don't feel the cold. I feel nothing."

"Well, come on, we have to get back," said Marshall.

The sun had burned away the mist and brought a clear blue day of dry winds. "It is forbidden to speak!" a lieutenant in sunglasses and a red beret had barked at them as they assembled yet again in threes. "Fill your knapsacks with rocks. Two minutes!" They rushed to do this, and in less than two minutes they were back in position. Sometimes they were tired, but, deprived of rest, they passed into active, lucid, energetic states. It was a great lesson. In the mornings, especially on sunny days, they always felt as if they had slept even if they had not.

"We are going to put these rocks on that mountain!" the sunglassed lieutenant bellowed, pointing to a rust-colored peak. "Because that is *our* mountain, and we are proud of it, and we want to make it *higher*." The company cheered. They had gained a sense of group courage, better at least than the criminals' usual nervous anarchy.

All one hundred fifty of them, rifles held slanting in unison in front of their chests, began a formation run out of the camp, and they looked for all the world like a group of elite commandos. The officers were shocked, and said, "Who are these soldiers?"

And they replied, "We are Company T. Criminals. Fighters." They chanted slogans such as, "We are black. We are black. We are black." And they were powered for an hour or two by the sudden discovery that they could run halfway up a mountain—outpacing fit officers unencumbered with rock-filled packs, rifles, grenades, and helmets—sweating until they were drenched and their burning eyes fixed ahead like bayonets in an Eastern trance of painless momentum.

After contributing to a sizable cairn on top of the mountain, the lightened platoons drifted down the side and bivouacked in the rocks. They listened to an interminable Hebrew military lecture, of which they understood mainly pronouns, proper names, and the numbers one to ten. Lightheaded, they viewed an almost African landscape. The rain had formed little lakes in basins between the hills, and these took on the pure color of the sky. From them, white storks arose and flew in graceful circles to clear the rock ledges. Marshall's attention had been devoted exclusively to the lakes and to the winds which whistled across the empty mountains, until one of the lecturers broke off some branches from a eucalyptus and placed them between his helmet and the rubber strap which girdled it. Antlered, he continued his lecture, which they then surmised was about camouflage. Soon they all broke off and were antlered. They looked like a lost tribe of antelope.

"Now," said a sergeant, "we will learn to walk with rocks." The idea was to walk on all fours, using rocks in each hand as improvised shoes.

"Begging your pardon, Sergeant," Marshall asked, "but what is the purpose of this?"

"To fool the enemy."

"How so? Will he think that we are reindeer?"

"Goats."

"Goats don't have antlers."

"Mountain goats."

"Tell me something. Who in the world would think that we were mountain goats?"

"Look," said the sergeant, indicating a patch of hillside across the ravine. "Do you see those mountain goats?"

Marshall saw a herd of ibex grazing calmly amid the outcroppings. "They're ibex, I believe."

"They're ibex, you believe. My dear sir, look closely, and you will see that they are not ibex; they are Platoon Three."

Marshall saw only ibex, beautiful silver-brown animals with white chests. The sergeant was just another *meshugah*. The real Platoon Three was in the midst of sneaking up on Marshall's position. With rocks in their hands and their antlers sweeping up and out from their helmets, they were extraordinarily conspicuous as they came over the hilltop. "Stupids!" yelled someone from below. "Where do you think you're going?"

That evening, they had their first free time. The weather was good and they were told that they could sleep until 4:30 the next morning. Marshall and Robert spent the hours before bed in a quiet corner of the hand grenade toss, but Lenny was nowhere to be seen. They thought that he had gone to visit Hannah, one of the half-dozen women in the camp. He had an affinity for female Army clerks, especially those in the Fourth Daughter, who did not understand that even a glimpse of their gentle forms could save a soldier from despair and insanity. Marshall was revived time and again by the sight of one of those girls—disappearing into a building, walking awkwardly past a battalion of hard men cut to the bone by privation and the ever-present sense that they were dispensable. The existence of those girls said emphatically that there was balance in the world, and the soldiers hungered for them in all possible ways.

Lenny skipped training sessions to sit in the tiny cramped office of Hannah, the junior social worker. She was a little blonde of rough and disaligned features. Her hands were strong, and her eyes were as blue as the rain pools which formed in the basins after storms. It was wonderful to see the wisps of hair, detached from the careful combing under her peaked officer's cap, touching her cheek and getting in front of her eyes. She always pushed them back gently with her thick hands. Because she had bad skin—

she was only nineteen—and because she was very short, and young, she was not used to men taking an interest in her.

Late one evening she had come with an old reserve captain to make the rounds of the platoons. Platoon Two had just returned from labor, and were not only filthy, but wet. Hannah and the captain set up a plywood table in the middle of the barracks. The bastardly sergeants were solicitous, and brought them three candles in paper cups. Hannah opened up an Army looseleaf book, and surveyed the soldiers, who were glued to her one and all. When, in the gold light, she perceived this, she cast her eyes down to the lines before her. There was not one soldier sitting on the straw in that dark smoky room who had not fallen in love with the rough-featured girl—for in the light and shadows dancing against a rack of oiled guns, she looked angelic.

She played with her pencil, and when she sensed that they were still staring, she blushed. This they loved, and a tall Kurd who looked like a wolf said something which sounded very beautiful. Marshall turned to Baruch and asked him what it was. He had said, according to Baruch's translation, that he blessed her, and that he wished for a woman like her to be the mother of his sons and daughters.

The captain made an incomprehensible speech, not realizing that the amused smiles on the faces of those to whom he spoke meant that they hadn't the slightest idea of what he was saying. Trapped in a world of no language, with poor quarter-Hebrew and less of their own abstruse native dialects, they were like the deaf and dumb. The captain ended his homily with the easily understood phrase, "Does this disturb you?" They shook their heads and said, "Oh, no, not a bit."

Then Hannah spoke. "Have any of you ever been in trouble with the police?" When thirty of the fifty raised their hands without hesitation, she gasped and her eyes opened wide. This sent Platoon Two into paroxysms of shared laughter. Their ivory teeth were bared in uncontrollable smiles. They slapped their knees and looked around. She too began to laugh. "Have any of you spent any time in jail?" Again, a forest of hands, and everyone thought it was a good joke. She closed her book, sat back, and said, "It's too much for me. I give up." It started to thunder. The captain went into his second incomprehensible speech, and Hannah could not help but glance again and again at Lenny, who was handsome even in his wretched state, and who was looking at her from an abyss of love and respect.

That Lenny skipped training sessions mattered little. Since the criminals were baffled by anything mechanical, an inordinate amount of time was spent in weapons lecture. Lenny was a light weapons expert, and knew far more than even the pompous well-fed armorers. When he arrived late, sometimes hours late, he capitalized on his sparse Hebrew.

"Where have you been! You can be court-martialed for this. You'll spend the rest of your days scrubbing pots. How do you explain this atrocious unmilitary conduct? And you'd better explain well, scum, fool, or I'll see to it that you get fucked," the sergeant would say with immeasurable venom.

Lenny would say, "Good morning," and sit down in complete self-assurance and satisfaction. The sergeants were always disarmed when he smiled pleasantly and sighed. One day, Lenny commissioned Maloof the sneak thief to get flowers from the General's walled garden. Maloof went out at two in the morning and darted through the camp like a black cat. He returned with three sleepy red roses and an unopened bottle of cognac. Explaining that he used only hashish, he gave Lenny the cognac. Lenny hid it in an empty barracks, and, the next morning, he took the roses to Hannah. They assumed that he and the roses reached her with appropriate effect, for he became in those last days marvelously happy and calm. They had learned to run with the wind in the precincts of the Fourth Daughter, and he had found a sweet-eyed girl.

When they returned from the grenade pitch, they found Lenny fast asleep, wound tightly in his four foul blankets. They wrapped themselves in their own foul blankets, and awoke at 4:30 eager and refreshed, greeting the mild starlight for the first time with a feeling of complete health and well-being. The rush proceeded; they washed at the freezing tap; they dressed and armed in darkness. As they assembled in threes Marshall and Robert realized that Lenny wasn't there. Robert went into the barracks, where Lenny was fast asleep in his blankets. Robert reported that he had not awakened even when the daylights had been shaken out of him. "He's sick," said Robert. "He breathed with his mouth open, and his breath was as hot as a fire."

"Let him sleep," the sergeant said, "and if he's still sick when we come back, then he can go to the hospital." It seemed reasonable, because they would be returning in just a few hours.

They went to a gully where for two hours they crawled over barbwire, goat dung, and thorns. The thorns stuck deep, and the soldiers developed extremely painful puncture wounds all over their bodies. The sergeants had to hold them down with their boots to make sure that they would really crawl. They envied Lenny.

But he was unconscious when they got back, and there were alarming spaces between each of his labored breaths. Robert picked him up in his arms and carried him in the blankets to the hospital, where a hundred soldiers lined the corridors. They had thermometers in their mouths and were sucking tongue depressors and lollipops. Most were malingerers or hypochondriacs. Robert and Marshall pushed through them into the emergency room. Because they had a body wrapped in blankets no one minded that they had broken line. Every now and then a soul was torn apart by a shell or hit by a ricochet on the rocky firing ranges, and it was not unusual to see limp bleeding forms being carried with utmost urgency through the rows of white buildings.

Robert put Lenny onto a stretcher in the middle of the floor. A corpsman at the desk glanced around and turned back to his papers. Then he had a second thought and looked again at Lenny, who had what seemed like two days' growth of beard, and whose eyes were open and glassy. He took a thermometer from a glass jar and was about to put it in Lenny's mouth when Lenny went into convulsions. "Get the doctor," shouted the corpsman. A nurse ran out of the room.

The doctor walked in. "Who are you?" he asked Marshall and Robert.

"We're his friends," they said slowly in their awkward Hebrew. "He stayed under a stream of freezing cold water for five minutes—yesterday." The doctor shook his head. Lenny was in the midst of a terrible seizure. Marshall was not at all shocked, as was Robert, by its power and explosiveness. It was as if his soul were warring to escape his body.

"Get out," the doctor said as he bent over Lenny. They moved to the door but hesitated there, looking on. A small nurse, almost a midget, kicked Robert in the shins and told him to leave.

Squatting in the white dust outside the hospital, they waited until finally the corpsman jumped from the steps and started to walk rapidly toward a square gray building conceived by the British as a fortress and used by the Israelis to house NCO's. Marshall and Robert ran up to him. Because they were trainees and he was a sergeant, he refused to acknowledge them and kept walking. They followed him at his irregular pace.

"Can you tell us how our friend is?"

"I don't know who you are. I don't know who is your friend."

"We just brought him in, at noon."

"At noon? It's five o'clock. You call that just?"

"But how is he? It's not against the law, is it, to tell us that?"

"Go ask at the hospital."

"They won't let us past the desk, and the soldier at the desk doesn't know anything."

"I don't know anything either." They were almost at the fortress courtyard. Tanks, halftracks, and ambulances were parked inside.

"But how could you *not* know?"

"I know that your friend was an idiot. That's what I know. Who asked him to stay under the cold water for so long? Are we responsible for all you criminals, idiots, and madmen?"

"To hell with that," shouted Marshall at the corpsman, who had drawn them into the courtyard, where they stopped next to a coffee-colored Russian tank captured years before. "To hell with what you think, or whether we are idiots, and your opinions of us. Just tell us how he is."

The sergeant shook his head, nodding it up and down as a bird might do. His contempt and assumed superiority enraged Marshall. He put his hand up against a bolsterlike external fuel chamber on the tank, and glanced around. Robert had already guessed, and leaned against the tread as if he had been suddenly taken ill.

"You don't care if I think you are madmen. You just want to know how he is."

"Yes!"

"Okay, all right. I'll tell you how he is. Why not? You want to know. I'll tell you. He's dead."

There had been only two days left in the Fourth Daughter, and Lenny had died on the day when conditions were eased. The suddenness of it hit Marshall and Robert like an artillery shell. They thought that the corpsman was lying. But the Major summoned them to his office, where they stood at attention and described how Lenny had stayed under the stream of water. All the while, the Major had a look of disgust. "He was not fit to be a soldier."

"Why?" they asked.

"Because he died." Strangely, and for once, the Major was right.

10

No less bare than other rooms in the Fourth Daughter, Hannah's office had white walls and a large barred window overlooking the parade ground. A heater glowed at her legs. It was November 22, and anywhere in the mountains that the sun did not reach was cold. Arranging envelopes and folders spread before her on the desk, she was consumed by the fervor such a task will sometimes elicit and did not see that Marshall stood by the doorpost.

She kicked off one shoe and put her bare leg underneath her, slowly swiveling back and forth on the chair. Marshall realized that he might have been able to stand in place unobserved for an hour. Then his eyes swept up as in an ascending scale, and he saw a little stuffed bear on a bookcase. He looked at Hannah again, trying to determine if she were a woman or a girl. It seemed strange. There he was, a free prisoner of sorts in a semi-prison company in a captured fortress. Having been placed there by mistake, he was about to tell of the completely senseless death of a dear friend of just a month, to someone his friend had known and perhaps loved, who had known him and perhaps loved him for only a week. And he did not know how to tell her or how to act, because she was doing the job of a full-grown woman and it was a very serious place, and yet she had a stuffed bear on the bookcase.

The roses were there, in a bottle of water. Outside, an entire battalion marched back and forth in mass and precision. Soldiers marching in ranks make for a special sight and sound unlike anything in the world. Hannah didn't look up. She was quite used to it.

Marshall began to phrase a statement, but everything he thought shattered as it was conceived. At first she would think that he had come to ask her help in assignment northward, to make sure that he would reach his own brigade, and to request that Baruch come as well. She was very sympathetic to these requests, truly so. Marshall had come to love her in much the same way that soldiers once loved the Virgin. He had assumed that Lenny would marry her, that sometime in the future he and Lydia and she and Lenny would eat in a restaurant in Tel Aviv and be able to look back on the hard times in the Army, on the West Bank—where no one wanted to be except Jerusalemites, who had an affinity for the thin air and who were near to home.

But he would not see her again, and there would be no meals over which they could talk. What was her office anyway? Where were they? In a fortress built by the British after they had taken Palestine from the Ottomans. It had been British for a long time. And then for twenty years it was occupied by the Jordan Legion, and then it was overcome by the Army in the uniform of which he stood. Occupation implies the ironical surrender of the victors to the attractions and history of the conquered place. He felt as if he were back in time much more than half a hundred or a hundred years. He sensed the fleeting presence of Janissaries and Mamluks, of administrations and empires so old and well-worn that they were impressed into the land as if they were its features. They had all stumbled into the light hard by the hills of Jerusalem and been possessed. It was a magnetic, intoxicating place. Forces unknown and immeasurable emanated from the rock, fell from the air, and did with souls and minds and bodies just what they pleased. It seemed to be a gateway, refreshing and dangerous in its turbulence.

It *was* a portal. He knew that, because when Lenny died Marshall had had a strong feeling that Lenny hadn't far to go. It was easy to die near Jerusalem, as easy as falling in the undertow of a history which surged in tides and currents and was unknown, but left its marks like wind eroding the rock. All things conspired there on a high part of the stage upon which they had come at their risk. He knew it when he looked past the window and saw that roses grew in abundance under a nearby wall. He realized that what he had come to tell her was there in as much profusion as the roses. He was certain that he would not have to speak. What he had to say already filled the room.

He stepped inside. At first she was surprised. She thrust her leg out from under her and put her foot back in her shoe. Then she leaned over the folders to look for Lenny in the hall. When she did not see him, she sat back in her chair and smiled at Marshall in the special way with which people greet the emissaries of those they have just come to love. They toy and flirt with the surrogate, knowing that the message will get through.

But as he moved a little way across the room her eyes followed him and her expression changed, plunging with perfect evenness. She winced in pain and shook her head from side to side. They could hear one another's breathing. Time passed. She knew from his continued stare that it was so. The room was filled with the unsaid.

Suddenly she stood up. She had a crooked, pitiful smile, like that of a woman who is mad. She went to the bookcase and put the stuffed bear on a lower shelf. Then she returned it to where it had been, and sat down. An expression of hatred came over her face. It was the most cynical look that Marshall had ever seen, harder and tougher than that of a battered old man, and it took form on the face of a nineteen-year-old girl. She placed her feet firmly on the floor as if it were moving like the deck of a ship, and began to shuffle the folders and envelopes, just as when Marshall had entered. As he walked down the echoing hallway he prayed that he would hear her cry. But she did not, and when he shut the outside door behind him, he was a different man. All had changed, just like that.

11

Lenny was dead. It was no one's fault, but it made Marshall angry. Hannah would never be the same. That too was no one's fault, but it also made him angry. In addition, he had been posted to an ammunition dump on the West Bank and had only thirty-six hours' leave before he was to report. That meant that he could see Lydia and not have time to contact the Second Mountain Brigade, or vice versa. He had to see Lydia, which meant that he would be staying in the ammunition dump for quite a while, since he had learned with considerable trouble that it was no breeze to extricate oneself from any kind of assignment.

Tight-lipped and full of rage, he returned to the barracks, where he was greeted by a very foolish Moroccan sergeant.

"Where were you!" the sergeant screamed, spraying Marshall with saliva. Marshall stared at him and built up steam.

"I asked where you were!" the sergeant said, pushing even closer, in imitation of drill sergeants he had seen in films. But he spun his wheels in midsentence and his arrogance subsided when he realized that a bomb was about to go off. He backed away; Marshall followed step by step. Then the sergeant turned and ran to the rear of the barracks, but someone had bolted shut the door. The sergeant burst into a little enclosure in which were kept a few dozen crates of hand grenades. Marshall followed him inside.

The sergeant breathed hard. He had many times threatened the Bengalis, and had been particularly fond of tormenting the weaker soldiers. He had suggested to those who were married that their wives were busy in the beds and arms of others, and he had done so in vivid, graphic terms. He had laughed as the frail ones broke and cried. Now he was shaking like Saint Vitus.

And no wonder. Behind Marshall were a dozen soldiers. To the sergeant, their eyes looked like rats' eyes, and it was as if they had pushed him deep into the skittering tunnels of their nest. Marshall approached, fists clenched, the veins in them standing out netted and elastic.

"You'll go to prison," the sergeant said, pointing his finger.

"Good," answered Marshall.

"It's against the law," he said, bumping against a crate of explosives. "They'll try you. You'll spend a year in prison."

"Good."

"Not the Fourth Daughter but Kelé Arba. You can die in Kelé Arba."

"You can die here."

"They shave your head with a razor blade."

Red hot, Marshall raised his fist. "I eat razor blades," he said, and then took after the sergeant in a cruel, mean, bloodthirsty, horrible way. He swung wide with his right fist and brought it against the sergeant's cheek. The blow wasn't particularly powerful, but the sergeant rolled so much with the punch that his hat flew off and he fell to the floor. Marshall was on him in a second, flailing with his open hand, leaving no marks. He beat the sergeant's face in rapid slaps—hard, sharp, and humiliating.

"I'm no saint," Marshall growled in a hoarse, terrifying voice. "I'm no saint. I fight back, you son of a bitch. Surprise." He picked up a grenade and held it over the sergeant's head. The sergeant began to whimper. He thought he was going to die.

"You see this?" Marshall asked. The sergeant nodded. "Eat it," Marshall commanded. The soldiers laughed. They would just as easily have killed the man right there. "Eat it!" Marshall yelled and began to choke his victim. The sergeant put the grenade in his mouth and actually tried to eat it. Marshall sickened so suddenly that tears began to stream from his eyes. He pulled the sergeant up off the floor and pushed him away. As the sergeant crashed against a crate, his spleen returned.

"This is the end of you, the end," he said, tasting it in his mouth as he stormed past the others. Marshall sat on a box, tears running down his cheeks. He made no sound, but the front of his shirt was black and wet. It all came out, and it was over. He felt relieved, but he knew that they were going to put him in Kelé Arba, and he believed that there he would die. He would not see Lydia for even thirty-six hours. It was possible to get through Kelé Arba relatively unscathed. But not for Marshall Pearl. He had once had that gift—back on the White Water, flaxen dam and Eakins and the Schuylkill—but he had lost it. The sergeant had disappeared and nothing was to be done. Soon the Major would march in and Marshall would be arrested.

But the White Water shook its mane. Marshall and the Bengalis looked up. A mysterious sound was coming toward them. As if a wide-winged bird of prey had entered the barracks, a whistling sound beat the air. The Bengalis ducked and dispersed just before a great blur pushed through the rear door, smashing the bolt like a dynamite charge. A puff of air rattled the broken windows. The sergeant flew in backward, four feet off the ground, and was carried across the room and dashed into a bullet-holed wall. Two strong hands held him motionless and astounded. All six and a half feet of Ashkenazi, bull-necked and balloon-armed, crushed the little sergeant against the concrete. Plaster began to fall from cracks in the ceiling. The soldiers looked in wonderment.

Ashkenazi freed one hand and drew from his pant leg a double-edged knife at least two feet long. It was so sharp that it buzzed like a bee as it came shining from the scabbard. Ashkenazi put the needle point against the sergeant's naked eye. The sergeant dared not move. Sharp steel touched an egglike membrane of white. Ashkenazi spoke.

"We are from Kfar Saba. And we were from Marakesh. Do you remember me in Marakesh? I was not so gentle there. I swear by Almighty God that if you say anything of what happened here, I will cut your eyes out. I will cut your mother's eyes out. I will cut your sister's eyes out. I will cut out your father's heart, for I know that he is already blind."

He carried the sergeant to the door and threw him from it like a bunch of dirty rags. Clearing his throat, Ashkenazi turned to Marshall. "They say— that is, Yakov said—that in America you are a millionaire, that you have made many inventions. If you return to America, take me with you."

There was an enormous, airy silence.

"I'll keep you in mind, Ashkenazi," Marshall just managed to say.

Then, like a dream, it was all over and he was free again—shorn, thin, and strong. In a state of shock and joy, he was on his way to Nablus, riding north in an Army truck with two dozen of his fellow criminals.

12

Marshall and Robert were granted the first takes of Lenny's brandy, and they finished half the bottle. Thus the ride was painless, and rather than fearing the truck's excessive speed, they fell in love with it.

They felt as if they had spent millennia on the West Bank, but for the first time its beauty rolled out before them without inhibition—the autumn air, the miniature villages, the mountains, and the valleys. The towns were feudal in appearance and they beckoned like Oz. Having often been described in monographs and magazines, they were familiar, and yet they were forbidding. They had been conquered and could lie very still—still like a dragon. Arab women beat the high olive branches with long switches. They had clothes of bright uncompromising colors Semitic in character and with no middle border or merging comfort, and their crackling fires burned a white quick smoke. As the truck sped past, they and their daughters machine-gunned it with their sparkling eyes.

Only Marshall was getting out at Nablus, since Kfar Yona was farther northeast in the Jordan Valley. The others were going to Haifa, and from there would make their ways. The truck did not stop, but, according to Army custom, it merely slowed. Marshall threw out his duffel and flew after it. A searing pain traveled through him as he hit the hard concrete. He toppled over and his magazines of ammunition scattered about. The truck disappeared.

He was drunk in Nablus, a city not known for its friendliness to the occupiers, and he collected his clips, shouldered his stuff, and staggered to the bus station. He had to wait an hour until a bus left for Bet Shan, and he went to an open-air cafe. The sun was shining bright and warm, and Marshall ordered tea and pastry. The way the people there gazed at him was like four hundred proclamations nailed on four hundred doors. The message was clear, but did they not understand that he too had his troubles? No, they did not. They would not have blinked one of their many eyes had he been ripped apart and quartered right then and there. And yet he was only a man, and he as they had been impressed into the matter as part of a supernatural levy. He had been born not far off, in the sea, while a battle raged. They had no exclusive claim to that coast. He had no desire to rule them. Since the tenth of June, 1967, he had been firmly against the occupation of Gaza or of the populated West Bank. He understood the hateful stares. But he felt the strong acid of his own imperative. They would have killed him there had they been able. And that was enough to make him happy that the gun he carried could fire 600 rounds a minute and would never jam. He was passing through Nablus on his way to Lydia. He grit his teeth. These people wanted to kill him. By force of arms, he would get through. To hell with them. The tea and pastries were sweet and he had paid for them, and the price had been steep, and he was not about to be marched backward into a grave. "To hell with them. To hell with them," he muttered. "Survival is moral. In itself alone it is right."

"Where are you coming from?" asked a young lieutenant as they boarded the bus. Marshall was shocked that an officer could speak with such kindness.

"The Fourth Daughter."

"No wonder you're drunk," said the lieutenant. "Let's sit in the back.

That way no one can grab us from behind. Look at how they look at us. We must be careful." He knocked Marshall in the ribs. "They want to eat us."

Speeding over arthritic roads and choked bridges, they passed lines of rolling hills and descended to dry grasslands. Wheat-colored late November light flooded in and filled the slick inner barrel of the bus. Marshall and the lieutenant sat wide-eyed and seasick in the back, over the motor.

"The most important thing," said Marshall, by this time only half drunk, "is to tell the truth."

"I don't think so. Only a barbarian doesn't dress his thoughts. It's civilized and correct to lie a little."

"No. Fire burns, but the best thing is to put your hand in the flames and hold it there."

"Why?"

"Because then you are most alive. Not telling the truth is like being dead. It doesn't hurt, but you might as well be dead."

"But why fire?"

"You feel everything."

"You feel the fire."

"And in the fire is everything."

"You are speaking like this . . . not because you are drunk . . . but, I think, because you've come from the Fourth Daughter."

Marshall turned to him. "The Fourth Daughter *is* fire."

13

In late afternoon, Marshall began the walk of several miles to Kfar Yona. Weighted with equipment, he sweated as he did double-time down the road. He pushed on. His heart beat wildly and it frightened him, but he used all his blood and strength to run, and he could not run enough.

Breathless, he passed the wire perimeter. Coming upon their white room, he threw open the door. She was not there. A letter tablet was on the table, and a coffee cup rested on a chair. In his absence, she had begun to drink coffee.

A man he didn't even know looked in. "You must be Marshall." Marshall nodded. "Lydia is in the cemetery, gardening. After work she gardens it. We think it's a little strange."

"*You* think. Who the hell are you?" He dropped his things and shot out the door like a horse leaving a starting gate. He ran down the road to the cemetery so fast that it frightened the birds. It was as if he had been in training all that time just to run down that road.

He didn't see her, but he knew that she was there because he felt her presence. Suddenly, she popped up with her back to him—she had been bending over. There she stood like an Englishwoman in her garden, with the sun lighting her hair as she pulled weeds off a rake. He saw the sweet, solid, beautiful shape of her back. She was wearing her dark blue cardigan. He knew it well: it was as soft as the underbelly of a lamb.

She stood calmly, framed by the high royal palms and the tendrils of a winding iron fence. His last steps were long astounding leaps. He choked on her name. She turned and it was an opening, time-lapse flowers, the slow crown of droplets, as they laughed amidst the shock and wonder and flight. Marshall cleared the vine-wrapped fence by many feet. He spread his arms wide and baffled the flow of air as he flew in deep, still, smooth slow motion. They watched one another's faces as they came together. They rolled on the ground. They touched, and it was like breathing again. It almost burst his heart.

14

They had very little time, and decided upon a night picnic in a hayfield. That evening they went to the kitchen and filled infirmary containers with freshly baked rolls, cold beef, salad, steaming hot tea, and what the cooks called Italian Chocolate Slice. Lydia pinched a carafe of wine from the religious stores, and they walked into the darkness, carrying what looked like aluminum models of Chinese silos.

Had they stayed inside they would have fought like hell, because the tensions were remarkable. Lydia had become good friends with new people that Marshall didn't even know. It drove him crazy. And when he mentioned Lenny, Hannah, Baruch, Ashkenazi, Maloof the sneak thief, and the rest, she too felt abandoned and as if he had jumped connections with insulting ease. Having been a woman waiting for her husband to return from the Army, Lydia was changed. Needless to say, Marshall was also changed. Like mating in the dark with a stranger, things just didn't slide so easily. She had little comprehension of where Marshall had been, and he wanted least of all to convey the full sense of the Fourth Daughter; but she was curious and kept asking questions. He was bound to leave at noon the next day, to travel via Nablus to an ammunition dump he had yet to see. The limited hours pressed on them like the lid of a tomb.

But the tension dispersed over the fields into a sky of whitened star-roads. The wind brushing the trees by the Jordan, the faint flow of the Jordan itself, the dewless cool grass, and the great and compassionate silence healed divisions as they appeared.

This was due in large part to Lydia's character and imagination. Dreading a catfight in their tiny room, she had pulsed with ideas to avert it. Her understanding of their natures had led her to bring him into a quiet field far outside the perimeter, the security lights, and the guard towers.

Slowly finding one another's speed, slowly joining together again, they could hardly speak. The time limit almost sickened them. When the moon came up it cleared the Jordan escarpment painfully fast, sending Marshall into a panic, but after he had finished his Italian Chocolate Slice and two thirds of hers (as was the custom in the case of things chocolate), she had him deep in her arms and she was deep in his. The distance disappeared; he told of how frightening it had been; she told of how lonely; and as a warm wind spilled over the mountains—a late autumn gift from Saudi Arabia—they fell back on the dry hay and slept under the traveling blond light of a bright flame-curled moon, unconscious in the rich protective din of crickets and tree frogs.

With the dawn came several combines moving parallel in the distance. They were green; they hummed; and they had come on a last foray into the hay. When the sun took fire on the lip of the escarpment, Marshall cursed the speed of astronomical processes. He discovered that, on leave, heavenly bodies rushed about the sky in madness, plotting against the slow drift of time. This reminded him of Major Pike and the great machinery hall of the Eagle Bay School. In illustration of an eclipse, the Major had cranked the orrery too far. Since the universe refused to back up, he had to bring it around again. "It's going to take five minutes," he said to his cigar, knowing that the children would go wild. "The only thing to do is dance. Dance. When Holly and I found that time passed slowly in the Philippines or in Nicaragua, we just danced. The British danced too, all over the world." He looked up at the children, who, because he was a wizard, would have done anything he said. "You kids do some dancing while I crank up the universe. Harlan Holmes, turn on the Victrola and put in cylinder sixteen—that's 'Camp Town Races, Doo Dah.'" Marshall danced with Francie Alden, a delicate little girl who was growing her long golden hair to drop out of a tower window. Around and around they went in a sort of waltz. "Can't you fox-trot?" asked Major Pike. "You're in the third grade." They tried to foxtrot, but failed, and returned to the waltz. Under the biplane, the battle flags, and other stuff hung from the ceiling, they heard "Camp Town Races, Doo Dah," five times before they drifted over to see how the universe was coming. Cigar ashes littered its green felt floor. The room was full of Havana smoke. The Major worked furiously. His glasses were in themselves moonlike and frosted on their rimless edges. Every now and then he would bend down and pat Frank's snow-white fur.

"Who was Frank?" asked Lydia, stuffing the last of the rolls into her mouth.

"He was the Major's dog, a strange-looking thing (looked just like a horseradish). Frank was a genius—the only dog in the world who could work a drill press. On military holidays, of which we had about forty in Eagle Bay, the Major would take him hiking. Frank wore a knapsack and a little green hat with a feather in it. It looked entirely appropriate. In first grade, we believed that he had been a student who had misbehaved. You should have seen how the little girls talked to him, and kissed him on his broad white forehead, hoping to change him back."

Suddenly dozens of jet fighters came roaring over the hills. They flew at 100 feet, far beneath the Syrian radars, to spring suddenly on the Golan. Their thunderous engines came wickedly close, each trailing a pyramidal torch of superheated fire. The noise shook the earth as, one after another, the Skyhawks and Phantoms from Ramat David passed above, quicker than silver and blue in the belly. The air smelled of kerosene, and the combines suddenly veered and began to paddle toward Marshall and Lydia.

"Let's get out of here," said Lydia, rising.

"You have beautiful legs," replied Marshall, still on the ground. "Quick, back to the room." They jumped on a trailer towed by an enormous tractor.

"Is your Hebrew good enough for you to talk to a general?" Marshall asked.

"My Hebrew is good enough for me to talk to God."

"Good. I want you to speak to the Commander of the Second Mountain Brigade. He seemed to be intelligent and nice. The idea is to get me back to my rightful place—a fresh start."

"Are you sure you want that?"

"Why not?"

"I don't know. It might be risky."

"Look. That way I might be stationed within half an hour's bus ride."

"You might also be stationed on the Syrian line."

"They can't do that. I'm an only-son."

15

Lydia could work wonders. When Marshall passed again through Nablus on the way to Camp Nashqiya, it seemed like a city of gardens, and its inhabitants were as friendly and talkative as the citizens of a Hudson town before a major thunderstorm. They appeared to understand completely Marshall's lot as a soldier. He returned to the cafe, where the waiter greeted him with a warm smile. The architecture was beautiful. The light struck the stone softly and sweetly, and the Arab girls were dignified and royal.

How amazing, thought Marshall, that everything works so precisely well. The streets are clean and dry. Lamb is cooking on the spits for tonight's dinner. Bread rises. Oranges sit in fragrant piles, and the orange vendor is clean, honest, and punctual. Everyone feels as comfortable and as good as if he had just finished a hard day's work. The flags and banners are washed and pressed. This is paradise.

The bus ride through cool autumn air had been a collage of beauty and quiet. The ride in a military truck had had the same effect. They traveled across enclosed plains and past ancient walled cities to a mountaintop on which a small camp was perched amid pine trees and rocky turrets. It was an ammunition storage dump protected by twenty-five soldiers and two armored halftracks. Besides sentry duty, they each served in the kitchen twice a year for a week of dishwashing and food preparation in aid to the Yemeni cook; they maintained the halftracks, heavy machine guns, mortars, small weapons, mine fields, and communications equipment; they (rarely) received and stowed shipments, or sent them out; and they gardened. The only plants in the Fourth Daughter had been highly armed roses. At Nashqiya, lawns were in abundance, beds of flowers climbed the hillside, and vegetable patches were placed between concrete bunkers. There were benches, badminton, chess, checkers, darts, and croquet. The officers were graduate students who spoke perfect English and were interested in *Beowulf*, Philip the Second, the economy of Japan, and bacterial chemotaxis. The beds had sheets and pillows; five soldiers shared a large, quiet, airy room; the food was fresh and nutritious; there was a radio; passes were arranged according to a rational system; and those who were married had supplementary leave. The wonders never ceased.

Marshall's job was to go on clear nights to a sandbagged redoubt overlooking the fragrant valley. Down a run of pine needles the camp reposed in dark blue. For eight hours, he sat next to a .50-caliber machine gun, staring past the wire as he inhaled fine resinous air. Roving patrols brought fruit, cakes, and tea, and stayed for conversation. When he was alone, he taught himself the names of stars and constellations in English, Latin, Hebrew, and Arabic. Far away, a medieval minareted city sparkled with tiny electric lights. In the mornings he returned to his quiet barracks and slept on clean sheets; before he fell asleep he would look appreciatively at the sunlit white curtains blowing inward.

He went to the Camp Commandant and explained that he had tried to contact Lydia to tell her not to work on the transfer, but the phones had been knocked out in a lightning storm.

"Yes. You know, to reach Bet Shan, it has to go through Jerusalem, Tel Aviv, and Haifa. It's silly, but perhaps it means that we're going to pull out some day. Wouldn't that be nice? We'll send a telegram. But I wouldn't worry. For better or worse, in this Army it takes a hundred years to obtain a transfer."

Marshall had only ten days until forty-eight hours' leave. What a delightful restoration. The bitter taste of the Fourth Daughter had fled. Falls and restorations taught the truth of the world, and provided dizzying rides. Ten months at Nashqiya would be perfect. Every night was starry and warm. The constellations blazed. Their names in Arabic were dazzling and mysterious.

16

Though born and bred in Norfolk, Lydia had been sent to a boarding school in Grosse Pointe. Her parents were rather old, and, foreseeing the eventuality of their own deaths, wanted to make her as independent as they could without making her bitter. It was begun during summers in Columbine, on sailing ships, in the Swiss mountains. And it continued in autumn, when she was sent lonely and beautiful up to Michigan, where the leaves died in early October and the cold was nearly unbelievable.

Her speech was a perfect combination of the considered Eastern seaward Virginia drawl, and the less sophisticated, slightly flat, rapid and charming upper Michigan trot. She threw out the middle of many words. For example, she did not say "animals," but "annils." Of all her characteristics, the most extraordinary was her smile.

Those with the misfortune of seeing her but briefly remembered her smile for the rest of their lives. God knows where and how it followed and haunted them. The best of gentleness and the best of strength were combined in the beauty of the ravishing lines of her mouth—her lips, the corners, the juncture between upper lip and cheek, the faint parallel lines along her lower jaw—and in the pure white of her teeth, which were as white as chiclets, and which looked as if she had just come out of a freezing mountain river. They were slightly uneven in the front, so that in kissing, there was character. Even when she wore sunglasses in obfuscation of her gentle eyes, or if her dress were sequined and low-cut, her smile opened up all that was gentle and fair and warm and kind.

Sometimes she forgot her disputational skill and fell into jargon, but the result was an illumination of the commonplace, which, held up for Marshall's consideration, deferred his impulse to shake it to pieces and elicited from him instead profound respect and understanding. Even when partisan for nonsense, she changed it, as if all things were possible, and she often had the effect of making irrelevant his best-protected principles and beliefs, of soothing anger, taming flared passion, etc. Though her external characteristics were splendid and admirable (those fools who think that beauty is nothing are the same as those who think that it is everything), they were best because of their saturation in the light of her spirit. Marshall did not need the golden light of an olive-wood fire in an oil drum underneath the autumn sky at Nashqiya. He needed only Lydia's smile. Therein the seasons were made obsolescent, and he understood the deeply felt warmth which had come to her and remained when, at boarding school by a dark lake shore succumbing to the advance of Canadian winter, she had felt rising within her certain conceptions and realizations which (by the greatest of luck) had combined into a sort of tender and happy perpetual motion.

She had no way of knowing what Marshall had found at Nashqiya. She knew only of the Fourth Daughter, of Marshall's fervent request. Thus, she rode on a bus full of Bengalis from Bet Shan to Haifa. It was the year for Bengalis—they were everywhere, and they were enthusiastic. The driver called out his stops, and they responded in spirited unison. "Afoola," he said.

"Afoola!" they cried.

"Ramat David."

"Ramat! David!" And so it went at every stop.

Lydia went to the great hotel on top of the mountain. High above the bay she watched from blue translucent shade as sunny little ships moved toward Cyprus and Crete, and she listened to the pines rustling cold to the touch because it was winter and the heights were deliciously cool. A girl came around with steaming white pots of tea on a pastry cart.

"Thee and pastry?" she asked.

"Thank you!" said Lydia, choosing a tiny strawberry tart on a dish with a golden rim. The fork was heavy and solid, as in all good hotels. The tea was magnificent. Its steam rose past the high windows through which the wide bay was always visible.

"Are you a guest, Mister?"

"Certainly," said Lydia, as graciously as she could.

"Without money, Mister," said the girl.

"Thank you very much."

Lydia sat in the elegant room high above the quiet city, taking in a sense of position and elevation which she hoped would help her with the general. It was so beautiful there. Because she was in love, the background and climate of the land seemed magical, and all the more so because she was in love with her husband. Marshall was somewhat strange and had not grown up in all the ways in which he might have. But she burned with love for him, for all the imperfections, all the roughness, and all the misunderstandings. She trusted him, and they had the same dreams, and they were for one another in many ways.

Staring out the high windows, she unleashed her transfixing smile, because she was lost in a plan that she had been developing since Marshall had left for the Army.

They had discovered that they loved life in agriculture. Perhaps they would stay on at Kfar Yona, but they missed America and Marshall never stopped complaining about how irrationally Kfar Yona was run. If *he* had a farm, *he* would do this and that, and the things he said were surprisingly true. On several occasions he had said that, after the Army, it might be nice to go back to America and buy a wheat farm somewhere in the West. This had moved both of them in that it was reaccess to a stirring memory. Enraptured by the idea, she had closed her eyes and envisioned a productive rational acreage; a big airy farmhouse full of books; and many lovely children growing up strong and happy; she had even gone so far as to envision a *pied-à-terre* in San Francisco.

"Wait a minute," said Marshall. "It's going to be a struggle. Maybe we can get going on a small farm, but you'll have to hold off awhile on a place in San Francisco." She neglected to tell Marshall, however, why she had allowed her dreams to be so explicit.

She had some money. She had never mentioned it, for it seldom occurred to her. The Levys had become wealthy when, after a vision, Levy had bought real estate and sold his ship provisioning business to a great corporation in exchange for a bloc of its stock. The corporation had then grown out of all proportion. Her parents willed most of what they had to Lydia, since she was the baby and the other children were well established.

Lydia had not been aware of the size of her inheritance until summoned to an elegant office in a new glass building near Dupont Circle in Washington, D.C. Her first impulse had been to give all the money away, but the trustee had informed her that she was not allowed to do that. In fact, she could not (without good reason) invade her principal, which Paul Levy would control until his death. The whole business was so unpleasant that she went back to Berkeley and forgot it, instructing the bank to pay her living expenses and re-invest the remainder. She associated the money with the death of her parents. Thus she had never mentioned it to Marshall, and seldom gave it a thought.

Now, high above the sea, she gave it plenty of thought in view of the wheat farm. She had arrived at the trustee's office, in blue jeans. The receptionist had given her an extremely dirty look, and later she had felt entirely out of place as the trustee attempted to delineate her wealth.

"Well, *how* much is it?" she had asked.

"I can't give you an exact dollar estimate," he had answered. "I can give you an inventory with assessments, but these are often imprecise."

"Can you give me an idea?" she asked, pained, for she knew nothing whatsoever about money, economics, or banking, and her checkbook was trench warfare. "Just an idea?"

"Sure. Let me illustrate it this way, Miss Levy. About two thirds of your holdings are in real estate. Of this, most is here in D.C. Of the real estate in D.C., about forty percent is represented in this building."

"What do you mean, represented in this building?"

"You own the building."

"This building? I own this building?"

"Yes," he said, "all eight floors, and you also own that one." He pointed to a similar building across the street.

"Oh God."

When Marshall finished the Army, they would buy a wheat farm in alpine country—in Colorado, in Montana, or in the high plains of Oregon, someplace like Columbine if not Columbine itself. It could be several hundred acres, or several thousand acres. That was not important. What was important was being on the land and what it taught in balance, restraint, redemption, love, and beauty.

Above the sea, she dreamed of the dry golden grasses, the cool clear sunlight, the air. She saw a white farmhouse with black shutters, workshops lit by fluorescent light, equipment sheds as extensive and clean as those at Kfar Yona, shiny new tractors and combines, a forest of blue pine growing on the hillside, waving wheat, and a view of mountains—all within reach.

After some minutes of this dream, she walked over to the glass and stared at the sea. The waves were like tiny scratches, like light rays dashing and breaking across an interferometer. She glanced at the lovely terraced city, the Hadar. It was time to go to the headquarters of the Second Mountain Brigade. She felt ready, for she had lost some of the simplicity of a kibbutznik, in the contrivance of eating a fancy pastry in a fancy hotel.

Arieh Ben Barak's deputy was a middle-aged colonel, a turkey farmer in real life, named Steimatzky. Steimatzky was rather portly. That is an understatement. He was the *Titanic*. Every now and then his chief would order him to reduce, explaining that no infantry soldiers, no, not even nonheadquarters units officers, could not afford not to be not slim. Then he gave up on beating around the bush by use of the infamous permissible and reversible Hebrew double negative and came right out with it. "Weigh your right arm, and then lose that amount of weight."

"But my right arm is where I wear my watch and my class ring."

"Take them off."

"I can't."

"Why not?"

"My fingers are too fat."

"What about the watch?"

"It stretches, but not enough."

"Steimatzky."

"Yes, Arieh."

"Weigh your right leg. You can take off your shoe, can't you?"

"My leg . . . ?"

"And Steimatzky, this is a mild climate. You don't need to eat those American things, what are they called . . . 'flapjacks'? Especially in the summer. That's what makes you fat."

A secretary poked her head in the office and announced that there was a visitor.

"Who is it?"

"A wife, General. A new immigrant."

"Bring her in. I'm not busy now."

Lydia was nervous and tense on a hard bench in the fortress courtyard. Soldiers walked rapidly from one office to another and from level to level. Messengers covered with dust sometimes ran up the wide stairs, clutching their pistols and their code cases. On her left, Lydia saw an arsenal. Two soldiers with automatic rifles slung from their necks guarded wide double doors. Inside, light effused from heavily barred windows onto two dozen armorers hard at work, bending over weapons in various states of disassembly, stacking cases on long counters, polishing, cutting, drilling. Against the walls and in the middle of a long corridor leading to the windows were metal racks on which were closely stacked thousands and thousands of rifles, machine guns, pistols, heavy machine guns, recoilless rifles, ATR tubes, rockets, mortars, and bangalor torpedoes. They glistened with light gun oil and were frightening to behold. A soldier leaned over and pointed inside. "In one hour," he said, "two thousand men can walk through there and come out fully armed. I bet you never saw anything like that in America."

Remembering that she had determined to win battles of station, Lydia turned to the soldier. "My brother," she said, "commands more than five hundred warships. This is a tiny little arsenal, a tiny, tiny little arsenal. In Norfolk, there is a place for small arms which has trucks and streets inside, and is five stories tall."

Arieh Ben Barak awaited Lydia. His office, too, had a high view of the bay. Map screens stretched across the walls; a large campaign table stood in the middle of the room; ten field telephones were arranged on a rack; a tattered Syrian flag was draped over a pole in the corner; and the Blue and White was hanging regally above the windows. Arieh Ben Barak wore his olive-colored uniform quite well, had a fatherly air, and had taken off his pistol belt to receive his visitor—the young woman that he did not know was his daughter-in-law. He was very gentle with her, understanding that wives who came on behalf of their husbands were always completely terrified.

Lydia was still somewhat nervous. The office was old-fashioned and rough, like a field command. Paul Levy's office was like a study, and his operations rooms were crammed with computers and electronic displays. But Arieh Ben Barak was surrounded by a purely utilitarian forest of maps, charts, and ancient telephones. His fat deputy was ready with clipboard and pen. Undoubtedly she had interrupted something of great moment.

"I know I should have made an appointment," she said, "but I didn't know where to call. I'm interrupting something. I'm sorry."

"No no no. You're not interrupting anything. What can I do for you?"

"My husband is in your command. But at Bakum he was sent to Company T in the Fourth Daughter."

Arieh Ben Barak leaned forward. "What did he do?"

"He didn't do anything; it was a mistake; his Hebrew isn't even as good as mine."

"How long has he been in the Fourth Daughter?"

"He's out now, but he was there for a month."

"In what classification?"

"Stage C."

"Stage C? Is he mad, retarded, a criminal?"

"Certainly not. He's wonderful. Now he's at Base 034."

"Nashqiya," said Steimatzky.

"He wants to get back to the Second Mountain Brigade. That's why I'm here."

"How long is he in for?"

"A year."

"Then it might be better for him to stay at 034. He couldn't have gotten any decent training at the Fourth Daughter. Our training cadres are inactive until June; I don't see how we could use him."

"He doesn't need training."

"Why not?"

"He's been doing dangerous things all his life. For example, when he was sixteen, he fought in the Jamaican back country and was badly wounded. My brother is Commander of the U.S. Navy Atlantic Fleet, which," she said quite demurely, "also includes the Sixth Fleet, and he says that Marshall is a born tactician. At home in Charleston we have a naval game. It's British; it's called Dover Patrol. Paul plays everyone, especially the NATO admirals when they come to visit, and he never loses. One day he played Marshall. Marshall had never heard of Dover Patrol, but he beat Paul easily. Paul thought it was beginner's luck. They played three times that weekend; Marshall won all three games and has yet to lose. I know it may not mean much for an infantry private, but he has a theoretical sense . . ."

"It sounds quite extraordinary. However, I'm not sure that we can use your husband even in light of his alleged capabilities. We have, for example, a commando force, but to be in it, you have to know Arabic."

"He knows Arabic. He studied it for years."

"But you say his Hebrew is not very good."

"It's not that bad, either."

"I'll tell you what. I'll get Steimatzky to look at his records, and we'll see what we can do." Lydia smiled. The General added, "And I'll make sure to try and get him back to the Second Mountain Brigade, which seems to be where he belongs."

"Her brother is the Commander of the Atlantic Fleet!" said Steimatzky after Lydia had left. "How can you say no to such influence?"

"First of all, I didn't say no. And sometimes you are very innocent indeed. That was the biggest lie I ever heard, but a charming, interesting lie."

"So why did you agree to get him back to the Second, if it's only for a year?"

"It's only a year, but then he'll be with us for reserves. He's educated. Maybe he speaks Arabic. Who knows? Look at his file, call Nashqiya, and send him wherever we can use an extra man. If he has Arabic and if his physical rating is above ninety-six, mark him down for training this summer with the Special Force at Tira."

"Okay. But that doesn't explain why you reversed yourself."

"Did you see her smile?"

Lydia walked down to the post office and sent a telegram to the trustee in Washington. It read: PLEASE PROVIDE INFORMATION ON AVAILABILITY OF APPROXIMATELY 1,000 ACRES HIGH COUNTRY WHEATLAND—CALIFORNIA, OREGON, ESPECIALLY NORTHERN COLORADO. SITUATION AND ESTHETICS PARAMOUNT. YOURS, LYDIA.

The telegraph clerkess turned to her partner after Lydia had left. "How much is an acre?" she asked.

"An acre is one kilometer square," her friend stated with great authority.

"Are all Americans crazy?"

"She was lovely."

"Well, yes, for a lunatic."

17

Looking north from Haifa, it is possible to see the mountains of the Lebanon. That they are only one hundred miles distant is unimportant. They are another world. From December until May, they are white, and appear to float above the horizon like a vast construction of linear cloud. Illuminated from before sunrise to beyond sunset, they shine with disconcerting brilliance as the rest of the land from the foothills to the sea darkens in soft night. They look to be a kind of heaven, and the city of Haifa is rigorously positioned so that their magic light may infill its various lucky chambers.

Quite often, civilizations turn on assumptions that they do not truly understand. As a minor example: archeologists are forever excavating special places in search of legend. Such a place is Carmel, and the scholars seek out its quality in close examination, combing the mountain as if it were their prize bay gelding, leaving not even spit unturned. They seek at their feet the Giants of Carmel, not realizing that the magic of the place is that *from* it one can see great masses of land floating above the horizon in an alpine

gleam. The Giants of Carmel did exist, but not in caves as some have con-
jectured: they were the mountains to the north, forever far, cut off by silence,
a thin air bridge to the world of light.

Looking at them from the comfortable sea slopes, it is hard to imagine
that men are there. But most frontiers have soldiers, and on this one, two
armies were stalemated in the snow. The Jews had captured the mountains
and built fortresses. With their great telescopes they could see palms in
Damascus and Syrian soldiers on the plain below eating dinner by their tanks
and howitzers, their knit caps pulled over their ears. The Jews had come so
high that they had only to pivot, and Damascus, Tyre, Haifa, Jerusalem,
and Amman would come easily into view. The Mediterranean was a foggy
blue band. The Jordanian desert was tan and purple. To the north—more
white mountains; to the south—Lake Kinneret, and, beyond a range of
stratified hills, the Dead Sea, the Red Sea.

Fortress Six was interminably separated from the lush valley of Kfar
Yona. The altitude made lungs ache, and, upon descent to sea level and
below, the fortress troops felt confused and dizzy, tired out by the miring air.
Marshall had traveled to the mountains painfully resigned. It had been his
own fault; his impatience had whipped about and struck him. He would
spend the winter in the mountains and rarely see Lydia.

Fortress Six really was a fortress—built on a cliff, hanging over a vast
Himalayan chasm, its concrete towers riddled with gun ports, heavy steel
doors sealing it off from a tortuous approach, underground chambers driven
deep into the rock. A cistern held a two weeks' supply of numbingly cold
mountain water. The wide courtyard was jammed with armored vehicles
intended to control the winding roads. Artillery pieces lined the ramparts;
great mortars were stationed below. In places, anti-aircraft guns stood five in
a row, pointing skyward with double barrels. Electronic arrays lined tall steel
towers; metal dishes were aimed at the army-choked plain. Soldiers were
everywhere—leaning against walls, cleaning the AA guns, tickling the
mounted aerials, exercising in drill, servicing their tanks and halftracks, returning from patrol, on line at the dispensary, praying to the East, rushing
from place to place, arguing, cleaning their weapons, cleaning their boots,
cleaning the ground. There was not a speck of dirt up there. The air was
pure. And yet everyone spent his days shining equipment—as balance for
the other major activity, which was to stare into the void and tire the eyes in
observance of the enemy army, which one came to know well.

There was no war, no peace. People danced in Tel Aviv, and tourists
came to Haifa for the gardens and the sea. But Fortress Six was in another
era. The commander, a colonel of the Second Mountain Brigade, looked
very much like Frederick the Great of Prussia. His cheeks were red, his
hair white; and many deep lines fled from enormous round eyes of slate
gray. He had been up there for half a dozen years. His life was war, validated

by the continual presence of the enemy, the rugged sleet storms, the all-night shelling, the commando attacks, the mines, the casualties, the problems of supply and morale. For him, it might as well have been the maneuver of armies in classical European war, far back in history, universal in its stroke. One day it snowed heavily and the troops wore white winter tunics. One day a truck came up from Tel Aviv, fragrant with oranges. One day the Syrians moved about in a frenzy, and Fortress Six came alive with alarm. Soldiers had breakdowns. There were accidents. Winds arose from nowhere and blasted at the armored doors. There were seldom enough men for patrol, and they worked outside during fourteen-hour days—sometimes in pure sun, and sometimes in wild storms which billowed like an explosion of gray cotton— which was just as well, for the barracks were chambers in the rock and dreadfully crowded with weapons and boots.

Guarding the northern border of the new Jewish State, within sight of a hundred thousand enemy soldiers in depressing steel brigades, nearly at the summits of snow-covered mountains, they were always active and alive. How could it be that there was war in this high white pocket, and love affairs down below in the sweet peace of the cities? It was true. It made them feel like soldiers in history, completely caught up and out of control. It made them feel as if they were in another time, a desperate untrammeled time, a time when cannon seemed to be the most important things in the world, when one awakened and went outside to assure oneself that the massed opposing ranks were quiescent. And it was all embodied in the face of their commander. Strangely, they took great pleasure in seeing him worry. When he rushed through the yard he looked like an eighteenth-century painting. The hart which symbolized Northern Command bounced on his shoulder patch. His insignia, trees and stems in dull green, made a soft muted statement against the mountain ice. He was tentative, suspicious, always thinking, always on guard, with red cheeks like those of Frederick.

18

Marshall awoke at four o'clock on a freezing January afternoon. For the fifth time in a row, he was going on an outside patrol. The barracks were quiet. A Russian slept soundly on an upper bunk and the others were off somewhere. Moving quietly according to the strictest code they had (not to disturb precious sleep), Marshall began to dress for twelve hours of lying at ambush in snow and sleet.

He pulled on a complete set of fishnet underwear, including fishnet socks. Over this he put silk underwear and silk socks. These two layers provided much warmth but were mainly to permit room for ventilation and to wick away moisture. He pulled on down-lined pants and a down shirt. A third pair of socks overlapped the cuffs of the down pants. Then a fourth pair of socks and heavy combat fatigues. Over this went a pair of pants and a shirtjack as thick and coarse as a rug, and yet another pair of socks. He pulled on his heavy winterized boots, and shoved his legs into an enormous pair of quilted battle pants, three layers thick. He covered all this with a heavy down parka and the standard battle jacket—like the pants, quilted in three layers. Both the parka and the battle jacket had thick hoods. Nevertheless, he wrapped his head and throat in a *kafiya* of soft gun flannel he had stolen from the artillery stores. An outer suit of drab nylon went over everything else. A pair of light gloves and heavy mittens with a gap for the trigger finger protected his hands. He strapped on an ammunition harness. It had pouches in which were seven clips of ammunition, three hand grenades, and toilet paper—the impossible of impossibles. He slung his submachine gun across his chest. One clip of ammunition was inside, another was held perpendicularly on a pivot. In a rucksack which slid over the small of his back, he put three bottles of Coca-Cola, a thermos of hot tea, and a dozen candy bars of the worst possible quality. Also over his chest he hung a pair of heavy weatherproofed night binoculars. So attired, he increased in weight from 145 pounds to 190, and he looked just like the Michelin rubber boy.

After staggering to the latrine, he checked himself out in the mirror. A little pair of eyes peeped from a great balloon of clothing and weapons. He posed and positioned in martial postures, trying to be like Marlborough, Kitchener, or Churchill. Then he lunged into the courtyard. Five more balloons emerged from other places. A bunch of NM's were ramrodding a big gun. "Here they come," said one of them, as the six rounded figures converged in the center of the yard. "The circus is in Tel Aviv."

A boxlike armored personnel carrier roared up to them and opened its rear door. The gunner jumped out and helped them board, pushing them into the light green interior as if they were fuel bladders or bales of cotton. The gates opened, and the lone APC chugged onto an ice-fleshed road. It climbed a ridge, and strung out the patrol like a chain of fat beads with several kilometers in between. Each time they stopped, the gunner braced his back against a bulkhead and pushed out the last man in line. They brought Marshall farther than usual to cover the flank. Then they withdrew, leaving him fifteen kilometers from the fortress. He had one flare with which to signal, and mobile patrols went by every hour or so. Otherwise, he was on his own.

It would have been dark, but the altitude and the snow made for a bright bluish tinge and a strange dreamlike visibility. On a flat overlook above the path of two trails, he unrolled a heavy groundsheet and lay prone upon it. It was comfortable at first, because of the thick snow. He pulled a white tarpaulin over himself, and arranged his equipment. The carrier would return in twelve hours.

He was watching for As-Saiqa, the Palestinian guerrillas with links to the Syrian Army. Unlike the cowardly domestic terrorists operating in milder regions for Al-Fatah, they were not insane revolutionaries and did not frolic in massacre after massacre. They only massacred occasionally, and were hardened soldiers, lifelong, much more professional than Marshall, and better experienced. Operating in winter and in storms, they had come to the very gates of the fortress, and their reputation kept the swaddled night patrols from sleeping.

It was terribly cold. The wind was intermittent, sometimes arising to play with swirling blue chains of glassy snow, sweeping it into mesmerizing breakers and rounded waves in the air. These mountains were Eastern. The Alps are noted for the feeling they convey of the absence of men, even in crowded valleys. The Eastern mountains suggest the presence of men even when there aren't any, and the history of ancient empires endows the thin-air passes with uncelebrated mystery.

Utterly alone in the cold air and dim confusing light, Marshall had been watching for only fifteen minutes when he saw a form moving toward him on the trail. He remembered High View, and the Rastas pacing like a tiger. But that had been in daylight and in another time. Here, whatever it was moved in the silence of the snow, in spite of night and mountain spirits.

He opened the breach of his gun, took it off safety, and laid out clips of ammunition on either side of him in places to which he could roll for a change of position in a fire-fight. He put the grenades in front of him, building a little ridge of snow so that they would not be seen. He pulled the white cover nearly over his head and clutched his gun.

His breathing came fast and hard, and he sweated. His face was flushed with blood. It *was* something, and it went along steadily. It seemed to be three or four men, as in Jamaica, moving in a group with the grace of a single animal. Though it came closer, reciprocal darkness obscured it. He could not believe that this strange creature which moved in sidling steps was real and of the world. It passed silently under the ledges. Clouds of breath issued from the head in white plumes, and it seemed to change shape before his eyes.

He was so frightened and so hot that someone might just as well have been in his thick clothes with him. For an instant he imagined Lydia caught up within the padded vestments, her rose-and-peach-colored skin hot and steamy against his own. How magnificent.

He heard muffled steps. It could not be. The light played tricks, but he could see that something in front of him was about fourteen feet tall, with many legs and three sets of eyes, one of which flashed like a cat's.

It stamped its feet and bellowed. Marshall was so frightened that he wanted to scream. He tried, and no sound came from his lips. He thought that he was mad when he heard a beating of wings and saw black flashes against the leaden sky. The wings circled above him while the body of the creature advanced. Then they fell upon him and sharp talons ripped into his clothing. A flashing beak struck and tore. He rolled, and the eagle kept above him. Soon its talons began to touch his skin. But a shrill whistle echoed in the valley, the eagle lifted, and Marshall was released.

Then he saw. A Druse chieftain sat high upon a white horse, and the eagle rode on his shoulder. Angry, ashamed, and still frightened, Marshall jumped to his feet as best he could, aimed the submachine gun at the hunter, and commanded him to dismount. The old man, who sat as straight as a steel rod, did not move or blink an eye. He was so perfectly still that it was hard to tell if he were living.

He wore a white robe crossed with bandoliers of bullets; a scimitar was tucked into his waistband; a shotgun was slung over his shoulder; a British pistol hung from his belt. His eyes were blue, or appeared that way in the deep blue haze. Perfectly impassive, he measured Marshall with his stare.

When Marshall had passed the point at which he might have killed him, the Druse said, "A boy does not order me off my horse. A Jew does not order me off my horse. A foreigner does not order me off my horse."

"Goddamnit!" said Marshall, enraged.

The Druse answered in English. "You may shoot the eagle if you wish." He spoke an Arabic command so ancient that it was Persian, and not Persian but Sanskrit. Almost as if it knew what lay ahead, the eagle hopped to the ground and began to brood in sad depressed circles.

Marshall let it be. The horse snapped its head, and the golden bridle clicked. Marshall could not but respect the Druse. He was so upright, a mountain lord from an ancient time. Marshall wanted to defer—youth to age, inexperience to experience, a man in soldier's clothes to one in robes, lack of ornament to careful masculine regalia, one who did not know the land to one who did, one who had not lost to one who had, a man on foot to a man on horse. He felt happiness in the ordained hierarchy and wanted to give way, like a son to a father. But it was not possible to allow the man within the lines. The Syrian Druse were not like those in Israel who with the Israelis fought against age-old enemies, but rather were closely allied with Damascus. Despite his nobility and his guise as a hunter, he might well have been collecting information. In running across Marshall, he had already found some. Besides, the soldiers of the mobile patrol—extraordinarily vulnerable in their loud armor with its arc lights—would shoot from a distance were they to see the flash of the eagle's eyes down the road, and the .50-caliber bullets would cut the Druse in half.

"You're not allowed to come here," said Marshall. "You have to go back. And don't come here again."

"I will cross the mountain at this point, as I have done all my life. A boy will not tell me that I cannot."

"First," said Marshall in Arabic, "you will not cross here. I'll kill you rather than see you cross. Second, you're a liar. You haven't been through this line in five years. I know it. You know it. And then, I am not a boy, but a soldier of the Kingdom of Israel, in its northernmost place, its highest frontier. I too go back in the centuries." An unexpected chill informed him of his profound connection with the past as he spoke in terms which made the old Druse feel like a newcomer. "*Thousands* of years before you . . ." Marshall's eyes sparkled and shone, "*thousands* of years, my King, David (it sounded pleasing in Arabic, *malakí, Daoud*), sent me to this high place. And I tell you now to go back."

Marshall's sense of triumph made it so, and the Druse called his eagle. The horse pranced like a horse in a medieval painting, and then he wheeled it into the enveloping darkness, the white mixing with white.

Marshall gathered his equipment from the churned-up snow and walked for half an hour to take up position in a different place. Before dawn, he played and replayed the scene a thousand times. It took on such colors and sounds and dreamlike qualities that at four, the most difficult hour, when he could hallucinate as easily as think, he was not sure if the Druse chieftain had been real or just an image of the moving snow.

The early morning was always difficult. By that time, he had been still long enough for his circulation nearly to cease. The temperature dropped to its lowest point, and his heart beat so slowly that he thought he would not make it out of the pause. It resounded throughout his body, knocking him each time like a slap on the back. He often had seizures and was locked in one position for an hour, his hands fused painfully about the wood and steel of his gun, his eyes far too wide, staring at an unseen horizon. Had the whole Syrian Army come up the mountain, he would not have been able even to blink.

But the silence and immobility allowed him in those hours to hear and feel the earth as it turned. He was aware of a massy rotation. Facing north, he sensed a steady rightward motion, as surely as he sensed gravity pressing him breathlessly into the snow and his acceleration lifting him away. Forgetting the Syrians and the cold, he felt as if he were being torn apart by elemental forces, as if he would soon crystallize into ice and dust and be flung about at random.

But the earth was spinning into the path of heat and light. The sky would brighten, a wind would arise from the pressure of advancing light, and he would see in the corner of his eye that over darkened Syria the sun came up from somewhere in the East, from a paradise perhaps near India. And from over Iraq a transient sliver would appear to Marshall's fevered eyes, blinding him in warmth and white, firing the ground and his bones, setting the world afire, steaming up the seas. Then he would sit up as if after a dreadful sickness and look out in half-crazed relief at the rising sun. The breezes across the snow were always mild and almost warm at that time of the morning. He was grateful, not so much for lasting through the night, but for the light itself, without explanation or implication. He was shattered by the love he felt for the light.

When the carrier came, Marshall hopped inside, the doors were closed, the heat turned on, and the next he knew he was making his way to his bed. He stripped off the many layers of clothes and, covered with just a towel, ran through a freezing wet gallery to the showers. There he stayed for a full hour under a steaming hot stream in a half-curtained stall. His clothes had indeed been torn, and others of the patrol had been visited by the Druse hunter. The fourth one down line, a wild insane Georgian, had immediately shot the man's horse, disarmed him, tied him up in his own leather belt, and sent a flare. The hunter had come for the Syrians to find out about the patrols. Frederick the Great rewarded the Georgian with a week's leave and was intensely proud. That winter, 1973, saw an enormous increase in Syrian attempts to gather information. Belatedly, or (in the larger perspective) early, Marshall began to wonder.

"How did the Georgian know? He had no way of telling that the Druse came to each one of us. How did he justify shooting his horse and arresting him?"

"What justify?" asked a soldier in another steaming stall. "He's from Tbilisi. If it had been Golda Meir on that horse he would have done the same."

"Where's the Druse?"

"They already have taken him to Northern Command. Nobody knows what the hell is going on."

Even in the hot shower Marshall was gripped by a chill and had to take hold of a pipe to steady himself. Suddenly everything fell into place—the artillery barrages, the air penetrations, the step-up in terrorism, the spying, the constant shifting of troops on the plain below. He knew exactly what it meant. The way was being prepared for a major war. They would make the Jews so used to crises that they could shield the beginnings of an all-out attack. Marshall had been amazed at the complacency of the Israelis. Sentries slept, went out with unloaded weapons, and actually deserted their posts to go to Tel Aviv and fool around with whores. Badly trained reservists with ancient weapons were sent to hold key positions. The network of supply was overloaded and tenuous at best. Morale was terribly poor, the Army divided by class and color. Force levels were down, artillery pitifully neglected. Just in his own peregrinations from base to base, Marshall had seen that the planes were badly maintained (despite reputations to the contrary), ECM was nearly nonexistent, communications were antiquated, and stocks were badly situated in relation to the new borders. He had wondered many times how Israel hoped to hold the Golan against a full-scale assault when only a few roads led to the heights where the battle would be decided—especially if the Syrians were to make determined efforts to cut these roads with their air power and paratroopers.

Everyone was overconfident. The image of efficiency and strength did the work of deterrence more and more, until real power receded and most of what kept the Syrians and Egyptians back was as empty and dry as a rotten tree. Marshall decided to tell Frederick. No, he would tell Arieh Ben Barak, for he was a general, whereas Frederick was only a colonel.

He always thought great worldly thoughts in the shower after all-night patrols when he was giddy and his mind was free. He had discovered that when in the shower, or in a pool, or a tub, he could make brilliant policy, predict the future, and think like a statesman. The trouble was, when he turned off the water and stepped shivering into a puddle of dirty suds, he became once again a miserable private with a toothache, vitamin deficiencies, and dirty linen. Thus he abandoned the idea of informing Arieh Ben Barak of his realization. Undoubtedly the Army chiefs and the political leaders already knew what he knew. After all, he had not even had the sense to arrest the Druse hunter, and had left it to the Georgian—who looked, moved, acted, and thought just like a monkey.

19

The three Mountain Brigades were an elite force. They took the best recruits; they were multipurpose and thus had experience in everything from mountain warfare to engineering; they had the most alert and intelligent officers; they were forever in the field fighting the real and minor wars; and they shared a special commando force of five hundred soldiers. Despite its small size, this battalion was earmarked for such grandiose schemes as the capture of Damascus, the abduction of Anwar Sadat (they prayed for the green light), destruction of Saudi oil facilities, the assassination of Yasir Arafat, the disruption of Egyptian communications, blocking Iraqi forces at the Syrian border, distant operations in Europe to rescue hostages, the capture of ships from the Soviet Fifth Squadron in the Mediterranean, and other specialized tasks.

Each of these soldiers had to satisfy a set of basic requirements—perfect physical condition, expert marksmanship, knowledge of Arabic, experience in an active infantry command, and a familiarity with explosives. Each soldier had to claim a specialty. There were linguists, engineers, pilots, doctors, mountain climbers, navigators, boxers, actors, miners, architects, physicists, police, demolitions men, sea captains, chemists, economists, hypnotists, locksmiths, historians, political scientists, dialecticians, forgers, Arabic typists, industrial designers, watchmakers, zoologists, weight lifters, tailors, teletype operators, distance runners, linemen, hydraulic engineers, memory experts, meteorologists, photographers, divers, and others.

They were trained and then formed into teams. Fifty at a time went to Tira for three months, during which they fought, swam, shot, learned special weapons, practiced languages, and had much free time. Arieh Ben Barak thought that the best irregulars were men of independent will. He believed that given the proper start and a little freedom, his commandos would apply themselves to problems, and that in the cross-fertilization of their particular talents answers would arrive at a staggering rate. He was right.

Tira was nothing more than a collection of tents in the dunes and two large warehouses for equipment, vehicles, and stores. Everything was improvised; they borrowed from all branches of the Defense Forces; and they were on the base only eight hours a day, with every Saturday off. Lydia had written to Paul, and he and the Livingstons made their anniversary present an apartment on the beach for three months. Summer arrived. Lydia took an intensive course in Middle Eastern history, while Marshall was trained and eventually put into a group specializing in ship capture. As she wrote a lengthy paper on the history and meaning of the Battle of Ain Jalut in 1260, he made dry runs against ships in the harbor and at sea—he often had to swim several miles into the bay before he could climb the chains of vessels at anchor.

Each evening, Marshall and Lydia returned to an apartment overlooking the sea. There they resumed their life together. By August only two months were left in Marshall's service, and they spent quiet evenings on their balcony, listening to music, cooking roasts over a pan of charcoal, reading, talking, and looking out at the Mediterranean, which in Haifa is active in summer and full of friendly green breakers, whereas in winter (except for the large storms) it is as quiet as a lake.

One evening in the middle of August when the air was mild and full of the sweet scents of flowers and fruit trees, Marshall and Lydia walked several miles down the wide beach to the camp at Tira. The stars were out full, but the moon had yet to rise. In the distance they could see the lights of cars speeding through the warm air on the Haifa–Tel Aviv highway.

Except for two sentries who watched over the warehouses, everyone had gone home for the Sabbath, and the tents were empty. But as they approached they saw firelight behind the dunes. When the camp came fully into view, they saw a gas flame burning brightly. Its plume was the size of a cotton candy, it roared, and it made the sand underneath gold and orange. Two men sat on deck chairs, talking and drawing diagrams in the sand. They were Arieh Ben Barak and Frederick, who invited Marshall and Lydia to share a cauldron of tea. Both men had their pantlegs rolled. Frederick scratched out a map with his foot, and when he noticed that they were looking at his bare shins he pointed sheepishly toward the ocean and said, "We were wading."

The General remembered Lydia, and, of course, Frederick recognized Marshall, who seized the opportunity to speak on equal terms with senior officers. He looked at Arieh Ben Barak, who had been busy making the tea, and saw eyes as diffuse and brown as his own. In fact, the General had a striking resemblance to this soldier far down in his command. But for their ages their coloring would have been the same, and there was much else which made them alike—even their teeth—though no one noticed.

Marshall presented a careful, well-analyzed case to support his point of view that the Arabs were preparing a big war for which Israel was not ready. He listed at least fifty signs that he had seen of laxness, overconfidence, poor planning, and lack of preparation. He spoke in phrases that ran together well because they had occurred to him repeatedly for many months, and the two high-ranking officers did not once interrupt. Sometimes they appeared concerned; sometimes they seemed to disagree; sometimes they toyed with their badges of rank.

At the end of his lecture, or plea, they said nothing and he began to go weak in the knees because he still harbored a considerable fear of officers. As long as he was a private on active duty he would be influenced by memories of the majors at Bakum and in the Fourth Daughter. He knew that Arieh Ben Barak could make him spend two months scrubbing pots in Afoola as easily as he could say one sentence to a deputy.

But the man with the soft brown eyes thought of the maps in the sand, looked up, and smiled.

"I'm interested to hear that you have given this problem some thought. When you finish your period of conscription . . ."

"Two months from now."

". . . come to see me. I'll look over your record, and if there is a place on my staff, we'll see . . . for reserve duty, that is. I would have to make you an officer. Would you object?"

Marshall barely managed to say, "Not at all . . . I'd be happy to be an officer, if it's possible."

"I don't promise anything. We'll see."

Lydia took advantage of the need to change the subject, and made a graceful transition to the Battle of Ain Jalut, explaining the inevitability of the Mongols' defeat. "They could have been stopped by the Ismailies in the mountains, but the Ismailies were in disarray." And then she gave an historico-military analysis which was so well done that Arieh Ben Barak, who knew nothing of the topic, joined in a spirited discussion of the failure of Rukn-a-Din to stem the Mongol invasion, and how Baybars the Mamluk had finally accomplished it. Afterward, at home, Marshall could not get to sleep.

He paced the balcony. By 2:30 he was in command of the Israeli Army. By three he was wild-eyed, but Lydia was up with him and she understood that the hot tea had stirred him to trances and splendors.

"Come're," she said affectionately, patting her knee. He strode over to her in large heroic steps. His heart was beating like a ton of bricks. He stared out to sea as battles criss-crossed his imagination.

"Sit here," she said, indicating her knee. He looked at her as if from a throne. "Even generals can sit on their wife's knee." He sat on her knee, eager to resume his pacing conquests. She began to stroke his forehead, which burned—her hand was cool. "You know what? You're crazy, and you'll never get to sleep if you keep marching across Macedonia. Just think of where we are," she whispered slowly. "It's a beautiful night. Come back to me."

He looked in her eyes and was no longer a general leading armies. Ambition was not even a thimble. The stars ceased their blistering and became soft, and the moon came up and whitened the sky and hills. They heard the wind rushing over the dunes and through the heather. It was warm and peaceful, and they lay fused together in the straight cool moonlight, gentle as the wind and the night birds on the slopes of Carmel. When finally the moon began to set behind Atlit, the villagers' fires were already flickering across the dark hill.

20

Marshall already had the alert and gentle hart on one arm, and the patch of the Mountain Brigade on the other, a white line of mountains with a II hovering above them in the azure blue. After the commando course at Tira, he was issued a pair of crossed swords in gold to pin over his left breast pocket. Arieh Ben Barak's deputy, Steimatzky, had been waiting early one morning at the circle of tents. When Marshall arrived he was shocked to find that he had been made a first lieutenant. Steimatzky explained. Thinking of Marshall, the General had ordered Steimatzky to check his records and (if they were satisfactory) to promote him. "Arieh said that this was a crisis, and that he was moving rashly, as in a crisis. I told him that you were due out on Eight October . . ."

"Eight October? It's the twenty-second, not the eighth."

"No. You're all to get a two-week present. But he said, 'Let him take charge of the commandos at Fortress Six for a month until the new captain gets there.' You were promoted to first lieutenant, because several of the commandos at Six are lieutenants, and we could not put you in charge unless you had rank."

He gave Marshall a box in which were several sets of insignia. Marshall was stunned. The fifteen commandos at Six would not take kindly to his apotheosis, but it would be only for a month, and he would be cautious and kind. His heavily accented Hebrew was not particularly incongruent with his new station. Even Arieh Ben Barak had a noticeable accent.

Perhaps his changed station had stimulated a review, but for whatever reason, one day in the hotel Marshall and Lydia made their decision. They sat on the hotel terrace at dusk. Before hopping into the *Carmelīt* to go down the hill to eat in a Rumanian restaurant and then see an Austrian mystery, they had stopped to look over the sea and have tea in the pine garden. "You see that ship in the middle, *Brigham Victory*? It has the black superstructure."

"That one?"

"That's right. Today we tried to capture it. We haven't had much trouble before. You know that I like scaling the anchor chains and storming the bridge. It's fun to climb while the wind whips the green water below. If you fall, nothing happens. But today when we got to the top we had a surprise. The *Brigham Victory* is an American ship, chartered out to the Navy. As I climbed over the rail, four men closed in on me with shotguns and pistols. They had me. All the other ships have been pushovers. I looked at their faces. They were the faces of plains farmers. They put down their guns and we talked. After all, I was in a bathing suit. What I want to say is that I was much more than proud. It was different and better than being proud. I felt drawn to the plains, the Rockies, Columbine—where we started. I seem always to be on the other side of the fence, but I'd like to go back to Columbine, and stay.

"We can never be what they are, the plainsmen, and we can never be like the Israelis either (maybe it's fine just to be whatever we are). But I want to make a home with you in Columbine. That's where I was happiest. If I belong anywhere, I belong in that valley. We could grow wheat, as we had thought—almost twenty years ago."

"That's what I want to do," said Lydia. "That's what I always wanted to do, what we're supposed to do. I was waiting for you to come around."

"Then we'll do it."

They yearned for the image and vision of Columbine. Even within the dream of childhood, it had been their dream.

"We'll go to Washington, to the Department of Agriculture, and get as much information as we can about the area. It's cold up there, and the growing season must be short. But I would imagine that you can grow spring wheat in the valleys. We'll check on taxation, mortgages, and the rest. Then, when we're ready, we'll go to Union Station and get on a train for Denver. And then we'll go north into the country. If there's a college nearby, maybe you can teach in it. I'll grow wheat."

"I'll grow wheat too," Lydia said. "I want to be a farmer."

As they watched the lights and the ships they talked about their plans. "We can have a little apartment in San Francisco," she said, knowing that it was true and that Marshall thought she was marching through Macedonia.

21

Early in September, Marshall returned to Fortress Six. He was just getting used to being an officer and times seemed easy, though he suspected that a shock lay ahead. He guessed that war would come in the winter, since the Israeli Air Force did not have all-weather fighters, and thus would be neutralized to an extent favorable to the Arabs—who, also unable to fly in bad weather, would be spared the agony of air combat with the Israelis. Because winter in the Middle East has always discouraged war, Israel tended to let down its guard, but the Arabs' Soviet equipment was suited to mud and cold. Had Marshall been in command of the opposing forces, he would have insisted upon a winter war.

Marshall took Lydia to the Bet Shan bus, through the barred windows of which he kissed her as dozens of North African women watched. Standing on a railing at the bus queue, he was a strange sight in his colorful uniform as he grasped her through the light aluminum bars and, from most angles, appeared to be kissing and stroking the bus itself. Then the bus backed out of the bay and Marshall jumped to the ground, waved to Lydia, and walked off in the direction of a motor pool in Bat Gallim, from which he got a ride to the fortress on Mt. Canaan above Sfat.

Sfat is in the mountains, and looks into valleys and depressions with much the same tranquillity as Delphi. There are terraces along the main street, and many quiet courtyards, and in fall the weather is unparalleled, being cool, clear, and dry. He found a room in a luxury hotel, and at evening he went to a restaurant on an open terrace cantilevered over a steep green precipice. Colored lights and paper lanterns were strung across the dining area and they swung in the breeze. There were many geraniums in carved stone boxes. The valleys, Lake Kinneret, and Tiveria were in dusk.

Marshall put his hat down and waited for a menu. A lieutenant with insignia of the First Mountain Brigade asked if he could join Marshall, who was pleased to have his company, but who had to ask him to speak slowly. They both ordered steaks, and Marshall told the story of how he had gotten his rank. The other lieutenant didn't resent Marshall's rapid rise, for he was young, and he too had risen rapidly. He was going home to Tel Aviv for a week. It was pitch dark when they started on their ice cream and tea.

"You won't recognize it up there," said the other lieutenant, who was from a strongpoint down the line.

"What do you mean?" asked Marshall, stirring his glass of hot tea.

"Don't you know? I suppose not, if you've been away. The Syrians must have brought in all but a few of their tanks, though they have recently thinned them out. Really, there are hundreds and hundreds, and all the support vehicles, APC's, and the rest, to go with them."

"You mean they're just sitting there on the plain?" Marshall was honestly astounded, and put down his spoon even as the tea continued to swirl seductively in an orange maelstrom.

"I suppose it's more of a shock if you haven't been there in a long time. They've built up slowly. They're defensively positioned, hull-down and dug-in—against our aircraft. It's a purely defensive deployment."

"Tell me something."

"What is that?"

"How many seconds does it take for a tank to lift itself out of its trench?"

"That's not the point. Their intentions are obviously defensive."

"How many seconds?"

"I don't know exactly."

"Just tell me. How many seconds?"

"Okay, thirty."

Marshall began to spoon his chocolate ice cream into his tea. It looked horrible, and it overflowed.

"What are you doing?"

"I don't know what I'm doing, but when you're in Tel Aviv, enjoy yourself. Eat well and see lots of movies. When you get back, we're all going to be fucked."

"I don't think so."

"Neither does anyone else. Maybe I'll see you up there."

Marshall decided to leave right away. He did not get out until 2:30 and arrived at Fortress Six as dawn was beginning to break. Climbing to the highest observation point, he surveyed the plain while the sun arose far behind Damascus, looking as if it were cradled in a fiery pit somewhere in Iraq. As usual, a tiny red sliver churned and bent on the land horizon like molten metal. The shadows of the hills grew severe, and green strips appeared to the northeast. The plain below was still a collection of dark crags. But then the sun came up and its blood red became yellow and blazing white. It was round and hot, and, as it climbed, Marshall thought he saw the surflike lashing of its corona.

A few lights and fires dotting the half-dark below faded or went out as the sun got higher. Someone in the fortress tuned a radio to the dawn chimes of the Army station. A sentry yawned and threw off his gray blanket. With the light he pulled the clip from his rifle and slung the weapon over his shoulder. He would wait an hour and then go back to bed, or to a shower.

When the sun was high enough for Marshall to make out colors and textures in the distance, he swung a pair of tremendous military binoculars on their tripod to scan valley and plain. At first he saw nothing unusual—boulders, rocky terrain, ditches, roads, an emplacement or two. But then his muscles twitched and he felt a surge of electricity run down his back. For in places usually empty of the Syrian Army he saw tank after tank after tank, rows of artillery, netting in so many places that it looked like Verdun, and what seemed like thousands and thousands of trucks, new emplacements, new cuts in the earth, and troops who had begun to get up and mill about in hundreds of camps.

He pivoted over to view the Israeli line. It hadn't changed. Marshall closed his eyes and imagined how the vast Syrian columns must have looked rumbling past Damascus on their way to the armed camp below, which burst into life in the sun's ascent and seemed to have a will of its own, as if it were a living creature spawned from steel.

22

Lydia too was up at dawn, wandering about carrying a notebook and a leaky fountain pen. Though they did not intend their primary instrument in Columbine to be recollection of the kibbutz (but rather remembrance of what they had envisioned long before), she thought anyway to take notes on agriculture at Kfar Yona. What they did right, they did beautifully.

She was full of early morning energy and lightheartedness, and she was happy. So that when the sun swept over the escarpment from Jordan and Iraq, instead of taking notes she found herself sketching the cows and chickens as they frolicked in front of her. Taken up as in the slow rhythmic ease of a float trip, she walked about for hours doing renditions of the hollow-brained chickens.

When she and Marshall had married, she had felt as if she were starting a new life. Riding in the helicopter to the *Royal George* had been much the same, as had the sudden inertia and Easternness of Tel Aviv, and the thick agricultural abundance of the Jordan Valley. And when, with a foolish grin, Marshall had come out onto the balcony above the sea, suddenly a lieutenant in a rakish hat, she had moved through another gate. As the gates opened and shut, each frame had about it the satisfaction of a good painting, and the engine clicked on in strokes of color.

When Marshall had returned from the Fourth Daughter, she felt as if she were suffering with him the privations of an Ottoman soldier. At the kibbutz she was generally content—and lonely. Then they went to Tira, where she became lost in a world of books and she and Marshall dashed through warm shallow waters undulating with smooth fishlike waves. Yet another picture awaited them in Columbine. Unlike Marshall, she knew that it might not last as long as they thought. They could well move on to something else. Most important was the energy of transit—for which it was worthwhile even to be driven in a breathless life.

At Kfar Yona, the cows thrust their thick padded heads through the round iron rails of the pens in continual efforts to reach the other side. Both sides were flaccid mud, but it was the crossing-over which magnetized them. She noted in her sketchbook that they looked as distrustful as bears, and could be smelled for miles.

Yossi Merzl, the secretary of the kibbutz, came by on his tractor and stopped the motor. "Hello Lydia," he said. "We'll miss you."

"Marshall and I are going to have a wheat farm, in America."

"I heard this. The capital! Can you do it?"

"Yes." She shook her head affirmatively, and smiled sadly when she thought of leaving them under siege and in danger. Yossi Merzl knew exactly what she was thinking, and dismounted from his huge tractor to sit beside her on the iron rail. He had wild white hair, and a face with so many places written into it that he could have been a gazetteer.

It was hot. There were flies. The valley almost burned, and a warm wind pushed through the trees, as loud as a freight train. "I want to tell you something," he said. "You may not understand, but . . .

"It was very nice of you to garden in the cemetery. Everyone appreciated it. But, you know, we left it untended almost on purpose. It's hard to explain. I'll try.

"When I was younger I lived in Poland. To make a very long story very short, the Nazis came. I went to the ghetto in Lodz. I was put in a camp. I escaped. I was in a camp in Cyprus. I escaped. I was skillful at escaping, but so what if I could walk around? Inside, I was dead.

"Then I came to Palestine. For many of us it was better than a new life, and even at the pier you could see people being reborn. They laughed, they cried, they even kissed the ground. But not me. I wondered if ever I too would emerge as had many of my friends. They had been broken and weak. Their selves had caved in. And suddenly, they came by one day and you saw that they were different, full of enthusiasm, as if their hearts had been replaced and they had taken new souls.

"Not me. I didn't understand. Would I always be bitter and unhappy? Nothing worked. I loved Kfar Yona, I loved to see it grow, but I was still a smashed-up Jew from a ghetto in Poland. Then the Arabs made the war against us in forty-eight, and I went with the others to fight. The war lasted for a long time. I did dangerous things. Many people died, people I loved.

"When it was over and the dust had cleared, and we started up again even though there were many new graves, I hardly knew what was going on.

The day that I got back, I looked around at this simple farm, I looked up at those mountains, and I cried.

"We were still alive. That was something. I'm not saying, you understand, that I worship survival. Despite the fact that it has been made the primary duty of every Jew, it in itself is not so special. The special thing was that life came back. Each war is the same, like holding your breath for as long as you can and then realizing how wonderful it is just to breathe; like a dry field suddenly feeling the flood.

"You tended the graves, a gentle thing to do. However, did you know that for everyone who dies in war, there are others who are born, and reborn? That is why veterans will never make the peace, and why, in denying the nobility of battle, pacifists cultivate war. To stop something so powerful you must at least tell the truth about it, and they don't. What I'm trying to say is, don't feel bad about us. There is a balance to everything— symmetry, compensations. A soul buried in the ground rises in the air. When you go to America and have your wheat farm, thrive in peace, but don't pity those in war."

He returned to the tractor and drove off to the hay fields. For Lydia, even in the space of minutes, a gate had closed, and a gate had opened.

23

When Marshall arrived at Fortress Six in the beginning of September there were actually fewer Syrian tanks than when he had left. But their positions had changed, and they were concentrated in such a way as to appear far more numerous, at least in those sections easily observed. During September itself the armor on the plain multiplied steadily until at month's end 900 tanks were in position. On the thirteenth, the Syrians pressed home an air battle over the sea, into which they flung and lost thirteen planes. Arieh Ben Barak decided then that war was imminent. The planes were sacrificed to lull the Israelis further into a stupefying sense of security, to probe their readiness, to test the wind. In the way that a farmer can sense a storm from the speed of clouds, the random electrification of the air, and the light in its gray and purple variations, Arieh Ben Barak smelled the full scent of war.

Not only did he go to the Chief of Staff and the Defense Minister (who sent only one extra armored brigade and put the Air Force on a high state of alert), but he began to take action independently. He canceled all leave, stockpiled ammunition and anti-tank weapons, summoned as many spare units as he could to the fortresses, impressed upon his subordinates the need for vigilance, and intensified efforts at gathering intelligence. There were 177 tanks on the Golan, and the Syrians were a few miles away with 900.

Marshall didn't go home. A strange collection of stray units streamed into Six, filling up all available space with tents and equipment. The ramparts were crowded and active. It was like a walled Arab town in the Middle Ages. Among those gathered in haste from other branches and divisions were Baruch and the three Bengalis, who had laid hold of an armored halftrack. Baruch drove and commanded (an unusual combination, to be sure); Wilson was the machine gunner; Chobandresh and Prithvi were mortarmen. Baruch wore sergeant's stripes, and the Bengalis had become corporals. Because they had been together for a year, they were well co-ordinated, and they lived with their machine day and night, maintaining it as if it were a new Rolls-Royce.

"A sergeant was mustering out," Wilson told Marshall, "and Baruch was senior in service. They gave us this halftrack. Then that unit (a reserve group where we had been sent to wash dishes) was deactivated. But we are conscripts, so Baruch asked what to do and where to go. The Commander said to take the halftrack and patrol the beach between Rosh HaNikra and Nahariya! That was in April. No one has bothered us except the tourists, who always take our pictures. We were very astute in our duties. In case you are wondering, the Commander was a Kurd—the uncle of Baruch's sister's husband. At the petrol dump someone told us that all miscellaneous forces were being sent to the Golan."

The new Captain of Commandos arrived, an Englishman who was so calm that he seemed to enjoy the heat of the moment as an Eskimo might enjoy a blazing fire. His name was Palmer. No one knew if in fact he were a Jew, or how he had gotten there. His Hebrew, though classical, was excellent and precise. He took half the force and assigned the other half to Marshall. They were busy that September, and they crossed the enemy line twice.

The first time, Palmer had taken two men out in early morning and returned several hours later, puffing up the road, a stick under his arm. He was noncommittal and emotionless, preferring not to describe the foray in detail except to give Marshall a few pointers on procedure, and to render his report—which attributed to the deployment of surface-to-air missiles a frightening density. "Looks like some real stuff," Palmer had said, "like a big holy war."

Marshall was impressed by Palmer's nonchalance about crossing the Green Line. "It's the Purple Line," said Palmer. "Are you afraid of those silly incontinent bastards, those . . . those crotchless half-wits?"

"Yes," answered Marshall. "And I don't have contempt for them."

Palmer gripped Marshall urgently by his lapels. "Neither did I, until the day before yesterday. But how do you think I got stiff enough to run around in their encampment?"

Marshall went out alone one day late in September, just before dusk. In addition to insulting the Syrians continuously and with verve, he had studied a route through the tels, consulted mine maps, and eaten carrots. On Palmer's advice, he took several belts of whisky before setting off, and tried to think of the whole thing as a lark. "If you're going to be a Russian, you should be a little drunk," Palmer had said. "In fact, you should be more than a little drunk. And scowl at them when you see them."

"You see them?"

"Of course you see them! You get close enough to kiss the fairies. And you'd better get that close. If you don't, you'll look out of place. Walk loose. Remember, there are a hundred thousand of them down there in vast confusion."

With the onset of darkness he made his way across the free zone, and approached Syrian lines just as the troops began to congregate about blazing gas fires and cookpots for their dinners. Marshall had carried with him all the way from Fortress Six a plate of stew and a bottle of lemonade. He went overland and then got onto a road. It was dark. He passed many troops. They too were eating, but their mess kits were shaped differently. It didn't matter, as it would not have mattered in Israeli lines. At choke points he passed right through, eating from his plate as he walked. He looked worried and preoccupied. He took many swigs from the lemonade bottle only to spit them back, and his bites were suitable for a tiny mouse.

The morale of the Syrians was not heightened and infused with vigor and destiny as before an assault. This perplexed him because he didn't know that even the Syrian commanders were ignorant of the plans for war until just hours before it was to begin. The soldiers behaved like soldiers on maneuver. There was a lot of laughing and joking—as in all armies at dinner-time unless it is raining.

Occasionally Marshall would remember where he was and what he was doing, and his eyes would cloud in absolute panic. In these moments his heart beat fast and then he would cool in his own sweat. His job was to get as close to as many tanks as he could, and check for night-vision equipment.

Knowing that the main counter to a mass wave of Syrian armor was the Air Force, Arieh Ben Barak guessed that the Syrians (aware themselves that Israeli planes were crippled at night) would break precedent and tradition to start their *jihad* in darkness. He wanted intelligence on the percentage of their tanks with infrared and starlight scopes. Men were sent out at various places along the line.

Marshall passed quite a few tank parks, keeping a running tally as best he could. "Two out of six, three out of seven . . . twenty out of thirty-one . . ." All the T-62s were fitted with scopes. Many of the T-54s had them as well. Within half an hour he started to make his way back along a different route, which led to a steep defile down which he wanted to escape.

A few hundred yards from the point where he planned to vanish down the precipice he passed a campfire around which a platoon sat picking its teeth. They had run out of conversation and were staring awkwardly into the fire, dealing with their decayed mouths. As Marshall passed, every tortured and suspicious eye was upon him. He heard a voice call out in Arabic, asking him where he was going. He responded in Arabic with a heavy Russian accent. (He and Lydia both had a knack for speaking other languages in various foreign dialects.) He said that he was Russian and spoke little Arabic, and that they should mind their own business.

To his disgust, a man jumped up and ran toward him yelling something in Russian, of which Marshall understood not a single word. He continued, but the man reached him just as the two of them passed completely beyond sight of those at the campfire. He ran up to Marshall chattering away happily, glad to have found a companion. Marshall smiled at him and tossed his plate of stew onto the road, revealing in the low moonlight his Webly and Scott pistol, angular and nasty, pointing at the Russian's heart.

"I hope you understand English," said Marshall. The Russian looked at him in panic. "Move!" He understood no English and balked at descending the cliffs, explaining in his own language that he could not do it. He was little and stocky and had two chisel-like buck teeth and reddish hair of which not too much was left on his shiny head. He seemed so human. He *was* so human. His knees were knocking. Marshall motioned for him to turn around.

He was a captain, and he began to cry. Marshall looked at the precipice. A Syrian patrol car was slowly winding its way along the road, playing an arc light in a side-to-side sweep. The captain started to lose control, and so did Marshall. He was tight inside. His eyes had never been opened so wide. He didn't want to kill the man who stood crying in front of him. The armored car got closer. Marshall was about to burst, when he took the pistol and hit the captain on the back of his neck, collapsing him onto the stones.

Marshall went down the cliff as if he were skiing—creating rock slides, falling terrified in darkness only to be arrested suddenly on a slim ledge over a sheer drop, speaking to himself in a slow encouraging voice. He reached the base of the cliff, and heard the Russian screaming and rocks falling into the wadi near him. "The little son of a bitch," said Marshall. "He's throwing rocks at me, the creep." As he ran he saw the lights of the armored car sweeping the tels. They would never see him. A volley of heavy machine gun fire signaled the end of their effort, and their light went off. Just after he raced across a flat half-mile in the U.N. Zone, a Syrian flare burst as white as phosphorus, casting stronger than moonlike shadows, like fireworks over a lake in a summer resort.

He screamed his coming to the Israeli lines, but no one was there. He ran along the fence until he reached a mine gap, climbed the wire, and threw himself down on the Army road—where he sat soaking wet, his heart pounding, his face flushed with heat.

The information he reported was received with close attention and he was commended. He got to bed by ten o'clock, and his sleep would have been peaceful had he not had one dream after another in which he was running a foot race. He was proud that he could run swiftly even in darkness. Before morning broke, the last chamber of the dream had him in China resting on a grassy river bank, while, on the water, junks and sampans moved quietly and in mystery, and above, a thousand star-shells burst over the night, flickering, falling, and darkening finally in the velvet stream.

24

On the sixth of October, Marshall was awakened just before dawn. Fully alert, they had prepared everything and were waiting for the onslaught, even though Jerusalem thought differently and the world knew nothing of it at all. When the light snapped on above his head he shielded his eyes and felt for his boots, assuming that the Syrians had begun to move. An agitated sergeant leaned over him, shaking as he spoke. "Definitive information," he said, "the attack will occur tomorrow, this afternoon that is, at four."

"Bar-Shalom."

"Yes?"

"Why did you have to wake me up to tell me that. Now I'll never get to sleep and I'll be too tired to fight."

"I was told to tell everyone," said Bar-Shalom, in exit.

Marshall did not even try to sleep. Instead, he took a long shower, put on a clean uniform, and shaved close. Because it was Yom Kippur, no one was supposed to eat, but everyone did. A lot of meat was served up, and even the orthodox were coaxed to partake of lunch. "God has sent the Syrian Army so that you can eat today," they were told. They ate nervously.

Enough ammunition had been stockpiled to last for days. The vehicles were tanked up, turned over, and assembled by order of sortie, with the Centurions first and the APC's following. There was nothing more to do, so the soldiers played basketball. At first, they tried to keep score, but they were too agitated to remember the numbers. Right after lunch a lookout screamed from the tower. "They come! They come! They come now!"

All the men rushed in a massed wave to the ramparts. They stood with weapons in hand and mouths open. Some whimpered and were told to shut up. A wind from the plain upwelled against the palisades, bringing with it the low unearthly sound of thousands of moving tanks and armored vehicles. It was a moment in which all time could anchor. The Syrian Army covered the world; the plains had arisen; dust filled the air; a deluge of columns approached.

The Israeli soldiers were frozen with wonder and fear. Frederick had come with his staff onto the rampart; he did not make an inspirational speech, though there were dozens within him. Few have ever seen such a sight. It was as if the ground were moving to swallow them up. The orthodox chanted in rapid discord, facing Jerusalem and running through the body of prayer. In the sound of their ancient words, the other soldiers despaired. They knew that only two armored brigades were in position, that full mobilization would take at least another day. They saw their own deaths.

Captain Palmer came walking across the courtyard. He was the only one who had remained in the dining room to finish dessert. They turned from one of the greatest sights in history, the noise of which was like a thousand muted thunderstorms, and looked at Palmer as he proceeded across the equipment-packed courtyard—his measured pace echoing off the walls—as if he were expected to check the distance and verify what they saw or tell them that it was a dream.

He climbed the long concrete stairs. His expression was a cross between a frown and a smile. Arriving even with the line of men, he squinted into the air and observed the unified mass of the entire Syrian Army. Then he turned to those who stood awaiting his verdict, and, speaking in English, he said, "Arabs?"

"Yes, sir," answered an Ethiopian tank driver.

"I didn't know there were so many."

"There are very many, sir, very many."

"Look, they're all worked up. Now, I suppose, we shall have to kill them."

Only Marshall had understood all his words, but the others had fathomed his tone, and, with a great cheer, they turned from the walls and rushed for their vehicles. Knowing that force ratios were ten to one against them, they realized that targets would abound on the fixed pre-ranged killing grounds for which they headed.

Three platoons of tanks and secondary armor rumbled through the iron doorway into the wide-open air. It had been practiced a hundred times. Marshall loaded Baruch's halftrack with five infantry soldiers carrying anti-tank rockets. With this tank-hunting halftrack he planned to match up against T-54s and T-62s despite their rapid fire, heavy armor, and gyroscopic and laser sights. Many halftracks were fitted out more or less the same way to help offset the dearth of tanks. On the .50-caliber machine gun, Wilson would try to handle opposing infantry and keep the tank commanders inside, hatches down. Baruch was the driver. The five ATR's would be used either in ambush outside the halftrack, or from inside, rocket tubes leveled over the armor plate to give a naval-style broadside. Prithvi and Chobandresh would use the mortar to limit the enemy's area of action, to break up concentrations of vehicles, drive them into the open, and put them out of commission.

Because Russian tank guns could not point very far downward, Marshall sought a depression in the road. If he could hold a ridge with his anti-tank rockets, the halftrack could sit in the hollow and supply a mortar barrage. A beautiful dip in the topography gave them just what they wanted, and needed—for several miles away a column of Syrian tanks moved toward them. Steeply banked, the road went downhill and was slightly curved. Thus the tanks could come at them only one or two at a time. They set up with supreme speed while the halftrack idled in the hollow. Baruch and Chobandresh manned the mortar, Chobandresh being gunner and Baruch shell-handler. Wilson stood at the machine gun, ready to cut down flanking infantry. Prithvi lay just atop the ridge, spotting for the mortar. The five rocket men were hidden—two, two, and one—in a position of enfilading crossfire. Marshall had a high point from which to command, and was ready with his submachine gun to fire at infantry. They waited until the Syrians came into sight, and the battle was enjoined.

When he could see the tank commanders stiffly upright in their turrets, Marshall turned to Prithvi. Prithvi's black hair was shining. He was small and intent. He said to Marshall, "I am not afraid."

"Very well," Marshall answered. "Begin." Prithvi signaled Chobandresh, and a mortar round soared over the ridge and landed fifty yards in front of the tanks. They stopped. The commanders went under. Prithvi turned to Chobandresh and said, "A minnow's head." Profoundly shocked, Marshall realized that because they did not know mathematics, they could not call out artillerymen's degrees. "Plus a minnow's eye," said Prithvi. Chobandresh adjusted the mortar and fired off a shot. It struck the lead tank on a corner and blew apart the tread. By this time the tanks were firing at the ridge, but they had no targets. "Chobandresh, a thick hair to that way," said Prithvi, pointing left. The tank blew up in flames.

The two Bengalis destroyed three tanks and forced the others into temporary retreat. Marshall was overwhelmed by the means with which they aimed the mortar. The phrases were extraordinary—"a grain of rice to that way; a finger to this way; a dog's bark; my sister's gold bracelet forward."

The sky was filled with planes, with the white trails of surface-to-air missiles, with the noise of shells. Marshall heard the familiar sound of Israeli tank guns, and the familiar crack of Syrian artillery. It seemed insane for a halftrack and some infantry to hold the road against a column of two dozen or more enemy tanks—but they were doing it.

Two Syrian tanks ripped around the corner and began to charge the ridge at full speed. The mortar was useless, and Marshall ordered the five rocket men out of the rocks. They aimed for a long moment and fired. Almost slowly, the rockets converged on the lead tank and blew it to pieces with a sound that echoed in the lungs of the Israelis. As the other tank pressed forward, Marshall shouted for them to reload. They didn't have time, and the tank got to the beginning of the slope. But there it had to stop short because Baruch had put three mines on the road. The tank commander's choice was to back off a little and machine-gun the mines, or try to fire on the halftrack. He chose the latter and, as expected, his gun would not lower enough. Only then did he back off, while his machine gunner sprayed the halftrack, in which Baruch and Chobandresh were crouched low. The machine gunner blew up the mines. Just as the tank started forward to confront the halftrack they hit it broadside with four rockets and it exploded in a muffled roar. The turret was knocked ajar.

They had destroyed five tanks, the last of which blocked the road. However, Marshall was apprehensive of the tank column's infantry, who he knew would next be sent to attack his men—who were not armed, positioned, or numerous enough to resist even a platoon of good foot soldiers. And if it were not infantry, it would be an air strike, against which they would have no chance whatsoever. They scrambled for the halftrack and drove east toward the U.N. Zone.

"Why here?" asked Baruch as he guided them down a wadi road.

"No mines. We can come around on the Syrian flank."

Chobandresh began to giggle and continued until he was wild with laughter. The others soon joined in. "What's funny, Chobandresh?" Marshall asked. Chobandresh tried to answer but was overtaken by a fit of giggles. Their encounter with the Syrians had been tense, fast, and lucky.

"I tink it is funny," he said, and then slapped his knee in the beginning of another fit, ". . . funny tat in tis little ting . . . oh . . . oh!" Whatever it was, he certainly thought that it was funny.

They burst through dust and small stones. The motors roared. The Bengalis had turned out to be excellent, excellent soldiers. They had wonderful courage, and, once over the giggling fit, they looked ahead calmly and unflinchingly.

25

They succeeded neither in reaching one of the main Syrian columns nor in coming close, because the Syrian advance was protected on its flanks by heavily reinforced anti-tank positions against which they dared not move. Too weak and with too little fuel to swing into Syria itself and disrupt lines of supply and communication, they turned back to Fortress Six to pick up supplies.

They were hungry and thirsty and, by evening, had lost the feeling of invulnerability which they had enjoyed for an hour or so after the tank battle. They understood from hoarse pleadings and confused orders coming over their radio that the Israelis were inflicting heavy losses on the attackers, but suffering many casualties themselves in their much smaller ranks. The Syrians had bypassed all but a few of the strongpoints, and, almost in the old Israeli style, were driving steadily toward the lip of the plateau.

Fortress Six did not answer. When they first saw it in the distance, Marshall made Baruch stop the halftrack. "What *is* that?" he said. He jumped out and stood on a boulder. Lifting his binoculars, he saw through the dusk that the Syrian flag flew over the citadel into which he had wanted to retreat. They could not understand how Six had fallen so easily, or why it appeared not to be battered. They imagined their friends lying dead in a pile just outside the gates, their whitened flesh slit in a hundred places.

They had enough fuel to reach the Israeli line west on the plateau, if they were to go straight through the Syrians. This seemed nearly impossible, but, saving a sudden Israeli counteradvance or coming upon a wrecked vehicle from which they could siphon gasoline, it was the only thing to do. Anyway, they wanted to make contact with another Israeli force, for they had been alone since they had peeled off from the column which left the steel gates of Six.

Moving in darkness, much less fighting, was impossible with the equipment they had on the track they were to follow. So they pulled off the road into a ditch and waited for the light. They tried to sleep, and could do so only for a minute or two at a time. In the middle of the night a Syrian infantry patrol passed by, leading a tank. When the halftrack had been parked in the ditch it had tilted sideways until it had almost turned over, and they left the doors flung open. In darkness, the Syrian patrol thought that it was a wreck.

When Marshall saw that nothing followed the dozen soldiers and the lone tank, he got everyone into the halftrack and started up the motor. After five minutes into which ten hours seemed to fit, they went forward, lights blazing. Coming upon the Syrians in a wide arena between two tels, they saw the tank turret slowly swing around. They honked their horn and yelled loudly. The Syrian turned on his floodlight to see if the vehicle approaching him were another Syrian. The floodlight would have blinded Marshall had he not turned off the head lamps of the halftrack and veered from the road onto the little plain. Coming up even with the tank, they fired their rockets in a broadside and hit it in several places. It banged open into a ball of orange flame, in the light of which Wilson shot the unsheltered infantry, but was killed by return fire directed at the flashes of the gun. He died before the others could wipe his blood from their sweaty faces.

Pulling out in the glow of the burning tank, they jolted across the field to a spot where they could not be seen. There they buried Wilson in hard ground which seemed, as gasoline-fired light flickered across it, to be orange-colored. The other two Bengalis went to pieces, crying and sobbing, and it was particularly dreadful to shovel raw earth onto Wilson's small upturned face, and then leave him in the suffocating ground. They marked the spot with a shovel and his helmet, and found a safer place, where they rested in expectation of dawn.

They started moving with the light. On their radio they heard of preparations for defending the Daughters of Jacob Bridge, which spanned the Jordan at the base of the Golan. They certainly hadn't enough gas to reach that far. Other Israeli units were fighting on the Heights not in a line, but in scattered pockets. The Air Force was all over the place. They saw many of its planes destroyed. Their picture was confused. But then they came upon a high hill which looked over everything. They had been trundling about on the northern flank of the Syrian Seventh Infantry Division and had never penetrated. The Syrian Third Armored Division had passed through the Seventh Infantry to press the attack. On the plain below, the patterns allowed Marshall to see that he and the others had been only on the fringes of battle. They saw Israeli tanks many miles away raising dust clouds in little wars of close maneuver. The Syrians were far to the west, but the Israelis had not stopped fighting around Kuneitra or Naffak, and in many other places downline. Marshall decided to head for Naffak and find an Israeli unit by the side of which they could fight. They had their second wind, and a cool breeze had washed over them when they came upon the overlook. Marshall turned to Baruch. "Do we have enough gas to get to Naffak?"

"Maybe."

"We'll try then. Chobandresh!"

"Yes."

"Fire a mortar round."

"At what?"

"Into the valley."

"Why?"

"Just to say that we're alive, for fun."

"What range?"

"An elephant's heart."

"It doesn't go that far."

"A sheep's heart." Chobandresh adjusted the mortar, threw in a shell, and, a little later, they saw a white puff in the valley. But the sound was indistinguishable from the explosions and reports which filled the air, and which the night before had made the sky waxen and white. Somewhat optimistic, they began their drive for Naffak. Israel was still fighting on the Golan, and the Reserves had not yet come into play. When that happened, they thought, they would all take their holidays in Damascus.

The noise of the halftrack was deafening, its color and weight mortal and earthlike. Marshall smelled the other soldiers near him. It was not pleasant, and he felt as if he and they were moles who had ventured into the light. They were frightened of fighting, frightened of the ripping steel, frightened of dying in blood-soaked dirt or burning to death in a slime of searing napalm. Then Marshall looked up and saw in infinitely intense blue two silver flecks tumbling and swooping. There were men in those shining, soundless, weightless spots—swaying in arcs of gravity and flight, fighting to kill, higher above the earth than effeminate clouds, surrounded by glass and steel and tailpipes burnished black by jets of fire. In the pines and thin air of the northern mountains, Marshall had thought that *he* was high.

For many hours the halftrack crew had gone without food or sleep. It was hard to see because of the sweat. It wet their shirts and dripped down their bodies, but they pressed forward in a cloud of their own engine smoke. One of the soldiers had brought a towel, and made it a present to his commander so that Marshall could wipe dry his sunglasses, his binoculars, and the knobs of the radio.

When Wilson was killed, the Bengalis had cried like babies. But then their courage had returned. Determination suddenly flooded the vibrating steel trap in which they rode. They lost themselves, and were refined from all they had known. Caught up dangerously in only one feeling and one idea, as they rode south toward the battle, they wished to die. But more than that they wanted to tear furiously into a Syrian column. It was the sleeplessness, the fumes, the lack of food, and the memory of Wilson's blood spattering all over them. They were angry. And they pressed on.

Marshall felt arising within him strength which he had not known, and was thankful. He thought that a man is like an ore, that difficulty and trial vaporize the earthly and the dross, and that in very hard times steel and gold and silver spring from the previously soft souls of the tried. He looked at the sleepless soldiers who had been driven from all corners of the world.

"I don't worry," he said to them, "about the outcome of this war. We ourselves may die, it is true. But you know, and I know, that we are the earth's sinew, rendered by force and death from almost every country, adept at paying any price. We hold on with shocking force, and we have stiff, leathern necks. We are now fighting ten times our number. They can burn us, and crush us, and slaughter our children, but we arise. Let them do what they will and say what they will. Let them come at night or in the day, in the winter, and in the dark. They can do anything they please, and we arise. Finally, we have come to enjoy this fight, and why shouldn't we. We can last a hundred of these wars.

"I want to find a Syrian column and attack it. We'll help stop them on the Heights even before the rest of the Army arrives. I want to slow those bastards, just for the thing itself."

The rocket men laid out their shells. Chobandresh and Prithvi did the same. Marshall organized belts of ammunition for the gun he had inherited from Wilson. At noon, they closed on the Naffak road in the midst of a battle. "You know what to do," Marshall said to Baruch. They were shaking. Their mouths were dry. But they were not unhappy.

Half a dozen Israeli tanks were battling five times that number of Syrian tanks as steadily advancing Syrian infantry fired anti-tank missiles. A rolling barrage fell on both sides from the guns of both sides. Aircraft fought above to clear the skies, so that they could give fighter support. At stake was the Naffak road, or at least some miles of it.

The halftrack sped toward the crossroads. Assuming that it would shelter behind them and lend its infantry to help counter the advancing Syrians, the Israeli tankists gave covering fire. But the tankists smiled when they saw what the halftrack did. It turned, for it had debts to pay, and drove left at the crossroads parallel to the Syrian column, firing from the row of rocket tubes menacing over its sides.

The Syrians could not move their guns fast enough because it was a great surprise to them that the halftrack had come in their direction. The infantry fired on it, and Prithvi was blown out of the cockpit. Marshall swung around and sprayed the ridgeline, driving back the Syrian foot soldiers. The rockets found their marks, knocking out several tanks through which the halftrack careened wildly amidst newly angered Syrian armor swinging its cannon, and too close to get a target. The commanders emerged from closed hatches to get to their machine guns, but Marshall was in white heat, his reflexes were perfect, and he pivoted quickly from side to side forcing the Syrian gunners back into their turrets with his sustained fire.

Now the Israeli tanks could move forward, and did. Their opposition was in panic, choked up in shrieking, clinking, metallic lines. The Israelis began their superior gunnery, but several Syrian tanks had escaped and were maneuvering on the sidelines for firing positions. "Baruch!" Marshall screamed above the gunfire. "That one over there." He meant a lone T-54 in a good firing point, swiveling its gun toward the approaching Israeli Centurions.

Baruch was not one to brook nonsense. He drove the halftrack full speed at the T-54 and did not slow or veer. He crashed directly into it. The halftrack engine seemed to explode. The tank tread was cut, and the tank itself was pushed up against a face of basalt. Its gun could not turn to fire because it bumped against the side of the halftrack. The drive wheels squealed on the rock. The soldiers in the halftrack laughed.

Another T-54 came toward them. Most jumped out in time, but two were still inside when the tank fired and the halftrack was destroyed. Marshall, three of the infantry, Chobandresh, and Baruch, ran into a cul de sac hewn from the rock as an ammunition dump. They assumed that the Syrian would not jeopardize himself by following them into such a narrow corner.

He did. His noise was deafening even over the exploding artillery shells. He came toward them—not firing, though he could have. He wanted to crush them. Baruch and Chobandresh started to run to the side. Then he opened fire. Chobandresh fell, nearly cut in half. The tank passed over him.

The others shouted. Marshall felt as if a bucking horse were inside him. "Hand grenades! Hand grenades!" he yelled. There were none. The tank rolled over the three infantrymen, and then over Baruch; they screamed high-pitched screams like birds crushed under wheels, and a sound arose from their smashed bones and flesh like that of cane crashing down in the field.

Marshall was so frightened that his feet did not touch the ground, and he felt no body, no time—nothing but electric motion all about. The tank kept coming, and he found himself jangling against a steep rock wall. He drew his pistol and fired at the ports. One shot, another, another, and several in rapid succession. He was ready to leap in the air to avoid the on-coming steel. But then he heard what sounded like the repeated banging of a scepter held in a clenched angry fist. Again and again, it struck.

Shells were falling in a walking barrage from the entrance of the canyon to its end. Marshall and the tank were frozen still as the explosions came closer, until one struck the tank directly, ripping it into a thousand pieces, throwing the armor plate about the rock chamber like chaff. Exploding over the mangled bodies, it roared upward and outward with great power, as if a surflike wave had burst into the cul de sac and finally taken hold of Marshall.

Morning at Hospital 10

Marshall had lost consciousness before his arrival at Hospital 10. Forever, they said, and it seemed so as weeks passed and he did not awake. With many tubes and plastic hoses leading in and out, he was painful to see, and the doctors said that the damage had been too severe, that he was not genuinely alive, that the wounds could not heal and would eventually drag him down completely and, in their view, mercifully. Until then, they had to keep him alive. The antiquated religious law of the state, a far cry from the wisdom of industrialized nations, forbade them the sensible measure of withdrawing support.

But the slightly plump nurse with two sweaters, one of the many girl "angels" in the Army, did not quite agree. She thought that sometimes she saw him move, and that sometimes in dead of night she heard faint words as if from a distant past. She did not mind standing watch at the glass table in the center of the room, the table by this time almost staggering under many copies of Israeli magazines, *National Geographic*, and *Paris Match*. The doctors refused to take her seriously, for she was, after all, just a sweet freckled girl who spent her days buried in the enticing images of far-away places. But she genuinely believed, or hoped, that he would revive.

By the end of October, only three soldiers remained in the high-ceilinged room near the sea. The others had died—attesting to the skill of the doctors, who had said that they would. They still did not know who Marshall was. The dental records office was unable to place him, and several slips of paper announcing this lay amid the magazines. Soon though, his family would come (as had many families of the missing) to look over the terminal ward. A score of fathers seeking their sons, and half that many distressed mothers and wives had been escorted past the bed in which Marshall lay. His family *would* arrive. There were only a certain number of missing, and the Army knew about this nameless one at Hospital 10. But it was difficult and complicated, because the war on the Syrian front was not over. Who had time for the missing? In striving to keep alive the living, commanders were too busy to pay heed to the dead and the dying.

Sometimes a warm wind would arise and carry into the ward the smell of pitch from the railroad ties and the voluminous sweetness of flowers in the war cemeteries clustered at the foot of Carmel. The nurses walked on the railway and crossed a muddy ditch to reach the cemeteries, where they went to rest and talk. Their favorite was the British because it was immaculate, the benches did not splinter, and there was much grass between the graves. Often a cold wind came in from dancing above the sea on luminescent spray, and it smelled of salt and great distance. The air in the ward was always cool and dark, and seemed to have a life of its own. It explored and circled as if it were searching. Sometimes the young nurse stared at it, in nearly angry puzzlement, and it answered by whipping a curtain, or by suddenly turning the pages of her magazines.

Paul Levy arrived in Israel for official reasons and because his brother-in-law was reported missing on the slopes of Mt. Hermon. The Livingstons followed. During the Second World War, Livingston had been in Jerusalem—for him a city of soldiers with guns, high above the mundane world, rarefied in action by the swirling magnetic conduct of war around it. Levy's position, his splendid blue uniform with a shock of decorations, and his physical presence, when combined with the age and dignity of Livingston, opened all doors. A full colonel escorted them.

Livingston became angry when the Admiral went to see politicians and generals, leaving in abeyance the search for Marshall. To Livingston's reprimanding eyes, Levy said, "I'm sorry, but I represent the United States. The business of nations, especially now, is more important than any one man's life—even if he is my brother-in-law and your adopted son."

"That's your military training is it," said Livingston, "duty?"

"Yes. That's my military training, and yours too. And it's right in both cases."

But it was Levy who had them in a records office in Tel Aviv one midnight, searching with harried clerks and translators through a pile of folders. They had converted Marshall's height and weight into metric, and they sat with their jackets off, perusing one file after another. The poor military clerks were astounded that the Commander of the NATO naval forces spent hours in their office going through casualty documents. They were further astounded when the American Admiral and Livingston began to read without the aid of aides, and to exchange comments in a strange mixture of English, Hebrew, and Yiddish. "What is this?" the clerks asked. "Who are these people?"

At two in the morning, Levy held up a folder. "I've got it," he said.

"Exact height. Lighter, but that could be because of wounds and surgery. What does this say?" he asked the colonel.

"He is in Hospital 10. That is just south of Haifa. He is asleep all the time. The case is terminal."

"We'll see about that," Levy replied. "Check these records with his Command in Haifa. I want to know if he might have been sent to this place."

"I can do it in the morning."

"You can do it now." Levy's authority was practiced and irresistible. The colonel rang up Second Mountain Brigade headquarters right then.

Arieh Ben Barak had flown in from the Golan a few hours before. He had not shaved for two days or slept for three. He was gaunt like a wolf but his eyes were bright and strong as he worked over maps late into the night, perfectly reconciled never to sleep. Few people were in headquarters. He had told his angels to go home and rest, for they were only children. When the phone rang he lifted it without looking, still absorbed in the maps. To the colonel's query he replied that, yes, the terminal cases would be in Hospital 10. Why hadn't the soldier been identified before? What was his name? The colonel told him once again, thanked him, and hung up. Arieh Ben Barak paused for a moment, angry that the war had taken the young man he had just promoted, and then he resumed his study of the fractured and faulted terrain on the road to Damascus.

Levy had the colonel call Kfar Yona. The phone rang forty times before the Druse night guard answered. His Hebrew was poor, so a major who knew Arabic was summoned from an all-night duty watch. "Awaken Lydia, the wife of Marshall. Tell her that Marshall is badly wounded but alive. Tell her to go to Hospital 10, south of Haifa off the Haifa–Tel Aviv road. We will meet her there."

"Shall it be proper for me to go alone to her?" asked the Druse.

"It is proper."

Levy and Livingston got in the colonel's car and drove through Tel Aviv's deserted streets to their hotel, where they summoned Mrs. Livingston. "I can drive," Levy told the colonel and a sleepy private at the wheel. "Give me a map. I'll get there. You people can get some sleep." At 3:30, the Army sedan pulled onto the Haifa road. It was misty and quiet as they crossed the Yarkon, and sheets of fog hung over its glassy surface.

Lydia was awake. She lay in the white room listening to the tenuous and feeble sounds of cicadas and crickets just before winter. It was misty in the Bet Shan valley too, and quiet. She had prayed for weeks. Her request and its unuttered vocalizations were not spineless importunities or passive begging. She parried; she struck; she struggled; she grappled and would not give up. It was as if for the time in question she held her breath and fought all along. She had been incredibly angry when the war broke out two days before

Marshall would have returned. She helped with defense efforts at the kibbutz when it seemed that the Syrians might invade the valley, or that, in the case of widened Jordanian participation, Kfar Yona would be in the path of armies advancing via a nearby ford in the Jordan. Then came the telegram. Marshall was missing. She walked about as if she had no body. Her gaze fastened on nonexistent horizons. She burst into tears over her tea and then scolded herself for imagining the worst.

The Druse had gone to his room, brushed his hair, and changed his clothes. He came to her door and stood stiffly in a military manner. Lydia heard something outside. She dared not be convinced that it was what she thought, and lay with the sheet clenched in her fists. The instant the Druse knocked on the frail door she jumped up with a gasp, knowing that Marshall was alive. She came to the door, and he told her the message, struggling admirably in his awkward Hebrew. She was like a madwoman, full of tears and laughter. She ran through the trees and past the cottages to get Yossi Merzl. Before long, they were on the road to Haifa.

Arieh Ben Barak had decided to sleep on the cot in his office. He lay down and stroked his bristling beard as he watched mist pour through the louvers. But suddenly he tensed. It was not possible, he thought. Still, he swung to his feet and strode down the hall to a records room. There he retrieved the file for Marshall Pearl. He suspected that he was going mad, for his throat was tight and he could hardly breathe. He opened the folder and his eyes swept down lines of penned and typed Hebrew. At the space for *Father*, a blank line had been drawn. Next came date of birth: twenty-eight June, 1947. His eyes filled with tears. He could hardly bring himself to read the next line, but he did, and he reeled. In the space for recording the name of the soldier's mother was the name of the one woman to whom he had been devoted all his life—Katrina Perlé. In his lonely headquarters the able General leaned against a row of steel cabinets and wept. Soon, though, he too was on his way to the hospital by the sea.

The gray-green room was both hot and cool, a paradox empowered by mist receding in anticipation of the breaking dawn. In the breathless space between dark and light, neither the night cicadas nor the morning birds were singing.

The nurse was wrapped in both her sweaters. She wanted to take one off but was too tired to move. She leaned against the glass-topped table. Immobile, she stared at the sea-green lamp which cast steep shadows and made her magazine colors too dazzling for a tired eye.

Then she heard the almost imperceptible singing of the sun in ascension. In a short time she would check to see if her patients were still alive. But she had some minutes until the first rays would strike through the half-opened door and throw a bright burnished beam about the room, warming it like a furnace, setting alight the powers of motion.

After his exhausting dreams, Marshall lay in a void. It was as if he had traveled the chambers of a nautilus. The first chamber had been that of birth, and those following had widened and lightened in glossy white and silver until he found himself on an open slope—from which he slid steadily and in perfect ease, as if by the trajectory of the shell he were to sail forever in the abstract darkness of sleep. But in an effort which pained him as much as or more than the wounds in his chest and legs, he spread his arms and pressed upon the smooth pearl glide, braking hard before the edge until he felt that he held a weight greater than that of the world.

As if in the field of another combat, his eyes opened aggressively. At first he saw only the white ceiling. But when his vision cleared he felt the pressure of advancing dawn. It served to push him up, and he lifted his head, but fell against the pillow in weakness. He was embroidered with plastic tubes; he had no sense of where he was, and did not know that they expected him to die that day.

He propped himself on his arms. The sun was beginning to light the half-open door. He managed to sit up and lean back against the bed posts. He was terribly weak and his hands and limbs trembled, but he found strength in anger. He was so angry that it was as if a war raged within him. He grit his teeth and took a breath. The beam of sun was rising and it began to flood his eyes. He screamed from deep inside his chest. The nurse started. Then she was unable to move.

In near slow-motion, he pulled the tubes from his body. First he whipped one of them to the right. Its fluid scattered across the room in an arc of shiny droplets. He lifted out a deep needle and flung it wide to the left, overturning a steel tripod and a bottle which smashed to the floor in a ringing clatter of crystal.

The stunned nurse shook her head back and forth and gripped the edge of the table as Marshall arose and fixed his gaze on the hot rays of dawn. "By God, I'm not down yet," he said. "By God, I'm not down yet."

And from the East, the sun came up with all its white thunder to light another day.

A Note on the Type

The text of this book is set in Electra, a typeface designed by W. A. Dwiggins for the Mergenthaler Linotype Company and first made available in 1935. Electra cannot be classified as either "modern" or "old style." It is not based on any historical model, and hence does not echo any particular period or style of type design. It avoids the extreme contrast between "thick" and "thin" elements that marks most modern faces, and is without eccentricities which catch the eye and interfere with reading. In general, Electra is a simple, readable typeface which attempts to give a feeling of fluidity, power, and speed.

Composed by Maryland Linotype,
Baltimore, Maryland.

Printed and bound by The Haddon Craftsmen,
Scranton, Pennsylvania.

Typography and binding design by Virginia Tan